Jennifer's Secret

Familiar Hauntings Series, Book 1

Kathy Madsen

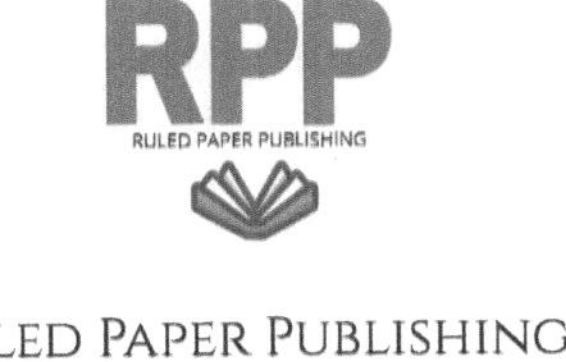

Ruled Paper Publishing

ISBN 978-1-953675-09-5 (ebook)

ISBN 978-1-953675-08-8 (Paperback)

Cover design by SelfPubBookCovers.com/DesignzbyDanielle

Chapter 1

"I ALSO HAVE THAT door upstairs that I'd like you to rekey," Jennifer reminded the locksmith, who was gathering his tools after having replaced the front lock.

"Yeah, I remember," he said with a pleasant smile as he glanced at her. "Let me wrap up here and take care of the side door first. Do you want that keyed the same as the front?" Jennifer hesitated. "Some people prefer one key for all exterior doors," the locksmith explained.

"Sure. Yes, that's fine." She was still a little distracted by thoughts of the upstairs room. "I'll let you work in peace. Call when you're ready for the interior."

"Sounds good," he replied and resumed his task, but not until his attractive customer was out of view.

Jennifer was glad to have the extra time to search the house while someone was within earshot. She would feel better knowing that she had looked under every bed, behind every curtain, and in each closet, making sure that no intruders were present. Last night was a restless one for Jennifer, despite being a bit sleep-deprived from the events of the past few weeks. She must have gotten out of bed at least five times to check the hallway. Just little noises here and there, but the feeling of not being alone in the house made her skittish.

The sight of a pair of black shoes placed directly beneath a hanging, long raincoat caused Jennifer to jump when she opened a closet in one of the spare bedrooms. "Oh, Aunt Ruth," she mumbled, shaking her head in exasperation. Jennifer pushed the shoes aside so that they no longer contributed to the impression of someone hiding in the closet. She took a deep breath to settle her nerves.

Sorting through her aunt's belongings would give Jennifer plenty to do over the next few months. She had inherited not only the house but all associated with Ruth Gaitley—her estate and personal effects. It came to quite the sum and was very much unexpected since Ruth was more of an aunt in name only. Jennifer recalled meeting her twice, and those visits were brief. Jennifer's mother considered herself estranged from her much older sister, Ruth.

Perhaps Jennifer simply needed to get used to the characteristics of an aging wooden house. After all, the rooms seemed cheerful enough when bathed in daylight, not in the least ominous. Maybe she was still a little spooked by the notion of her aunt dying here in home hospice just the month prior.

By the time Jennifer received notice of Ruth's failing condition and that Jennifer was the sole inheritor of her aunt's estate trust, Ruth was no longer capable of speaking.

Supposedly, Ruth wished to see her niece one last time, so Jennifer quickly packed a couple of suitcases and embarked on the twelve-hour road trip the following day. Although a home health companion warmly greeted Jennifer upon arrival and attempted to make her feel welcome, Jennifer had doubts that Aunt Ruth was cognizant enough to be aware of her niece's presence. Nonetheless, Jennifer dutifully sat by her aunt's bed and made one-sided small talk, not sure whether the elderly lady could hear or understand. It was the least she could do for a woman who had decided to leave everything she owned to her.

The grudge, if that's what it had been, was between Ruth and her only sibling, Elizabeth. With Elizabeth, Jennifer's mom, herself now deceased, Jennifer didn't feel an obligation out of loyalty to distance herself from Aunt Ruth. This elderly woman was Jennifer's last remaining family member on her mother's side. She just wished that either she or Ruth had attempted to reconnect earlier when they could have had a real conversation and answered one another's questions. As Jennifer observed what remained of her frail, sleeping aunt, she felt little more than sadness and loss of what might have been.

Jennifer's thoughts snapped back to the present when she shoved aside a curtain in the next room and sent a cloud of dust shooting forth, flecks sparkling in the morning sunlight. "Ugh!" she remarked in disgust. Overall, the house was clean and well-maintained, but these draperies probably hadn't been cared for in decades. Since two rooms had no window coverings, Jennifer was glad she had set up a consultation appointment to solve that issue. It would be a good day's work to change the locks and take the first step in getting some sort of blinds in all rooms. Jennifer assured herself that she'd sleep sounder tonight.

"Okay, no intruders in this area either," Jennifer mumbled. Not that she had expected to run across anything sinister or suspicious, but this systematic investigation of her new home was already making her feel better about living here.

She had no apartment to return to, even if this adventure didn't work out. Aunt Ruth only survived two days after Jennifer's initial arrival. Once Jennifer made sure her aunt's final wishes were followed per the detailed papers left in place, Jennifer made the return trip "home" to give notice to the landlord and finish packing what remained. A moving van brought the little furniture she possessed and her boxed belongings. Jennifer had the van's contents mainly stored downstairs in what appeared to be a den but had the movers bring about half of the well-labeled boxes upstairs to one of the spare bedrooms.

Being highly organized, Jennifer appreciated the detailed planning Aunt Ruth put into transitioning her property and estate responsibilities. Likewise, Jennifer had no doubt her aunt would have approved of her niece's ability to make sense of and implement what Ruth had laid out.

The shrill ring of the telephone in the main bedroom caused Jennifer to jump. She was used to the mellower ringtone of her cell but had given the landline number when contacting businesses. Jennifer debated letting the call go to the answering machine but then thought better of it.

"Hello," she answered with a hint of guardedness.

"Yeah, hi," came a youthful female voice from the other end of the line. "Is this Jennifer Shemmer?"

"Yes, speaking."

"Great! I'm Teresa Degra from Jake's Got You Covered. I'll be the one coming to your place this afternoon to discuss window treatments, and I have a few initial questions to help with the process."

"Oh, yes, hello, Teresa," Jennifer replied, relieved to be getting the project underway. "Good luck with your questions, though, since I'm new to this home. I haven't measured any of the windows, and I'm not sure what I'm looking for. This home is relatively old—I'd say from the late 1800s to the early 1900s—so I want something that looks appropriate but is still easy to maintain. Sorry. I should have thought things through better."

The young woman laughed good-naturedly. "It sounds like you're talking to the right person! I'll bring a variety of sample books of what we offer, and we'll see what we come up with. There's no pressure," Teresa assured her prospective customer.

After a few minutes of chit-chat about business details that went beyond Jennifer's current level of understanding, Teresa made her phone goodbye, promising to see her client shortly. Instinctively, Jennifer liked Teresa and was glad she was the one assigned the task of assisting her. Even over the phone, Teresa came across as genuine. Jennifer wouldn't feel embarrassed pondering the different options and asking for Teresa's aesthetic preferences between the offered samples.

"Hello, ma'am," a male voice boomed from the front entryway.

Oh, the locksmith. He must have finished with the side door. "I'm coming!" Jennifer yelled, descending the stairs quickly yet at the same time cautious not to trip. She wasn't used to stairs, but it would be good daily exercise, another plus for the house.

"Ready to take a look at that upstairs lock," the middle-aged man announced.

"Right this way." Jennifer led him back up the steps she had just descended. "I'm sorry, I forgot your name." Actually, Jennifer didn't recall him introducing himself other than saying that he was the locksmith.

"Steve," he answered from one step behind.

"Well, Steve, this upstairs room has a keyed lock. I don't have the key, so that's the problem."

"What about the other bedrooms? Do you need keys for them?" His hand automatically tried the nearest door.

"No. The other rooms lock with a twist of the knob."

"I can change those out. They're not as secure," Steve offered, although he admired the look of the older hardware.

"Um ... not at this time. I don't think that's necessary, but I do want to get into this room, of course. I recently inherited the house from a relative." Jennifer wanted to be pleasant but wasn't quite sure why she was giving out unnecessary information to a stranger.

Steve inspected the door. "Want just a key made? The other option is to change out the lock."

"Let's go with a brand-new one," Jennifer answered after a moment's hesitation. She didn't know why she had opted for that. A simple replacement key should have sufficed, but the odd noises in the middle of the night and the feeling of being watched no doubt impacted her decision.

"Sounds good," the ever-affable locksmith said and got right to the task.

Although Jennifer again promised Steve she'd let him work in peace, she stayed near this time, in and out of adjacent rooms. She wanted to be present when Steve made it into the not-seen-before room, the room of mystery, simply because it was the only one with the added security.

By the time the locksmith finished, Jennifer was confident no strangers lurked in her home, having had time to assess possible hiding places to her satisfaction. Steve advised Jennifer to try the new key to ensure it worked easily for her.

"Man, you'll have some antiques in here!" Steve exclaimed, glancing around the newly opened room.

"Some dusty ones," Jennifer blandly agreed.

"Did you say you inherited this place?"

"Yes, I did." Jennifer felt slightly self-conscious.

Steve nodded slowly, in an appreciative way. "Looks like some nice things. Were you close to your relative?"

"No, but I was here for her death, and that in itself has made me feel closer to her." Jennifer realized she was being vague and added for clarity, "Closer to my aunt."

"Lost my aunt and uncle about a year ago." Steve said in a sympathetic tone. "Sorry for your loss."

"Thank you. I'm sorry for yours, too. It's never easy to lose loved ones."

"Well, let's have you try out the other keys before I go." Steve gathered his tools one last time. "Whoa, did you feel that chill?" he suddenly asked as he straightened and turned his head to survey the hallway. "The hairs are standing up on my arms! Look at that!" Steve shoved both muscular, tanned arms in front of Jennifer for her observation.

Jennifer had felt the coldness herself and was a little taken aback. "I did feel it," she said after a brief pause. She glanced at her own arms and then briskly rubbed them.

"That was weird." Steve gave a short, uncomfortable laugh.

"We just had the door open to a room that's been closed off for who knows how many years. I guess you'd expect cold air." Jennifer offered the explanation, but even to her, it didn't seem to account for the sudden and brief temperature drop in the hallway after the door was shut.

Steve seemed to be satisfied, however, and nodded. "Yeah. I think they call them air pockets."

They walked down the stairs together, Steve remarking that the house seemed pleasant. Jennifer meant to ask him if he knew anything about her aunt or the home, but it was apparent that he didn't. His conversation and questions would have been different had that been the case. Before departing, Steve presented Jennifer with a cute refrigerator magnet business card in the shape of a key.

Teresa would be coming by in approximately two hours. Jennifer walked to the kitchen and positioned the newly obtained business card on her refrigerator before checking its contents to see what she might have for lunch. There was still a box of lettuce blends and some tomatoes. She'd make herself a salad soon, but first, Jennifer wanted to discard her former keys and get the replacements on her chain.

On second thought, she would keep the mystery room key hidden upstairs.

Upstairs. Hmm. Jennifer climbed the steps once again and immediately went to the room of intrigue. She turned the key in the new lock, and it opened as easily as it did when Steve was present. Jennifer cautiously walked into the room, trying not to scrape against the dusty boxes and bric-a-brac. It was undoubtedly cooler here than in the hallway, but the air was a consistent temperature. The hairs on her arms weren't standing on end. Jennifer glanced around and thought about the time and effort it would take to go through everything in this one room alone. She sighed but then focused on the joy she'd get from discovering what was here and learning about her aunt through the process. Who knew what treasures she might find? Photos, documents, letters? Steve was right about the antiques. Apparently, this room was used as secure storage. It was larger than the other upstairs rooms, including the bedroom that Jennifer took over. Perhaps this had been considered the main bedroom when the house was designed.

Forty minutes quickly passed after Jennifer began rummaging through a selection of the room's items. She became intrigued with the contents of a box labeled "specimen plates of flora." There was also a collection of outdated biology books, the pages fragile and yellowed, not nearly as attractive to look at as modern texts. Aunt Ruth had been a research biologist, and her love for her chosen field showed in this room and throughout the house. Considering that Ruth was born in the 1920s, it was a massive feat for her to receive an advanced degree and be employed in a field primarily regarded as a man's domain at that time.

If Jennifer was going to have a leisurely lunch and focus on the topic of selecting window coverings, she knew she had to pull herself away from the mystery room. The air inside was already feeling a tad warmer. Jennifer debated locking the door or leaving it open. After all, she might have Teresa walk through the entire house and assess what needed replacing. Something told her to always keep the door locked, however. Aunt Ruth obviously did. Neither Ruth's caretakers nor her lawyer had the key. Since everything within these four walls had a coat of dust, Jennifer had no reason to suspect that anyone had rummaged through the contents for years.

Teresa was punctual. Based on their brief phone conversation that morning, she was pretty much what Jennifer had expected. Teresa appeared to be in her thirties, perhaps early forties. Jennifer was forty-two, and to her discernment, she thought the saleswoman looked a little younger. It could be the fashionable clothing, though. Black leggings, silvery ballet wedge shoes, large red-beaded earrings, and an exceptionally charming, colorful floral tunic top. The woman looked as if she'd stepped off the cover of the clothing catalog Jennifer loved to browse but from which she had yet to order. She was more of the jeans and t-shirt type herself but could appreciate a variety of fashion choices, and Teresa's was certainly artistic.

It didn't take long to feel at ease with the saleslady, especially after giving the young woman a full tour of the house and sharing details of how she had come to live in this small town. Jennifer even confided about her relatively recent divorce due to her husband's infidelity. The mostly private Jennifer blushed at her surprising willingness to divulge as much personal information as she had to a stranger who was here solely to make a sale of window coverings. Apparently, the move to Tilbrook made her feel lonelier than she had realized.

It wasn't that Jennifer had such a wide circle of friendships back home, but she did miss lunches with her longtime pal Angie. Of course, she still felt pangs of grief over the loss of her mom. After all, she had taken care of her mother, Elizabeth, for the final year of her life. It had been rough but, in hindsight, one of the best decisions Jennifer had ever made, even if it had meant taking a leave of absence from her teaching career. Although the plan was to return to her third-grade classroom, circumstances said otherwise. But with her parents' inheritance and that of Aunt Ruth, Jennifer considered herself extremely fortunate to have financial freedom. While short on social connections, she gained a sense of peace that came with the ability to start a new chapter of life.

"I didn't know your aunt," Teresa said, her back momentarily to Jennifer as she carefully measured a window, "but I did meet her. Back in the day when I worked for Benton's." Teresa jotted down a few numbers.

"Really? You met Ruth Gaitley?" Jennifer was surprised.

"Yeah. I thought the house seemed familiar and recognized the blinds in that room." Teresa pointed the end of the tape measure in the direction of the den. "We picked them to blend with the architectural style of the house. Didn't you notice they're newer than the coverings in the rest of the place?"

"No." Jennifer seated herself on the sofa, feeling a little awkward while Teresa worked solo. "I haven't lived here for long. Plus, I have so much stored in that room now."

"There're some portraits of Ruth in there if you didn't know." Teresa glanced in Jennifer's direction. "I remember admiring them, and she told me they were of her. They're on the wall. From wherever she worked, I think, like business portraits, or something like that."

Jennifer was curious and immediately got up to check the den. Sure enough, there were two photos of a woman. In one, she appeared to be late twenties to early thirties. In the other, sixtyish yet bore a striking resemblance to her younger self.

"Hi, Aunt Ruth," Jennifer whispered to the portraits, feeling affection for this lady who had given her so much but of whom so little was known.

When Jennifer returned to the living room, Teresa had already moved on to another window. "These are high quality," Teresa said, gently fingering the material of the drapes. "These are keepers and worth cleaning unless you want to update or redefine your space."

Jennifer laughed. "I'm fine with those curtains, draperies, whatever. I will be making this place more mine with time, but I like vintage for the most part."

After the two women finalized decisions on what to do about the bare windows upstairs, Jennifer prodded to see if Teresa had further information about Ruth.

"All I remember," Teresa mused, "was that she was quiet. Maybe a little aloof. I wouldn't call her unfriendly, though. A little too much," at this, she paused, "a little too much science motif for my taste."

"Well, Aunt Ruth was a biologist. I agree with you, though. Now that I look around, I see that there's not a lot of variety for wall hangings. I think those two portraits of Ruth are the only people I see. On the other hand, there are butterflies, birds, frogs, leaves, feathers...." Her voice trailed off, having made her point.

"Exactly!" Teresa nodded and laughed.

"Do you recall any other details about Ruth? It's frustrating getting to this stage of my life and discovering that I had a family member who cared more about me than I realized."

"Not that I can think of. If I do, I'll let you know." Teresa turned and winked. "I'll be back several more times to install the products as we get them. I'll have to order the blinds custom."

"Oh, you do the installation yourself?" Jennifer winced at the surprise in her voice and instantly regretted having asked that.

Teresa laughed and didn't appear offended. "Yes, but I also have a co-worker, and we help each other with two-person projects. I can do the blinds myself. I might bring in reinforcement for the long draperies. We'll see. We'll also arrange for the items you want dry-cleaned."

Jennifer led the way downstairs, surprised by a sudden chill. It reminded her of earlier that day when Steve the Locksmith had been at the house.

"Ooh. That's almost icy!" Teresa exclaimed behind her.

The two women continued down the steps. Once safely on firm footing, Jennifer nonchalantly asked, "What was icy?"

"The air! All at once, it was super cold. Then all at once, it wasn't," Teresa explained. She smiled calmly.

"I felt that, too. In fact, this isn't the first time. Any theories on why that would be?" Jennifer tried to make her voice sound matter-of-fact.

"Ghosts?" Teresa laughed. When she saw Jennifer's facial expression, she recanted. "I'm kidding. I don't know. Old house?"

Jennifer nodded but had an odd sense that she and Teresa were not the only ones who had been on those stairs.

"It's been a real pleasure to meet you." Teresa looked sincere, and Jennifer felt the same about her.

"Do you think when you return, you'll have time to sit for a chat and iced tea or lemonade or...?" Jennifer suddenly realized that she didn't have a wide choice to offer and zero alcohol.

"Tell you what; I'll make time! Iced tea with lemon?" Almost as if Teresa could read Jennifer's thoughts, she added, "I'll bring wine on another occasion or, better yet, the makings for this delicious fruity-tasting concoction I recently discovered. Unpack those cocktail glasses." She winked.

After seeing off her potential friend, Jennifer slowly walked up the stairs, rechecking for cold spots. Nothing out of the ordinary. She still had the key to the upper room in the pocket of her jeans from when she had given the grand tour. Teresa mentioned that this accumulation of Ruth's possessions over the years might include memorabilia of Jennifer's maternal grandparents and mom. That was of far more interest than the antiques and other bric-a-brac.

The notion of finding mementos regarding her mother's early days left her both excited and sorrowful. Jennifer felt guilt that she was now the home's owner, even though intellectually, she knew she had nothing to feel guilty about in this situation. Elizabeth Lowingwood, Jennifer's mom and Ruth's only sibling, resented her older sister for not sharing the house. Legally, Aunt Ruth had no responsibility to do so since the sisters' parents had made Ruth the sole inheritor of the property. As Jennifer recalled, Elizabeth did receive a small sum of money when the will was settled, but the house and most of its contents went to Ruth. It could have been because Aunt Ruth was twelve years older than Elizabeth, and their parents believed this was the proper order of inheritance. It could have been because Ruth had not married and, at least according to her sister, had no interest in dating.

Elizabeth, on the other hand, was already engaged at the time of her parents' fatal automobile accident. Jennifer couldn't even remember the full name of her mom's first husband but did know that before being Mrs. Lowingwood, she was Elizabeth Daniels. The marriage hadn't lasted long, but neither Elizabeth nor her parents could have predicted that. In the 1950s, divorce was neither common nor well-accepted. Elizabeth's parents likely assumed their younger daughter would be cared for by a doting husband for life.

Elizabeth Daniels' story did not have a fairy tale ending, however. The marriage only lasted three years. In desperation, Elizabeth arrived on Ruth's doorstep, the entryway of her childhood home, suitcases in tow. She anticipated a warm welcome and an invitation to live with her older sibling as long as she wished. Elizabeth half-expected her old bedroom to look the same as it had on the day she departed to join her husband-to-be. Much to Elizabeth's astonishment, Ruth found alternative lodging for her in a boarding home. Ruth paid the bills, gave Elizabeth cash for necessities, and even helped her young sister obtain training to become a secretary, a job Elizabeth maintained throughout her working days. Elizabeth felt no gratitude, however. She cut ties with Ruth as soon as she felt capable of standing on her own two feet and moved from the boarding home Ruth had chosen to another.

Her first secretarial position was for a law partnership, two brothers who teamed up to share resources and camaraderie. Elizabeth had remarked more than once over the years that she envied the connection and loyalty the brothers had for one another. It reminded her of what she lacked with Ruth. At the same time, Elizabeth felt like family in that small law partnership. Her job was intriguing, and both attorney brothers enjoyed training Elizabeth to become somewhat of a legal assistant. Eventually, as their practice grew, more routine tasks were delegated to a front desk receptionist, freeing Elizabeth to do more specialized secretarial work for the lawyers.

In 1975, just a few years short of two decades since her divorce, Elizabeth Daniels became Mrs. Peter Lowingwood, wife of a prominent attorney in a neighboring state. A few years later, Jennifer was born to two highly appreciative and loving middle-aged parents who had not thought it possible to be fortunate enough to experience parenthood.

How ironic, Jennifer lamented, to become the owner of the very house her mom had desired to share with Ruth, the focal point of so much bitterness. Elizabeth labeled herself as estranged from her sister and implied that Jennifer was also distanced from her aunt. Although Jennifer had met Aunt Ruth a couple of times, she could only recall that her relative didn't show any particular emotion. In hindsight, it seemed that she might have been sad and perhaps a little regretful. Had Aunt Ruth willed Jennifer the home to make amends to Elizabeth? Jennifer was reconciled to never fully knowing the answer. She was grateful, however, because everything could easily have gone to charity, probably to support an environmental cause or scientific research. Still, Jennifer wished her mom could have been one of the home's owners.

Jennifer jumped when the doorbell chimed. Who could that be? She hadn't scheduled any further appointments for the day, plus it was nearing dinner time. She was tempted to ignore the bell, but what if it was a friendly neighbor coming to welcome her? Although she preferred not to see any further visitors today, Jennifer didn't wish to get on anyone's bad side.

She peered through the peephole, a habit she was accustomed to, coming from a larger town than this. "Yes?" Jennifer called out without opening the door.

"Hello. My name's Ted Filston," came a muffled voice from the other side. "I was a friend of Ruth Gaitley. I thought I'd drop by and extend my condolences."

Jennifer cautiously opened the door. The man framed in the peephole had looked harmless, but one could never be sure. Tilbrook was a relatively quiet town, though, and to her limited knowledge, appeared to be fairly safe.

Ted grinned broadly upon seeing Jennifer standing in the doorway. He extended his hand and repeated his name. "I don't mean to barge in on you, and I realize it's getting a little late in the day. I drove past earlier and saw vehicles here. However, I couldn't stop at the time because I was on a call. I sell annuities, you see, and had a client in the area."

Jennifer thought Ted was one of the most handsome men she had seen who wasn't a celebrity. His well-groomed blonde hair glistened in the late afternoon rays. When he removed his sunglasses, he revealed eyes that were either a blue or gray shade—very attractive and somewhat unusual in hue. His warm smile radiated to his eyes, giving him extra appeal. It didn't hurt that he wore a well-fitted suit complete with a tie. When Ted asked if he could come in, Jennifer didn't hesitate.

"This brings back memories," Ted remarked as he swiveled around, gazing in evident appreciation of the old house. "It's been ages, but in some ways, the place hasn't changed much." Ted proceeded to seat himself on the sofa, although Jennifer had not yet invited him to do so.

Jennifer positioned herself in the adjacent floral chair. She attempted to readjust the pillow against her back and then moved it to her side. "You said you were friends with my aunt?" she prodded, hoping to learn more about Ruth in addition to getting better acquainted with the picturesque man in her living room.

"Yes. I met Ruth through work. In fact, I lived here briefly, in this house." Ted registered amusement as he watched Jennifer's facial expression, knowing that would pique her curiosity.

She had expected Ted to continue, but he merely sat looking at his hostess with a pleasant smile. Obviously, he anticipated a reaction from her. "When was this?" She heard the guardedness in her voice.

Ted knew that Jennifer was mentally doing the math to understand how someone his age could have worked with someone her aunt's age. Possibly she was wondering why she hadn't heard of him before if he had lived with Ruth.

"I was only in my mid-twenties at the time," Ted elaborated. "Ruth had already retired but chose to work part-time on a study. She must have been in her seventies, I believe. Anyway, I do know she collected social security." He paused to give Jennifer a disarming smile, which he could tell had served its purpose well.

"Oh! So, you were once a researcher yourself?"

"No. Not me!" Ted laughed, still smiling broadly, his dimples deepening. "I have zero aptitude for science and am in no way geared for a life of hypothesis forming and testing. I wouldn't have the patience even if I did have the skills. No, I was on the business side of Tenger. That's the company your aunt and I worked for. Now they've tagged 'Bio' onto the name. It used to simply be called Tenger."

"How did you come to live in this house?" Jennifer asked the foremost question on her mind, aware that her visitor was enjoying keeping her in suspense.

"I was going through a rough spell." The smile left Ted's face as he shifted his weight on the sofa. "I had gotten married early, too early, and that came crashing down in divorce. Here I was, only about twenty-five, suddenly single and without a home. Ruth was kind to me. She would come in several days a week to work on her project and stay to eat with me in the cafeteria. Eventually, that lunchtime friendship led to her asking me if I'd like to move in with her until I got back on my feet."

"I didn't know my aunt," Jennifer admitted. "We weren't close, but from the little I do know, that sounds out of character. She was pretty aloof." Jennifer couldn't imagine that her aunt would refuse her own sister to coinhabit the house yet allow a young co-worker to move in—not only allow, but extend the offer.

"Ruth was quiet, but I wouldn't call her aloof," he remarked, appearing to mull over the notion before speaking. "It was a long time ago. I think I was probably the one who said I didn't know what I was going to do. Anyway, the end result was I lived here, in this same house, for a short time." Again, Ted threw Jennifer one of his enchanting grins.

"What do you mean by *short*?" Honestly! She felt like she had to pull each detail from him.

"Maybe six months," Ted replied with a shrug.

Jennifer chuckled. "That means you've lived here longer than I have!"

Ted joined in the laughter and asked Jennifer a few questions about herself and her life before moving to Tilbrook. His visible pleasure upon learning that she was now single was flattering. After finishing off a couple of rounds of iced tea, he asked if he might be given a tour of the house. Jennifer jumped up with pleasure to escort her new acquaintance, describing the plans she had to make the home seem more like her own. Ted paused and remarked about the computer and large-screen television.

"My aunt was surprisingly into technology. She had a laptop, desktop, tablet...." Jennifer let her voice trail off, realizing that she was forgetting a few items.

"Once a scientist, always a scientist."

"Well, yes. You're right." She nodded. "Of course, Aunt Ruth would have to be computer literate if she wanted to stay abreast. Plus, you've now told me she continued to work at least into her seventies."

"A brilliant woman. Always curious."

When they'd reached the upstairs, Ted pointed out what used to be his room. It was one of the smaller ones but still had a bed and dresser. Ted confirmed that they looked to be the same furnishings he had used.

Jennifer showed him Ruth's former bedroom, the one she had taken over. She hoped he wouldn't think lesser of her for choosing that room for herself so early after her aunt's death.

If Ted did think this, he didn't show his feelings. Instead, he said, "I can almost feel Ruth's presence." At that, both he and Jennifer stood still and glanced around.

Could that be the presence Jennifer had felt on multiple occasions? Auth Ruth? Odd, she hadn't considered that. Of course, though! Her aunt lived here all of her ninety-six years. If the house *did* have a ghost, and she wasn't convinced that it did, most likely it would be the spirit of Ruth.

Jennifer pondered this when she followed Ted out of her bedroom to the locked room. Ted tried the doorknob. It mildly surprised Jennifer that he'd be so bold, but she quickly dismissed her initial thought. After all, he had lived here, and Jennifer was giving him a tour.

"Locked?" was all Ted said as he looked at Jennifer.

"Yes. I don't have the key with me. It's just a storage room now."

Ted paused as if expecting her to get the means to unlock this upstairs room, and it dismayed Jennifer that she made no attempt to retrieve the key. She was becoming oddly protective of the room's contents. Instead, she merely asked, "Was this room locked when you lived here?"

"No." He also seemed surprised. "No, it wasn't. It was used as a place for keeping odds and ends, though."

Ted remained firmly footed in front of the door, even though Jennifer had moved on to the next room. She sensed that the tour was now over and initiated the walk downstairs, half-expecting to feel another one of those cold spots. She was pleased on both accounts—that Ted had followed her down and that no chilly air pockets had materialized.

"Would you care to join me for dinner tonight?" Ted asked unexpectedly.

Jennifer turned to face him. "I'd invite you to eat with me, but I'm a little low on supplies."

"I'm asking you out, my treat." Ted laughed. "Do you like Italian?"

Jennifer did but hesitated. He stood before her in suit and tie. She could change out of her jeans but hadn't settled in enough yet to really get dressed up for an evening out.

Ted seemed to read her mind. "Perfezione is a great little Italian place in Bilmore. That's about thirty minutes from here. You don't need to dress up." He removed his tie as he spoke.

Jennifer thought twice but agreed. Bilmore was the nearest town, and she would like to start exploring the area. She also liked Ted, and spending more time with him was no sacrifice. It wasn't as if she had anything planned for the evening outside of unwinding before the television.

"Give me about ten minutes," Jennifer finally responded. "I'm just going to change to black pants and some nicer shoes. Make yourself at home." She paused at the foot of the stairs. "Make yourself at home, *once again*."

Ted laughed at the joke and nodded.

It was nice being with Ted. Jennifer felt at ease since he proved to be a safe driver and excellent conversationalist. The half-hour trip passed pleasantly, and she was slightly disappointed when she saw the neon sign of Perfezione coming up. Although Jennifer's stomach announced it was ready to have dinner, she would have liked the excursion to continue for many more miles.

"Is Bilmore larger than Tilbrook?" Jennifer asked as Ted held the restaurant's door open for her.

"Yes. Probably at least triple in size," Ted ventured. "Two, please," he addressed the host.

When they settled in a quiet booth near the fireplace, Ted added, "I live in Bilmore myself."

"Oh." Even Jennifer heard the hint of regret in her monosyllabic response.

It was evident that Ted caught the tone of her voice, as well. He laughed, again giving her one of his disarming smiles. "I'm in Tilbrook from time to time, though. I travel a lot for my work. I go where I'm needed."

It occurred to Jennifer that he would have to spend an additional hour in transportation time to take her home and return to Bilmore. Had she realized that Ted didn't live in Tilbrook, she would have insisted on eating in a café local to her. Jennifer hoped he wasn't intending on bringing her to his house afterward. That would be awkward since she would refuse the invitation at nighttime.

Ted again appeared to read her thoughts. "I don't mind driving in the least. In fact, I enjoy the freedom of being on the road. That's one of the appeals of my job. Plus, the clients. I love the opportunity to help people with financial planning and goal setting."

Dinner was fantastic! Jennifer didn't know whether it was simply the tastiness of the food, the dimly lit cozy ambiance of the ristorante, or the pleasure of Ted's company that made this evening rival the English translation of the restaurant's name, "perfection."

They lingered in the comfortable booth another half hour after the dinner plates were cleared. Ted offered tiramisu, but Jennifer was too full to accept any dessert. He ordered a sweet sparkling wine instead. Jennifer only drank socially but appreciated his selection. It was a nice finish to the delicious meal.

"I think you know all about me now," Jennifer said to Ted. He had asked her numerous questions and learned that she had no children, although she obviously loved kids or wouldn't have gone into elementary education. Ted was curious about Jennifer's parents but didn't press too much on the topic upon learning that her dad had passed five years ago and her mom last year. He extended just the right amount of sympathy when she explained the joys and hardships of caring for her ill mother.

Jennifer hoped that Ruth had told Ted about Elizabeth, Jennifer's mom, but that hadn't been the case. When Ted lived with Ruth, he was unaware that she had any family. He didn't know of Ruth's death until he saw the obituary in the newspaper. Ruth, the consummate planner, had even thought to write her own obit. It was short, simple, and humble. No mention of relatives outside of Jennifer Shemmer, her niece. No accolades about Ruth's accomplishments, either. She described herself as having a love for biology and was grateful for the opportunities Tenger-Bio had presented her. The obituary seemed to be more of a tribute to Tenger-Bio, an environmental and biological research center on the outskirts of Tilbrook.

However, Jennifer did pick up a few new facts about her late aunt. Ted shared a couple of amusing anecdotes. One involved Ruth "saving" Ted from what he hyperbolized to be a giant monster of a spider. Jennifer laughed, knowing that Ted was joking but enjoying the way he acted out the events in such a humorous way. The other story centered around Ruth making her own bath salts in the kitchen. Ted had mistakenly taken it as seasoning for his steak. He acted that out in a charmingly hilarious fashion, as well. Jennifer didn't remember the last time she had laughed so hard. She missed those days when she was carefree and had the illusion of a happy marriage.

"I have the feeling there's a lot more to be learned about Jennifer Shemmer." Ted leaned forward, folding his arms on the table. He admired the way she looked at that moment. She still had her hair in a ponytail, but a few more strands had managed to free themselves and were glimmering a soft golden brown in the candlelight.

Jennifer blushed. She hoped he wouldn't notice. "Tell me some more facts about Ted." She paused. "I know you told me your last name, but I've forgotten."

"Filston. Ted Filston." He extended his arm across the booth to Jennifer.

She obliged by shaking hands with him, going along with the playful reintroduction. "Pleased to meet you, Mr. Filston."

"Well, I think I've filled you in about myself," Ted mused. "Let's see. What else? I'm forty-five. I used to live with your aunt, but you knew that," he said teasingly. "I like most foods, I am single, but then you knew that."

"Kids?" Jennifer asked.

"I was only married that once, and no, we had no children. I had a dog, Max, but he died a few years ago. I thought about getting another, but since I travel so much, I decided against that idea for now."

The conversation continued until Ted excused himself and returned to the table to ask Jennifer if she was ready to leave. She offered to contribute to the bill, but he announced it was taken care of, his treat. Jennifer slipped into the jacket he held open for her.

She sighed. It was time, probably past time, for the date, or whatever this was, to end. Again, she hoped that Ted would not drive her to his house. Although she liked him—a lot—she didn't want to deal with any next steps.

To her relief, Ted got back out on the main road to Tilbrook. He chatted most of the way home about his last visit to San Diego and some of the changes he'd seen. Jennifer had only been to California once, to Los Angeles. It crossed her mind that it would be fun to travel with him.

Listening to Ted's tales and watching the night landscape illuminated in the headlights made the return trip home thoroughly enjoyable. But, as the saying goes, all good things must end.

As Jennifer anticipated, Ted insisted on walking her to the front door. She pulled out her keys and turned to face him, hearing herself ramble on about what a lovely evening it had been, profusely thanking him for stopping by to introduce himself. He returned the pleasantries and pulled a business card from his wallet, placing it in Jennifer's hand.

"If you don't mind, I'll come by again soon. Perhaps you'd like to try another restaurant, or maybe you'd like to see more of the area?" Ted took a step backward.

"I would like that."

"Then I will leave you for now," he said with a warm smile and outstretched arm. Jennifer put Ted's business card in her other hand so she could return his shake. He didn't release his grip until she gently pulled away. "You bear a little resemblance to Ruth," he remarked, almost to himself. "That's a compliment. I noticed it at the restaurant."

"Oh, well, thank you." Jennifer felt foolish for acting awkwardly.

"Sleep tight!" With that, he walked off. Jennifer quickly unlocked the door but looked back to glance at Ted. Before getting into his SUV, he turned and waved. She reciprocated before retreating inside.

"Oh, Aunt Ruth!" she said out loud, giggling. "I just had the best time with your friend Ted Filston!"

She hadn't expected an answer, of course, but she felt a strange presence. Again, there was a slight chill, and this time the hairs on the back of her arms did stand. She rubbed her arms to calm the goosebumps.

"Thank you, Aunt Ruth," Jennifer addressed the empty room. "Thank you for this house, a chance at a new life, and for leaving me all you owned."

The sense of being watched continued. Jennifer turned on the lamps as she progressed through the living room into the den. She switched on an overhead fixture and confronted the portraits of her aunt, studying them to detect the resemblance Ted thought he saw between Jennifer and

Ruth. Maybe a little. People often think they see a similarity when they believe someone is related. Jennifer's dad's side of the family felt she took after her dad. Jennifer thought she looked more like her mom.

"Thank you, Aunt Ruth," she reiterated in a hushed voice. Jennifer wondered if the alcohol was affecting her because she so keenly felt the presence of a spirit in this room. She gave a start when she felt something brush the right side of her face. Jennifer put her hand on her cheek and vigorously rubbed the skin. No doubt a cobweb. She shook her head slightly to clear her mind.

Time to switch off the lights, go upstairs, and unwind from what had turned out to be an eventful day. She would have a nice, relaxing bath and then catch up on her journaling. "Goodnight, Aunt Ruth!" She paused at the base of the stairs before ascending for the night.

Chapter 2

JENNIFER AWOKE FEELING UNUSUALLY refreshed and ready to face the day. She had slept soundly, not knowing whether to attribute that to the sense of security she felt with the new locks or the fun she'd had in Bilmore with Ted Filston. She recalled a portion of a dream in which she was aboard a gondola in Venice, serenaded as it moved along the canals. Jennifer smiled, acutely aware of the connection between that and her ambient Italian-restaurant evening.

Speaking of dining... One look in the pantry reminded her that she needed to get serious about stocking up on food. Jennifer snacked on the little that remained of the cereal while starting a grocery list. Maybe she'd try the larger market that was further away. As much as she liked the convenience of the nearby one, its choices were limited. It wouldn't hurt to check out the larger malls on the opposite, newer side of town. Still, Jennifer wanted to support local small businesses as much as possible. The older side of Tilbrook continued to be dominated by mom-and-pop shops and service businesses. Chain stores gravitated to the newer part of town.

The melodic notes of Jennifer's cell spurred her to scribble the next item to her list illegibly. She inadvertently let the pen roll to the floor in her hurry to pick up the phone.

"Angie!" Jennifer greeted her closest friend with enthusiasm. "How are you?"

Angie Calberto was happy to hear Jennifer's voice, too. "I'm good! We're all fine. Well, Mike's got this battle going with a squirrel, but that's beside the point. Anyway, just checking in to see how it's going with you. Liking your new space? People treating you well?"

"So far, so good." Jennifer didn't have to pretend, not that she would with Angie. She had known her since college, and their bond had only strengthened over the years. "I miss you, though. That's the drawback, Ange. I don't get to have those fun outings with you."

"You're not so far away that we'll never see one another, Jen," Angie mildly reproached her pal. "And as I recall, you don't have to work for a living anymore, right?"

Coming from any other person, Jennifer might think there was a bit of envy behind that statement. Angie knew what Jennifer had been through, however. One major life stressor after another. Plus, she genuinely cared about her best friend.

"Are you trying to tell me something?" Jennifer replied with a short laugh.

"You bet I am! You know we have a guest room, and most of the time, it's waiting for an occupant."

"I remember," Jennifer said with fondness. Angie, her husband, and her daughter were warm, welcoming people, but Jennifer didn't like to intrude. She also felt slightly uncomfortable being a guest in the home of a family. If Angie were single, she'd take her up on her offer more frequently.

"How are you coming with the house?"

"Not bad. I'm prioritizing." Jennifer carefully considered her next words. "I got that mysterious room upstairs unlocked yesterday. It's full of more items to sort. Some of it looks pretty interesting, though. My aunt apparently liked antiques, or maybe she simply kept most of what her parents, my mom's parents, owned. Also, Aunt Ruth had lots of old books, posters, and displays related to nature."

"I don't know whether to congratulate you or offer my condolences." Angie chuckled. Jennifer assumed she was referring to the amount of work needed to go through the personal belongings.

"I'm going to take it slowly," Jennifer assured her friend. "Yesterday, I looked through a box of specimens of flora. I wish I knew who to donate it to."

"What's that place called that Ruth worked at for all those years? They'd know, right?"

"Tenger-Bio?" Jennifer didn't think the company would be interested and certainly didn't think they'd appreciate a phone inquiry over something that trivial. However, she promised she'd keep the thought in mind, not wanting to belabor the topic.

Angie moved on to her next question. "Meet any interesting people yet?"

"Funny you should ask," Jennifer said in such a sing-songy voice that it embarrassed her slightly.

"Oh, my! Tell me more," Angie gushed in an exaggerated way that made Jennifer want to divulge every detail of her evening spent with the handsome friend of her aunt.

By the time Jennifer finished, Angie was up-to-date on everything her pal knew about Ted Filston. Jennifer anxiously awaited the feedback she knew was coming.

"He sounds very promising, Jen," Angie said with a surprising note of solemnity. "Proceed slowly, though. It takes a long time to get to know the real someone."

Jennifer's own internal guidance had communicated the same warning. Still, there had been no red flags as far as she was aware. "I promise you I have no intention of rushing into anything. I will admit that I very much enjoyed Ted's company, and I do find him attractive. I got the impression that he felt the same about me, although I don't really understand why. Ange, this guy is *so* nice-looking, gracious, and humorous."

"First off, don't sell yourself short," Angie admonished. Sure, Jennifer wasn't gorgeous, but her friend was attractive nonetheless. She kept herself in good shape and had a nice figure, a pretty smile, and somewhat delicate features. "Second, you have much to offer! I think that jerk you were married to did a number on you." In all fairness, Angie had liked Alex Shemmer once, but that was long ago, and she couldn't recall why. She'd have to think about it, and she didn't care to do so. Angie was thankful her own marriage was strong and that she could trust Mike.

Jennifer began to protest, but Angie reminded her that she was starting a new chapter in life. New town, home, financial freedom, friends, and fresh possibilities. Jennifer couldn't argue with that, and why would she want to?

"You're just what I need, Ange. If I haven't told you lately, I appreciate you."

"I know, and right back at you. But for now, I have to go. I've got to take Jolie to a dentist appointment."

"Does she have a toothache?" Jennifer liked Angie's teenage daughter. If Jennifer were to have a child of her own, she would wish for one as loving as Jolie.

"Oh, she's fine. It's just her regular checkup and cleaning." Angie's pace quickened. "Got to go, honey, but keep up the great work. We'll talk later."

"Definitely," Jennifer ended, letting her friend attend to her own life.

She put her cell phone in her purse so that she wouldn't forget it for her trip to the grocery store. Talking with Angie made her miss her best friend all the more. Angie was the one remaining person Jennifer felt utterly free to be herself around. She could wear her heart on her sleeve, and for the typically private Jennifer, that was a big deal.

As Jennifer walked upstairs, she thought of Teresa, the window-covering salesperson, recalling her remarks about the icy air felt on these same steps. Teresa seemed interested in sharing social time with Jennifer, but perhaps she was only being courteous because of the rather large sale she had made. Time would tell, but Teresa did seem to be someone Jennifer might connect with for local friendship.

Jennifer passed the mystery room and tried the knob, relieved when it wouldn't turn. She had left the door locked, and it remained so, just as it should. This afternoon, Jennifer planned to sort through another box or two with dust rags in hand. For now, though, it was time to get ready for some needed shopping.

Tilbrook certainly was varied, Jennifer concluded as she compared this side with the older section in which she lived. She was glad she had decided to drive around the newer part of town today. Frankly, this more modern side of Tilbrook looked much like what she was accustomed to in her former hometown of Reddington. Then again, she had lived only one state away. Jennifer decided to explore a bit on foot before loading her car with perishables from the grocery store.

She parked her Toyota and set forth for a bit of leisurely walking, carefully noting the street signs. It occurred to Jennifer that she'd have to visit the motor vehicle department now that she had moved. She could take care of some of the business online, but she'd better get to this task soon. She pulled out her phone and typed a reminder.

The air was crisper today and refreshing. Jennifer enjoyed her morning, promising to do more of these jaunts to become better acquainted with Tilbrook. She picked up a town map in the small chamber of commerce and, noticing the map of neighboring Bilmore, grabbed that as well. Armed with the Tilbrook map, Jennifer noted her location with precision. The supermarket was approximately two blocks away. Nearby, but since she'd be carrying groceries on the return trip, best to make her way back to the car and drive over.

Jennifer almost opted to walk past her vehicle to extend her exploration in the other direction. However, she told herself that was enough for now. After all, there would be plenty of days left for future strolls.

The supermarket was part of a modern-looking strip mall and was easy to spot. Jennifer parked a little distance from the crowded section of the lot. She got out of her car and swiveled to view the signs of the other businesses occupying the mall. A barbershop, nail salon, tax accountant, and Jake's Got You Covered.

"So, this is where Teresa works," Jennifer said under her breath. She found herself walking toward the draperies and blinds shop instead of her intended destination.

She hadn't meant to go inside or even get close enough to peer in the storefront window. It was mere curiosity that caused Jennifer to stride steadily toward Jake's. Teresa Degra exited the door and almost instantly recognized her client, Jennifer.

"Hey!" Teresa shouted without slowing or missing a step. Teresa pressed a key fob to open the back of her hatchback. Jennifer felt embarrassed, as if she had been caught stalking the lady. She reminded herself that she had done nothing wrong.

"Uh, hi, Teresa," Jennifer responded, close enough now that she didn't have to raise her voice. "I'm here for some groceries, actually. I wanted to check out what was in the area, and then I saw your sign." Jennifer was annoyed at herself for defending why she was now standing in front of Jake's Got You Covered.

Teresa was busy loading and rearranging what looked to be displays and sample books. She lowered the hatchback door, apparently satisfied. "I'm glad to see you. I have a call to make in an hour but want to grab a bite to eat beforehand. All I have time for is Tito's. If you'd care to join me?"

"Lunch?" Jennifer looked perplexed. She glanced at her wrist to look at a watch that wasn't there. When Jennifer had been a teacher, she always wore one to help with scheduling and planning. Now, she usually found that an occasional glance at her phone sufficed for the little she needed to know the official time.

Teresa laughed. "It's 12:30. Tito's is over there." She pointed a short distance behind Jennifer.

"Oh, that would be great! I've obviously lost track of the time. I thought it was still morning."

Teresa led the way, walking quite briskly in cute yellow-strapped sandals that matched the yellow trim of her blouse.

"Aren't you a little chilly?" Jennifer was comfortable and warmed from her morning wanderings, but Teresa had come from inside and wore no sweater.

"Not one bit." Teresa smiled and glanced at her client. "Today's very pleasant!"

Teresa led the way into Tito's and was greeted almost immediately by staff that evidently were well-acquainted with this petite, perky lady. Once again, Jennifer felt underdressed in her jeans and turquoise knit shirt, golden-brown hair gathered into her usual casual ponytail. The women settled into a booth by the window, and Jennifer snuggled into the overstuffed seat.

"I almost always get the garden salad and cup of minestrone soup," Teresa explained, not bothering to read the menu placed before her.

"That sounds perfect for lunch." Jennifer continued to browse the selections, making a few mental notes for future meals. Teresa beckoned the waiter and placed her order. Jennifer made it easy, requesting the same.

"Thank you for inviting me to join you," Jennifer continued now that the food was on its way. "I don't know anyone here in town." She reconsidered, thinking of Ted, but since Ted lived in Bilmore, that was a true statement.

"I'm glad for the company!" Teresa leaned forward with her arms folded on the table. "What have you been up to?"

Jennifer told her about her morning wanderings, and Teresa gave her a few tips on places to check out. Jennifer liked her potential friend more and more. It wasn't a chore to make small talk with this dynamic lady.

Service was speedy at Tito's, rivaled only by Teresa's pace of eating. Jennifer noticed that she still had half her meal left, but her companion was nearing the end of hers. Then again, Jennifer did the bulk of the talking, giving Teresa extra time to munch her salad. If Jennifer was going to bring up the subject of Ted, she figured she'd better start now before Teresa was out the door. Jennifer hesitated. Part of her really wanted to discuss him, but in the end, she sat quietly. Perhaps she was afraid she'd jinx the likelihood of a second outing with the man.

"I like the section of town you live in," Teresa continued. "The old part of Tilbrook has the charm. It has character." She briefly waved her fork back and forth before spearing her next piece of lettuce. "It's becoming pricey to live there, though. I doubt I could afford to buy a small home in that vicinity now. I'm glad I bought when I did."

"Where do you live?" Jennifer asked, hoping that wasn't a bit forward since she was technically little more than a client at this point.

"I'm not too far from you. Have you seen the picturesque stone Presbyterian church?"

"I recall a beautiful stone church, but I don't know the denomination. It looks old." Jennifer wracked her brain to remember further details.

"I live on the street behind the Presbyterian church."

"That's a handy reference point," Jennifer said, half-listening to Teresa, who had turned the conversation toward architecture. Jennifer mulled over the possibility that her aunt Ruth had attended that same church at some point.

Teresa pulled out her phone and showed Jennifer a photo of a green-eyed black cat basking in the sun. "My baby!" She proudly grinned. "Hooligan."

"You named your cat Hooligan?" Jennifer asked, not sure that she had heard correctly.

"A bit of a mischief-maker," Teresa explained but beamed as she glanced one more time at her obviously beloved pet. "Here's my house." She pushed her phone across the table once again.

"Very nice!" Jennifer said with sincere appreciation in her tone. "You strike me as an artistic person. You chose a home that reflects that. What did you say earlier? Charm and character?"

"Yes, indeed." Teresa retrieved the phone. "What's your cell number?"

Jennifer gave it to her, and her phone soon played its familiar soft ringtone. She started to reach for it, but Teresa motioned to the contrary.

"I just phoned you. Now you have my personal number. The card I gave you yesterday is the business one. I need to leave if I'm going to make it to my next appointment on time. It's been a pleasure, really, and we'll do this again," Teresa rapidly spoke as she stood to make her exit. She had already paid her tab when Jennifer still had about a third of her meal left.

"Oh, I'm sorry!" Jennifer started to rise, but Teresa motioned her to remain seated.

"Finish your food. I've got to go, but you don't. Catch you later!" Teresa smiled and winked.

Jennifer watched her lunch companion quickly walk out of Tito's and across the lot toward the hatchback. Teresa was no follower. On the contrary, she seemed very much the leadership type. Jennifer wondered if Teresa's ambition was to have her own store someday.

Now that she had the booth to herself, Jennifer leaned back to relax and study the view from the window. She leisurely sipped tea as she watched cars enter and leave the parking lot. Lunch had been quite pleasant. Eventually, she pulled the grocery list from her purse to read through the items—time to restock the pantry.

The locked room upstairs held an allure for Jennifer, and she couldn't help thinking about it. Having completed the chores outlined for the day, she decided to reward herself with time to rummage through more of its contents. She retrieved the key in anticipation. Where to start?

She picked up a vase that caught her attention due to the delicate landscape encircling it. Carefully, Jennifer turned the vase to see if the bottom bore a label or inscription. Hand-painted. She set the vase in the hallway to take downstairs later. She would—

An odd crackling noise startled Jennifer, interrupting her thoughts. Cautiously, she made her way to the opposite side of the "mystery" room, brushing against furniture and boxes to get to the source of the sound.

"That's one way to dust," she mumbled with a hint of disgust that she hadn't thought to put on an old shirt.

Books? She hesitantly bent down to survey the area for signs of anything that could have accounted for the noise. It might be a good idea to have the interior treated for pests. Jennifer heard the sound again, this time about two feet from her left. She stooped to lift the topmost books from a stack on the floor. Beneath was an old book, perhaps a journal, tied shut with a mauve ribbon that had seen better days. Intrigued, Jennifer absentmindedly set the books she had in hand aside. She picked up the one with the ribbon and examined it closer, gently fingering the knot that held it shut. The fact that it was "locked" by a strip of material made her want to see what was inside all the more. She had satisfied her curiosity for the moment with two new-found treasures, the vase and now this book. Jennifer exited the room, turning the key in the knob again out of habit.

She carefully dusted the china vase and eyed the living room for an ideal spot for display. Then she turned her attention to the book. It would be a shame to cut the ribbon. Jennifer washed her hands well and got a toothpick from the pantry. Painstakingly, she worked the knot with the tip of the wooden pick, slowly loosening it. Ten minutes later, her efforts paid off. She opened the book to confirm that it was indeed a journal—the diary of Ruth Gaitley from 1939.

"Ah!" Jennifer squeaked with delight. "Aunt Ruth! You would have been," she paused to do the mental math, "you would have been fourteen?"

The book was delicate but had held up well. Ruth's cursive handwriting, pleasing and legible, increased Jennifer's desire to read the contents.

Dinner could wait a bit. It was even possible that Ted would show up after seeing his last client of the day. Jennifer was prepared to offer spaghetti if that was the case. For now, she curled up in what had become her favorite chair in the short amount of time she'd lived in her aunt's old place.

"Ruth Gaitley, 1939," Jennifer read out loud, "January 1."

Her initial enthusiasm turned to slight disappointment. Aunt Ruth mainly recorded observations of nature and wrote of school assignments. Jennifer gathered that Mr. Johnson had been the science instructor that year and obviously a favorite teacher of Ruth's from the amount she wrote about him. In contrast, Jennifer's mother, Ruth's baby sister, had only received one mention so far. Jennifer paused to estimate Elizabeth's age at that time—a little over a year old. It didn't appear that Ruth took much interest in helping with the child. To Jennifer, Ruth seemed different from most teenagers. So far, no mention of get-togethers with friends, no gossip, and no crushes. Not the most riveting diary.

Jennifer glanced at the clock and gave up on the possibility of Ted dropping by. One frozen dinner later, she returned to read more of the fragile diary.

"March 1," she noted. "Let's pick up the pace, Aunt Ruth," Jennifer said under her breath. "You're even more bookish than I was at your age."

She hadn't noticed the series of unused pages before. Jennifer flipped back and forth, comparing the dates. March 5 through March 26 were completely blank, odd for someone as diligent as she envisioned Ruth.

"March 27," Jennifer picked up and continued. "God has left me to wonder if I bear responsibility for the death of dear Doctor Ephraim. I wish to blot out the memory, but I fear it will linger with me for eternity."

Jennifer bolted upright in the chair. Had she read that correctly? She repeated the words more slowly. Did her aunt kill someone? That couldn't be possible, could it? Jennifer now purposefully skipped over what she viewed as mundane, anxiously seeking elaboration on the March 27 entry.

"March 29," she continued. "Mother and Papa do not discuss Doctor Ephraim in my presence, but the walls have ears, as do I. The newspaper says he was murdered. I weep myself to sleep with guilt." Jennifer put her finger on the smudged words and slightly puckered paper, evidence that Ruth had been crying when she penned this journal entry.

Again, Jennifer reread her aunt's jarring words, attempting to absorb all meaning from them. She jumped ahead to subsequent days' entries but saw little more than further mentions of grief and attempts to cope. By June of 1939, Ruth returned to her more objective recording style. Jennifer reverently placed the worn mauve ribbon in the diary to serve as a bookmark.

"Aunt Ruth," she addressed the empty space around her, "I'm so sorry you felt bad about Doctor Ephraim's death. I don't know why you felt guilty, but I'm sure it wasn't your fault. You were only fourteen."

Suddenly the lights flickered, and the air seemed a tad cooler. Momentarily, Jennifer was taken aback.

"Aunt Ruth?" she said in a faintly questioning tone, although certain she could feel the presence of her aunt around her. "I don't know you, but I do love you. Don't feel bad. Whatever happened is part of the past. Okay?"

Again the lights flickered, and this time the cool air manifested as a slight breeze. Jennifer experienced no fear, however. If anything, she felt a stronger connection. Tonight, she had learned something about her aunt. Ruth Gaitley wasn't a cold person. She had wept for the death of Dr. Ephraim and her possible involvement, whatever that was. Ruth had a secret of some sort, and perhaps that bonded her to this house.

Chapter 3

ANOTHER DAY PASSED, AND still no sign of Ted. Jennifer stowed his business card in a top kitchen drawer but had no intention of calling him. She might have to reconcile herself to the notion that Ted had asked her to dinner solely out of respect for his recently departed friend, Ruth Gaitley. That would make sense—to take the niece out to offer condolences and reminisce. He probably had no intention of seeing Jennifer again despite how he had left it when they parted that night.

Jennifer had been faithful to her resolution to continue exploring Tilbrook. First on the itinerary had been the old stone Presbyterian church. Since the office was open, she inquired inside if anyone knew of Ruth Gaitley. It was a unanimous no. However, all, including the interim minister, appeared to be younger than Jennifer. Ruth most likely wouldn't have had the mobility to continue attending services in her later years. Jennifer asked if the church had membership records. She knew they would and was surprised no one had offered to look up Ruth on their own. By the time Jennifer left the church, she was rewarded with a peek inside the serene sanctuary, a welcome packet, and the knowledge that her aunt had been made an inactive member in 2007.

Teresa Degra's house was easy to spot, almost directly behind the old church. Jennifer recognized it from the photo Teresa had shown her. It looked a little smaller in real life but was cute and well-maintained, at least outwardly. Jennifer knew little about Teresa but imagined that the interior was colorful, somewhat modern, and stocked with cat toys. She envisioned a plethora of wall hangings, tasteful yet eye-catching.

Although Jennifer had never been a habitual procrastinator, she was proud of how she had tackled her long list of chores and errands. For once, she had overestimated the amount of time it would take her. She could honestly tell herself that she was well on her way to settling in.

Angie Calberto made sure to phone daily if she hadn't already heard from her loyal friend Jennifer. Angie took a keen interest in Ruth's diary entries and Jennifer's belief that her aunt was still present in the house. Today was no exception, and Jennifer correctly guessed who was calling before looking at her phone screen.

"Good afternoon," Jennifer answered with mock formality.

"Hey," Angie greeted. "What's new on the home front?"

"I am now an official Tilbrook Public Library card carrier," Jennifer explained with put-on enthusiasm.

"Well, you always did like to read. Speaking of reading, how's the diary coming?"

Jennifer knew she was referring to Aunt Ruth's diary and not to Jennifer's own journal writing. "Not much that's really of interest to me. There are a few references to my mom and my grandparents. Those I enjoy reading. So far, I'm into September. Ruth has only mentioned Doctor Ephraim one more time. She wrote that the police still don't know who killed him. She doesn't think they ever will."

"That doesn't sound like your aunt murdered him, right?" Angie said reassuringly.

"No. I doubt Aunt Ruth did. I still can't figure out why she'd feel guilty about Doctor Ephraim's death, but maybe she meant she felt guilty to be alive when he was dead."

"Maybe he was protecting her," Angie countered.

"Maybe we have overactive imaginations," Jennifer played along.

"Maybe we do! Still, try talking to your aunt! Keep on trying to contact her." Angie was a firm believer in ghosts. She and her daughter, Jolie, had several favorite paranormal shows they watched regularly. Jennifer was open-minded but couldn't call herself a true believer. The house was turning her into one, however.

"I *do* talk out loud to the walls," Jennifer admitted, "quite a bit."

"Good." Angie's tone communicated complete approval. "Ask Ruth questions, too. Have you thought about hiring a paranormal investigator?"

"No!" Jennifer spoke with uncharacteristic sharpness. "I don't want that. I don't think my aunt would have wanted that either."

"Okay, Jen," Angie said soothingly. "Just an option, right? So, now let's focus on the living. Who else have you met in town?"

Jennifer filled her in on a couple of conversations with some people she'd run across during her explorations of Tilbrook. She had already told her friend about meeting Teresa, and Angie asked if Jennifer had heard further from her but noticeably avoided inquiring about Ted. Jennifer figured Angie shared her doubts about whether he would keep in touch.

The two ladies spoke for an additional hour until Jennifer heard the doorbell and bid Angie goodbye. She peered through the peephole and immediately smoothed her hair and straightened her pink blouse when she realized who was on the other side of the door.

"Ted!" Jennifer greeted him with a smile that matched his own.

"I hope it's all right that I dropped by. You see, I don't have your phone number. I remember giving you my card, but I didn't ask for your number, unfortunately. I'll have to remedy that." Ted put his hands in his pockets and took a small step backward. It finally dawned on Jennifer that she was blocking his way into the house.

She quickly stepped aside and motioned him to enter. "Of course, it's fine that you stopped by." Ted wore khakis with a deep blue-gray polo shirt, quite the contrast from his suit and tie several days prior. In her estimation, he looked equally handsome today. The shirt perfectly matched the irises of his eyes. She searched for something to say. "Your day off?" Jennifer chastised herself for asking something so lamely obvious.

"Saturday," he reminded her. "I'm off tomorrow, also. I thought I'd take my chances and see if you might like to go out for a drive. We can get something to eat afterward."

Jennifer hesitated. She wasn't a spontaneous person. Perhaps she should offer to cook that spaghetti she had planned in case he showed up.

"I know it's short notice, and once I have your phone number, I'll call in advance." Ted seemed to read her mind as he spoke. "It's a sunny day, warmer than usual, and I thought we both might like to spend some time along the river."

Jennifer mentally kicked herself for her delayed response. "That sounds like a nice plan. I do like the idea. Give me about ten minutes to get ready."

When she returned downstairs, he was sitting on the sofa leafing through Ruth's diary. She bit her lip in time before saying something that could be taken as a reproach for going through private property.

"I see you found my aunt's journal." Jennifer was pleased that her voice sounded relaxed. She extended her hand for Ted to turn the diary over to her. When he didn't pick up on the hint, she gently put her hand on the book. "It's fragile, I'm afraid. It took me a while to salvage the ribbon." The ribbon that Ted had carelessly let fall to the floor.

He didn't appear flustered to have been caught snooping. Perhaps Jennifer was overly protective of the diary, but she didn't feel it should be treated like a coffee table book for company to pick up and browse.

"Have you learned anything from it?" Ted continued to eye the eighty-something-year-old book.

"Nothing you didn't already know," Jennifer answered, purposefully vague. She hoped he hadn't read about the Doctor Ephraim murder.

Ted smiled but said nothing. There was silence between them for what seemed like an awkward amount of time.

"Are you ready?" Jennifer half wondered if he still wanted to go on an excursion with her.

"You acted a little odd about the diary. Is there something wrong?"

"No." She debated how to handle this. "I can sense my aunt's presence in the house. That's all. Maybe that sounds crazy. Maybe it's because Aunt Ruth just recently passed. I don't know."

Ted genuinely looked concerned. His eyes widened slightly, and his smile vanished. "What do you mean by *presence*?"

Jennifer gave a few examples. Ted seemed more at ease, his casual smile returning.

"So, her diary makes you feel connected to her, which makes you feel that she's here in the house with you," Ted stated his interpretation of what Jennifer had said.

She was about to argue the physical aspects—flickering lights, cool breezes, icy cold spots, and the occasional sensation of an ultra-light touch. Those didn't come from reading a diary.

Ted rose and looked at his watch. "We should get going, Jennifer, if we want to spend a little time enjoying the river before the sun sets."

They drove along a country road that soon lost its pavement, causing Ted to lower his speed. Already it seemed a little cooler, and Jennifer was glad she had brought a light jacket.

Ted knew quite a bit about the area, including the predominant birds and other wildlife. She had her own private tour guide, a handsome one at that. Ted, now fully relaxed, very much seemed to enjoy the outing.

When they reached the river, he parked and unloaded a pair of camping stools from the back of the SUV. "I wish I had thought to bring a couple of sodas." He waved Jennifer's hands away when she attempted to lighten his burden by carrying one of the stools.

Ted walked with determination to a spot that was postcard-worthy in itself. Then he unfolded both camp stools and positioned them to face the river at a forty-five-degree angle. Jennifer took a seat as silently directed and gazed at the stunningly beautiful water, now reflecting shades of teal tinged with yellow and orange. She zipped her jacket further toward her neck and stuck her hands in her pockets. When she turned to address Ted, she noticed he was busy observing her.

"Oh," she briefly gasped in surprise, feeling a little awkward. "It's so lovely here. Thanks for asking me to join you."

"My pleasure," he said with one solemn nod and slowly moved his gaze from Jennifer to the water. He breathed in deeply, obviously enjoying the fresh, fragrant air.

"What was that large building in the distance that we saw when driving here?" Jennifer inquired, attempting to keep the conversation going.

"Which direction?" he asked absentmindedly, transfixed by the river's colors in the lowering sun.

"Probably that way." Jennifer pointed, and Ted glanced at her finger.

"Tenger-Bio, I imagine," Ted said without much inflection to his voice. "I believe that's what you're referring to. Tenger-Bio owns quite a lot of acreage across from here, butted up to the river. It's been around for ages, I think."

"That's where Aunt Ruth worked!" Jennifer sat upright with enthusiasm, craning her neck to look past the river, expecting to see something on the other side that was not visible from this vantage. "Oh, and you, too," she added, remembering that Ted had worked there in his early years.

He nodded. "I did. Of course, it wasn't as large back then, but still, Tenger was a major employer in the area. Tilbrook is a small town, fortunate to have a stable source of jobs with decent wages."

Jennifer thought about Ted now selling annuities when he once worked for Tenger. "Why did you leave if it's such a good place to work?"

Ted looked momentarily surprised. "I prefer the open road and variety I have every day compared to working in an office. Don't get me wrong. I still think Tenger-Bio is a good company, especially for a scientist such as your aunt. Remember, I am not a research biologist." He laughed. It was a soft laugh, perhaps a little sad or wistful.

"I can see the lure of being on the road and having variety. That's what I liked about teaching. The variety. Of course, I wasn't on the road." Jennifer turned to Ted, who met her gaze and smiled. "I think you would have made a great biologist, though," she continued. "I learned more from you on the drive over here than I would have gleaned from a guidebook."

Ted contemplated that for a moment. "Ruth and I shared an appreciation for nature. Perhaps that was the basis for the start of our friendship."

"Is that what you and she discussed over lunch?"

"We did. That and a lot of other things." He sighed.

"The few, and I mean few, people in Tilbrook who remember anything about Ruth emphasized that she was quiet and aloof," Jennifer said, puzzled how a senior woman and young adult male bonded, given that the woman was not known for idle chatter.

"Ruth was friendly," Ted reminded her. "I never viewed her as aloof. People often tack that word onto people who are quiet. I don't think aloof is a synonym for quiet. Most likely, those you've talked with don't actually know Ruth other than in passing."

Jennifer appreciated that Ted stood up for her aunt. He was a loyal friend. She'd have to remember to tell Ruth that. Jennifer laughed out loud when she caught herself thinking of what to say to the ghost of her aunt.

Ted misunderstood the laughter and immediately cast Jennifer a frown. "What was amusing about what I said?"

"Nothing, nothing. I laughed because I thought Ruth would appreciate you standing up for her. I liked that. I liked what you said."

Evidently, Jennifer chose the right thing to say because Ted resumed smiling and even reached out to touch her shoulder. She pulled a hand out of her pocket and rested it on his arm in a return gesture, prompting Ted to enclose her hand with his. She noticed that he didn't let go as they continued to watch the sun lower over the water.

Jennifer appreciated this additional night in which she did not have to cook. Ted took her to a seafood place, which seemed fitting for the end of their afternoon at the river. Jennifer pulled out her cell phone and asked Ted for his number, attempting to imitate Teresa's smooth move at Tito's. However, Jennifer wasn't as polished as Teresa, and Ted pretended he didn't know what she was up to. He teased her, saying that he didn't have his number memorized. Finally, Jennifer pulled a strip from her napkin and wrote her contact information on it. Ted laughed and took out his cell, punching in her number. Once finished, he quickly recited his own.

"You said that pretty rapidly for a guy who never memorized his phone number," Jennifer teased in retaliation.

"I think it was temporary amnesia. Yes, I'm sure it was." Ted smiled. "But now, I have the prize." He held up his phone. "I finally possess Jennifer Shemmer's number."

"Yes, you have my number, all right!" Jennifer blushed, aware that the flirting had turned to silliness. It was fun, though. She and her ex-husband Alex never had conversations like this. Ted was easygoing, spontaneous, fun, and somewhat of a charmer. Alex was, well, just Alex. Serious, goal-oriented, and not so romantic. Perhaps that had changed once he swapped Jennifer for his gorgeous, young office assistant. Hadn't Alex accused Jennifer of being too solemn and lacking in the fun department?

The half-hour trip back to Tilbrook wasn't nearly long enough as far as Jennifer was concerned. She wished Ted would keep driving, but that was unreasonable and impractical, as the evening had to come to a close. After walking Jennifer safely to her door, Ted kissed her briefly but firmly on her lips. Since it was already late, she didn't invite him inside. He didn't ask either—once again, a gentleman. Jennifer shut the door after watching him return to his SUV.

"Aunt Ruth," she said as she switched on the nearest light. "I really like your friend, Ted Filston! And he is so loyal to you," Jennifer continued as if her aunt were sitting on the sofa awaiting her niece's return from her date. "Everything Ted says about you shows that he admired you. Admires you." She didn't know whether to use the present or past tense when speaking to her aunt's spirit.

The lights flickered briefly. Jennifer sat in the floral chair, shifting the pillow to the side. Perhaps Angie was right, and she should try communicating with Ruth more often.

"I can feel your presence in the room, Aunt Ruth." Jennifer slowly swiveled her head, first left and then right. "I hope you're fine. Actually, I hope you're more than that. I want you to be happy."

Again, the lights flickered, and this time, the chill settled on Jennifer. She shivered and folded her arms across her chest. Then she reached for the pillow and used it for added warmth.

"I love you, Aunt Ruth. I am much happier here in your home in Tilbrook than I was in Reddington. Sure, I miss some of the people, but I can still visit them. I needed to reset my life, and you gave me that opportunity. I felt I had lost everything. Well, almost all that really meant something to me—my parents and my marriage. I couldn't imagine how I'd rebuild my life, and then you blessed me with this." Jennifer let go of the pillow long enough to wave her arms in an encompassing gesture.

The lights continued to flicker a bit longer, but the chilliness subsided. Jennifer reached for the diary and took it upstairs. She was too wound to fall asleep, even though it was already past her usual bedtime. Jennifer changed into her gown, washed her face, and brushed her teeth. The plan was to read in bed until she felt the urge to close her eyes. Usually, she liked to write in her own journals; a gratitude journal plus a diary she was accustomed to keeping. However, those could wait until tomorrow.

Jennifer noticed that she had lost her place in her aunt's diary when Ted removed the ribbon to read it for himself. She flipped pages back and forth, looking for where she had left off. Her eyes briefly focused on the words "unexplained" and "sinister." That caught her attention.

"October 28," she stated aloud, deciding to read this entry even though she hadn't yet gotten that far in the journal. "I am increasingly aware of an otherworldly presence in this house and on the grounds. I try to rationalize what I observe, but it must go unexplained. Is it of a sinister nature? I pray to our Lord that this is not the case. I pray for protection, in the name of Jesus Christ and all that is good, but I am frightened."

Jennifer bolted out of bed. "Oh my God!"

She hadn't had time to fully process what she had read, but her instinct was to get out immediately. Obviously, it wasn't the spirit of her aunt that was present in this house. Who or what it was, she didn't know. Hurriedly, Jennifer changed into jeans and a top and grabbed the diary. She hadn't realized how quickly she could descend stairs. Snatching her cell phone along with its charger, Jennifer stuffed them into her purse and fled the house.

She didn't know where she was going yet drove with speed and purpose, only forcing herself to decelerate when she noticed the high speedometer reading. Jennifer took deep breaths and reminded herself that she was safe. Even if she hadn't packed a suitcase, she had brought the means to pay for a motel for a few days until she had "this" sorted—whatever it was.

Chapter 4

THE PHONE RANG AROUND 10 a.m., gently bringing Jennifer out of her troubled sleep. She was too groggy to do much more than turn on her back and rub her palms over her forehead. Reality came crashing back, and she opened her eyes, remembering that she was in a motel, somewhere between Tilbrook and Bilmore.

Jennifer forced herself to get out of bed to place the "Do Not Disturb" sign on the other side of the door. She dampened a washcloth with lukewarm water and held it to her eyes. That felt good. She thought about brushing her teeth and then remembered she hadn't brought toiletries.

On the dresser lay her cell phone, plugged into its charger. Jennifer swiped the screen to see who had called earlier, hoping it was Angie. Sure enough. She unplugged the phone and sauntered to the window to push back the heavy curtains. It was overcast and dreary outside, matching Jennifer's mood.

She plopped on the edge of the queen-sized bed to return Angie's call. Her friend promptly answered in her usual upbeat manner. It didn't take long, though, for Angie to realize that something was amiss.

"I'm staying in a motel for a few days," Jennifer announced after telling Angie what she had learned from Ruth's diary. "When I thought it was my aunt's spirit remaining in the house, I could live with that. Now that I know it's some other spirit, well, no. I don't know. I don't know if I can deal with that." She shook her head and stared out the window, noticing the light rain.

Angie listened to Jennifer's narration of the previous night without interrupting. She empathized with her friend and then asked, "When you fall off a bike, what's the advice?'

Jennifer knew she was referring to getting back on and trying again. "This isn't the same," she said, upset with herself for the irritation she detected in her own voice. "I'm sorry. I don't mean to be prickly. It's just an emotional rollercoaster. I was so happy yesterday, so thankful to have the house and live in Tilbrook. I had spent a fantastic afternoon at the river with Ted, who did show up again yesterday, by the way. We had a nice dinner together, and then I decided to read Aunt Ruth's journal some more, and then I learned *this*."

"I know, I know. Listen to me, though, Jen," Angie soothed. "Take a step back. You have been fine while living in the home, right? Nothing bad has happened to you. Some weird stuff with the lights and some cold air. You've told me many times that you felt a friendly presence, which is why you assumed it was Ruth."

Jennifer was silent, only forcing herself to give a noncommittal "hmm" when Angie didn't continue.

Her friend took that as a positive signal and proceeded to advise. "Why don't you finish reading the diary while staying at the motel? You might find out that it's not what you think."

"I brought the journal with me, and that's what I did last night—read. I was way too stressed to sleep, at least until the early morning." Jennifer sighed. "I don't feel better! Aunt Ruth mentions the same hauntings I'm experiencing, Ange. She was afraid herself."

"If there was one diary, the odds are there will be another, right? You keep journals, Jen. You hang on to them, don't you?"

"A few," Jennifer conceded. She didn't like where this was going, that she should return to the house to search for another diary.

"Keep in mind that Ruth wrote about this weird haunting stuff in 1940."

"In 1939," Jennifer corrected.

"Even better. She lived in that house well into her nineties. Ruth wouldn't have stayed if there was something to be frightened of. If you find some other diaries, you might learn more about what Ruth experienced. You'll probably feel a lot better. At the very least, you'll know more about what's going on."

Jennifer relaxed some as she listened to her good pal. "I guess you're right." Angie made sense, but Jennifer wasn't totally convinced.

"Did Ruth write anything about her parents and their reactions to the house?"

"Yes. Actually, she did. It appears that her parents discouraged her from talking about the subject. Her father told her it wouldn't reflect well on the family." Jennifer paused. "Whatever that meant."

"Did either parent think the house was haunted?"

Jennifer imagined they did but replied, "I'm not sure. Aunt Ruth didn't come out and say that."

Angie gave a short groan. "Look for another diary, Jen. Try to find out more. Listen, would you like to stay with us for a while until you feel more yourself?"

Jennifer would like nothing more, but that wasn't a practical solution. She had an exterminator coming on Monday and was expecting Teresa to call any time now about the window covering installations. She also wanted to see Ted again—soon.

"When I checked in last night, Ange, I asked to stay two nights. The guy at the desk told me I'd get a discount if I booked for three. That's what I did, so I've already paid for tonight and tomorrow night. I'll have to go home today to pick up a few things, but at least I don't have to sleep in the house." She paused, then added, "Yet."

"That's a good plan," Angie said encouragingly. "Things aren't as scary in the daylight as they are at night. Spend some time looking around the house today and tomorrow. You'll feel better knowing you're leaving before dark."

They spent another nineteen minutes talking, and Jennifer was pleased to realize that she had temporarily forgotten the upset she felt upon waking. Angie filled her in about Jolie's latest crush, and Jennifer smiled because it reminded her of how she had felt at dinner last night, flirting with the charming Ted Filston.

After ending the conversation with Angie, Jennifer searched her phone for Ted's number. "Darn," she said softly, frowning. She hadn't entered his number after all, and his business card was at home in a drawer. Jennifer double-checked her contact information, annoyed with herself for her oversight. He was off today, Sunday. If Jennifer needed an incentive to return to her house—and she did—this was the carrot on the stick that worked for her. She pulled a comb from her purse and tidied her hair the best she could. She was ready.

Jennifer overestimated the time it would take to drive back to her home. The motel seemed much further away last night. No wonder the man at the front desk looked at her strangely when she presented her temporary driving permit for identification. He had seen the Tilbrook address. Much to his credit, he discreetly asked no questions. Jennifer declined help with her luggage, failing to mention that she had none.

She tried the doorknob, checking to see if she had remembered to lock up before fleeing yesterday. She was relieved to find that she had. Once in the entryway, she loudly called out, "Is anyone here?" Jennifer didn't know why she had yelled that silly question. Who did she expect would answer? A rodent? A ghost? She set her purse on the table.

How to prioritize? Should she brush her teeth or call Ted? She chose the latter but first transferred the number from Ted's business card to her cell.

"Ted?" She was afraid she had reached his voicemail.

"Yes. Jennifer?" Ted sounded delighted to hear from her. "I was just thinking about you. I'm glad we chose yesterday for our river trip. It's a little soggy today." He laughed.

"Ted, I had some trouble in the house last night, so I'm staying at a motel for a few nights. Would it be possible for you to come by today?" She got straight to the point and hoped she wasn't putting him on the spot.

"Trouble in your home? Last night after I left? Are you all right?" He sounded alarmed, and Jennifer realized she was being too dramatic.

"Yes, Ted, I'm fine. Let me start again because I didn't do a good job of wording it. Those physical things happening in this house—the flickering lights, the breeze, the odd noises—happened again. Then I read in my aunt's diary that she experienced these things, also. She was scared. At least she was back in 1939. I was frightened, too, so I took off for a motel." Jennifer hoped he wouldn't laugh at her.

"I'll be over in," Ted paused, probably calculating how long the drive would take and whatever he needed to do first, "let's say half an hour or so."

"Thank you!" Jennifer's delighted relief was endearing. "I really appreciate it."

"I'm on my way."

"See you soon," she replied and heard the reassuring click ending the call.

She barely had time to freshen up and change clothes before Ted arrived, although she had managed to wolf down a slice of buttered toast. Knowing that Ted would soon be there gave her fortitude and a restored appetite.

Ted bent for a quick kiss when she opened the door. Jennifer greeted him with a hug before ushering him inside. He made his way to the living room and motioned for Jennifer to sit next to him on the sofa, a welcomed invitation.

"Do you believe me now when I tell you there's something strange about this house?" she asked with an I-told-you-so tone.

"You wouldn't be paying for a motel if you didn't truly think so," Ted replied, somewhat begging the question. Jennifer appreciated the supportive arm he'd slipped behind her shoulders.

Suddenly, it dawned on her that Ted might know more than he currently realized. "Didn't you notice some odd things when you lived here?"

"No." He slowly shook his blonde head. "Nothing out of the ordinary. Ruth never warned me about the house or told me stories about hauntings."

"That's strange." Jennifer sighed. Surely, she wasn't imagining things. No, she had Ruth's writings as proof. "Will you help me look for another diary? There are a lot of belongings upstairs."

"Absolutely!" Ted quickly rose, startling Jennifer. She hadn't meant immediately, but why not? As he followed her upstairs, he gave practical counsel about having an electrician and an exterminator come to the house. Jennifer contrasted his advice with Angie's. Angie had not doubted the presence of a spirit for a moment. Ted apparently didn't believe in the supernatural.

"I've got an exterminator coming tomorrow," Jennifer informed him. "I guess I could call an electrician, but since the lights were flickering decades ago, why bother?" Still, it wouldn't hurt to rule out all possibilities. Jennifer left Ted standing by the mystery room door while she went to retrieve the key.

"I found the first diary in the stack of books over there." Jennifer pointed across the room once she'd unlocked the space. "It's still dusty in here," she continued apologetically.

Ted was already making himself at home, picking up bric-a-brac and inspecting the bottom inscriptions. "Oh, don't worry about that," he said absentmindedly.

"Over here," she directed. "Let's start with the books."

Jennifer hadn't worn a watch, but she guessed at least half an hour had passed. She noticed that Ted was highly methodical and slow in his search. She wondered what it would be like to go shopping with him. Evidently, he wasn't the type of man who walked in and out with the sole intent of making his purchase and leaving. That's how her ex-husband had been. Browsing was unimaginable.

"I'm a little discouraged," Jennifer broke the silence, aware that they hadn't been chatting but instead focused on the task at hand.

"There's still a lot to sift through." Ted shot her an encouraging smile. "There are boxes upon boxes. What about the rolltop desk?" He motioned with the hand that still held the figurine he'd been studying.

Jennifer had tried the desk earlier and couldn't get it to open. "Locked," she informed him but walked over to try once more. "Do you think you'd have better luck?"

Ted made an attempt and then asked Jennifer for a paperclip. She returned with both a bobby pin and a small paperclip. Ted unbent the clip, and when that didn't work, he tried the hairpin. "And you don't recall seeing any small keys anywhere?"

"No," Jennifer replied, clearly disappointed. "I'll call Steve tomorrow." When Ted looked at her with slight surprise, she added, "Locksmith." Ted nodded.

She opened one additional box, and the pair carefully unpacked it. Since the contents revealed no books, Jennifer offered, "I'll treat you to a late lunch or early dinner. There's a café about three blocks from here that looks inviting."

"I am hungry!" Ted patted his stomach with a grin.

Unfortunately, the small diner Jennifer had in mind wasn't open on Sunday. However, the newer side of town had multiple choices. Ted joined her in ordering a garden salad and iced tea. Alex would never have ordered salad for an entree. She smiled, realizing that she had compared Ted with her ex several times today, and Ted came out ahead each time.

He noticed her facial expression and commented that she looked much more relaxed and happier than when he first saw her at the house that morning. Jennifer nodded, sipping her tea through a paper straw.

"I think I should stay with you tonight," Ted announced bluntly, eyeing her directly.

At that, Jennifer set her glass down. "I'll be fine." She was flattered that he offered but didn't want to deal with possible expectations on his part at this early stage of their friendship. "I'm not staying at the house, anyway. I've paid for two more nights at the motel."

"You might be able to talk them into a refund." Ted flashed her one of his most enchanting smiles.

It would be nice to have him around, but no, not yet. "I don't want to ask for my money back, plus I accepted a discount deal. You sure made going into my home easier today and much more pleasant." Jennifer hoped he'd accept this praise and be satisfied.

"Another option is to give me your house key and let me stay there the night. I can investigate any strange occurrences."

The suggestion surprised Jennifer. Perhaps if she had known Ted longer, she would have jumped at his offer. She pictured Ted alone in her house, with his habit of making himself comfortable. The image of Ted reading Ruth's diary the other day flashed through her mind. Although this was a small thing, it was still enough to remind her to follow her initial instincts.

"That's so nice of you, Ted," Jennifer said appreciatively, "but I'm fine. I have a plan now, and I'm feeling better as you noticed yourself."

His grin faded slightly, but he nodded in agreement. "Keep in mind that my old room is still pretty much as it was back in the day," he added persuasively.

So, Ted wasn't suggesting he sleep in Jennifer's bed. She felt mild guilt and sheepishness over not letting Ted help. Still...

"I'll keep that in mind," she said with some uncertainty.

Ted dropped her off at her home and insisted he check inside before departing to make sure Jennifer felt safe. Since it was late afternoon, she had no qualms about being there alone for the little time it would take her to pack a small overnight bag. Ted made one final offer to stay, but Jennifer stood on her toes to kiss him goodbye on the cheek. He put his hands on her shoulders and found her lips with his. It was a longer kiss than the previous ones.

Steve showed up around noon on Monday, just as he had estimated. Jennifer had already been at the house an hour. Still no sign of a second diary, though. This time, she left the mystery room open since the point of Steve's return visit was to unlock the rolltop desk.

The locksmith admired the antique furniture piece and had it unrolled in no time. He praised Jennifer for not damaging the lock by attempting to force it. Jennifer tried each drawer and found another need for Steve to employ his skill. Once that drawer was also unlocked, she pulled it fully open to see what secrets it guarded. A diary—one with a lock, but its tiny key had been left in place.

"Looks like you've got some reading material," Steve said. He glanced around the room with the same appreciation he had the first time he'd opened the mystery room. "If you're thinking of selling some of this stuff, I'd try Bilmore. You'll get more for it there. Tilbrook has a small antique shop, but nothing compared to Bilmore."

"Do you have any recommendations?" She tried to make herself forget the diary long enough to focus on the locksmith.

"Yeah, if you have some paper, I'll write down two places I've used. Don't know the addresses, but you can look them up. One's a pawnshop. Try the antique place first."

"So, you like antiques," Jennifer stated bluntly.

"Well, my brother and I inherited some stuff." Steve shrugged. "You know."

Yes, Jennifer did know. She got the information from the locksmith and walked him out. He thanked her for the repeat business and drove off just as her next appointment pulled up. A highly productive day, she noted.

The exterminator wasn't as personable as either Steve or Teresa, but he was competent and professional. Jennifer tried following him around the house and grounds but eventually gave up. She imagined he was relieved. When he presented Jennifer with a pesticide package that included quarterly treatments, she cringed at the cost but agreed. Maybe she'd skip the electrician for the time being and not reserve the motel for additional nights. However, it was a relief to hear that the only pests in the house appeared to be a few crickets and cockroaches. Too bad there was nothing the exterminator could do for a ghost infestation, she thought wryly.

Jennifer relocked the mystery room after the exterminator took off and got ready to leave for her final night at the Cozy Cottage Motel. It was still early afternoon, but she had some reading to do, and for that, she preferred to be leaning against propped-up pillows in the motel's queen-sized bed, sipping a vending machine diet soda. Jennifer left the tiny key on her nightstand and carefully placed the newly-found second diary in her tote. On impulse, she packed her own gratitude journal and diary. Maybe writing in those would help her see the silver lining to living in a potentially haunted house. She noticed that she no longer fled her home in fear and felt no pressure to leave. That pleased her.

The drive toward Bilmore was pleasant since today was better weather-wise than yesterday, at least if you were inclined toward sunshine as Jennifer was. Still, the rains kept the grass green and the narrow river flowing. Jennifer bought a can of soda from the outside vending machine, happy that it accepted the worn bill with no issues. Before settling in, she grabbed the ice bucket to stock up on cubes for the remainder of the day.

The drink tasted good. Usually, Jennifer avoided cola, but there was something about motels and soda that, for her, went hand in hand. She imagined it was nostalgia from childhood trips with her parents, who tended to bring in beverages and ice for the evening. Not much else to do in small motels except watch TV, read, talk, and snack.

Jennifer had her motel comforts in order. Now, she pulled back the bedspread and untied her sneakers. She leaned the pillows against the headboard and sat in bed, ready to tackle the latest edition of Aunt Ruth's diary.

"Nineteen forty-nine," Jennifer read. "Hmm. Aunt Ruth would turn twenty-four that year, so still a young woman, but a decade later than the first diary," she pondered aloud.

"Ephraim," Jennifer said, noticing that this name was mentioned frequently. She randomly flipped through the small book and discovered that Ephraim was a regularly occurring character in 1949. Surely this wasn't Doctor Ephraim, the man who had been murdered, the man Ruth had felt guilt over?

In contrast to Aunt Ruth's teenage diary, Jennifer was engrossed in this one. She absentmindedly sipped her soda, so much so that she quickly drained it. Eventually, she decided it was worth the effort to slip back into shoes and head to the vending machine with more money.

Jennifer popped the tab and poured part of the latest can's contents into a glass with fresh ice. Her feet were out of her sneakers in no time.

"I do not know what I would do without Ephraim," Jennifer read aloud, "who brightens my life enormously. I can spend infinite time within my own head, fascinated by pursuits others find unfit for my age and gender. Ephraim understands me. In the strangest sense, it is through him that I find connection to the outer world."

Jennifer skimmed the pages this time, wanting to complete the diary today while she was at the motel. The more she read, the more it appeared that this Ephraim character seemed very much alive to Ruth. There was no mention of ghosts or being frightened by anything other than a party Ruth felt she had to attend or whenever college exams were oral rather than written.

Jennifer tried to piece together the fragments of information. Apparently, Ruth wasn't living at home. She was still in college. If she was twenty-four, she was probably a grad student. When Ruth returned home for vacations, Ephraim's name came up in her diary frequently. Elizabeth, Jennifer's mom, was twelve at the time, making her an upper-elementary student. Ruth mentioned her sister but only in terms of how she had grown and how Elizabeth didn't share her sister's aptitude for science and math. Per Ruth, Elizabeth was primarily interested in boys. Jennifer could see how the age gap and personality differences separated the siblings despite being raised by the same biological parents.

"Well, Aunt Ruth," Jennifer talked to the diary on her lap, "who was this Ephraim you liked so much? He seems to have been a close friend, yet you don't actually describe him. Was he your boyfriend? Did he live in the neighborhood?"

When Jennifer noticed the light dimming outside the curtains, she closed the book and once again put on her shoes and coat. She recalled a fast-food place about five minutes away. Tonight, she might even opt for fries and a cheeseburger. Not health food, but she was simply looking for comfort and convenience at this point.

No one was in line ahead of her in the drive-through, but this was Monday. Jennifer brought her goodies back to the motel, careful to spread enough napkins on the nightstand she used as her dining table. She ate while halfway watching a sitcom repeat, still wondering if there was a connection between Ephraim in this latest diary and Doctor Ephraim, who was murdered. She finished the last of the fries and carefully washed her hands so as not to damage the pages of her aunt's diary.

Again, she plopped down on the bed and grabbed the little book, searching for more clues. Ephraim seemed to be present a lot, yet there was a surprising lack of detail about him. When Ruth mentioned being with other groups, Ephraim's name was missing. Also, there was no apparent interaction between Ephraim and the other members of

Ruth's family. And what's this part about Ephraim growing stronger? Was he ill? Sickly but still able to visit the Gaitley house on a regular basis?

"Eureka!" Jennifer exclaimed about an hour later. "Ephraim," Jennifer read aloud, "let me know that he approves of my new dress by manipulating my lamp. A single light flicker signals an affirmative. Two rapid light flickers signal a negative. We don't communicate this way when we are not alone. Mother and Papa know he is here but can't admit it. Myself, I think it's wonderful that Ephraim is here."

Jennifer contemplated what she had just read and repeated the passage several times. Ephraim is a spirit. Aunt Ruth no longer calls him Doctor Ephraim, but it must be him. Ruth seems to have peace with his murder and doesn't appear to feel guilty. If anything, Ephraim has become Ruth's closest ... friend?

Jennifer glanced up from the diary and, in a muffled voice, pondered, "Closest ghost friend?"

Chapter 5

HOME SWEET HOME. JENNIFER unlocked the door and placed her overnight bag inside. What a contrast. Three days ago, she had been terrified to sleep in her own bedroom. Now she felt serenity when stepping inside the entryway.

Teresa would be here in an hour with the first batch of blinds, the ones for the upstairs. Jennifer unpacked the little she had taken with her to the motel. She unlocked the mystery room and placed both of Aunt Ruth's diaries inside the rolltop desk so they wouldn't be on public display.

Ted had called several times to check on Jennifer, and his concern touched her. Of course, he still believed there was a practical, easy-to-explain answer for the strange happenings in the house. She couldn't blame him. Jennifer hadn't mentioned Ephraim to Ted. If Ruth had chosen not to tell him about Ephraim, then she wouldn't either.

Angie, however, was a different story. She was a daily part of Jennifer's life via phone. Her friend was thrilled that Jennifer had taken her advice to look for other diaries, and Angie readily romanticized Ephraim. She imagined a touching, soulmate connection between an introverted young woman and a lonely ... ghost?

Jennifer had a new mission that energized her. She wanted to learn as much as she could about this Doctor Ephraim. Surely there would be some record of him.

The doorbell rang, and Jennifer looked through the peephole to confirm the presence of Teresa, who was a tad earlier than expected.

"Hi! Good to see you!" Jennifer opened the door widely to allow Teresa to bring in the first load of slats.

Teresa bypassed the customary greetings and small talk. "Can I take these directly upstairs? It's just me today because my partner's on another call. I should be able to handle the blinds myself, but if you could help me carry and hold a few things in place, that would make the process easier." She turned and winked at Jennifer.

"I'd love to help in any way." Actually, Jennifer was pleased to learn that it would just be Teresa and her today, allowing for girl talk.

She followed Teresa to her hatchback several times, and the two carried their loads upstairs. Teresa apparently had an excellent memory because she knew precisely where each package went. They started in the room adjacent to the main bedroom. Although Jennifer could do little more than hold parts or locate items, Teresa expected nothing more than this and not once did she ask Jennifer to hand her a specific tool.

"Will it distract you or bother you if I talk?" Jennifer finally asked. Teresa was on the top rung of the medium ladder, and Jennifer's glance traveled to Teresa's shoes. Today's choice was practical; a sturdy yet flashy sneaker with fuchsia laces.

"Nope."

Jennifer waited for her to expand her answer, but when she didn't, Jennifer continued, "Have you ever heard of Doctor Ephraim, who lived in Tilbrook in the early 1900s and was killed in 1939?"

Teresa initially laughed, then stifled herself since the man in question was deceased, and Jennifer looked serious. "I'm sorry, I don't know anything about him. I guess I laughed because I wasn't expecting a question about someone from that long ago. Why do you ask?"

"He may have been a friend of Ruth's." In case Teresa had forgotten details of their past conversations, she added, "My aunt, Ruth Gaitley."

"I don't recall a Dr. Ephraim, and we don't have any Dr. Ephraims in Tilbrook now. Doctors of all types are in short supply here, and some people head to Bilmore."

"Any tips on where to check for past records?"

"Have you tried the library? They might have newspaper archives." Teresa stepped down from the ladder. "It's located—"

Jennifer cut her off, explaining that she'd already been there and obtained a library card. "I should have thought of that myself. That would be a good starting point. Thanks."

She watched Teresa skillfully use the power tools and position the blinds single-handedly. When she voiced her admiration, Teresa humbly brushed the compliments aside.

"Practice, practice, practice," the perky installer said, pushing her almost-black hair from her eyes as she looked up at the next window top. She repositioned the ladder to tackle the next job.

"You seem to really enjoy what you do."

"I do, yes." Teresa sighed. "I like the freedom to get out of the shop, drive a little, and meet new people, but the best part is seeing the final result. I have something tangible to show for my efforts."

Jennifer saw the similarity to how Ted had described his job. "Do you ever think about owning a business? Being self-employed?" Obviously, Teresa was quite capable.

"Yes, but I probably won't go that route." She reached for a bracket that Jennifer held. "Owning a store is a ton of work and responsibility. I get paid well for what I do, and I'm content. I have free time and a stable enough schedule. I can ask for time off, plus I like my co-worker. I don't have the ambition it requires to take that idea further."

It was an honest answer, and Jennifer had heard small business owners talk about the horrendous hours and stress. Like anything else, there were advantages and disadvantages.

"What about you?" Teresa repositioned the ladder again. "What do you plan on doing in Tilbrook?"

"Good question," Jennifer replied, "and I don't have a good answer. I'm going to allow myself time to settle in, which may take a few months. Then I may either get part-time employment or do volunteer work. It won't be in teaching, though. That was my past life. I might do something that involves social service."

"Tilbrook could always use volunteers. You'd be welcomed."

Teresa worked her way through the three rooms that were recipients of the new blinds. Jennifer admired the results. The blinds looked sharp, a combination of modern with an antique heirloom curtain look.

Teresa grinned broadly and fished for a compliment. "What do you think?"

"You were right to suggest these. I think they're perfect for this house!" Jennifer softly clapped.

"As do I." Teresa stood with her arms folded across her chest, admiring her work.

"Do you want something to drink, iced tea or pomegranate juice, or do you need to take off?" She hoped the young woman would stay, at least for a few minutes.

"I made a little time today," Teresa replied with a wink, "just as I said I would. Could I have iced tea with a little of the juice added?"

Jennifer hadn't thought to do that, but it sounded delicious, so she prepared two pomegranate teas and brought them to the living room. Her guest had already made herself comfortable on the sofa, slipping off her sneakers to reveal socks you might see in an art museum gift shop.

"Cute socks," Jennifer remarked. "All of mine are white. No, I take that back. I have a couple of pairs of black socks."

Teresa laughed. "What can I say? I like color."

The two ladies conversed for another hour, both enjoying the companionship. Jennifer shared that when she visited the old Trinity Presbyterian Church, she looked for Teresa's house in the vicinity. A pleased Teresa promised to invite

Jennifer over soon to see the home's interior, which she then described in some detail. The doorbell interrupted Jennifer in the middle of one of her stories about her pre-Tilbrook life. She excused herself and squinted through the peephole of the front door.

Ted! She was surprised he hadn't called first, especially now that he had both her landline and cell numbers. Jennifer unlocked the door and gestured, alerting him that she had company.

"Yes, I saw the car." He strolled into the living room, walked over to Teresa, and extended his hand. "Pleased to meet you. I'm Ted Filston." He didn't go into detail about his connection to Jennifer.

Teresa introduced herself and let Ted know she was there both for business and social reasons. With that, she gulped down the last of her tea and made the excuse that she should return to the shop before she was missed.

Ted sat in one of the floral chairs and set its pillow on the floor. Jennifer walked Teresa out, carrying her satchel of tools while Teresa lugged the ladder. Jennifer was surprised Ted hadn't offered to help, but his back was to them, so perhaps he was oblivious. The two ladies returned from Teresa's hatchback to haul out the last few items.

After seeing Teresa off, Jennifer noticed that Ted had moved to the sofa. He'd left the pillow on the floor, however, and Jennifer stooped to return it to the chair before taking a seat next to him.

"I dropped by to see how you were doing on your first full day back here." He made an encompassing gesture with his arms.

She glanced at the clock. "You got off early."

"I work overtime some days, but not today." Ted squeezed her hand. "Would you like to have dinner with me?"

This was getting to be a habit, and although Jennifer liked seeing Ted, she had hoped to spend the rest of the day in solitude, watching a little television to unwind. However, she still had the fixings for spaghetti and garlic bread, so she graciously offered that option to Ted. He, in turn, gallantly gave her a choice of cooking or allowing him to treat her to dinner. Since Jennifer preferred to stay home, she rose to start the meal even though it was still relatively early. Ted followed her into the kitchen and offered to help.

"I'm fine," Jennifer replied with a smile. "Let me get the water boiling and the meat defrosting in the microwave." Ted watched her as she moved, which made her slightly self-conscious. "Something to drink?" she offered, with the dual purpose of being a good hostess and distracting Ted.

"What do you have for alcoholic beverages? Red wine?"

"You know, I was just commenting to Teresa that I don't have alcohol. I'm not much of a drinker. I guess if I'm going to have friends over, I should buy a few bottles."

"I'll bring something next time." Ted gave a simple shrug. "I'll have whatever your friend was drinking. Teresa, right?"

"Yes. Teresa Degra." Jennifer got another glass from the cupboard. "Iced tea with pomegranate juice?"

"Great." He walked to the kitchen window and commented on the lovely view.

Ted mainly did the talking while Jennifer worked on the meal, and she was glad because she was a little tired. She would rather be soaking in a warm bath right now and hoped

Ted wouldn't be offended if she cut the evening short after dinner. He had been so nice to help her out on Sunday, though, plus Ted had checked on her several times a day since. Jennifer felt she owed him her attention and company if that's what he now wanted.

"And," Ted continued his story about his time in Las Vegas, "that's how I came to love garlic bread." He looked at her with a broad grin, confident that she had found his story amusing.

In truth, Jennifer had only been half-listening and had missed the bulk of the story, but she covered for that fact. "Well, sir, garlic bread you shall have, but it's the frozen kind that comes in a box."

"My favorite!" He beamed. Ted truly was quite charming and a great conversationalist. She could see what an asset that would be in his line of work. Jennifer had never developed the gift of gab past asking a few questions about the other person. She admired him.

Ted insisted on setting the table and took it upon himself to pull out the candlesticks from the china cabinet. Jennifer hadn't even noticed them before. The melted tops of the candles suggested that they had been lit at least once. She wondered if Ted planned on burning them tonight.

She brought out the spaghetti sauce while Ted carried the bowl of pasta. When Jennifer returned from the kitchen with the garlic bread, the candles flamed, and he already had her chair pulled out for her.

"Mmm, excellent!" Ted gave his approval. Jennifer was thankful the sauce turned out as well as it did. Sometimes she didn't get the seasoning right, and the sauce was bland.

This time, there was the perfect amount of tanginess. The garlic bread was soft in the center with a crispy edge, just as she liked it.

Ted complimented her cooking multiple times as they ate. Even though he did the bulk of the talking, Jennifer was the last to finish. She wished she had more to offer for dessert than packaged cookies, but her guest didn't seem to mind.

"So," he began after they had cleared the plates. "I am prepared to stay the night with you if you'd like."

Jennifer hadn't seen *that* coming. She thought they'd been through this earlier. "Not now," she said, hoping he'd understand and not take offense. "I don't want to jump into anything too quickly. I had a messy divorce during an already trying time."

"I'm flattered, Jennifer, but I was thinking I'd sleep on the sofa or in my old room."

"Oh!" Jennifer was embarrassed and turned several shades of pink. "I'm so—"

Ted laughed. "I'm kidding, Jennifer. Of course, I'm attracted to you, and if you were ready, that would be terrific. It's also fine that you're not. I offered because you just spent three nights in a motel rather than sleep in this house. I thought you'd feel better if I was available nearby."

Jennifer was a little ashamed of herself. Ted was sweet and considerate. Oddly, she was no longer frightened of the house, though, and looked forward to some alone time. Plus, she felt drained.

"I need to face this by myself for now, Ted. I hope you understand. If there's a problem, then I'll reconsider, but I'm not anticipating trouble."

He looked a little perplexed. Jennifer hadn't told him about Ephraim or fully explained how she went from freaked out to totally relaxed—well, mostly relaxed. She still had to get used to this Ephraim spirit.

Ted made a couple more persuasive arguments for staying with her but realized that she was only digging in her heels all the more. He decided not to press further and took his cue to exit, complimenting Jennifer again on the meal. He leaned in to kiss her and was pleased that she still seemed to have interest in him. Ted took his leave, finally giving her the house to herself.

Jennifer ran comfortably warm bathwater and added lavender Epsom salts from a clear glass container on the shelf. Despite knowing she was alone in the house, she shut the door tightly. She hoped the ghost respected privacy.

The library proved to be a dead-end for information on Doctor Ephraim, although Jennifer did receive a tip to try the historical society. She didn't know Tilbrook had such a thing, but it made sense, being an older town. It was close to where Teresa lived, too, but if Teresa was aware of the place, she hadn't thought to mention it.

After two failed attempts to spot the building, Jennifer parked her Toyota and set out on foot. She glanced at the address scribbled on the small scrap of pink paper, although Jennifer had the numbers committed to memory by now. No wonder she had driven past. The only thing identifying the house as anything other than a residence was a hard-to-read metal plaque to the left of the entrance.

She was pleased that the knob freely turned when she tried the door. An older, slightly stooped man greeted her almost immediately.

"Hello. Welcome!" He gave a slight nod of his head.

"Hi." Jennifer took a deep breath. "I'm new here in town, and I was hoping to find information about a Dr. Ephraim. Unfortunately, all I know about him was that he was killed in Tilbrook in 1939. I wondered if you'd have any records from Tilbrook that go back that far."

The man motioned her to come further into what once had obviously been the living room but now functioned as a museum-like display area. "I'm not familiar with that name, at least not off the top of my head, but since you have a specific year to work with, you might be able to find a newspaper clipping that mentions him."

Jennifer felt a wave of optimism. "You have old newspapers from that long ago?"

The man's eyes glanced upward at her, although his neck couldn't fully straighten. "We have microfiche and dedicated volunteers, like myself, who are working on digitizing our research library holdings. Besides, 1939 isn't that far back in time."

"You're right. Of course. That's great." Jennifer smiled. She hoped she hadn't inadvertently offended him. Suddenly, it occurred to her that she had been so focused on her mission to get information that she had skipped the introduction stage. "My name's Jennifer Shemmer, by the way. I've lived here about a month now, so I figured I should learn more about my new town."

"I'm Samuel," he said, and although he didn't offer a last name or a handshake, Jennifer's impression was that Samuel was a kind, friendly man, perfect for greeting the public. She wondered how large this public was, however. How many days did Samuel sit at his perch in what used to be the dining area, with zero visitors entering?

"Pleased to meet you, Samuel," she made sure to repeat his name as she followed him into a back area of the house.

"Nineteen thirty-nine?" he questioned. "Do you have a particular month in mind, or do you want to see all we have from the local paper for that year?" He motioned for Jennifer to sit at a table that reminded her of the old library at her college.

"Prior to April." Jennifer thought back to Aunt Ruth's diary. "I believe Dr. Ephraim died either in February or March, but I can't be sure."

Samuel said nothing as he readied archived material for his guest to view. Jennifer took the time to gaze around her, noting the details of the room. "Was this the den of the original house?" she inquired to break the long silence.

"This portion was completely remodeled in 1996. The kitchen was gutted and a wall removed." He paused and added, "But you're correct. Part of this room had been a den of sorts at one time."

"Nineteen ninety-six? So, were you living in Tilbrook at that time?" Jennifer asked while Samuel slowly and meticulously directed his attention to loading the past for his visitor to observe.

"I was born in Tilbrook in 1940." Samuel volunteered the information with a hint of pride in his voice.

Jennifer registered surprised, not that Samuel was born here, but that he wasn't as old as she had estimated. She had figured him to be around her aunt's age, in his nineties. "I inherited the Gaitley place," she explained. "I'm the niece of Ruth Gaitley."

"Ah, yes!" Samuel stopped what he was doing and stiffly turned to Jennifer. "I remember Ruth. She was a smart woman! I liked her."

Jennifer could feel the enthusiasm spreading to her facial expression. "What else can you tell me about Ruth?"

He directed Jennifer to view a screen that now displayed newspaper articles from February 1939. "She was older than me, and she kept to herself mostly. We attended the same church, Trinity Presbyterian. After service, people gathered in the courtyard to socialize. Sometimes Ruth and I talked. She had a fascinating job at Tenger!" He laughed. "I knew she was smart because most of what she said about her research went straight over my head. She did teach me to identify some of the different butterflies we have around here, though."

"But she never mentioned Dr. Ephraim?" Jennifer bluntly asked.

"Not that I recall. If she did, it would have been in passing. I'll leave you to look through February." He pointed to the screen. "Holler when you're ready for March." Jennifer would hardly need to holler because Samuel chose to sit in the same room. She figured it was a security measure. After all, she was still a stranger, even if she was Ruth Gaitley's niece.

Jennifer skimmed article after article but saw no mention of Dr. Ephraim. When she told Samuel she was ready to look at the March archives, he obliged and then returned to his seat.

There was nothing of interest to her from the early weeks of March, but vigilance paid off. "Dr. Ephraim Walson, fatal bullet..." She checked back for the article's date—March 15. "I found it!" Jennifer yelped, surprised that she announced this out loud.

Samuel slowly made his way from his chair to view the screen over her shoulder. He leaned in close, so much so that it slightly irritated Jennifer. She quickly reminded herself that he had done her a huge favor.

"It has to be him because of the date," Jennifer told Samuel. "I had only heard him referred to as Doctor Ephraim. I wasn't aware of his surname."

Samuel said nothing, squinting a little to read the article. Jennifer hadn't yet finished it herself, so she began with the headline, aloud for Samuel's sake. "Beloved Doctor Killed. Tilbrook lost one of its prominent citizens Tuesday evening to a fatal bullet to the heart. Dr. Ephraim Walson was shot from behind when responding to a house call on Gearson Drive." Jennifer stopped reading. "I live on Gearson Drive!" she exclaimed.

She could detect Samuel's slight nod from her peripheral vision. "Yes," was all he said.

She continued to read, "He was exiting his vehicle when the gunshot occurred. Police report that he likely died immediately. Dr. Walson treated patients in the Tilbrook area for over a decade, filling the void left by Dr. Joseph Tatum's retirement in 1926." Again, Jennifer stopped. "That's around the time my aunt, Ruth, was born. I think the year after."

"Ah." Samuel smiled.

Jennifer resumed reading, "He regularly kept long hours, responding to medical emergencies both day and night, sometimes traveling many miles. Minnie Lando fondly recalls Dr. Walson's calm and pleasant bedside manner. Joseph Emerson says he owes his life to Dr. Walson. Lawrence Cummings says that the doctor always put others' needs first and wonders when Dr. Walson ever got a full night's sleep. Police are treating this case as a murder. No arrests have been made at this time."

Jennifer pulled a small notepad from her purse and made a few notations. Samuel walked away, apparently to another room. Jennifer was mildly curious that he would now leave her alone among the historical treasures of Tilbrook, but she was primarily focused on the fact that Dr. Walson had been on a house call on Gearson Drive the evening of his murder. Since it was highly unlikely that Ruth or any of her family had been the perpetrator, Jennifer wondered if Dr. Walson was coming to the Gaitley home that night. Maybe that's why Ruth felt guilty. Jennifer suddenly remembered all the blank pages in her aunt's diary in the month of March. Perhaps Ruth had been ill, and that's why she had let her journal lapse for a while. That could explain it. Maybe Dr. Walson was shot in front of the Gaitley house when getting out of his vehicle to attend to Ruth. A fourteen-year-old could very well feel guilty about that. Ruth might have reasoned that if she hadn't been sick, or if her parents hadn't called the doctor, he wouldn't have died.

Samuel strolled across the room toward her, bringing Jennifer's thoughts back to the present. She noticed that Samuel had a framed photo in his hand. Could it be...?

"This is Dr. Ephraim Walson," Samuel confirmed. "It's undated, but I'd guess this was taken when he initially took over the medical practice."

"Around 1926, then," Jennifer read from her notes.

Samuel paused to reflect. "I think that would be right."

"Would it be possible...?" She almost hated to ask. "Would it be possible for me to have a copy of that photo?"

Although Samuel didn't answer verbally, he turned to walk toward the Xerox, and Jennifer knew her request was about to be fulfilled. She remained seated at the table until he returned with the copy. Samuel handed it to her and asked, "Do you want to see if there are further articles?" Yes, she did, so Jennifer stayed an additional half-hour with Samuel dutifully posed nearby like a sentinel.

"There's another short article, but it's just about not having any leads in his case," Jennifer informed Samuel. "Also, his death caused Tilbrook to be without immediate medical care for quite a while. I still haven't run across an article about his replacement, but I'm going to call it quits, at least for now."

Samuel stood. "We're open four days a week, Wednesday through Saturday, 10 a.m. until 3 p.m."

Jennifer thanked him and said her farewell before returning to ask if he had any idea where Dr. Walson might be buried. There were two cemeteries in Tilbrook, the older, smaller one on the outskirts and the newer cemetery that Jennifer was familiar with because of Aunt Ruth's passing. Jennifer asked Samuel for directions to the older cemetery and was almost out the door again when, this time, he called *her* back.

"By the way," the older man said with a shy grin, "I had a crush on Ruth's sister when I was a lad. Her name was Elizabeth."

"My mother!" Jennifer exclaimed.

"Yes, Elizabeth Gaitley." Samuel smiled more broadly now. "She was a little older than me and had her eye on," at this, he had to stop and think, "Peyton Daniels, I believe."

Peyton. Of course. Jennifer had blanked out on his first name. "Yes," she agreed now that Samuel had reminded her. "My mom married him. He's not my father, though. My mom and Peyton got divorced after a few years." She watched Samuel's attempt to straighten his slightly bowed head. How much he knew, Jennifer hadn't a clue, and Samuel didn't say more on the subject. "My mom died recently," Jennifer added, in case he wanted to ask about Elizabeth but was embarrassed to do so.

Samuel looked more solemn now. Evidently, he hadn't heard that news. "I'm sorry you lost both your mother and aunt," he sympathized. Jennifer nodded and successfully made her exit.

She needed to pick up more toothpaste and salad, so she swung the Toyota into the rutted parking area of a mom-and-pop grocery. On a whim, she added a small bouquet of white daisies to her purchase. Since she planned to make a detour to the old cemetery before returning home,

Jennifer thought she'd do something "nice" for Dr. Walson on Ruth's behalf if she could locate his grave.

Samuel's directions were excellent, and Jennifer had no difficulty finding the cemetery, although if she hadn't been on the lookout, she might have driven past. With no caretaker in sight, Jennifer combed grave markers looking for the one she wanted. Some of them were sadly unmarked. Another aisle over, Jennifer noticed a stone capped with a caduceus, the staff slightly extending upwards and the serpents entwining, flanking the sides. Since that would be an appropriate choice of markers for a medical person and because this was a grander gravestone than most of what she'd seen so far, Jennifer headed over.

Sure enough. "Dr. Ephraim Walson, 1886-1939," Jennifer read out loud. She lay the daisies on his grave. "Dr. Ephraim Walson," she repeated, "I'm Ruth Gaitley's niece, Jennifer. She was very sorry for your death. I am, too." Jennifer had a habit of talking to herself anyway, yet she felt that she was directly speaking to the spirit of Dr. Walson. "I just read a newspaper article from March 1939 about you. People truly respected and appreciated you. My aunt wrote about you in her diary. She referred to you as Doctor Ephraim. Your headstone is lovely, by the way. Whoever chose it had excellent taste. I think it suits a physician like yourself." Jennifer felt she was babbling on and laughed because some of it sounded a little silly, yet she didn't quite know what to say to someone deceased.

She bent down a final time to touch the name inscribed on the headstone. Jennifer stood there, lost in thought for a moment. She was proud of herself for making the time to pay respects to this man whose life had been cut short. As she turned to leave, her eyes briefly caught the name etched on the plainer, adjacent gravestone.

Jennifer gasped and then read under her breath, "Ephraim Walson, Jr., Born in 1907-Died in 1938."

Chapter 6

"So, what are you going to do now?" Angie asked the following morning.

"Return to the historical society and see if I can find a few more clues," Jennifer replied. She put the phone on speaker so she could hold her coffee mug with both hands.

"Anything further from Ruth's diaries?"

"Nothing."

Angie sighed. "Well, I agree with you that Ephraim Walson, Jr., must be the son. Otherwise, the graves wouldn't be side by side. How old would he have been when he died?"

"About thirty-one," Jennifer instantly answered. She'd already done the math. "Dr. Walson would have been fifty-three when he was killed. Maybe fifty-two since he died early in the year. I don't know his birth month."

"And no other Walson headstones, right?" Angie queried. "No Mrs. Walson?"

"Those are the only two in the cemetery. I checked carefully before I left yesterday."

"I wonder why Junior died," Angie stated more than asked.

"The historical society is open today, so I plan on making another trip to see Samuel. Maybe I can find an obituary or article on the son."

After the two ladies speculated about the past for another few minutes, Angie turned the focus to her friend's new love interest. Jennifer didn't mind Angie's well-intended teasing. In fact, Ted was rapidly becoming one of her favorite subjects to discuss.

"We have a date this evening. Ted's dropping by after work. This time he's taking me out for Chinese food," Jennifer informed Angie.

"Lucky you, Jen! I have to cook for three people practically every night. I think the last time Mike took me out to dinner was for my birthday."

"Oh, poor Ange, happily married with a wonderful daughter who still enjoys dinner at home with her parents."

Angie laughed. "Yeah, poor me. Make sure you tell Ted that I said I want to meet him sometime. Since you're settling in fairly well, you'll probably be ready for a visit by next month. You won't have to put us up, either. We can stay at that motel you were at."

Jennifer insisted that Angie and her family were welcome in her home but was glad that her pal was thinking about a future trip rather than an imminent one. Right now, Jennifer felt she still had too many loose ends to deal with before turning her attention to hosting guests.

"I probably should let you get back to the mystery of the two Ephraims," Angie stated as she wound down the phone conversation.

"Yes, the historical society is already open," Jennifer confirmed as she glanced at her watch. "Time to find out more about Ephraim Junior."

She wasn't kidding about finding out more information. She was already dressed and ready to leave as soon as she checked in with Angie for the morning. With that accomplished, Jennifer was on her way, this time by foot, combining the fact-finding mission with exercise. Once she had strolled two blocks left, the old Presbyterian church was well in view and served as a guide.

Samuel was not at the Tilbrook Historical Society today. Jennifer thought about coming back later rather than going through the story again. However, the woman who greeted her was friendly, and there were no other visitors to interact with the docent. Jennifer took a deep breath and gave the woman an abbreviated summary of her quest and yesterday's findings.

"Walson sounds familiar," the helpful docent said. "I m afraid I don't handle anything on the technology end, so you'll have to come back when Samuel or Megan is here. That won't be until next week."

Jennifer tried to hide her disappointment. "You said that the Walson name sounded familiar. Do you have any idea why? Is there an exhibit here with that name? Any photos?"

"You just missed our history intern, Torrey. He's doing a project on local murders and planning a future exhibit around that theme. We were discussing it, and Torrey found the portrait of Dr. Walson in the back. Torrey says he, Dr. Walson, is one of the cases featured. I don't know more than that, though."

"May I see the portrait?" Jennifer asked, satisfied once she confirmed it was the same one she had been shown yesterday. Samuel must have set the portrait down to walk Jennifer out and forgot to put it back. "When will Torrey be here? I'd love to speak to him about the Walson murder."

"I don't know because he's not a docent, per se. He's a college intern. I do have his number, however." The historical society woman hesitated. "I'll tell Torrey you'd like to talk to him about this case if you leave me your number."

Jennifer agreed. That was the best way to handle this situation, better than the docent giving out Torrey's number without his permission. Jennifer thanked the woman and asked for her name.

"Sally," she answered, simultaneously reading the note Jennifer handed her. "Okay, Ms. Shemmer. You have excellent printing. I can clearly read your name and number. I'll make sure Torrey gets your message in the next couple of days."

Jennifer hoped it wouldn't take that long but resisted the urge to ask Sally to call him today. After all, this wasn't an emergency. Both father and son had been dead for approximately eighty years. What did a few days matter?

When Jennifer got home, she saw the flashing light of the landline answering machine and half-expected it to be Torrey the Intern. Instead, it was Teresa. The cleaning service Jake's used for the draperies had upped their prices unexpectedly. Teresa sheepishly broke the news to Jennifer, hoping she'd be agreeable to the added expense. What reasonable option did Jennifer have? She returned the call and agreed to the latest terms. Teresa then offered to pick up the check to cover the amount due.

"I'll be by around 4:30 if that's all right," Teresa said apologetically. "I'll make it up to you by bringing a couple of wine coolers."

"I'm expecting Ted, the guy you met yesterday, around 6:30 or so."

"Then let's hold off on the wine coolers until another time," Teresa replied without hesitation. Jennifer was slightly surprised. She figured Teresa would simply say she'd leave when he showed up. That was fine, however, since Jennifer wasn't a particular fan of alcohol.

She spent the interim doing a little house cleaning, curious that she hadn't felt any cold spots in the home since returning from the motel. No flickering lights, no indoor breezes, and no eerie feeling of being watched. Wouldn't that be something if all of that ended now that she had read the second diary?

The timer sounded to remind her to switch gears and get cleaned up for the meeting with Teresa and date with Ted. Since she didn't know how long Teresa planned to stay, Jennifer decided to dress for her evening with Ted.

When she opened the door for Teresa, she could tell that at least Teresa approved of her choice of outfits for the night. She hoped Ted would, as well.

"Very nice," Teresa remarked, with no opening greeting. "I like your hair down like that. Not that the ponytail doesn't suit you, but now you look like you're ready for a dinner date."

Jennifer blushed. She didn't recall mentioning that she and Ted were going on a date, just that Ted would be coming by. "Um, thanks," was all Jennifer could think to say.

Teresa reminded her a little of Ted, also making herself at home with confidence, and it was she who led Jennifer into the living room. Jennifer quickly detoured to the kitchen to grab the checkbook from the counter, having everything but the amount already filled in. While she was there, she poured two blueberry teas.

"Thank you again, and sorry!" Teresa grimaced after confirming the amount due. "Usually, we get advance notice. We don't overcharge our customers, so we can't afford to cover the extra cost ourselves." Jennifer noticed that Teresa spoke as if she were part of the small business, one big happy family.

"That's okay, I understand." Jennifer sat in her favorite floral chair after handing over the now-completed check. "Prices are going up for everything."

That was apparently the opening line to get Teresa started on a diatribe about inflation, the challenges of living today, and the difference in prices between cities. Jennifer enjoyed listening to Teresa and learned a bit more about Bilmore. Jennifer shared the story of her one trip to Bilmore to dine at Perfezione with Ted.

"He lives in that town," Jennifer added.

Teresa nodded. She didn't seem surprised. "I don't recall seeing him around here," she confirmed what Jennifer had assumed.

"He was a friend of my aunt and lived with her here in this house for several months; I think maybe half a year. Ted also used to work for Tenger-Bio, but he was in the business office. Ruth had already retired but still had projects going, so she and Ted sometimes ate lunch together."

Teresa sipped her tea silently. Perhaps she was tired from her earlier monolog, or maybe she wanted to make sure Jennifer had equal time to share. Still, Jennifer was slightly disappointed that Teresa hadn't shown the enthusiasm that Angie had for her new suitor. Angie hadn't yet met Ted to see for herself how handsome he was. Jennifer knew that looks were subjective, but she was surprised Teresa hadn't commented on Ted in the way many women did when they were among friends.

Jennifer moved on to other topics. She had a lot to tell Teresa about the historical society, the old cemetery, and finding out about Dr. Ephraim Walson. Teresa visibly perked up, not realizing that there even was a historical society, let alone one within walking distance of her own home. Jennifer then described the second Walson gravestone she found, that of the son. Although Teresa knew about the old cemetery, she hadn't been there in ages. Teresa implied that she would visit it in the near future, curious to see the caduceus headstone that Jennifer mentioned and to read the old dates inscribed on the markers.

It was slightly after 6 p.m. when the doorbell rang. Teresa had just mentioned taking off so Jennifer could be ready for her date but hadn't left in time to avoid encountering Ted. He shook Teresa's hand, and Teresa was just as polite to him in return, yet Jennifer could see that neither of them had an interest in the other. Jennifer contrasted this scene with Angie's expressed desire to meet Ted soon. She was glad she had Angie, even if she did now live one state away.

Jennifer saw Teresa out and closed the door. She was startled to see Ted when she swung around. She thought he had stayed in the living room.

"Oh, I'm sorry I scared you," he said in a concerned tone, smiling tenderly. "I have missed you!" He sealed his apology with a long kiss.

"I've thought a lot about you, too," Jennifer confessed. "I've been looking forward to seeing you tonight."

"You look great," Ted added, just what Jennifer hoped to hear. "I haven't seen you with your hair down like that." He was gentlemanly enough not to tell her he preferred this look to her usual casual tied-back hairstyle.

This was a suit-and-tie day for Ted, and he had chosen different shades of blue for his ensemble, all of which blended perfectly and went well with his fair skin tone. Jennifer couldn't help but glance at him repeatedly on the drive to the Golden Dragon. She tried to keep a dialog going so that her gazes seemed natural.

"Can I lose the tie?" Ted asked before exiting the SUV to get the door for Jennifer. She had been surprised he had worn it for as long as he did. Maybe he had known she was admiring his appearance during the short drive.

"Certainly!" Jennifer did a mock bow of her head while Ted masterfully whipped off his tie and laid it on the backseat. She waited for him to open her door. Alex, her ex, had lost these chivalries over their years of marriage. She wondered if Ted would also if he ever remarried.

Ted ordered moo shu pork, and Jennifer chose the chicken with pea pods. They decided to share their entrees and finished the meal with hot tea and the extra fortune cookies that Ted requested.

"You will be wealthy in all things important," he read the tiny slip of paper pulled from half his cookie. "Not a bad fortune. What does yours say?"

"A handsome stranger will enter your life," Jennifer blushed as she read the message and hoped he wouldn't notice in the rather dim lighting.

"Hasn't a handsome stranger already entered your life?"

"Yes." She was annoyed at herself for giggling. "So, my fortune already came true. Let me try this other cookie." She broke it open and read the slip. "Follow your instincts as more clues come your way."

"That's an odd one." Ted leaned forward. "My second fortune says to ask Jennifer out again tomorrow."

"Let me see that." She teasingly reached forward. "Who's writing these fortunes? Someone in the back room?" They both laughed. "My fortune about clues coming my way reminds me of what I've learned over the past couple of days." Jennifer proceeded to tell Ted the tale of the two Ephraims. Although she didn't reveal specifics of what her aunt had written in her diaries, Jennifer informed him that Ruth repeatedly mentioned an Ephraim.

Ted listened quietly without interruption. Then he said, "I don't recall Ruth ever talking about anyone named Ephraim." He shook his head. "No strange phenomena in the house, either."

"I wondered." That was one of the reasons Jennifer wanted to share this information with Ted. She wondered if any of what she had to say would strike a chord with Ted and bring some memory to the surface.

That was enough speculation about Ruth and Ephraim for one night, however. Jennifer told Ted stories about her closest friend Angie and the town of Reddington. In turn, he spoke in detail about his parents and their setup in an active retirement community near Phoenix. Jennifer appreciated how easy it was to converse with Ted. Three hours passed quickly, and she reminded him that the restaurant would probably close soon. Ted nodded and placed extra cash on the table as a tip. Although Jennifer offered to pay or at least split the cost, he declined once again.

It was much cooler outside now, and Jennifer huddled in her coat. She didn't know how long it had been since she had worn a dress in the evening. Pants were undoubtedly warmer, but she knew Ted would appreciate seeing her in a skirt for a change, just as she liked occasionally seeing him in a suit.

When they returned to Jennifer's home, Ted assumed he was to follow her inside. She offered coffee, but Ted held up a hand, remarking that he'd partaken of quite a lot of the hot tea served at the restaurant. She joined him on the sofa and asked if he'd like to watch television or listen to music. He opted for the latter, and Jennifer gave the voice command to play instrumental music appropriate for conversing.

"Did Ruth have wi-fi?" Ted asked.

"Yes, she did. Cable, wi-fi, and Alexa."

"What more could you ask for?" he replied and then put his arm around Jennifer, pulling her closer. "Except for maybe..." They embraced for a long while. By Jennifer's standards, Ted ranked up there as a great kisser. Tender, yet firm at the same time. Once they pulled apart, Ted surprised her by saying, "My lease will be coming up for renewal in another month. It would be convenient for me to live here since we're seeing each other often now."

"Live in Tilbrook?" Jennifer wondered whether he meant to get a place in town or move in with her.

"Yes, in Tilbrook," he replied with a laugh. "You have a lot of space, Jennifer. I don't mean to pressure you, so I could make my old upstairs bedroom my lodgings."

Jennifer didn't know what to say. She was torn. Part of her wanted Ted to move in tomorrow, but part of her was reluctant. After all, she had gone through a number of major changes within a single year. She was a recent divorcee, a grieving daughter still recovering from being a caregiver, and the inheritor of an estate in a different city. Plus, Jennifer was still getting used to the house, and there was the mystery of Ephraim and whether his spirit remained here. Furthermore, Jennifer liked being on her own, at least for now. On the other hand, Ted was rapidly becoming a big part of her new life, and she didn't want to jeopardize that future.

"Can I have time to consider?" Jennifer finally responded after an awkwardly long pause. She saw the look on Ted's face and quickly added, "In a sense, I'm still grieving. I'm trying to make my way through to a new life. I really do like you, Ted, and I enjoy your company. It's simply the timing. I need to stop the world for just a bit and learn how to adjust.

I need to take things slowly, and I hope you can understand that."

When Ted reached out and covered Jennifer's hand with his own, she turned her wrist to entwine her fingers in his. He didn't say anything but kissed her gently on the forehead. Jennifer leaned her head against his shoulder and sighed deeply, causing Ted to shift so he could cradle her in his arms. They sat like that, listening to the sweet sounds of orchestral music until Jennifer drifted to sleep.

"Hello," Ted said very softly, jostling Jennifer just a little. "It looks like someone needs to get to bed."

Jennifer lifted her head from Ted's chest and brushed a hand over her hair. "Oh, I'm sorry. I guess I felt very relaxed."

He leaned over to kiss her again before standing up. "I will be on my way."

"I had a great time tonight, Ted. Thank you."

"My pleasure, Jennifer, truly," he answered while walking to the door.

Jennifer felt a little anxious. She hoped he wasn't offended that she hadn't jumped at his suggestion to move in with her. She took a deep breath before asking, "Will I hear from you again?"

Ted turned abruptly to face her. "Of course. I'll call you tomorrow, I promise." He rubbed the nape of her neck with his left hand and then gave her a quick kiss goodnight.

Jennifer felt a combination of relief and worry as she watched Ted's SUV lights recede into the darkness. She hoped she wasn't making a mistake by slowing their relationship.

Jennifer shut off the music and downstairs lights to head for her bedroom. What would be the harm of allowing him to live here? He was right that there was plenty of space. Jennifer kicked off her shoes and sat on the edge of her bed.

A daisy? She leaned diagonally to pick up the single white flower from her nightstand. How did that get there? She gasped. It looked exactly like the daisies she had placed on Dr. Ephraim Walson's grave yesterday. There had to be a logical explanation. Ted? He hadn't been upstairs, though, and she had been with him the entire time. On the other hand, she had fallen asleep. Yet, Jennifer wasn't such a sound sleeper that he could have moved her head off his chest, gotten up, and then returned to resume their cuddled position. Still...

Jennifer made the trip downstairs to retrieve her cell phone. She looked in her contact list and dialed before heading back upstairs to her bedroom.

"Jennifer? Are you all right?" Ted greeted her with surprise.

"Yes, fine. I found a flower upstairs and wondered if you put it there."

"A flower? No, Jennifer, I didn't bring any flowers." Ted sounded genuinely perplexed. "You found it upstairs?"

"Yes, after you left."

"Would you like me to return? I'm not in Bilmore yet. I can easily come back." His foot automatically backed off the accelerator.

"No, Ted, but that's very nice of you. I'm not frightened, just puzzled." Jennifer hesitated, debating how much detail to give him. "I put a bouquet of white daisies on Dr. Walson's grave yesterday, and now this flower appears."

"One must have come free from the bouquet. Perhaps you left it behind yourself," Ted offered a plausible explanation.

"No, because I went straight from the store to the cemetery."

"Are you sure?" Ted persisted. "Or did you take one flower out and bring it home?"

Jennifer was irritated but didn't want to stress their new relationship further. She reminded herself that it's natural to seek logical explanations. That's why she phoned Ted, to rule out the remote possibility that it had been him.

"You could be right," she placated. "Maybe I'm overly tired. Thanks again for a lovely evening."

Ted reassured her before ending the call. Jennifer set down the phone and walked to the nightstand where she had found the daisy. Was it a coincidence that the flower had been placed on top of her gratitude journal? Was it possible that Dr. Walson found a way to demonstrate appreciation for Jennifer's visit to his gravesite? She picked up the daisy again and examined it closer. Since it was wilted, it probably had come from yesterday's bouquet.

"Thank you," Jennifer said as she glanced around the room. "How sweet of you," she added, pointing to the little daisy.

Chapter 7

THE LANDLINE RANG WHILE Jennifer unpacked the last of her groceries. She let the call go to the answering machine. "Hello, I'm calling for Jennifer Shemmer. I'm Torrey, the intern at the historical society. I was told—"

Jennifer rushed to pick up the receiver. "Hi, Torrey? I'm here. Sorry. This is Jennifer Shemmer."

"Hello," the young man started again, unsure how much of his message he needed to repeat. "This is Torrey. I was told you wanted to speak to me?" His tone registered uncertainty.

"Yes, if you don't mind. A docent at the historical society said you're working on a project involving local murders. I'm interested in learning more about Ephraim Walson. I live in the house once owned by the Gaitley family. I believe he was killed nearby." Jennifer gave the young intern background information while she pulled out a small notepad and pen from a drawer.

"There isn't much information about the Walson murders, but I have been looking into them, and they'll be included in the upcoming exhibit," Torrey confirmed. "I hope to—"

Jennifer cut him off. "Did you say Walson murders?" She must have heard wrong.

"That's right, ma'am. Both of them were named Ephraim, father and son. The son, Ephraim Walson, Jr., died as the result of an alleged hunting accident. He was shot with an arrow. The father, Dr. Ephraim Walson, was fatally shot from behind with a bullet."

Jennifer was surprised to notice that her hand shook while jotting down notes. "I only found out recently that there was a son, and I had no idea how he died. You said in a hunting accident, though, so that wouldn't be a murder."

"Alleged hunting accident," the intern clarified. "Mr. Walson was on his own property, well, to be technically accurate, on the property he rented at the time of his death. One arrow. That ended his life. The police at that time assumed a careless hunter was responsible. No one came forward, however."

"So, Mr. Walson, the son, wasn't hunting, correct?"

"Yes, ma'am. It was early morning, and he was on the grounds near his rental," Torrey confirmed.

"Where was he killed exactly? Do you have a street address, or is that confidential?" Jennifer subconsciously held her breath as she awaited his answer.

"I won't include specific addresses in the exhibit," he assured her. "I want to be respectful to homeowners such as yourself."

Jennifer was surprised at how he worded his response, so she pushed a little further. "You know I live in the Gaitley house. That's on Gearson Drive." She gave him the house number. "Can you confirm if this is the address of Dr. Walson's murder, the dad?"

"Yes, ma'am. The son was killed next door. The father was murdered in front of the Gaitley home." The intern's voice was solemn, and she appreciated that he appeared to treat his history project with respect.

"Next door? Why would a hunter be in this area? There's quite a bit of acreage between lots, but still, this neighborhood isn't appropriate for hunting," Jennifer pointed out.

"In 1938, that neighborhood was different. There were no homes behind Gearson Drive until the late 1940s. The Gaitley house and neighboring homes butted up to a forested area."

"I didn't realize that." Jennifer sighed. "Torrey, what makes you believe that the son might have been murdered instead of accidentally struck with an arrow?"

"It's purely speculative, but I think it's too convenient that the son was fatally shot with an arrow approximately five months before his dad encounters a fatal gunshot. Both happened on Gearson Drive in the same vicinity."

"What did the police think?" Jennifer probed.

"Again, remember that we are speaking of a different time, the late 1930s. Also, Tilbrook is not a large city. From my investigation, it appears that the police were satisfied to believe that the son's death was an accident. The hunter who shot the arrow might not have been aware of what happened. It's possible the hunter wasn't from Tilbrook. That being said," the young college student paused before proceeding, "I am going to include this in the Tilbrook exhibit as the father and son murders. The son was killed. Whether it was accidental or not, we'll probably never know."

"I see what you mean." Jennifer turned the focus to Dr. Walson's 1939 death and told Torrey what she had learned from her visit to the historical society. She asked if he had anything to add.

"You're correct that the police had no suspects. They treated his death as a homicide. The Gaitley family was questioned, but the police didn't appear to think there was a connection."

Jennifer remembered her aunt's guilt over Doctor Ephraim's death but didn't seriously think any of her family members could have killed someone. "Any theories, Torrey?"

"Wrong place at the wrong time? Mistaken identity? Perhaps he had figured out who killed his son," the young intern speculated. "That last bit is strictly my own theory. The police never connected the two deaths."

"And you don't believe Dr. Walson's death was also the result of a hunting misfortune?" Jennifer queried.

"His death was in front of the house, not in the back wooded area. Also, it was nighttime. He had been on a house call."

Jennifer shuddered. "How horrible! Do you know if that medical visit was to the Gaitley house?"

"Yes. According to police records, Mr. Gaitley called Dr. Walson on behalf of his daughter."

Jennifer briefly considered telling Torrey about Ruth's diary and her declarations of sorrow and guilt over Doctor Ephraim's death. However, Torrey was a historian. Naturally, he would hope to gain access to the diary and most likely want to look for others. Jennifer's loyalty sided with her deceased aunt, as appreciative as Jennifer was of the intern's information.

She thanked Torrey and wished him success with his college project. He promised he would keep her informed of any further clues.

Jennifer grabbed an ice cream bar out of the freezer and took it to the living room. She bit into the cool chocolate as she mulled over what she had learned from Torrey. What an incredible tragedy! Jennifer waved the nibbled ice cream bar toward an invisible audience. "If anyone is still in this house, I am sorry for what happened to you. Is it you, Doctor Ephraim?" Jennifer said out loud, addressing the spirit by the name her aunt used in the 1939 diary. "Or is it your son, Ephraim Junior? Or both of you?" Jennifer hadn't thought of that possibility until now. She pictured the daisy placed on her gratitude journal. Her gut feeling was that the spirit responsible was Doctor Ephraim, especially since she had put the bouquet on his grave, not the son's.

Jennifer continued to nibble the now-melting bar in silence, her palm underneath to catch any drips. What to do next? There was only one adjacent neighbor since the houses to the back had not been built in 1938. She had no idea who occupied that home. Indeed, no one had come over to introduce themselves or see Ruth before she died.

Jennifer had considered taking the first neighborly step but hadn't gotten around to it. No time like the present.

She changed her shoes and looked in the upstairs mirror to make sure her teeth showed no signs of chocolate. Satisfied that she looked presentable for an introductory visit, Jennifer grabbed her coat and keys. What if no one was home? She prepared for that scenario by writing a brief note that included her phone number. She put the tape dispenser in her purse, just in case.

Jennifer assessed the property as she walked purposefully toward the neighboring house. There was a surprising amount of land separating the two homes, even for this section of town, the old historical portion. Jennifer paused to survey the view from several angles, picturing the wooded area behind the buildings prior to the late 1940s.

The house she walked toward looked very little like the Gaitley home. Instead, Jennifer's impression was that the neighboring house looked foreboding. But maybe that was her overactive imagination, especially after learning today that Ephraim Junior died there. Of course, Ephraim Senior was shot next door in front of her own place, so...

She climbed the steps to ring the doorbell. Just as her instinct had predicted, no one answered. Since Jennifer didn't see any vehicles near the house, she pulled the note from her purse and used a small strip of tape to attach it to the door. That was all she could do for now, but at least she was taking the time to get to know her neighbor.

On the walk home, Teresa Degra's name popped up on Jennifer's phone screen. She greeted her friend with curiosity, wondering if Teresa had to work on a Saturday afternoon.

"Listen, I know it's short notice, but I suddenly find myself with free time, and I recall promising you wine or some sort of alcoholic beverage. Two questions. First, are you free this afternoon or evening? Second, do you like margaritas?"

Jennifer was pleased with the prospect of company since Ted was out of town on business until tomorrow. "Yes, to both. My house or yours?"

"Either one. Would you like to come over here? Kick back a little, get out of your own home?" Teresa's tone further suggested she'd prefer to be the host today.

"Why not?" Jennifer said with some enthusiasm. "Should I bring anything? Snacks?"

"I have plenty of refreshments, so just bring yourself, say around 4:15? Why don't you drive instead of walk? Then you can stay late. We'll have our margaritas early, and you'll be fine to drive home."

"That sounds good. I'll see you then. Thanks for—" Jennifer smiled when she realized that Teresa had already ended the call.

It felt nice to be making new friends. She still missed seeing Angie in person. That reminded Jennifer that she should call her longtime pal before heading over to Teresa's. Angie had loved hearing about the daisy left on Jennifer's gratitude journal. Unlike Ted, Angie didn't dismiss it as Jennifer's own absentminded doing. Instead, she readily attributed the deed to a male spirit, Ephraim, whom Angie had already romanticized. She would be intrigued by what the history intern had to say about the death of Ephraim Junior.

⊶

"Make yourself at home," Teresa warmly greeted Jennifer. "Mi casa es tu casa."

"Very nice window treatments!" Jennifer teased. "I sincerely mean that," she added, to be clear.

Teresa laughed. "Employee discount. Have a seat. Don't be alarmed when Hooligan jumps on your lap. You aren't allergic to cats, are you?"

"No." Jennifer looked around for the feline but couldn't spot her friend's beloved pet. "You have great taste. Your place is colorful, warm, and cozy. Even though it's a little nippy outside, it feels warm in here. Some of that has to do with the décor."

"Why, thank you kindly," Teresa said with a demure nod and a broad smile. She was confident. She didn't blush when given compliments, nor did she minimize her accomplishments.

The women chatted a while before Hooligan made his appearance and, right on cue, jumped on Jennifer's lap. His paws tickled her upper legs, but soon the cat settled in and stopped squirming. Jennifer petted the purring feline. Teresa looked quite pleased and got up to make two margaritas.

"How did you meet Ted? I believe you told me once, but I've forgotten." Teresa returned, sipping from the broad rim of her glass.

"He dropped by the house to offer condolences. Ted knew my aunt decades ago from Tenger-Bio. He worked in the business office, and Ruth was still doing part-time research. Anyway, he was going through a divorce or newly divorced, I'm not sure which. Ruth offered to have him stay with her for a while." Jennifer sampled her drink. Hooligan shifted position but didn't leave Jennifer's lap.

"Tenger-Bio might be a source of more information about your aunt." Noticing Jennifer's blank look, Teresa elaborated. "You've asked me several times if I knew anything about Ruth. You also asked me about some doctor friend of hers. It occurred to me that Tenger-Bio might be useful."

"Aunt Ruth was well into her nineties when she died. She had retired before Ted met her, and he was in his twenties at the time," she reminded Teresa, implying that too much time had lapsed.

"You never know." Teresa squinted in contemplation, or maybe due to the margarita she again sipped. "Ruth worked there for decades and would have stood out as a pioneering female in their industry. You just told me that she did research after her retirement. Who knows for how long? It's worth a phone call or, better yet, go in person. Take the photos of Ruth from the den."

Jennifer already had a slight headache from the alcohol. The margarita was delicious, but she wouldn't have another if she were to drive home that night. "That's a good idea, Teresa." She could see from her friend's facial expression that she had said the right thing. Jennifer wasn't keen on visiting Tenger-Bio, but she could agree that the idea was sound. Maybe she could convince Ted to go with her. He'd probably enjoy that.

"Do you have any gentleman friends?" Jennifer asked since she'd inquired about Ted. It was the hostess's turn to share. Instead of speaking, Teresa picked up her phone and scrolled before handing the displayed photo to Jennifer. It was a picture of Teresa and a young woman with their arms around each other. Jennifer wondered who the woman was but, since Teresa was silently watching, merely said, "She looks friendly, and you two appear to be very happy."

Teresa took the phone back and smiled. It was the same doting smile she had flashed when she looked at Hooligan. "Yes, she is. We're discreet. Tilbrook isn't tiny, but it still is a smaller town. Her name's Maria. She's originally from Yuma, Arizona. Maria works in Bilmore at an art supply shop but lives here in Tilbrook, in the newer section."

Jennifer nodded. "When did you meet?"

"Almost three years ago, in Bilmore. I walked into the shop to browse, and we hit it off immediately. At that time, she had an apartment in Bilmore. Six months later, she traded it in for an apartment here."

"I'm happy for you. It's nice to have a special someone."

Teresa agreed. Jennifer wondered if she was relieved to have that out in the open. It was bound to come up if she and Teresa continued their friendship. "I'll have you over sometime when Maria's here. She's running errands and doing chores today."

Hooligan finally had enough of a cat nap and leaped from Jennifer's lap to run upstairs. His owner's gaze followed him. "Would you like a tour of the house?"

"Definitely!" Jennifer set her glass aside and followed Teresa. "Do you paint?" She noticed the vivid oil paintings similar in style in multiple rooms.

"Yes, but those are Maria's. You'll see some of my work in the bedroom. Also, the large painting in the entryway—mine."

Jennifer had noticed. She wished she had even half the talent. Although Maria's paintings were engaging and pleasing, Teresa's appealed to her more. They were somehow more original and eye-catching. That summed up Teresa.

Once they had settled again downstairs, this time to nibble on chickpea salad sandwiches prepared by Teresa, Jennifer shared a little more about her relationship with Ted. She told her new friend about Ted's suggestion that he move in with Jennifer. To Jennifer's surprise, Teresa shook her head and grimaced. Her reaction was a stark contrast to Angie's nudge to accept Ted's suggestion to take up his old room upstairs, at least for the time being. Angie didn't want Jennifer to hesitate too long, perhaps pushing him away in doing so.

"You two haven't known one another long enough," Teresa warned. "You did ask my opinion, so I'll be frank for that reason. Ted is very handsome and charming. One day he shows up at your door to offer condolences. You have a few dates, but what do you truly know about him? From my experience, once you allow a person to move in, it's difficult to get them to move out."

"That's happened to you?" Jennifer frowned.

"Oh, yes. I've had my share of life's lessons. My advice—that you asked for—is to follow your instincts. Take it slowly. I'm surprised he's asking you so soon."

"Well, he did offer to move into a separate bedroom," Jennifer said in Ted's defense.

"How generous of him," Teresa remarked bluntly. At that, both women chuckled.

"I do like him, and he has been great company," Jennifer added, feeling a hint of guilt over joking at Ted's expense.

"I didn't say dump him. I said take it slowly. If he cares about you, he'll give you your space. You have been through a lot. He knows that. Maria can show him around her apartment complex if he wants to move to Tilbrook. The rates are quite reasonable."

Jennifer nodded. She agreed with Teresa and was glad to get her honest perspective. Angie, as much as Jennifer loved her, viewed Ted as the leading character in a romance novel. Angie viewed Ephraim in a similar way. Jennifer laughed out loud when she thought about that, causing Teresa to look up and smile, waiting to be filled in on what had tickled her.

"Um, I was just thinking about my friend, Angie, back home. She'd probably have me married to Ted by Monday if that were a possibility, and she hasn't even met him yet."

Teresa joined in the laughter. It had been a fun night, but it was getting late. Jennifer thanked her host and made her way to the Toyota. Hooligan tried to follow, but Teresa scooped him up, thwarting his plans. Jennifer paused to admire the nighttime lighting cast on the old stone church across the street.

"Picturesque view!" Jennifer shouted back to Teresa. Her friend nodded and waved.

Chapter 8

JENNIFER SET HER PURSE on the dining room table and tossed Trinity Presbyterian's Sunday order of service pages next to it. On the one hand, she was glad she had ventured out to meet other people and perhaps find a church she would like to attend regularly. On the other hand, she was disappointed that introducing herself as Ruth Gaitley's niece hadn't produced the results she anticipated. People smiled and nodded, but that was the extent of it.

Oh, well. Jennifer picked up the church pamphlet again and sat down to read over the list of activities happening this month at Trinity. Perhaps they offered a class she might like or had a movie night. Jennifer jumped when the phone rang. She hadn't realized she was so preoccupied.

"This is Mrs. Nandez from next door," responded a rather forceful voice in response to Jennifer's greeting. "I got your note. Sorry I didn't get back to you yesterday, but I've been busy."

Jennifer lowered the phone from her ear and switched it to speaker. "Oh, thank you for calling. I thought it was time I introduced myself. As I said in my note, I'm Jennifer Shemmer. I inherited the house from my aunt, Ruth Gaitley." She paused, waiting to hear her neighbor's reaction.

"Yeah, I knew she'd died," the gruff voice replied. "The grapevine said a middle-aged niece had moved in. They didn't think she had kids."

Jennifer wasn't sure she was going to like her new neighbor. "I'm sorry, but I didn't catch your name?"

"Mrs. Nandez."

"Okay, thank you, Mrs. Nandez," Jennifer said, a little perplexed that no first name was offered. Maybe there was a conflict between Ruth and this woman. Jennifer carefully chose her wording before proceeding. "Did you know my aunt? Did you sometimes get together?"

"Oh, not really." Mrs. Nandez seemed to shake off the questions. "We waved when we saw one another."

Jennifer was silent for a moment, waiting for a more fully developed response from Mrs. Nandez, but none was given. "Well, I'd like to have you over to the house. I think it would be nice to connect with the neighbors."

"I'm pretty busy," Mrs. Nandez said firmly.

Jennifer bit her lip. "I didn't mean today, but in the future. Perhaps you'd come for lunch when you have an afternoon free? Or just stop by for a chat?"

"We'll see," Mrs. Nandez stated, but from her tone, Jennifer inferred she wouldn't be seeing much of her neighbor. Better ask any questions now while she had the chance.

"I won't keep you on the phone long, Mrs. Nandez, but I wonder if you've heard of the deaths of the Walsons that happened right near our houses back in the late 1930s?" Jennifer softly cleared her throat as she waited for a reply.

"Yeah, I know about that. Why?"

"It's part of the history of the neighborhood, and I just found out that Dr. Walson was shot in front of my own house," Jennifer explained. "I'd like to learn more if possible."

"That's history now, my dear. It's before our time, and I've always felt safe here."

"Right. I'm not implying that I'm worried about the neighborhood, but I recently learned that the younger Walson, the son, was shot with a bow and arrow on what is now your property. Do you have any further details?" Jennifer cringed as she said the last part, hoping she wasn't pushing too hard.

Fortunately, Mrs. Nandez didn't appear phased when she answered, "From what I understand, he rented the guesthouse. It was just a small guesthouse. It hurt the property value, though, you know—to have a death there—and that's why it was eventually torn down. All I know is that when my late husband bought the property, it was gone. No memories of the death. Don't you think that's for the best?"

Jennifer was a little taken aback. "Right. We won't bring it up after today. Just to clarify, there was a guesthouse between your home and mine back in the 1930s, and this was rented out to the young Mr. Walson?"

"Correct." Mrs. Nandez didn't offer more.

"I noticed considerable space between our properties, so it makes sense that a guesthouse was built there at one time. Thank you for that information, Mrs. Nandez."

"Okay," the neighbor replied. "I've got to go. Nice talking with you."

Jennifer doubted the sincerity of that last statement but extended pleasantries to the woman on the other end of the line. She could understand why Aunt Ruth and Mrs. Nandez had never formed a neighborly bond. At least Jennifer had a phone number for her now, and Mrs. Nandez, whatever her first name was, had hers. Good to have in case of an emergency.

Once Jennifer was off the phone, she realized how close it was getting to the time Ted would arrive. The two of them were going to the fall festival, and Jennifer looked forward to a leisurely afternoon of soaking up whatever Tilbrook offered in the way of a hometown craft fair and autumn carnival. Ted told her to expect local bands, solo acts, games, and plenty of good food. She was ready for such a day.

Jennifer had just descended the stairs when Ted rang the doorbell. He gave her a quick kiss and placed a bottle of wine in her hands.

"For when we return," he said with one of his charming grins. "A nice way to end what I think will be a perfect day."

She returned Ted's smile and set the wine down on the nearest table. "Do I need to bring anything? A blanket to sit on?"

"Nope. I have canvas chairs. We'll get all our food, our goodies, there. I'm looking forward to homemade pie, onion rings, roasted corn on the cob, and probably a burger, but I might be swayed when I see what else is available."

"All of that sounds great." Jennifer nodded her approval.

The festival was quite well-attended, obviously a favorite Tilbrook tradition for all ages. Jennifer watched children run about, unsure of what they wanted to do next—the petting zoo, games, or face painting. She recalled her days as an elementary school teacher. Although she didn't miss the paperwork, planning, and discipline, she did have fond memories of her time with the students.

"Petting zoos are not just for kids, you know." Ted took Jennifer's hand in his. "Let's you and me say hello to the Shetland pony and potbelly pig." He handed a few coins to an elderly gentleman, who gave Ted two small cups of pellets in return. Ted gave one to Jennifer and then proceeded to offer treats to the closest critter. She set her cup down to take a photo of the pair.

"I think this one would eat every pellet we have!" He laughed, withdrawing his hand. "Did you see the little donkey?"

Jennifer gently petted the animal and offered it a snack. It had been years since she'd been to a fair, and she was already having great fun. This time it was Ted who pulled out his phone and snapped a photo of her.

"Where to next?" she asked once they'd made the rounds amongst the animals.

"Any interest in karaoke?"

"Listening to others do karaoke, fine. Doing it myself, no," Jennifer replied adamantly. "And you?"

“I have done it before, and I’m none too shabby if I do say so myself.” Ted gave a slight bow. “However, I will not be performing today.”

“Oh, no,” Jennifer responded with mock disappointment. “Don’t let me put a damper on your singing career.”

Ted laughed and grabbed Jennifer around the waist, pulling her against him. “It’s a sacrifice I’m willing to make.” He kissed her.

“You two need to tone it down,” a reproaching female voice said from behind.

Ted quickly let go of Jennifer and swung around. She also turned in surprise. There stood Teresa with a scolding finger pointed at them. Teresa burst into laughter, joined by the petite lady at her side. Jennifer recognized the woman from the photo Teresa showed her the previous night.

“We thought we were in serious trouble,” Jennifer said with a chuckle. “You got us!”

Teresa smiled at Ted and extended her hand to him. “Do you remember me from Jennifer’s house? I’m Teresa, and this is my friend Maria.” The petite woman stepped forward and offered her hand to him, as well. Maria then turned her gaze to Jennifer and nodded with a smile.

“I was just at Teresa’s place yesterday,” Jennifer explained to Ted. “Teresa has some of Maria’s paintings. I was very impressed.” Maria lowered her gaze temporarily, but Jennifer could tell she appreciated the compliment.

“Ah, yes,” Teresa joined in. “Her work deserves to be displayed in galleries across state lines.”

At this, Maria decided to speak. “Personally, I believe it’s Teresa’s art that should be displayed.”

"I'm obviously surrounded by talent here." Ted grinned and again pulled Jennifer close to him. "I had no idea you were an artist, Teresa."

"It's more of a hobby for me." She shrugged humbly.

"Tell me, Teresa and Maria," Ted threw them a winning smile as he spoke, "what attractions and food booths do you highly recommend?"

Teresa did most of the talking, but Maria chimed in with her opinion if it differed from her friend's. Jennifer thought that the four of them might wander the fair together or at least hang out for a bit, but Teresa discreetly backed away and wished the couple a fun afternoon. Ted returned the pleasantries and didn't ask the pair to join Jennifer and himself.

Once the ladies were out of earshot, Ted said, "It looks like you've made a friend in Teresa. She's been to your house and you to hers."

"Yes. I think so, too. I really like her. She lives nearby, which is also a plus, not that any of the places in Tilbrook are far away."

"Bilmore isn't far away, for that matter," he emphasized.

"Good thing!" Jennifer hugged Ted firmly.

"I think I'm ready for course one of our four-or-five-course dinner. What do you think? Roasted corn on the cob? Onion rings? How about one of each, and we share?"

"Sounds good. Let's go for it." Jennifer reached for his hand, and they walked off, fingers entwined, tempted by the food choices offered.

The afternoon passed quickly, and the evening chill crept in once the sun set. Jennifer zipped her jacket as high as it would go. Ted put his arm around her to keep her warm but didn't offer to fold up the chairs and take off. The band continued to play as a few people danced.

"Would you care to?" He gestured to the dancers. When Jennifer nodded, Ted stood and offered his hand. He led her to an area near but a little apart from the other couples and took her in his arms. It was a sweet, slow dance, all the sweeter with Ted as her partner. Darkness was closing in quickly now, and the first stars to be visible added to the ambiance. Jennifer glanced up at the crescent moon. It was magical. Ted chose that moment to kiss her gently. They danced like this until the music changed to a tempo not conducive to romantic dancing, prompting Ted to lead Jennifer back to their chairs. When he put his arm around her again, she rested her head against his shoulder, content to listen to the music and drink in the atmosphere of the early autumn evening in the town she was beginning to love.

"Did you notice the sponsor sign over there?" She pointed in the general direction of the dancing couples. "One of the sponsors of the festival is Tenger-Bio. There's a big Tenger-Bio sign."

"I was too busy looking at something else to notice, or should I say someone else?" he replied softly.

Jennifer gently laughed. "Would you like to visit Tenger-Bio with me when you have a free weekday?"

"Not really."

Jennifer was surprised, so much so that she lifted her head from his shoulder to look at him directly. Despite the festival lighting, it was too dark to make out his facial expression. She wondered if he was teasing her. "Are you serious, Ted?"

"For me, Tenger was part of my distant past. I don't know anyone there now. It wouldn't be the same."

"Okay, but it might be interesting to check it out, don't you think? You could see the changes in it over the years," Jennifer countered, still hoping to convince him to go with her.

Ted remained silent for a while. Jennifer was pondering what to say next when he finally spoke. "It seems that you are the one interested in visiting Tenger. Why?"

"I'd like to see where you used to work, where my aunt used to work. It's also the largest employer around here, right?"

"Are you considering applying for a job?" Ted inquired, but Jennifer could tell by his tone that he was teasing. He knew the answer to that.

"Yes," she went along with the joke. "I have such an extensive background and credentials in biology that I've decided to try to get a research job. If that fails, I'll use my equally impressive background in business to work in the section you worked in."

Ted laughed. "I don't think Tenger's ready for either one of us."

"So, you honestly don't want to visit Tenger-Bio with me?"

"No, Jennifer, I don't, and I don't think you should either. Tenger-Bio isn't the same place it was when your aunt worked there. You can't, and shouldn't, try to go back in time."

She nodded and laid her head against Ted's shoulder again. "You've made a good point. Teresa brought up the idea yesterday. I somewhat had the same reaction that you did." Jennifer was silent for a moment but then asked, "Ted, why didn't you keep in contact with Ruth over the years? If you were good enough friends to live under the same roof for a while, then..."

Ted sighed deeply. "I regret that. Not the living under the same roof part, but the part about not keeping in touch. I believe we did for a while, but keep in mind that I moved out of state. I traveled. Time passes, and things change."

"Didn't you move to Bilmore when Ruth was still living?" Jennifer continued to prod.

"Yes, and I regret not letting Ruth know. First, I wasn't sure she was still alive. Second, I didn't know if Ruth had moved. Third, I wasn't sure she'd still remember me. Fourth, I simply procrastinated, and now I regret that."

Jennifer felt empathy for Ted and was sorry she had brought up the subject. "I've done the same. I've put things off, too. I don't blame you in the least. I'm sorry." She reached to squeeze Ted's hand. He responded by kissing the top of her head as it rested against his shoulder.

They enjoyed the remainder of the festival in silence, enjoying each other's embrace. Finally, Ted asked if she was ready to leave. The last band of the night was wrapping up.

When they got back to Jennifer's house, he reminded her of the wine he had brought. By the time Jennifer freshened up and returned to the living room, Ted had poured two glasses and had the lights dimmed, with soft music playing in the background. He stood as she entered and handed her one of the wine glasses he had gotten out of the china cabinet.

"To a wonderful day, Jennifer. I highly enjoyed it," Ted toasted as he raised his glass to hers.

She was about to put her lips to the edge of the glass when she felt something akin to a slap across her hand. The forceful sensation sent the wine glass sailing out of her grasp, flying through the air and shattering on the wooden floor. Simultaneously, the lights flickered, and the atmosphere became chillier than the outside air at the festival. Ted cursed under his breath, obviously caught by surprise, just as Jennifer was.

"I'm sorry, Ted," Jennifer finally found the ability to speak. "I don't know what happened! Did I get wine on you?"

"No, I'm fine." Ted set his own glass down on the nearest table.

Jennifer surveyed the damage. The wine missed the rug, which was good, but the glass was in multiple tiny pieces. She was embarrassed and annoyed by her apparent clumsiness. She also was irritated that Ted had taken it upon himself to use the delicate glasses from her china cabinet without first asking. Jennifer quickly got to work mopping up the spill while he cleaned up the glass fragments.

"Again, I'm sorry, Ted," Jennifer said when the situation appeared under control. "No real harm, though. I have sturdier glasses in the kitchen that I prefer to use anyway. Let me get those." She quickly returned and poured two glasses from the open wine bottle. She handed one to Ted, who reached out and accepted the glass but seemed somewhat detached. Evidently, the mood was broken for him. He had planned a romantic moment, and it derailed.

The two finished their respective drinks, and Ted didn't stay long afterward. Jennifer again apologized, and this time Ted reassured her that it wasn't her fault and that he still had a wonderful time. Jennifer was grateful for that.

Once Ted had driven off, Jennifer returned to the living room to reflect on what had just transpired. She could have sworn she felt someone slap her hand, her arm, with enough force to send a wine glass sailing. Did she simply experience a muscle spasm? No, different sensation. What about the flickering lights and the iciness of the air? Ted didn't seem to notice. Well, at least he hadn't mentioned it. Ted, though, was focused on the spilled wine and broken glass that had side-tracked his romantic moves.

She didn't know what to think, except that it had been an accident on her part, resulting in no actual harm. It had been a fantastic day despite the awkward ending. Jennifer switched on the stairway lighting. She was exhausted, and it was time to adjourn upstairs to get some needed sleep.

Chapter 9

WITH THE LAST OF the five boxes loaded in the back of the Toyota, Jennifer set off for Bilmore in her first attempt to sell some of Ruth's belongings. The time had come for Jennifer to unpack and assimilate more of her own possessions to make the house feel more personal. But to do that, she needed to free up space. Over the past few weeks, she selected items of her aunt's that didn't suit her taste and put them aside. Today, Jennifer had a nice assortment of bric-a-brac and headed out with the addresses of an antique store and a pawn shop in Bilmore, leads given to her by the locksmith, Steve.

Of course, Bilmore reminded Jennifer of Ted, and she was sorry he would be working today. Initially, she planned to wait for a weekend to run this errand, but the antique store recommended by Steve was only open by appointment on Saturdays and closed on Sundays. Today, Jennifer was highly motivated to get rid of the accumulating "for sale" boxes.

Besides, she liked the idea of having time to tour Bilmore independently. When she visited with Ted, they inevitably seemed to be on a mission to get to a specific place. After accomplishing the task at hand, Jennifer looked forward to a leisurely drive to scout out Tilbrook's larger, neighboring town.

As Jennifer passed the Cozy Cottage Motel, she chuckled, recalling the night she frantically fled her house to take refuge there. In hindsight, she could laugh, but at the time, she was petrified. How empowering to feel comfortable in her own home once again!

She slowed the car, recalling that the speed limit dropped somewhere in this vicinity. Several times on past trips, she noticed motorcycle cops parked in waiting. Ted always slowed in this area, as well. She was pleased that she was getting to know the ins and outs of living here.

Ted's apartment was on the way to Jennifer's first destination. On a whim, she decided to drive past, not that she expected to see him there but because she liked Ted and wished to see the exterior of his place one more time. As anticipated, his car was not in its reserved spot or anywhere in the smallish parking lot. Jennifer pulled into the visitor area and got out to stretch her legs and admire the façade of the building Ted currently rented. Overall, it was a cute complex. If she were in the market for an apartment in Bilmore, this would certainly be on the shortlist.

Jennifer got back into the Toyota and, this time, headed for the antique store without further detours. The shop was much smaller than she expected, but since it was Steve's number one recommendation, she ventured inside carrying one of the five boxes. She'd feel out the situation first.

"Hello, welcome! How may I help you?" inquired a friendly and enthusiastic voice.

"Hi. I have several boxes of odds and ends, mostly bric-a-brac, that I am thinking of selling," Jennifer said. She stopped short of telling the man behind the counter that she definitely wanted to get rid of the items and sell them today.

"Let's have a look. I can't promise you anything, of course. We have to be able to move our inventory, and we have a lot in stock at the moment."

Jennifer nodded. "Actually, I have four additional boxes in the car." She hoped that wouldn't put off the store owner or manager or whoever this was. He seemed open to the idea of her bringing in more merchandise, however. When Jennifer got to the Toyota, she was surprised he had followed to help carry the load.

"Why don't we do this," advised the man, who had resumed his position behind the counter. "Give me about twenty minutes to look through what you have. Either you can unpack it yourself, or we can. Feel free to watch, ask questions, or look around the shop." The man smiled and then called for someone from the back room. An elderly gentleman came forth and joined the other man. "My dad, the founder of the store," the son said to Jennifer by way of introduction.

"Pleased to meet you." The older man gave a slight bow. "What do we have here?" He turned to his son.

"We're just about to find out." The younger man looked at Jennifer, smiled, and spread his hands in a gesture that seemed to ask what she wanted to do next.

"It's fine for you to unpack the boxes. I'll probably do a combination of looking around the store and watching your assessment. Or should I say appraisal?" Jennifer's pitch went up. It was painfully obvious she had no idea what she was doing and no knowledge of the worth of the objects she presented to these gentlemen today.

"Very well," the younger man replied and nodded. The father-son team carefully unpacked and examined the items. Although they worked on separate boxes, they seemed well aware of what the other was doing. Occasional comments interrupted the blocks of silence. Overall, the younger man deferred to the judgment of the senior.

It was closer to thirty minutes when the father called Jennifer to the counter closest to him. He handed her a pink slip of paper with an itemized list of prices that Jennifer found staggering. She adopted her best poker face.

"We can accept these." The dad made a sweeping motion. "Unfortunately, we'll have to decline those items for now." He pointed to what had already been repacked into two boxes. "Feel free to come back, though. We're always open to looking at what our customers have to sell."

Jennifer's eyes were still glued to the pink sheet of paper. She mentally added the figures. There were no miscalculations. She had no idea Ruth's "stuff" could bring in this much money.

Apparently, Jennifer's facial expression or body language gave away more than she realized. The elderly shop owner explained, "You had more than mere knickknacks." He chuckled softly. "Did you decide if you want to accept the offer? You can sell one piece or all on that list."

"All," Jennifer said bluntly. "I'm trying to make room in a house I inherited."

"Oh?" The shopkeeper shifted his weight. "Someone close?"

Jennifer assumed he was referring to the person who bequeathed the house to her. "My aunt," she responded, without directly answering whether the relationship was close. "In Tilbrook," she added. Jennifer handed her driver's license to the younger man, who requested to see it for identification to write out the check.

Jennifer thanked both men as she slipped the license and check into her purse. She picked up one of the remaining boxes while the son carried the second. The older owner bid her goodbye before adding, "You know, years ago, I used to get items very similar in style to some of what you brought in today. I used to look forward to seeing the young gentleman come in. All at once, he stopped coming around. I guess he eventually ran out of things to sell!" He shook his head as he laughed.

The next stop was the pawnshop, about ten minutes from the antique store. Despite not managing to sell everything, Jennifer was pleased. She fared far better than she could ever have anticipated. Steve had not steered her wrong.

Jennifer spotted a branch of the bank she used in Tilbrook and stopped to deposit the check, which still seemed too good to be true. From the bank, she randomly drove to discover what additional amenities Bilmore offered. When she saw the movie theater, she suddenly knew how she wanted to spend the rest of her afternoon. Tilbrook lacked a cinema, although it had a quaint theater for live performances put on by local actors. Jennifer hadn't realized until now how much she missed seeing movies in an actual theater. At this point, she didn't much care what she watched as long as it wasn't a horror movie. Unlike her ex-husband, who enjoyed all gory films, she never liked anything gruesome.

Since it was a weekday, only two matinees were offered, and only a handful of patrons attended the theater. Jennifer settled into what she perceived to be the best seat for viewing, put her cup in the holder, and began munching on popcorn. Being in a cinema was already fun, something she hadn't made time for in years. She felt a slight twinge of guilt, however. Here she was in Bilmore, Ted's town, at the movies. Perhaps she should have bypassed the theater today and suggested to Ted that they come here together another time. Well, too late now. Besides, Jennifer reminded herself that there were other films they could see as a couple. Plus, she had a life of her own, independent from Ted.

To her surprise, she continued to think about him long after the movie ended. She swung past his apartment again, but he still wasn't there, and it was probably too early to wait for him. It wasn't like she had a key to his place. As Jennifer neared Tilbrook, the sight of the Cozy Cottage Motel triggered memories of Ted comforting her and offering to stay at the house when she was frightened. With Ted's apartment lease soon ending, maybe it was time she let Ted move in with her.

She continued to mull over the possibility as she pulled up to her house. Odd that she had set off today to begin the project of making the Gaitley house feel more like the Shemmer house. Hours later, Jennifer leaned toward making the home a Shemmer and Filston one. Hmm.

Jennifer's desire to talk to Ted intensified. He might still be working, but she could at least leave him a phone message. It didn't take long for Jennifer to settle on the sofa, hoping for a conversation with Ted. To her delight, it was not the voice message system that picked up.

"Jennifer. Hey, how are you?" His voice was enthusiastic and warm.

"Great! I had a fantastic day. Guess what? I made a trip to Bilmore! I did stop by your place on the off chance I'd catch you there, but you're working, so I didn't expect to see you. I had a few errands I wanted to do, though, so that's what brought me to Bilmore today." Jennifer winced when she heard herself rambling. She hoped Ted wouldn't be offended that she'd chosen a time he wouldn't be available.

"I'm glad you had a nice day, Jennifer," Ted said evenly. "You mentioned you had errands to do in Bilmore? Something that couldn't be taken care of in Tilbrook?"

"I wanted to go to a specific antique store there. When I had the locks changed, the locksmith recommended it if I ever decided to sell some of Ruth's items."

There was silence for a moment before Ted spoke. "Did you just go to check out the antique store, or did you take items to sell?"

"I had five boxes, Ted. The antique place accepted the majority of the things I brought, and most of the rest went to a pawnshop. You'd be surprised how much I was offered! In fact, the next dinner is on me, I insist. Let's go to a nice restaurant in Bilmore. We could go back to Perfezione or any place you'd like to go." Jennifer hoped he'd take her up on the offer as early as that evening.

"Why didn't you mention that you planned to sell Ruth's things?" He sounded displeased. "Why didn't you tell me you planned to go to an antique shop in Bilmore?"

Jennifer was caught off-guard. "Are you upset that we didn't do this together? Is it because I came to Bilmore today?"

"Jennifer, we talk on the phone almost daily. We see each other several times a week at a minimum. Of course, I thought you'd tell me if you intended to come to Bilmore. Yes, I thought you'd clue me in that you had items of Ruth's you hoped to sell."

It was her turn to be silent. She was stunned. After a few seconds, she found the voice to say, "I am sorry I didn't give you a heads-up about me coming to Bilmore, but Ted, honestly, it was on a whim. Even last night, I didn't know I'd decide to go to Bilmore today. As for my aunt's belongings," Jennifer paused, "first of all, I didn't realize she had some things of significant value. On the other hand, they are mine to sell if I choose. I don't understand why you seem to be upset with me."

"I'm not upset with you." Ted's agitated tone contradicted the message. "I guess it's because I have more sentimental attachment to Ruth than I realized. I know it's been ages ago, but I have strong memories of being a guest there. I'd actually like to see what items you want to get rid of before you dispose of them. Maybe I'm being overly sentimental. I don't know."

Jennifer felt a pang of remorse, although she knew she had done nothing wrong. She had no idea Ted felt so strongly about Ruth. "I'll keep that in mind," she said soothingly. "It never occurred to me you'd care one way or another."

"Forgive me, Jennifer." He recovered his composure and was almost back to his usual self. "It was a rough day. I'm tired or at least mentally exhausted. I'm afraid I came off as a little testy, but I don't mean to be. Again, I'm sorry."

"That's okay," Jennifer said softly. She felt bad for Ted. She hadn't even asked him about his day before going into length about her own. "Do you want to talk about your work? I assume it was work that made today rough."

"It was, but no, I try not to talk shop. I have, or more likely had, a client who misunderstood the terms of his contract with us. He's trying to make my life miserable. I care about my clients, too, so it bothers me that he's not happy. There's only so much I can do, however."

"I had the occasional angry parent when I taught," Jennifer sympathized. "Sometimes, the people you do the most for complain the loudest."

"Exactly! Needless to say, I wouldn't be good company tonight. Perhaps tomorrow evening?"

"Sure, Ted. You take care of yourself tonight. Relax and get some rest. Would you like me to treat you to dinner out tomorrow, or would you like to stay in, and I'll cook?"

"If it's not too much trouble, I think a night in sounds best. Are you sure you don't mind cooking? I could pick up food for us on the way," Ted offered, obviously aware that Jennifer didn't love to cook.

"I don't mind, Ted. I want to. Would you prefer salmon, chicken, or lasagna?" Jennifer named three dishes that came to mind instantly.

"Salmon sounds exquisite. I'll see you tomorrow, probably a little after six."

Shortly after they hung up, Jennifer texted Angie. Her pal phoned almost immediately. "You're not interrupting," Angie initiated the conversation in response to Jennifer's message. "I already have dinner in the oven, and it will take twenty minutes. What's up?"

She gave Angie a synopsis of the day, including her recent conversation with Ted. "Don't you think his reaction was strange?" Jennifer ended her monolog with a question.

"Yeah, Jen. A little. I mean, you are entitled to do what you want. He isn't a co-inheritor. Ruth left everything to you. Notice she didn't leave anything to anyone else, meaning him. And, Jen, if you want to go to Bilmore or anywhere else, by yourself or with a friend, you can do that, too. You don't need to check with Ted first." Angie sounded quite passionate.

"I agree, but I still feel slightly guilty," Jennifer confessed. "Ted did say he had a rough day. He also said he hadn't realized how strongly he felt about Ruth. I guess she filled a role in his life at that time, like a mentor or even a surrogate family member."

"Yeah, maybe." Angie softened a bit. She liked Ted right from the start, although she hadn't met him. For that matter, though, Angie liked Ephraim Walson, both the son and the father, and she certainly wasn't going to have an opportunity to meet them.

Jennifer sighed. "I just needed to get that off my chest. I probably should let you go. It won't be long till your dinner's ready."

"Jen, listen. Follow your instincts. You've got good ones. That's about the only advice I can offer at this time. Hang in there. Take it slow, and keep me posted."

Jennifer expressed her exasperation with a short groan. "Will do. Thanks for talking with me, Ange. Give my love to Jolie and Mike."

She ended the call and made for the den. "Hello, Aunt Ruth," she greeted the two portraits on the wall. Jennifer took both down and held the photos before her. "Aunt Ruth, how would you like to accompany me to Tenger-Bio tomorrow?"

The lights flickered momentarily.

"I'll take that as a sign of approval," Jennifer whispered.

Chapter 10

FOR THE PAST THIRTY minutes, Jennifer rehearsed what she'd say once she got to Tenger-Bio. Now that she was actually here, standing at the front desk, she felt uncomfortable and didn't know how to proceed. The young man behind the tall counter gave her an empathetic look as if encouraging a nervous public speaker.

"Sorry. My name is Jennifer Shemmer. A long time ago, my aunt worked here as a research biologist. Her name was Ruth Gaitley."

The young man continued to smile pleasantly. "Yes? How may I help you?"

"I know it's a long shot. What I mean to say is, well, I'm hoping someone here might remember my aunt, Ruth Gaitley. I didn't have much contact with her, so I'm..." Jennifer hesitated, feeling foolish. Ted was right about it being too long ago, and Jennifer wished she hadn't come. She opened the file folder with the two portraits of Ruth. At least she'd been wise and left the frames at home. She placed the photos on the counter, facing them toward the receptionist.

"Follow me, please," he suddenly requested. A surprised Jennifer gathered the photos and trailed behind the young man. They didn't go far, only a short distance down the hallway. "Your aunt?" He pointed to an enlarged, beautifully framed portrait identical to the one she had of Ruth when she appeared to be in her sixties.

"Oh, my goodness!" Jennifer noticed the frame bore a plaque with her aunt's name. Next to the portrait was an impressive list of Dr. Ruth Gaitley's accomplishments. Jennifer felt her eyes brim with tears of pride. She was genuinely touched to see her modest, introverted aunt commemorated in such a manner.

"Since you're a relative of Dr. Gaitley, I'm sure Dr. Benton will want to meet you." The receptionist led Jennifer back to the front desk and motioned for her to have a seat. It wasn't long before a tall, well-dressed man approached Jennifer confidently, his hand outstretched in welcome.

"Hello. I'm Jerome Benton. Ramon tells me you are the niece of Ruth Gaitley?" He spoke rapidly without giving her time to respond. "She was a brilliant woman, a pioneer. I'm honored to meet you. Would you like a tour of our facilities? Ramon, could you hand me a welcome packet? Thank you." Dr. Benton pressed the packet firmly into Jennifer's hand. She felt slightly overwhelmed.

"You're probably too young to have worked here when my aunt did," Jennifer speculated out loud. "Did you ever meet her?"

"Unfortunately, no. She is part of the dynamic history of Tenger-Bio, however. Like many of us, I walk past her portrait every workday."

"I'm hoping there might be someone left at Tenger-Bio who did know her. Maybe someone who could tell me a little more about her." Jennifer studied Dr. Benton's reaction.

"Not many, if any, I'm afraid." Jerome Benton shook his head in sympathetic regret. "We have a young staff overall, with frequent turnover." Dr. Benton motioned for Jennifer to follow. "Tenger-Bio is part of a larger organization. This facility is in an ideal location for its research goals and training due to the area's biological diversity. However, as far as many of our young staff are concerned, the area lacks diversity in terms of attractions and nightlife." He shrugged. "Rotan is the largest city near here, an hour's commute."

"That surprises me." Jennifer frowned. "I thought most people working at Tenger-Bio would live in Tilbrook, like my aunt. Even Bilmore is closer than Rotan."

"Rotan has much more to offer in terms of entertainment, sports, and higher education," Dr. Benton explained. "However, Rotan can't compete with the locations of our parent company. After three years of positive evaluations at Tenger-Bio, an employee can usually receive a transfer, with a generous moving allowance."

"Are you in for the long haul, Dr. Benton?" Jennifer asked, half-teasing.

"I enjoy working at Tenger-Bio for now. I doubt I have the longevity of your aunt," he said good-naturedly, "but I haven't put in for a transfer."

Jerome Benton continued to lead Jennifer through a maze of hallways. She hoped someone would show her the way out after the tour because she was completely disoriented. "You certainly get your daily exercise walking these halls," she commented, attempting to make small talk.

"Cindy," Dr. Benton called to a redheaded female, "can you give Jennifer a tour of the research facilities and also introduce her to Hank? Be sure to tell him this is Ruth Gaitley's niece." He turned and shook Jennifer's hand before receiving a reply from either woman.

Evidently, Jennifer was now to follow Cindy. The young woman was pleasant enough, but her body language indicated that she preferred not to be giving impromptu tours. Although Jennifer found behind-the-scenes at Tenger-Bio interesting, this wasn't her mission for the day. After a while, Jennifer let Cindy know that she mainly wanted to see the area where her aunt worked and that an abbreviated tour was fine, emphasizing that she didn't want to be a nuisance. Cindy nodded, obviously liking the idea of cutting the tour short, leading Jennifer into yet another area of the Tenger-Bio maze.

"Hank, meet Jennifer, Ruth Gaitley's niece." Cindy confronted a gray-haired man who was busy positioning a rather large, technical-looking piece of equipment.

"Pleased to meet you, Hank." Jennifer extended her hand after repositioning her welcome packet. "My aunt was a researcher here decades ago, but she continued to work after her retirement, into her seventies."

"I do remember her," Hank mused after a moment's hesitation. "Your aunt was a very kind woman. I admired her."

Jennifer's jaw dropped. "Oh, it's nice to find someone who knew her! I hope you have a few stories about her or at least can fill me in on what she was like."

"Excuse me, Hank, but can you see this woman out once you two are caught up?" Cindy inquired, impatient to get back to her own project.

"Sure," Hank agreed and paused while Jennifer quickly thanked Cindy. "I didn't know Ruth well, mainly by her reputation. You see, she was already semi-retired when I came to work here. Her research was part-time. Mostly, we exchanged pleasantries. I remember how unpretentious she was, though. Have you seen her portrait displayed in front?"

Jennifer nodded. "Yes, I have a smaller copy that hangs in my den."

"You don't see *my* portrait at Tenger-Bio!" He chuckled jovially. "That speaks of her prestige, yet she was very humble."

"I understand that she was aloof, possibly a little unfriendly."

Hank adamantly shook his head. "She was quiet, intensely focused, and no-nonsense. That's not the same as unfriendly. In fact, I recall she befriended some young guy who worked here at the time."

"Ted Filston?" Jennifer blurted out his name without thinking.

"I don't remember, but it's been so long ago," Hank lamented. "All I know is that Ruth had taken him into her house and later had to ask him to leave."

"Excuse me?" Jennifer couldn't believe what she was hearing. "My aunt asked the young man who was staying with her to leave?"

"That's right." Hank gave a singular nod.

"Did she tell you why?" Jennifer was still stunned.

"No, and I didn't inquire. It wasn't any of my business. I remember Ruth was troubled at the time. I think that's the only reason she told me. She felt bad about the situation."

"Did you ever meet the young man? He used to work in the business office or the finance office—something like that. He and Ruth had lunch together in the cafeteria." Jennifer tried to fill in as much detail as possible in hopes it would trigger a memory in Hank.

"I know I did see him around, and I know he wasn't in research. All I can tell you is that he appeared to be very young. I'm sorry I can't help you more with details."

"That's fine, Hank, and you actually have been a big help," Jennifer assured him. "I've taken up enough of your time. I will need help finding my way out, though. Oh, and can you show me the section where my aunt worked?"

"You're standing in it now. Of course, the equipment is much more modern. I imagine I won't recognize the place myself in twenty years." Hank navigated his way toward the main entrance with Jennifer trailing behind. He stopped in front of Ruth's portrait. "I'll leave you here, Jennifer. It was a pleasure to meet you. Again, I greatly admired your aunt. Such a nice woman." He looked up at the large wall photo with obvious appreciation.

"Thank you so much, Hank. I truly am grateful for your time." Jennifer said a heartfelt goodbye and walked towards the reception area, waving briefly to Ramon.

"Oh, one more thing," Hank's voice boomed from the hallway. Jennifer turned to look in his direction. "The young man had blonde hair. I doubt that helps you, but you asked for details."

Jennifer brought the last of the grocery bags into the kitchen. Earlier today, she looked forward to having a quiet dinner at home with Ted. Now it seemed like a chore to be completed and checked off the calendar. She removed the salmon from one of the sacks and put it in the refrigerator. Some of the produce needed to be prepped for tonight, so she tackled that task once everything was unpacked and put away.

"Jeez!" Jennifer yelped when she nicked her thumb with a sharp knife. She observed the blood and held the injury under a stream of tap water.

Suddenly, Jennifer was aware that the atmosphere in the kitchen had changed. It was cooler, no doubt, but there was more to it than that. She couldn't explain the subtle distinction, but she sensed the difference, enough to shift her attention from her wounded thumb. The blood continued to ooze, however, so Jennifer grabbed a paper towel and headed for the bandages she kept upstairs. With her thumb securely wrapped, she returned downstairs, darkened the living room by closing several blinds, and sat on the sofa. The kitchen chores could wait.

"Ephraim," she said hesitantly. "Doctor Ephraim or Ephraim Junior, are you here?" Jennifer heard nothing. The living room felt "normal" and didn't possess that strange atmosphere she noticed in the kitchen when she sliced her thumb.

Jennifer held her bandaged hand up above her head. "See, I applied first aid. It still hurts, but it's not bad. Was it you, Ephraim, who was with me in the kitchen?" Still nothing. She didn't let the lack of response deter her, however. "I felt someone with me in the kitchen, and I believe it was you, Ephraim. I think you were concerned about me."

She lowered her hand to her lap and sat in silence for at least a minute. The stillness of the room was unusual. If possible, it was a quieter quiet than normal. Jennifer pondered that notion. A quieter quiet. It made no sense, yet the expression fit the situation. Someone was definitely here right now.

"I can feel your presence, Ephraim," Jennifer finally spoke. She surveyed the room slowly but without leaving the sofa. "I want to talk with you, even if you aren't able to answer, or maybe it's that I'm not able to hear you."

Again, Jennifer paused. As she sat in silence, she noticed the air chill slightly. It wasn't a considerable temperature drop, just a cooler sensation, and it wasn't unpleasant. She felt an unusual energy, atmosphere, or perhaps vibration. Jennifer had stayed away from recreational drugs, but her experience at present reminded her of a heightened sense of being and awareness. She couldn't recall ever feeling this way before. It was as if she were one with the house and all that was in it. It was as if she were united with all of the universe. Jennifer liked this newly discovered sensation.

"I want to thank you, Ephraim, for caring about me. At least, I think you do," she continued out loud to her invisible audience. "I believe you cared about my aunt, too. I think you and Aunt Ruth shared a connection for decades. Maybe that's why she couldn't have my mom stay with her in this house. That's okay, Ephraim. That's fine, Aunt Ruth. I'm only beginning to understand the presence, or whatever it is, in this house. There's something here, though, and I am aware of it."

Jennifer was a little disappointed to receive no clear response. The same unusual atmospheric sensation continued, but nothing out of the ordinary presented itself visibly or audibly. Jennifer placed her palms over her eyes. It was soothing.

"Did you leave me the daisy that day?" she suddenly asked. "The day I put flowers, those same flowers, on Doctor Ephraim's grave."

No answer.

"Did you push the wine glass out of my hand?" Jennifer was surprised she thought of that question.

No answer.

"Obviously, I don't know much about you, Ephraim. I don't even know which Ephraim this is or if there are two of you here. My instinct says that it's you, Doctor Ephraim, the one my aunt wrote about in her diary. Anyway, I hope you are okay. I'm very sorry you were murdered. That was so unfair. I think you know that Ruth felt terrible about that. She felt guilty because you were coming to check on her. If this is Ephraim Junior, then I'm sorry you were killed with that arrow. You were much too young, and that was tragic. I can't even imagine how much your father, Doctor Ephraim, mourned. I wish things could have been different for both you and your dad. I want everything to be fine for you now, however. I wish you nothing but peace and happiness. I hope you have that."

Jennifer thought she felt a brief, soft brush against her left cheek. Her bandaged thumb stopped throbbing, and she had an odd sensation of her hand having another placed on top of it. She didn't move because she enjoyed the feeling of contentment, protection, and love. Jennifer didn't want the spell to break, so she sat this way in silence for close to an hour.

If it hadn't been for the obligation to start preparing dinner for Ted and herself, Jennifer would gladly have remained with Ephraim longer. Reluctantly, she stirred from the couch to start cooking. Jennifer noticed the kitchen felt "normal" once again, and for that, she was disappointed.

Ted arrived promptly on the hour, this time bearing gifts of flowers and chocolates. "Sweets for the sweet," he said. "Oh, that sounds awfully cliché, doesn't it? It fits, though." Ted placed the bouquet in Jennifer's hand as he kissed her on the cheek.

"Thank you, Ted. They're lovely," Jennifer replied, thinking that also sounded routine.

"Whatever you're cooking smells delicious!" He grinned broadly. "Can I help in any way?"

It was difficult not to be pulled in by Ted's charm. Jennifer had contemplated telling him about today's visit to Tenger-Bio. She rehearsed confronting Ted about Ruth asking him to move out of her house years ago. In the end, Jennifer decided to say nothing. If Hank was incorrect or there was a misunderstanding, any hint of accusation would surely ruin any prospects of a long-term relationship with Ted. Instead, Jennifer decided to observe with an open mind while being cautious. One thing for sure, she would not invite Ted to move in with her at this time. True, she leaned toward the idea only yesterday but not after what she heard at Tenger-Bio.

"This looks good! I like the seasoning," Ted announced after having sampled the simmering sauce she'd prepared for the salmon.

"Thanks," Jennifer said bluntly. Maybe Ted's tendency to make himself very much at home was the reason Ruth asked him to leave. Jennifer knew she found that trait of his a little annoying. When she was in someone's home, she always asked permission before doing anything. Ted had no compunction about opening her china cabinet, sampling food, reading her aunt's diary, etc. On the other hand, that probably was part of Ted's overall charm—his confidence, ability to show initiative, and his follow-through. Jennifer didn't know what to think.

"I am truly sorry about yesterday," Ted said, perhaps picking up on Jennifer's subdued tone. "I know I had a bad day, but I should never have let that creep into my conversation with you. Will you accept my apology?" He looked so contrite it was difficult to remain perturbed.

"I've cooked you a salmon dinner," she reminded him, somewhat evading the question.

He interpreted that as acceptance. "And I thank you for that, Jennifer. I could use a quiet night. We both probably could."

She agreed and turned her attention to the side dishes. "Is iced tea okay for the meal?" She didn't feel that either of them needed alcohol tonight, and she was relieved that Ted chose to bring flowers and chocolates instead of a bottle of wine.

"Absolutely. May I pour?"

"Yes. Let's use the glasses in that cabinet." Jennifer directed him to the ones she intended.

They sat down to dinner about fifteen minutes later. While Jennifer was finishing up in the kitchen, Ted managed to take the two candlesticks from the china cabinet and set them on the table. He was in the process of lighting the second candle when Jennifer entered with the main course. Many people would find this a romantic, charming action, but Jennifer was irritated with Ted. Why couldn't he ask permission? She should call Steve and have him put a padlock on the china cabinet. The notion made her laugh out loud.

"What's funny?" Ted inquired with a broad grin.

"Oh, nothing really. I think it's relief that I managed not to burn the meal. I'm not the best of chefs." Jennifer circumvented the real answer.

"I have no complaints, as you will soon see while I eat everything on my plate! You've put together an amazing dinner, Jennifer. Thank you."

She softened. Ted could be so nice. Alex, her ex, was never one to extend many compliments. She was surprised to find that by the end of the meal, she felt close to Ted once again. He insisted on clearing the plates from the table and offered to load the dishwasher. Jennifer allowed him to do that and watched in appreciation. Although she insisted that the things needing to be hand-washed could wait until tomorrow, Ted began filling the sink. Jennifer grabbed the dishtowel.

After the chores were finished and Ted pronounced the kitchen spotless, the two adjourned to the living room sofa. Ted put one arm around Jennifer's shoulders while using his dominant hand to manipulate the remote of the television.

"Is there anything special you'd like to watch?" He flipped to the guide.

"No. I don't have any favorite shows anymore." She sighed.

Ted nodded as if he felt the same. "Have you seen this movie?" He paused the guide so Jennifer could read the details.

"No. That's fine. Let's watch that." She was agreeable. It truly didn't matter to her.

Ted dimmed the lights and then settled in again to watch the two-hour film with his sweetheart. He put his head on Jennifer's shoulder, and she smiled. As lovely as this moment was, she couldn't help but contrast it to her earlier encounter with Ephraim. Ted had a physical body, warm and real. Ephraim had a presence—an atmosphere and energy.

Although Jennifer liked the feeling of Ted's body next to hers, she couldn't honestly say she preferred this over the sensations she had when Ephraim "sat" next to her.

Jennifer did her best to follow the movie and be present with Ted, but her mind wandered. Sometimes she was at Tenger-Bio. Sometimes she was at the Bilmore antique store. Sometimes she was in the cemetery kneeling before the graves of the Walsons. She noticed that Ted had drifted to sleep. He needed his rest, she thought. Ted was a nice guy, Jennifer told herself. Look at how he helped out in the kitchen. Alex, on the other hand, usually left the clean-up to her. Ted appeared to want to share life with Jennifer. She and Alex shared the same roof for years but hadn't been partners in the sense of being a team. Alex had his concerns; she had hers. Alex had his chores; she had hers.

Aunt Ruth lived alone most of her life. When she invited Ted to stay with her, Ruth wasn't used to someone like Ted confidently making himself at home without asking permission for every little thing. Jennifer further reminded herself that Ted was coming off a divorce in his mid-twenties and was accustomed to sharing with a partner. Perhaps that accounted for the conflict that caused Ruth to ask her boarder to leave.

There was also the possibility that Hank was mistaken. Maybe Ruth and Ted had a misunderstanding at the time, and Ruth was only contemplating asking him to live elsewhere. Perhaps the young man wasn't Ted. Did Ruth have other houseguests who lived with her besides Ted ... and Ephraim? Jennifer glanced down at the top of Ted's resting head. He was definitely blonde. Very blonde. What were the odds it would be someone else? Not good. No, it most likely was Ted.

"What did I miss?" He stirred and rubbed his eyes with his right hand before raising his head from Jennifer's shoulder. "I'm sorry I fell asleep. It's so peaceful here."

That's precisely how Jennifer felt when Ephraim was beside her. "The guy in black there," Jennifer pointed as she spoke, "is the murderer. Carrie has fallen in love with him and has no idea he shot his wife. Meanwhile, Nathan is suspicious and has called in a friend of his who's a private investigator."

Ted reached for his iced tea. "Are you in the mood for a chocolate?" He was already starting to get up.

"That sounds welcome."

Ted returned with the box opened and offered her first choice. He tempted her to take two pieces, and he did the same. The candies were delicious, and Jennifer appreciated the sweetness of both the chocolate and her companion. He settled back into position on the sofa, and this time, Jennifer rested her head on Ted's chest. He kissed the top of her head multiple times.

Yes, this was nice. Pleasant and real. Jennifer could get used to this kind of life very easily. She snuggled in for the remainder of the movie.

Chapter 11

"I CAN FEEL THE presence of a spirit in your house," Maria Guzman announced suddenly after sitting quietly on Jennifer's sofa for most of an hour while Teresa and Jennifer dominated the conversation.

"Oh, she *does* have a ghost here, Maria." Teresa turned to give Jennifer a teasing wink. "Jennifer, do you remember the day I came to measure your windows? Remember how icy the air became?" Teresa used one hand to point to the stairway while using her other to pat Maria's adjacent knee.

"I do remember," Jennifer replied with a twinge of disappointment. She liked being the only one outside of Ruth to feel Ephraim's presence and was slightly taken aback that her guest had sensed him.

"Maria worked at the Yuma Territorial Prison," Teresa informed Jennifer. "She had some unusual experiences there." Teresa smiled and squeezed Maria's hand.

"You once worked in a prison?" Jennifer was genuinely surprised. "What type of work? Did you enjoy it?" She tried picturing the petite, quiet woman as a corrections officer.

Teresa answered for Maria, "Yuma Territorial Prison shut down in the early 1900s." She turned to her partner for confirmation, and Maria nodded but remained silent. Teresa continued, "It's a tourist attraction. Due to its history, it's allegedly haunted. Maria witnessed some weird things there."

"You were a tour guide or something like that?" Jennifer looked directly at the young woman.

"I worked in the visitor center and museum. That prison has its own energy. I could feel the spirits, especially when I walked past certain cells."

"So, what weird things did you witness?" Jennifer used Teresa's phrasing.

"In the visitor center, items would mysteriously move. Once, coins from the register flew out of the drawer. Several times, I was touched," Maria said all of this in a very matter-of-fact tone.

"Don't forget the young man." Teresa gestured for her partner to elaborate.

"I was near what they call the Dark Cell. I saw this man, probably in his twenties, standing by the entrance. I thought he was a visitor, and I didn't think much about it, except he was dressed kind of odd. I thought maybe he was in a uniform or costume. Many people visit the prison, and some are obsessed with its history. When I turned to look at him, he looked right at me, and then," Maria stopped talking momentarily, taking a longer than average pause for full effect, "he vanished."

"And she doesn't mean he went running off," Teresa added, having heard this story multiple times.

"No, he faded. He disappeared," Maria said in an almost whisper.

Jennifer experienced goosebumps and shivered. Maria was quiet but knew how to use her tone and timing to increase suspense. "Did anybody else experience similar things?" She already knew the answer but felt compelled to ask anyway.

"Oh, yes." Maria nodded but said no more. Her eyes were wider than usual.

"Yuma Territorial Prison is pretty well known for being haunted. There are books and TV shows about it," Teresa added. "You can easily find more information on the internet."

Maria nodded vigorously. "Why don't you get some paranormal equipment?" she asked, bringing the topic back to Jennifer's own house.

"Oh, I don't know about that!" Jennifer immediately balked at the idea. Angie had already suggested this and, after Jennifer's reaction, didn't bring it up again.

"Just a simple recording device," Maria continued. "You might capture some EVPs."

"Electronic Voice Phenomena," Teresa clarified, in case Jennifer was unfamiliar.

Again, Maria nodded. "That's a good starting place. You can buy other types of equipment, too, but that's a start.'

Jennifer didn't know how to respond, so she changed the subject. "Did I tell you that Ted's moving to Tilbrook? He took a six-month lease at Montgomery Haven Apartments."

"I live at M. H.," Maria said. "It's a nice place. I think he'll like it there."

Teresa looked dubious. "Jennifer, you'll have the same issue to deal with when his six-month lease is up." She turned to Maria to fill her in on Ted's desire to move in with Jennifer.

Jennifer waited patiently for her to finish. "Six months will give me time to know how I feel about Ted and our future. Personally, I think it's a good idea. It will allow us a chance to spend more time together but still retain our space."

Teresa shrugged but did manage an affirmative nod. Maria offered to help Ted if he needed anything at the apartment. Jennifer liked the idea of Maria being nearby and supportive.

"Have you met the neighbors?" Teresa asked Jennifer abruptly. "Your own neighbors, I mean. Not Ted's neighbors at Montgomery Haven."

"Yes, I met Mrs. Nandez. Not exactly warm. Let's just say that I'm not expecting to be invited over anytime soon. She did tell me that there used to be a guest cottage on her property that's now torn down. That's where Ephraim Walson, Jr., was killed by a bow and arrow."

"He was murdered?" Maria asked.

"No. Well, who knows," Jennifer tried to answer. "It was considered a hunting accident. No one came forward. The area behind the houses was undeveloped forest in those days."

"You have a fascinating place," Maria responded, looking as if she genuinely meant it. "May I see the upstairs?"

"Oh!" Jennifer had cleaned and straightened the downstairs for company but hadn't thought about needing to do anything extra upstairs. "Sure, if you don't mind an unmade bed and some general disarray."

Maria stood, apparently ready for a tour. Teresa remained seated and said, "Jennifer, we don't need to go upstairs today. That might be asking a little much on such short notice." She turned to Maria and made a face that communicated that perhaps Maria had overstepped.

"It's okay, really," Jennifer assured the two women. "After all, you're both friends, and I doubt you imaged that I always live in an immaculate, orderly house."

"Hear, hear!" Teresa raised her iced tea glass in a mock toast. She gave Maria a playful wink as she rose from the sofa to join the impromptu tour.

"I still have the mystery room locked. That's my pet name for this particular room because it's the only one with a keyed lock. I had to get a locksmith to open it since Aunt Ruth left it closed without a key," Jennifer explained once the women were upstairs.

Maria stood facing the door, obviously expectingly her host to retrieve the key. Jennifer hesitated but went to get it. "I've made a small dent in going through things, but this room seems to have been Ruth's main storage space."

Teresa walked up to Jennifer and quietly whispered, "Keep the door locked."

"What?" Jennifer asked with surprise.

"Ted. He's living in Tilbrook now or will be soon," Teresa said pointedly.

Jennifer glanced toward Maria, who seemed oblivious to their side conversation. Maria was busy admiring, but respectfully not touching, Ruth's collection of memorabilia

Jennifer flashed Teresa a disapproving gaze, which caused Teresa to raise her eyebrows. This marked the first time Jennifer had been irritated with her new pal. "I trust Ted," she said but immediately wondered if she had just lied to herself. Teresa appeared to sense this revelation and winked at Jennifer.

"Simply friendly advice to be cautious and don't let your guard slip," Teresa persisted. "It's a small bit of precaution that doesn't hurt a thing."

Jennifer neither spoke nor nodded. She focused her attention on Maria, who seemed satisfied that she had seen enough of the mystery room.

"I found two of Ruth's diaries here," Jennifer finally broke the awkward silence. "I've sold some of the antiques. Ted's nostalgic and hasn't wanted me to part with some of them, so I'm not quite sure what I'll tackle next."

Teresa said nothing and looked at the floor. Jennifer reddened as she realized the connection between Teresa's advice to keep the room locked and Ted's feelings for Ruth's antiques. Maria turned and removed the key that Jennifer had left in the mystery room's lock. She pressed the key into Jennifer's palm and gave her a sympathetic half-smile.

With her visitors gone and Ted away for the weekend, Jennifer felt a bit of a let-down. She retrieved her computer and did a search for paranormal equipment. The number of options and the overall reasonable prices surprised her.

She had no idea there was so much interest in ghost hunting and paranormal detection devices. Jennifer contemplated several items but, in the end, opted to follow Maria's suggestion and start with a digital recorder. At least Angie would approve, although Ted would probably think the notion silly. Jennifer was oddly excited by the idea of trying out the recorder and didn't know why she balked in the beginning. Maybe she was afraid of what she might learn. Perhaps she was even more fearful of not getting any evidence of the supernatural.

Several hours passed before she noticed the darkness outside. How easy it was to become absorbed by the internet. Jennifer returned the laptop to its rightful niche, double-checking that it was plugged in to recharge.

After finishing off the leftovers from today's luncheon with Teresa and Maria, Jennifer snuggled into her favorite chair. She missed Ted. He'd be back in town on Monday. It wouldn't be long until Jennifer would help him move to his new apartment at Montgomery Haven, or M. H., as Maria called it. She wondered if Ted would also pick up that habit. Well, she had already seen her Tilbrook pals today. Angie had phoned earlier, and Ted was unavailable, so that left...

"Hey, Ephraim," Jennifer laughed as she addressed him out loud. "How was your day? I'm alone tonight, as you already know. I had company over today, my friends Teresa and Maria. Maria said she could feel your presence. She didn't mention you by name or have a particular spirit in mind, but she could feel someone else in the house."

Jennifer sat in silence for several minutes. She didn't know if it was wishful thinking on her part, but she swore she could detect a slightly cooler feel to the air, a little more stillness, and perhaps a bit more energy. It was difficult, if not impossible, to describe. Electric charge? Positive ions? Negative ions?

"I've ordered a highly sensitive digital recorder for paranormal investigations," Jennifer finally broke the silence. "Not that I'm investigating you, per se," she quickly added. "I would like to know more about you. After all, you apparently live here or visit here. It would be fantastic to hear from you."

No answer. No further change in the living room's atmosphere.

"Would you like to communicate with me, too? You did with Ruth, didn't you?" Jennifer recalled the 1949 diary entries of her aunt.

Of course, Jennifer wasn't expecting a direct answer from Ephraim, but it didn't hurt to try. Maybe if she regularly conversed with him, she'd get results. Perhaps it was a matter of practice like anything else. Even Ruth herself didn't appear to be able to communicate with the ghost in the house initially. It seemed to take a while. Speaking of her aunt and the 1949 diary, Jennifer got up from her chair to retrieve her aunt's journal from upstairs. She'd like to reread the passages that involved Ruth's communication system with Ephraim.

It didn't take her long to locate the diary. As she descended the stairs, she felt a particularly icy air pocket. Jennifer wasn't deterred, however, since she no longer feared the spirit in her home. Jennifer moved her drink to the coffee table and sat on the sofa, just in case Ephraim wanted to sit near her. She thumbed through the diary to find the first entry about Ruth's communication using light flickers.

It was a straightforward system, at least in the beginning. One flicker of the light meant yes. Two flickers meant no. Jennifer wondered if, in later years, the system became more complex. She hoped that someday she'd run across further diaries of her aunt. For now, though, this was it.

"Ephraim. Can we communicate with light flickers the way you did with my aunt? One flicker for yes. Two for no. Can you do that?" She got up from the sofa to switch off one of the two lamps, wanting to make it as simple as possible. "Ephraim, can you make this light flicker? Once for yes."

The steadiness of the light disappointed her. She waited patiently for a full minute until she tried a different approach.

"Is your name Ephraim? Please make the light flick off and back on one time if your name is Ephraim. Please turn the light off and on twice if it isn't."

Again, no change in the lighting. Absolutely no change. Jennifer sat quietly, looking around the room. She knew a spirit was present by the feel of the atmosphere, even though she could see nothing unusual.

Jennifer tried another question. "Do you know my name?"

The steady shine of the light bulb irritated her. She repeated her experiment using a different lamp, first demonstrating for Ephraim. The result was the same, however—nothing.

"Oh, Ephraim!" Jennifer shifted her weight on the sofa and crossed her legs, simultaneously frustrated and disappointed. "I thought you might communicate with me as you did with my aunt. You two could have developed a different system over the years, but you used this simple one to start with, at least in 1949. I know you can make the lights turn off and on. You've done that before. The next step is to do it in a meaningful pattern. I'd love to talk with you, even if only through yes and no questions. Wouldn't you like that, too?"

Suddenly she laughed. It struck her funny that Ephraim and her ex-husband, Alex, had something in common. Both were stubborn and immune to Jennifer's pleas.

"I like your company anyway, even if you won't or can't talk with me. Maybe I'm asking too much of you. It could be that you can't make the lamps flicker on command. I thought you could, but maybe you don't have that ability. It was worth a try, though. I did enjoy our experiment."

Jennifer continued her one-sided conversation. "I think I have a lot in common with Aunt Ruth. She must have felt lonely at one time, at least when she was young. I can tell from her diary entries that she very much considered you a friend. You gave her comfort, you know. I'm beginning to realize that you're giving me that gift, too. At first, when I realized that Ruth wasn't the ghost inhabiting this house, I was scared. You probably saw me run out of the house that night, the evening I first discovered that Ruth was also frightened of a presence. I want you to know that I'm over that now. You probably already know that. I think I'm rambling on...." Jennifer's voice trailed off.

There it was again, that blissful peace she'd felt the other day around Ephraim. Jennifer sat silently on the couch, taking it in with all her senses. She thought about trying the lamp experiment again yet hated to break the magical spell that left her absolutely content, not wishing to leave the sofa ever. She could hear the pleasant ticking of the mantel clock. The air around her seemed to smell oddly sweeter but not perfumy. It reminded Jennifer of a man's cologne. Whatever it was, it was subtle and appealing. Entranced by this pleasant moment, she didn't care that she was unable to hear from Ephraim directly. She knew he was here, and she didn't need visual or auditory proof.

"I wonder if I would still like it here in this house, in Tilbrook, if it wasn't for you," Jennifer's words amazed even Jennifer. "I mean, even though I enjoy Ted's company and my new friends Teresa and Maria, living here is a huge change for me. I miss seeing Angie. Sometimes I miss the familiarity of my former town and even my old apartment, although that can't compare to the benefits of this house. I think the main draw to making this place my home is you, Ephraim, and that surprises me. I have a sense of well-being I haven't felt for a very long time. Maybe that has to do with getting further removed from the stresses of caring for my mom before she died, adjusting to divorce, and finding out that my aunt, who I didn't even think of as actual family, made me the sole beneficiary of her entire estate in another town. It's been overwhelming, yet..." Jennifer's voice lowered until she stopped in mid-thought.

She remained in this meditative mood until her cell phone's ring slowly brought her to present reality. Ted. That was good. She'd wondered if he'd call tonight.

"How's my favorite Tilbrook friend?" Ted started the conversation.

"I don't know. Who is your favorite Tilbrook friend?" Jennifer teased.

"Here's a hint. She will be helping me move in a few days. It's a good thing that she has a car to help me haul things. It's even better that she has a heart of gold and patience with me!" He laughed. "Seriously, Jennifer, thank you. I think this move will be great. It's a real step in the right direction for me, perhaps for both of us."

"I missed you this weekend," Jennifer admitted. "I did invite Teresa and Maria over today, though, and I learned that Maria also lives in the Montgomery Haven Apartments. She offered to help you out if needed."

"See? I'm fitting in with the locals already. There's only one Tilbrook resident I'm really interested in, however, and that's you. I can't wait to see you again."

She smiled. Ted was such a charmer. They spent another few minutes catching one another up on the latest events of the weekend. Ted ended the conversation by saying he wanted to take a shower and get to bed early. Suddenly, a relaxing bubble bath appealed to Jennifer, perhaps followed by hot apple cider while listening to music downstairs. She could almost feel the coziness of her robe, fluffy slippers, and the soothing taste of hot cider.

Jennifer plugged her cell phone in to charge and headed up the stairs. "Okay, Ephraim," she said lightly, "I'm going to take a bath now. Can I trust that you will give me my privacy? Will you stay out of the bedroom and bathroom?" Jennifer laughed, closing the door behind her.

Downstairs, a gentle breeze slightly swayed one of the lampshades. The bulb flicked off and then back on a single time.

Chapter 12

"YOU'RE NOT ALL PACKED and ready to go?" Jennifer asked Ted, although the answer was evident with even a cursory glance inside Ted's soon-to-be former Bilmore apartment.

"I thought it would go smoother and quicker with the two of us." Ted sounded genuinely surprised by Jennifer's question. "I hope you don't mind. I guess I didn't think it through. I am prepared, however." He proudly held up a large roll of bubble wrap. "There's plenty of tape, loads of boxes, string, scissors, and markers for labeling." Ted beamed at Jennifer, pleased that he had planned so well.

Jennifer sighed, and Ted shot her a concerned look. "Oh, I'm up for it, but I pictured that we'd be loading my car and your SUV right away to head over to Tilbrook," Jennifer picked up a box and surveyed the situation as she spoke. At least it was a one-bedroom, furnished apartment.

"I'm sorry, Jennifer," Ted said ruefully. "We should easily be fully moved today, though. I don't have as many belongings as most people my age."

She nodded and shrugged. "Well, where do we begin?" He pointed to the kitchen and stooped to pick up packing materials.

"I thought we'd get the kitchen set up first," Ted said, this time speaking with enthusiasm. "Let's go room by room. When we have enough boxes to fill both vehicles, we'll head over to Tilbrook and unpack what we brought. I'd rather set up piecemeal like that instead of winding up with boxes stacked upon boxes that we might not get to today. Besides, I still have a few days on my lease, so it's not like everything must be moved out immediately. I can hope, though." He directed his best smile toward his partner.

"I doubt you have so much that we can't get it all moved today. Since we don't have to move furniture, it should go fairly quickly." Jennifer paused, not sure that would be the case but not wanting to be a wet blanket on Ted's plans.

Ted quickly organized a two-person assembly line, with Jennifer doing the wrapping and taping while he sealed each completed box and penned a short label. Every so often, he'd excuse himself to carry a few boxes to one of their vehicles.

"At least we're on the ground floor," she said when Ted returned to the kitchen. "It could be worse. You might be lugging things up and down stairs." Jennifer laughed but noticed that Ted had a strange expression.

"Did I mention that I'm on the second floor at Montgomery Haven?" he asked a little sheepishly. "My apartment there has a small balcony with a nice view overlooking Tilbrook."

"Is there an elevator?" Jennifer bluntly inquired. He was silent, so she elaborated on the question. "Ted, is there an elevator between ground level and the second floor, or are there only stairs?"

"Stairs, Jennifer. My guess is that Montgomery Haven was built in the 70s." With that, he put his arm around her waist and pulled her against him. "I'll do the hauling," he whispered in her ear and then kissed her temple. "I appreciate you helping with the packing and transport. Most of all, though," he cut his remark off to give her a long, passionate kiss, "most of all, though, I appreciate your company. That is why I'm making the move to Tilbrook in the first place."

Jennifer felt a stab of guilt over her irritation, albeit mild irritation. "Well, I guess you'll get more exercise with stairs," she said with a hint of a grin.

Ted noticed the smile and kissed her again, briefly. "I'll be toned, Jennifer! I'll be an even better me," he kidded. "Besides, you'll like the balcony. When the weather's pleasant, we can eat out there."

"Speaking of eating, I guess we should get back to the business of getting your kitchen ready to be set up." She gently pulled away from Ted's embrace.

"I think we're about ready for our first caravan over to Tilbrook. I've got your car pretty much loaded. I've got the SUV partially filled, but I'm going to take my clothing over in stages by draping it on the back seat." Ted didn't wait for a response from Jennifer before heading into the bedroom.

He quickly returned with a selection of shirts on hangers and made directly for his vehicle.

Jennifer followed him outside this time to check out the situation. She was impressed. Ted did an excellent job of making the best use of the space available without overdoing it. Everything looked stable. Even if Jennifer had to hit the brakes, she didn't believe anything would be in danger of shifting precariously. Ted was even considerate enough to place towels on the seats of her Toyota before piling boxes on them.

"I'm going to grab another armful of clothes, and then we'll take off," he directed. "I'll drive ahead of you, so trail me. I don't see how we can get separated, but if we do, can you get to Montgomery Haven?"

Jennifer didn't tell Ted that she had swung past M. H. out of curiosity the same day she learned from him that he had signed a six-month lease. Instead, she found herself saying, "I believe so. It's in the newer portion of town, near a bank."

Ted nodded. "That's it. You've got your phone anyway, correct?"

"Once I get my purse from your apartment," Jennifer agreed, following him inside again to retrieve what she needed while he made his way to the bedroom. "Need help carrying?"

"This is enough for one trip. I figure two more will do it. Not as bad as you thought it was going to be, right?" Ted grinned as he addressed his partner in packing.

"It's too early to make that judgment call," she remarked dryly but then laughed when she made eye contact with him. "You are going to feed me today, I hope?"

"Absolutely!" Ted didn't miss a beat. "I thought we'd do a little grocery shopping after we get the kitchen arranged. If you don't mind, I'll make us lunch, either sandwiches or frittatas, your choice. It will be our first meal in our new home."

Jennifer noticed that he included her by saying "our," which was sweet but unnecessary since only he would be living there. "You make frittatas?" she asked lightly.

"Your choice of toppings *if* you go to the grocery store with me."

"Deal," Jennifer said, and Ted laughed at her single-word reply, squeezing her hand.

"Okay, we're ready for trip one," he announced, moving toward his SUV. "I don't anticipate any problems, but I'll check my rearview frequently. If you need to pull over, I'll circle back."

Jennifer thought Ted's concern was endearing, especially since it was only a half-hour to Tilbrook, and she knew the route well. Because it was Saturday, traffic would be slightly less than on a weekday. On the other hand, Tilbrook residents did like to come to Bilmore to shop.

Ted pulled out and waited for Jennifer to position her Toyota to caravan over. Fortunately, the weather was cooperative, and whatever rain had been forecast had not materialized. The light cloud cover made the temperature warmer than average. All in all, it was a pleasant day, and she was surprisingly glad that Ted had decided to team with her in tackling the packing. This was turning out to be a nice project for them, one that would bring them closer.

Jennifer daydreamed about the upcoming holiday season as she traveled the familiar route between towns. Ahead, Ted's SUV passed the Cozy Cottage Motel, Jennifer's landmark for gauging the remaining distance between Tilbrook and Bilmore. She recalled Ted's kindness when she phoned him from the Cozy Cottage, frantic about the strange occurrences in her aunt's house. Jennifer's memory drifted back to Ted's comforting offer to stay with her so she wouldn't be frightened. In some ways, that seemed like a longer time ago than it actually was. Here she was today, helping her boyfriend move to an apartment in Tilbrook to be closer to her home.

She felt a surge of appreciation and fondness for Ted. Jennifer glanced at her reflection in the rearview mirror and caught the grin on her face, attributing that smile to Ted. He was such a sweetheart. Thank heavens he had decided to introduce himself when he noticed that a new person had taken up residence in Ruth Gaitley's old house.

Jennifer followed Ted's SUV through Tilbrook towards the east side of town. She spotted the Montgomery Haven sign just before Ted signaled and pulled into the lot. He stuck his arm out the window to point to a sign indicating visitor parking. Jennifer pulled into the first available spot, although only one other vehicle was present. Ted backed into a numbered space, apparently reserved for him.

"I'll let the office know I'm here for the key," he told Jennifer as she joined him. "They're expecting me anyway." He winked at her in a manner that reminded her of Teresa. Jennifer wondered which apartment belonged to Teresa's significant other, Maria.

Ted emerged from the Montgomery Haven office within five minutes, keys in hand. "Let me go up first, unlock the place, and check on things. Then I'll come back down, and we'll start unloading." As an afterthought, he added, "Remember, I'll haul the heavier boxes. You can take a few shirts up at a time, but nothing heavy."

Jennifer nodded, appreciating his concern for her. "I'll be glad to help with what I can, Ted. Congratulations on your new home."

He beamed at those words and headed toward the stairway while Jennifer dutifully followed instructions and stayed put. She watched Ted ascend, and although he quickly disappeared from view, she heard the clunk of a key turning in a lock. Within minutes, she heard Ted's footsteps overhead near the stairs.

"I like it!" Ted affirmed when he had almost descended. "I think it's going to be perfect for me ... at least for now." Ted shot her a meaningful glance to remind her that his goal was to room with her eventually.

Jennifer gathered as many shirts as she could safely carry up the stairs without dropping any. Ted lifted a single, heavy box from his SUV. They continued in this fashion until they had unloaded both vehicles. Ted slit the tape from several of the boxes, and the pair commenced unpacking and arranging the contents in the kitchen cabinets and drawers.

She could understand why Maria said these were nice apartments. Ted only opted for a one-bedroom, but it was a decent size. The kitchen had a small pantry, and the bedroom contained a walk-in closet. For apartments built in the 70s or 80s, these were nicely designed. The landlord had the walls repainted before Ted took occupancy, which gave the place a fresh, clean look.

"May I see the balcony before we tackle another box?" Jennifer asked, hoping for a short rest. She hated to break the news to Ted that her back was already hurting a bit.

"It's just over there." He pointed to the obvious. The balcony extended off the living room, in plain view.

"I mean, can we go out on the balcony? I see they included a table and chair set." Jennifer's voice registered appreciation.

"Oh, of course, we can go out there. Would you like a break? I only have tap water to drink, I'm afraid. We'll need to do that grocery shopping before I have more to offer."

She answered by way of a smile as she walked across the medium-sized living room to the patio door. Jennifer seated herself before Ted joined her with two newly unwrapped amber glasses he had just filled with tap water.

"Thank you," she responded, briefly grinning. "I am a little thirsty."

"Remind me to get some ice going. I don't care for room-temperature tap water but in a pinch..." He took a sip.

"Should we make a toast to your new apartment?" Jennifer lifted her water glass.

"Yes, we should make a toast, but let's wait for a more fitting beverage. At least we'll wait for some ice."

She involuntarily made a face. "I think you should pick up a filtration pitcher or one of those on-the-faucet things. This water is a little heavy on the chlorine."

"Um," he nodded, taking another sip, "yes, too much chlorine taste for me. I prefer a subtle bouquet of chemicals in my drinking water."

Jennifer coughed to prevent herself from choking as she giggled. "Oh, you! Seriously, I think we're accomplishing a lot today. Just getting the kitchen settled and a few of your shirts hung in the closet makes this place seem homier."

"Wait till we get the bedroom set up," Ted said smoothly, with obvious flirtation. Jennifer ignored the innuendo and took in the view from the balcony. "I'll be able to watch you from here," he said in response to Jennifer's gaze.

"What?" Jennifer gasped in surprise.

"I can see your house from here. Maybe I'll pick up some binoculars along with that water filtration pitcher."

"You can't see my house from here!" she exclaimed, but her facial expression and voice registered doubt and unease.

"Oh, sure I can," he briefly teased before reassuring her. "Of course, I can't see your house from here, Jennifer. It would be impossible from this level with the trees and the distance."

She sat silently for a moment before logic kicked in. "Oh. Sorry, Ted," Jennifer said meekly, feeling herself blush.

"I wouldn't do that to you anyway." He got up to put his arm around her shoulders. "I wouldn't snoop on you even if I lived next door with full view into your bedroom window. I respect you and your privacy."

"I know that," Jennifer replied, recognizing that wasn't entirely true because, for a moment, she had taken Ted's joke seriously. In the years she was married to Alex, she couldn't recall Alex teasing or joking. She liked Ted's humor, and she also appreciated his ability to stop as soon as he realized it might be going too far. Jennifer felt Ted's lips caress her temple. She liked that about him, too. She responded by putting her hand on Ted's arm and giving it a light squeeze.

"So, what do you think," Ted changed the subject, "about either grocery shopping now or making another jaunt to Bilmore first?"

They decided to make another trip to Bilmore. Ted tackled the living room and brought a few more armloads of clothing. Several hours later, almost two-thirds of the apartment was arranged, with all the boxes from the second trip unpacked. Ted made a haul to the dumpster before announcing that it was time to bring in food. He noticed Jennifer wincing with pain every so often and insisted that she rest at the apartment while he did the shopping. Jennifer didn't protest and gave her input on what she thought Ted should get regarding cleaning supplies. He asked her if that was what she wanted on her frittata, which made both of them chuckle.

With Ted gone on his errand, Jennifer positioned herself in what she deemed the most comfortable chair in his new apartment. Granted, it wasn't as comfy as her own furniture, but it was still welcome on the back. She surveyed the living room from her seat. It all came together nicely. They still had a final trip to make, but that should do it. She'd be extra careful to let Ted do all the carrying, and she would mainly be there to drive the Toyota.

Jennifer stood gingerly to retrieve her cell phone from her purse. She hadn't talked to Angie yet today, and this was a perfect time since it would take Ted at least half an hour to complete his shopping. She punched in Angie's number.

"Hey, Jen," Angie quickly greeted her. "What's up?"

"I'm at Ted's apartment in Tilbrook. We've been moving his things today, and he's gone to do the grocery shopping now. I stayed behind because the move's been a little hard on my back," Jennifer explained to her friend.

"How do you like the place?"

"It's cute, actually. Second story, with a nice balcony and a great view. One-bedroom. Good closet space. Personally, I think it's better than his Bilmore apartment."

"And closer to you," Angie said teasingly, always the romantic.

"That too." Jennifer gave a short laugh. "Ted's going to cook lunch for me, a late lunch, once he's back with some food. He's going to make me a frittata with cheese and veggies on top."

"That's a good sign, Jen. The man can cook. So, it sounds like the relationship is going well? You're no longer concerned about what that guy said from the place your aunt used to work?"

"All Hank from Tenger-Bio said was that Aunt Ruth asked the young man staying with her to leave," Jennifer explained, "and Hank couldn't be sure of any details. He never asked Ruth why she asked the guy to go. For all I know, Hank is mistaken or incorrectly remembering the incident after several decades."

"Well, Jen, you were troubled about it at the time," Angie reminded her. "Hank did remember that the young man was blonde."

"So are many other people, plus there are multiple shades of blonde. I'm brunette, yet some people describe my hair as golden-blonde," Jennifer countered.

"Color-blind people." Angie clucked her tongue skeptically.

Jennifer ignored her friend's comment. "We also should consider Ephraim's presence and the fact that Aunt Ruth had a bond with him. Maybe my aunt felt she had to ask Ted or whoever to leave for that reason. She might have been afraid Ted would begin to sense a spirit in the house. Maybe she didn't want questions asked, or perhaps Ruth simply realized that she preferred living alone and thought it was time for her guest to move on. After all, as I understand it, my aunt was trying to help Ted through a rough patch in his life. She wasn't seeking a permanent tenant. It could be that she—"

"Okay, I get what you're saying," Angie interrupted. "I trust your judgment, Jen. You don't fall for men easily, so Ted must be doing something right. When do I get to meet him? Thanksgiving?" Angie had invited Jennifer for an extended holiday visit.

Jennifer hesitated. "I'd bring Ted if we lived near you. Since I'll stay overnight, actually for two nights, no, I don't think so. It would be awkward, considering he still hopes to move in with me. Besides, Ted and I have only dated a few months."

"Separate rooms?"

Jennifer bit her lip in contemplation. "Still no."

"What if you brought Ephraim instead?" Angie gave a hardy laugh.

"Yeah, I'll ask him tonight," Jennifer went along with the joke, "but I don't know if my ghost can travel."

"Oh, yes, you do!" Angie quickly retorted. "He left you a daisy from that bunch you placed on his grave."

"We don't know for sure that was him," Jennifer replied but secretively hoped Angie was correct.

The women continued their lighthearted conversation until Ted returned home with an armload of plastic bags stuffed with groceries. Jennifer pointed to her cell phone, and Ted nodded, quietly removing items from the bags. When he exited again to get the remaining grocery sacks, Jennifer said her goodbyes to her longtime friend. She couldn't wait to see Angie, Mike, and Jolie later in the month.

Ted whipped up exceptional frittatas, accepting no help from Jennifer. She was impressed that he possessed such quality cookware and utensils, better than her own. Obviously, he wasn't a novice cook. The last time Jennifer made an omelet, it stuck to the skillet and ended up more reminiscent of partially scrambled eggs. She complimented Ted, who was humble but visibly pleased that she appreciated his culinary efforts.

She debated mentioning her Thanksgiving plans to Ted, but the prospect of disappointing him kept her from broaching the topic. It was likely he expected to spend the holiday with her. On the other hand, he had family, just not nearby. Today was Ted's first day in his new apartment, though, and Jennifer didn't want to jeopardize their celebratory mood. When or if Ted brought up the subject of Thanksgiving, she would simply tell him she had accepted an invitation from Angie long ago. She could always have Ted over for a turkey dinner before or after the holiday. Judging by his cookware, it might be better to prepare the meal here in his apartment. Even better, have Ted do the cooking. Jennifer chuckled at the thought.

"Did you want more lemonade?" Ted asked as he cleared her plate.

"No, I'm fine, actually more than fine. Thank you, Ted. This was terrific!"

"Thank you for your help with the move. I guarantee you that's worth much more than one lunch."

Jennifer slowly and cautiously rose from her chair. She was sore, but the pain was manageable, at least to drive. Ted returned from the kitchen with a glass of water and two small pills. "What's this?" she asked as he handed them to her.

"When I did the shopping, I bought something for your backache. Just don't take anything else for eight hours."

Jennifer studied the pills. She wished he'd left them in the bottle. She liked to know what medication she was taking but appreciated that he had been thoughtful enough to pick up something for her. Ted appeared to read her mind and silently handed her the bottle.

"Oh, thank you," Jennifer responded.

"Keep them. You might need them later tonight or over the next few days. I did ask the pharmacist for a recommendation, and this is what I was given."

"That's so sweet, Ted. Thanks for doing that for me." Jennifer smiled at him after obediently swallowing the two tablets.

He sighed deeply. "If I were that sweet, I wouldn't ask you to make another drive to Bilmore today, but I would like to get my bedding so that I can sleep here tonight. Do you think you're up to one last trip? I'll do all the work this time while you sit and relax. Once we're back here, I'll unpack your car, and you can go straight home."

"I think I can handle that, Ted. Besides, I imagine I'll be fine once those pills kick in."

"We won't take any chances, Jennifer." He spread his hands and shrugged. "I would love to spend the evening with you in my new apartment, but I think you'll be better off at your own place."

Ted took the now-emptied glass out of Jennifer's hand and set it on the table. He gently pulled her in for a kiss, careful not to jar her aching back. They remained embraced for several minutes. This was nice. Jennifer wished she could spend the evening with Ted, too.

Jennifer soaked her achy body in the luxury of her deep bathtub until the water got to the point of feeling lukewarm. She debated adding hot water or exiting. Eventually, the thought of the raisin bagel that Ted had insisted she take home lured her out. Gingerly, she used her toe to unplug the tub stopper before reaching for the grab bars. Initially, Jennifer felt relaxed, but her back muscles spasmed with the movement. Still, she managed to dry off and drape the softest, coziest nightgown she owned over her head. She removed the hairpins she had put in prior to her bath and let her hair fall loosely around her shoulders. Jennifer glanced at herself in the mirror. She grimaced, slightly alarmed by her less-than-becoming appearance. Maybe the dark circles under her eyes would vanish with a good night's sleep.

To be on the safe side, Jennifer descended the stairs barefooted, with fuzzy slippers in hand. Now wasn't the time to risk a fall. Once her feet were properly clad, she entered the kitchen to retrieve the coveted raisin bagel from the bag on the counter. She cut it the best she could and settled for a thin coating of margarine. Hot tea and a buttered bagel sounded perfect. Cautiously, she made two trips to carry her light meal to the living room. Usually, she ate in the dining area, but tonight she thought her back would appreciate the comfort of the sofa.

Jennifer picked up the remote to power on the television and channel surf, finally settling on an old 1940s black-and-white film billed as a thriller. The movie was more engrossing than she had anticipated, causing Jennifer to forget the second half of her bagel. She started to rise to get another cup of hot tea but decided against it when her back rebelled. The bagel half, however, was within easy reach, so she began to nibble while reflecting on the movie she'd just viewed.

When this film came out, Doctor Ephraim and his son were already deceased. Aunt Ruth's 1949 diary didn't yet exist. It seemed surreal when considered in that context.

"How did you like the movie, Ephraim?" Jennifer suddenly asked out loud.

Of course, there was no response. Jennifer was used to that by now, so it didn't deter her. She enjoyed talking to

Ephraim and didn't need a reply, although she was looking forward to the arrival of the digital recorder.

"Nineteen forty-two," Jennifer added, "was when the movie was released. I wonder if you used to go to the theater at times. Did you?"

No response.

She continued to make idle chit-chat, telling the invisible Ephraim about her day helping Ted move. Was that appropriate, though? Jennifer abruptly stopped her monolog, feeling a strange pang of guilt over talking about Ted to Ephraim. It was as if she were cheating on Ted ... or Ephraim. That was silly, however! She reflected on this in silence, eventually concluding that she was being ridiculous.

Jennifer tried to stand again and yelped in pain. She put her hand to her aching back and groaned. Interestingly, the sensitive area began to experience a pleasant warmth. Jennifer lifted her hand from her back, noting that it instantly felt like another hand had been placed on the sore area. The sensation was quite relaxing and therapeutic, allowing her to bask in the feeling of comfort and relief. It was like having a heated massage chair, only better.

Her eyelids grew heavy, and the last thing she remembered was her head gently being lowered to the sofa cushion. When she awoke, she noted that the lighting had been dimmed to a soft glow. Jennifer considered spending the night on the couch but thought she'd be better off sleeping in her bed, even though that meant the trek upstairs. With some reluctance, she raised her head from the pillow and sat up. Surprisingly, she felt better! Jennifer gingerly touched her back. She studied the pillow her head had rested upon.

Hadn't it been at the opposite end of the sofa? Jennifer didn't recall putting the pillow in its current location.

She attempted to stand and found that she could do so without pain. Hmm. Was this due to the warm bath plus pain meds at Ted's or Ephraim's supernatural help? Well, she was grateful for whatever caused the temporary relief—something else to record in her journal.

Jennifer removed her fuzzy slippers to make the journey upstairs. Despite the downstairs nap, she knew she'd fall asleep again instantaneously. She snuggled under the covers, delighting in the coziness. Unfortunately, she'd forgotten to flip the light switch in her rush to get into bed.

"Ephraim, would you please turn off the light for me?" Jennifer asked, her body relaxed and her eyes closed. After a second's pause, the room was in darkness. "Thank you, Ephraim," Jennifer mumbled, already half asleep. "I knew you would."

Chapter 13

TED SHOWED UP LATE morning, unannounced, catching Jennifer off-guard. She had slept longer than usual and hadn't yet changed out of her nightclothes. Jennifer grimaced. She knew that she'd see more of Ted now that he lived in Tilbrook, but she hadn't anticipated that he'd show up without a phone call.

Jennifer cracked open the door slightly. "I'm afraid I slept in, Ted. I'm still in my robe."

She could see half of his face through the opening between her and the door. He smiled broadly. "I don't mind at all, Jennifer." He softly chuckled. "However, I can wait until you've changed if you'd feel more comfortable."

Jennifer opened the door fully and motioned for him to step inside. "No, that's fine. I guess I'm just a little embarrassed that it's this late, and I'm not dressed."

Ted kissed her before responding. "Hey, it's Sunday, a day of leisure. I worked you pretty hard yesterday. I wanted to check on you." He kissed her again.

When he finally pulled away, Jennifer said, "I'm surprisingly better today. Still a little stiff and achy, but not like I expected to feel."

"Those pills I got you must really work. I suggest you keep taking them today, though, to be on the safe side."

"Sure." She didn't tell him that she hadn't taken any further pills. Jennifer attributed her remarkable recovery to Doctor Ephraim, not to over-the-counter medication. Suddenly, she felt a little self-conscious in nightclothes with both Ted and the invisible Ephraim present if, indeed, Ephraim was around. She could feel herself blush and was relieved to see that Ted had already turned to make his way to the living room. It would be difficult to explain why she was growing more visibly embarrassed.

"Would you like to do something today, Jennifer, or would you prefer a day in? I could go either way, so decide what's best for you."

"Let me think on that while I get dressed." She watched from the base of the stairs as he took his usual spot on the couch.

"Have you eaten?" It suddenly dawned on him that Jennifer might not have had breakfast.

Already halfway up the stairs, she paused to answer. "Not yet. I am hungry, so let's have brunch or an early lunch if you don't mind."

"Do you want me to fix something? What about a sandwich picnic at the river? It's a little chilly to sit outside, but we could eat in the SUV." Ted immediately rose to head toward the kitchen.

"I like that idea," Jennifer assured him, "but give me time to get dressed before you attempt to make sandwiches. I'll help you once I'm ready."

Ted nodded, and Jennifer continued up the stairs. She knew she needed to be more spontaneous if she was going to make this relationship work. His plan sounded fun, much nicer than her usual routine, although a typical Sunday meant a visit to church if she hadn't overslept.

Instead of her Sunday best, Jennifer put on the usual jeans and sweatshirt. After applying moisturizer to her freshly washed face, she tied her golden hair into a ponytail It suddenly occurred to her that this morning was the first time Ted had seen her completely devoid of makeup. Jennifer considered that as she applied eyeliner and mascara. Well, Ted hadn't flinched when he saw her. Judging by the passion of his kisses, he wasn't put off by the fact that she wasn't wearing her usual rose-shimmer lip gloss.

When she finally descended the steps, Ted rose from the sofa and walked toward her. She was pleased that he hadn't gone against her wishes and attempted to organize their picnic without her input. Ted had something in his hand, but she couldn't quite make out what he held.

"Digital recorder?" Ted inquired as he presented the object to Jennifer in his outstretched palm.

"Yes, it is." She had forgotten that she had left the opened package on the coffee table. She hadn't even read the instructions for it, let alone used it to attempt to hear from Ephraim.

"What do you need a recorder for?" He looked genuinely perplexed.

Jennifer hesitated, not sure how to respond. Although Ted knew about her early concern that the house was haunted, he had not bought into that theory, and Jennifer chose to refrain from telling him about further developments. "I-I just ordered it on a whim. Angie has one and suggested I get one, too. I don't have any specific use for it. I guess I could record grocery lists, etc." She hated to lie, but the idea of discussing Ephraim with Ted was even less appealing.

"You can use your phone for that," Ted pointed out. "I can show you. Where's your phone?" He turned to look towards the dining area, knowing Jennifer's habits by now.

She got the phone and handed it to him, playing the part of an eager student. "Here you go." Ted put one arm around her shoulder as he demonstrated skills her phone could do. Jennifer liked his physical closeness and appreciated his sweetness as he patiently and enthusiastically "taught" her how to use the phone's microphone.

"We'll get you into the twenty-first century yet." Ted winked and gave her a peck on the cheek.

"You can try!" Jennifer laughed, relieved that he apparently had lost interest in the topic of her digital recorder purchase. She headed into the living room and moved the packing box and recorder out of sight. By this time, he was already in the kitchen browsing through the refrigerator.

"Turkey sandwiches?" Ted held up an unopened package of lunchmeat. "I see you have salad, so we can have lettuce on our sandwiches. Oh, and you have tomato, mustard ... you don't have mayonnaise, but that's fine." Jennifer didn't respond. She knew he was talking to himself more than to her. She joined him at the kitchen counter and proceeded to get the needed bread and the foil for wrapping their sandwiches.

Ted craved potato chips and insisted on running into the mom-and-pop grocery on their way to the river, the same store where Jennifer bought the daisies the day she visited the old cemetery. She stayed in the SUV while Ted did his impromptu shopping. Since he assumed her back was still a little achy, he didn't press her to join him. It gave her time to reflect on that trip to the cemetery and how much closer she felt to Ephraim since then. She envisioned the single white daisy placed atop her gratitude journal, Ephraim's symbol of appreciation for having brought the flowers to his grave.

"Great timing," Ted said upon opening the driver's door, startling the lost-in-thought Jennifer. "They had just opened. I might not have gotten my chips if we'd been five minutes earlier. I got us chilled sodas, too. We can also drink the iced tea you brought, but, you know, impulse shopping." He positioned himself behind the wheel, pulling his seatbelt taut.

"Sunday hours," she remarked, responding to the first part of Ted's comments. "We're on the older side of Tilbrook."

"Mmm. Nice little shop. Have you ever been in there?"

"Once, briefly. I thought it was nice, too. I like those types of places. They can't carry as much variety, but..." Jennifer trailed off, not bothering to finish. Ted didn't appear to notice, however. He was preoccupied with getting to the river so they could eat.

Jennifer noted Tenger-Bio in the distance, pointing it out to Ted, who only smiled and nodded. She cautioned herself against telling him about her trip there. Maybe someday, but this lovely afternoon wasn't the appropriate time.

They reached the part of the country road where the pavement ended. Ted parked in an area that looked familiar, probably the same place he'd parked several months ago when he'd brought her to the river to watch the sunset. Jennifer disembarked from the SUV when Ted did, pulling her jacket closer to her throat.

"What do you think? Eat inside the vehicle?" Ted asked, looking rather chilled himself.

Jennifer was already pulling on the door handle. "Good idea!"

"Whew!" He seated himself again, placing both the lunch bag and his grocery purchases on Jennifer's lap. "I think it's colder than when we started."

"It's hard to believe that we ate outside on your balcony just yesterday," she reminded him. "Yesterday had cloud cover, though, and was unseasonably warm."

"Well, look at you, Jennifer, talking like an old-timer," Ted teased.

She handed him a soda and a sandwich. "Yeah, you'll profit from my numerous years here in Tilbrook." She opened the bag of chips and offered Ted first honors of scooping out a handful.

They sat in silence, enjoying their lunches and the beauty of the river. Jennifer felt a peaceful satisfaction, and from all appearances, so did Ted. Finally, she broke the spell by commenting on the mustard just below his lip.

"Oh, and I was aiming for a mustard mustache," Ted joked as he wiped the condiment away with his fingers. Jennifer handed him a napkin. "Speaking of turkey sandwiches," he continued, even though nothing had been said about the topic, "Thanksgiving's coming up soon."

Darn. Jennifer hoped to delay talk of Thanksgiving plans, but now it was unavoidable. "Ted, Angie invited me to stay with her and her family over Thanksgiving, and I accepted. Angie's my best friend, and we have a history together. She was my strength when I went through the divorce and when my mother was ill. Then, after Mom died, she helped me through that. Leaving Angie was one of the biggest drawbacks of moving to Tilbrook and living in Aunt Ruth's home. I had to think long and hard about that. I—"

"Jennifer, it's okay," Ted cut into her lengthy explanation. "I waited a little too long before inviting you to spend Thanksgiving with me. Besides, I have people I can visit. You don't need to feel bad."

She was relieved he'd taken the news so well. "How about Christmas, Ted? We can spend that holiday together unless you're going to be with family or have some tradition with other people."

Ted grinned and gently caressed the nape of Jennifer's neck. She already knew his answer before his response. "Absolutely, we'll spend Christmas together. I'll bring the mistletoe."

Jennifer returned his smile and leaned in to kiss him. Neither she nor Ted complained about the cold for the rest of the day.

Where had she put that digital recorder? Jennifer remembered moving it out of sight, hoping that Ted wouldn't press the subject of why she thought she needed one. Evidently, Ted hadn't read the vendor's name on the outer packaging, indiscreetly labeled for anyone to see that the contents came from a company that dealt in paranormal investigative equipment. Ah, there it was! Jennifer pulled out the instructions and briefly read through them.

"Ephraim," she said upon turning on the recorder, "this is a new way for us to communicate. It's called a digital recorder. It may allow me to hear what you say to me. Well, I mean that it will record voices, and it can pick up things that I might not be able to hear without the device. Does that make sense?" Jennifer was aware that she was talking to someone born in the nineteenth century. "Anyway, let's give it a try because I'd love to be able to hear what you have to say. Are you willing to try? Do you have a message for me?"

Jennifer silently counted to twenty before pressing the play-back. Although her voice came through with clarity, she focused on detecting any softer voices, especially male, which the device might have captured. Nothing. It was the first try, however, so she wasn't daunted.

"Is your name Ephraim?" Jennifer asked, trying a more guided tactic. "Is your name Ephraim?" she repeated, allowing what she deemed sufficient time for a spirit to answer.

She played back the segment, disappointed to have no response. She deleted what she had recorded, ready to begin anew.

"I'm just going to talk. Please speak if you have something to say, and I hope you do. I'm going to leave the recorder running, and you can jump in to comment at any time."

With that, she turned on the device and began to chat with Ephraim as if she were talking to an old friend. She brought up a myriad of topics, including her day with Ted, mindful to leave long pauses to give the spirit a chance to respond. Finally, Jennifer glanced at the time and decided to end her session so she could get to bed before midnight.

"I'm going to wrap this up for tonight. Any last words for me?" After an additional thirty seconds of silence on her part, Jennifer shut off the recorder.

She was groggy by now but couldn't imagine sleeping soundly tonight knowing that she potentially had a recording of messages from her ghostly housemate. Jennifer made herself a cup of decaffeinated tea with a touch of honey before returning to the living room to review her conversation. Gently, Jennifer set the cup on the table and positioned the pillow on the sofa to better support her slightly achy back. She reached for the small digital device and pressed play-back.

The recording sounded pretty much like a very long monolog. However, in several sections, she thought she might have heard a male voice. It was tedious to stop, reverse, and replay so many times. Jennifer concluded that there was nothing she could definitively point to as evidence of a response from Ephraim. However, there was just enough to give her hope that he had tried to converse, but his voice was either too faint or too ... something.

Jennifer stood and picked up her empty teacup. "That ends tonight's session, Ephraim," she told him as she made her way to the kitchen. "Thank you for humoring me. We'll try again another night. I think I might have heard your voice, but it just wasn't loud enough for my human ears. Not that you aren't human," she quickly amended. "Let me rephrase that. It wasn't loud enough for my ears since I'm in a physical body. Oh, I'm tired, and I don't know what I'm saying! It's past my usual bedtime, but this has been fun and a great experiment for one evening. I'll see you tomorrow, okay?"

Jennifer was at the base of the stairway when the light flickered a single time. Suddenly, she felt wide awake.

Chapter 14

"I THOUGHT FOR SURE you'd want to visit the art museum, Maria," Jennifer said over her left shoulder, directing her comments to the young woman seated in the back of Ted's SUV.

"Bus driver's holiday," Teresa spoke from behind Jennifer.

"Bus driver's holiday?" Maria reiterated as a question.

"That means you aren't necessarily keen on doing what you do in your work life in your free time. Someone who drives a bus five or six days a week might not opt for a vacation where she has to drive a long distance. For instance a cruise might be more relaxing," Teresa explained.

"But she might want to take a road trip," Maria objected.

Jennifer glanced towards Ted, who was intent on the traffic. He didn't say anything, but Jennifer could tell by his slight grin that he was amused by Maria's unfamiliarity with the expression.

"Well, if you don't want to see the art museum in Rotan, is there another place you'd like to visit?" Jennifer directed her question toward her friends in the backseat. "Ted and I didn't have any specific plans in mind. We just thought it might be nice to do something different for a change. I suggested Rotan since I've never been there."

"What about you, Ted?" Teresa queried. "I'm surprised your line of work doesn't frequently bring you to Rotan."

"Oh, it does." Ted briefly looked at Teresa in the rearview mirror. "I am there often. I don't do much sightseeing in Rotan, however, but I am very familiar with the city's layout and the location of some of the main attractions." Ted reached toward Jennifer in the passenger seat beside him and patted her knee. "I should have offered to take Jennifer to Rotan earlier. I guess since I lived in Bilmore when we met, I was more focused on the area on our side of the river."

"And I was still getting used to Tilbrook," Jennifer added. "Between our two towns, there were plenty of novel things to do and see."

"Teresa," Ted directed his comment to the more dominant lady in the backseat, "what about you? Don't you get into Rotan for business?"

"Not very often. Jake's mainly does business in Tilbrook and Bilmore. Rotan has more competition."

"Thank you for inviting us," Maria interjected. "I've only been to Rotan once, and I'm looking forward to it. I don't care what we do, but if I have a choice, I'd like to see a play."

"Splendid idea, Maria," Ted quickly concurred. "If everyone agrees, I'll swing us past the playhouse first thing, and we can make arrangements. The rest of the day then revolves around the time of the performance." Ted looked toward Jennifer to determine her reaction.

"Fine by me." As far as she was concerned, she was game for anything. Rotan was simply a chance to explore something different with all her new friends.

Ted glanced in the rearview mirror. "How about you, Teresa? Is that acceptable?"

"Of course."

The foursome drove in silence for several miles. According to Jennifer's calculations, they'd already been on the road for about forty-five minutes. The mileage sign ahead indicated that it would take longer than an additional fifteen minutes for them to make it into town.

"I thought Rotan was only an hour's drive from Tilbrock," Jennifer said without directing her comment to anyone in particular.

"It's almost a two-hour drive from Bilmore," Ted answered. "I'd estimate that we have another twenty minutes to go. Not bad, though, right?" He turned to smile at Jennifer and gave her another reassuring pat on the knee.

"Since this is Sunday, Ted, I'd like to be home at a reasonable hour tonight," Teresa said. "By that, I mean before ten. Tomorrow's a workday for some of us."

"For me, as well." Ted directed his rearview-mirror gaze toward Teresa again. "As I suggested, we can see what plays fit into our schedule and plan accordingly."

Jennifer wondered if Maria detected the subtle tension between Ted and Teresa. Probably. It was likely that Teresa shared her feelings openly with her young partner. Also, if Maria was sensitive enough to pick up on the fact that

Jennifer's home included the presence of a ghost, Maria was keen enough to recognize vibes among the living.

"If the plays are too late, we can do something else," Maria offered. "I wasn't thinking about it being a Sunday." Her tone was apologetic.

"Oh, it's fine, Maria," Ted said soothingly. Jennifer appreciated his quick response. "Rotan has several venues for the theater, two of which I know for certain have weekend matinees. If you wish to see a play, then you shall see a play. Barring tickets have sold out, of course," he added with a shrug. "The sidewalks don't roll up here as quickly as they do back home."

"Speaking of sidewalks...," Jennifer began an exaggerated account of her latest experience in Tilbrook, more to change the subject than anything else. It worked, though, because both Teresa and Ted recounted their own tales, filling the SUV with laughter.

Ted gauged the arrival time into Rotan with amazing precision. Jennifer was impressed by the city. Rotan definitely offered a variety of entertainment, business, restaurant, and shopping options. Ted acted as impromptu guide, pointing out locations with the same familiarity he had with Bilmore. Evidently, he had spent considerable time in Rotan.

Ted parked in front of an impressive neo-classical building that sported large banners streaming downward, each advertising a current production. He instructed his passengers to hold tight while he scouted for information.

"I like Rotan already," Jennifer confessed to her friends when Ted left the vehicle. "In some ways, Tilbrook seems divided—old versus new. Not that I don't appreciate Tilbrook, but Rotan seems better balanced."

"It has its areas that have gone into decline, Jennifer, like almost everywhere else," Teresa explained, "but I know what you mean. The overall architectural planning is well-thought-out. I also think that when you come from a smaller town, it's natural to feel excited about all a larger place has to offer."

"Especially if you enjoy doing things at night, like go dancing or bar hopping or...," Maria trailed off.

"Or attend an opera or a comedy club," Teresa continued seamlessly.

"I remember those days," Jennifer joined in wistfully. "When I was married to Alex, we used to go to comedy clubs frequently, which is odd now that I think about it because Alex didn't seem to have much of a sense of humor. He didn't dance, but he wasn't against bar hopping," Jennifer added with a laugh.

"He must have dragged you along." Teresa chuckled. "You, Jennifer, who prefers your iced tea straight."

"And on the rocks," Jennifer joined in the joke, then told the ladies about the time she'd accidentally dumped Alex's homemade beer out, thinking it was stale tea that had been in the fridge for ages. She's replaced it with a new fusion tea she'd never tried before, and Alex thought it was the smoothest brew he'd ever made.

"So," Teresa was laughing pretty hard by this time, "did Alex get drunk on it? On your tea?"

"He sure acted like it had an effect on him," Jennifer squealed, her face reddened by laughter. "Alex used to—" She stopped short at the sight of Ted.

He opened the driver's door to the SUV and climbed in. "Why did it go silent in here the moment I returned, ladies? What have you been up to? Can't I leave you unattended to run a simple errand?" Ted feigned a reproachful tone.

"Oh, just girl talk," Teresa jumped in, sparing Jennifer from mentioning Alex to Ted. "What did you find out about performance times?"

"Two options, ladies." Ted handed a pamphlet to Maria in the backseat and gave one to Jennifer. "Comedy versus drama. Both well-received. Both within our time frame. I have no preference but am here to make sure you all have a good time in Rotan."

Jennifer leaned toward Ted with the pamphlet in case he wanted to read it with her. She hoped that Teresa appreciated Ted's chivalry. Teresa's partner, Maria, was the one who asked to see a play in the first place. Many people, including Alex, would have imposed their own agenda.

"I think the comedy sounds good," Maria finally broke the silence that had settled on the four while they studied the descriptions of the performances. "However, like Ted, I could go with either."

"I know we all enjoy a good laugh," Teresa chimed in. "I don't see why a comedy wouldn't be welcome today."

Jennifer pulled cash from her purse and discreetly tried to hand it to Ted. "Four tickets for the comedy," she whispered to him, indicating that she intended to pay for everyone.

"Let's do the early matinee and eat afterward before heading home," Teresa suggested. "I'm paying for our two tickets, Ted."

He didn't argue. In fact, he said nothing as he accepted both Jennifer's and Teresa's payments. He winked at Jennifer as he exited the vehicle, though. In hindsight, Jennifer felt she hadn't handled the situation well. She should have at least offered to accompany him. Instead, she'd pretty much assumed it was his job to go purchase the tickets for them.

Maria and Teresa were having a quiet conversation between themselves in the backseat. Jennifer couldn't make out what was said but thought Maria mentioned Ted's name. Maria liked Ted, however, so Jennifer figured it was most likely a positive reference.

Jennifer observed Ted as he returned to the vehicle, tickets in hand. "Do you want me to hang on to these, or should I divvy them up?" he asked once he'd shut the driver's door. Ted reached behind his seat to pass Teresa's change to her. Then he laid Jennifer's money on her lap.

"I trust you with the tickets, Ted, but I would like mine," Teresa answered. He quickly handed two tickets to the ladies in the back. He put Jennifer's in his wallet along with his own.

"Thank you for getting them for us," Maria said. "That was nice of you."

"Yes, yes it was, Ted," Jennifer quickly added. "After you got out, it occurred to me that I should have gone in with you. I'm sorry."

Ted shook his head and gestured with his right hand as if to negate her words. "Not at all. It's a little nippy out there, anyway. I suggest limiting today's activities to indoor places or driving around Rotan."

"We have about an hour before we can get into the theater," Teresa remarked after noting the seating time on her ticket. "Jennifer and Maria might like to see more of Rotan via car since neither is familiar with the city, and both seem to like it. Everyone will have a better idea of what they want to do here in the future if we, or you guys, come again."

Ted looked at Jennifer, who simply smiled at him. "All right," he concluded. "The Rotan tour continues with me, Ted Filston, as your guide. Look to your left, and you'll notice..." For all of Ted's jesting, he was an excellent guide and a good sport.

"I didn't need that last glass of champagne." Jennifer rubbed her forehead and giggled.

"Who really needs it, Jennifer?" Teresa responded, also laughing. "I think Maria's asleep already."

"No. I'm awake," Maria said quietly, but it was apparent from her tone that she was groggy.

"Ted, it's a good thing you're the driver," Teresa observed. "You showed tremendous restraint tonight," she added, referring to his limit of a couple of sips of Jennifer's champagne.

"What did they used to say? What was that phrase?" Ted asked, obviously talking to himself. "Precious cargo. That's it. Precious cargo. I am responsible for the safety of my passengers."

Jennifer laughed again. That should score Ted points with Teresa. "You did very well today, sir," she complimented.

"You enjoyed your day in Rotan?" Ted smiled, already knowing the answer.

"Oh, yes, I did! I can see why the guy at Tenger-Bio said most of the young people who come to work there choose to live in Rotan over Tilbrook. I'd do the same thing," Jennifer announced.

"I still prefer Tilbrook," Teresa countered, "especially the side we live on, Jennifer. I think we have it best. We have all the quaintness and small-town feel with the conveniences and razzle-dazzle of the larger cities nearby."

Maria burst out laughing, unusual for her. "Razzle-dazzle," she repeated. "We got some razzle-dazzle today."

Teresa and Jennifer giggled, and Teresa added that the choice of plays was a good one. She also praised Ted for his restaurant selection for dinner. A second compliment for Ted from Teresa, Jennifer proudly noted.

"It's one of my favorites," he agreed. "I've taken clients there over the years. It has a modern feel with an energy that adds to the ambiance, especially at nighttime."

"Are we going to be back home by ten, Ted?" Teresa asked with what appeared to be teasing reproach. "You know I'll turn into a pumpkin by ten."

Ted played the game well. "Jennifer turns into one at twelve, so you've got two hours on her. But to seriously answer your question, yes, I should have you home at ten, if not a little sooner. Maria, are you coming back to the apartments with me, or are you staying with Teresa?"

"I'm staying at Teresa's," Maria said after a considerable pause.

"Her car is at my place, Ted," Teresa reminded him.

"Of course," Ted said. "I forgot. I'll drop you both off first."

Jennifer commented on how different everything looked at night and how dark the road was. Ted responded by flicking on his brights. The beam only irritated Jennifer's eyes, already sensitive from the excess alcohol. "Umm," she groaned slightly.

"Your head?" Ted asked Jennifer. "Do you want me to dim the headlights?"

"No, Ted. Do whatever is safe for you. Yes, though, I do have a headache. It's my own fault."

"Why don't you close your eyes and get some rest? I believe the ladies in the backseat are already doing that."

Jennifer turned to glance behind her as much as the seatbelt would allow. Since neither Teresa nor Maria spoke, Jennifer figured they were dozing.

"I want to help keep you awake, Ted," Jennifer told him but wondered how long she could remain alert under the circumstances.

"We only have about twenty minutes to go, Jennifer. I know the road well, and I'm fine with night driving. Remember that I'm the only one in this vehicle who's alcohol-free. I'll immediately pull over if I start to feel sleepy, but I don't think it will come to that."

"You make a convincing argument." Jennifer smiled, feeling ready to drift off at any moment. "I'll take you up on your offer." She positioned her head comfortably on the seatback. "Thank you, Ted," she added softly.

If he answered, Jennifer was unaware. She was in the middle of a pleasant dream when Ted gently woke her with a slight nudge. "We're home. Well, at least we're at Teresa's. I'll let you wake the two in the back."

Jennifer did so, and both women responded with sizeable appreciation for the fun day and Ted's chauffeuring. He waited until Teresa and Maria were inside the home before backing out of the driveway.

"The church sure is pretty at night." Jennifer was mesmerized by the soft lighting against the stone building.

"I have something I want to discuss with you," Ted said, ignoring her comment about the church.

"Can it wait until tomorrow?" Jennifer still felt tired from the day trip. "I'll be better company tomorrow, I promise." She yawned as if on cue.

"I'm away the next two days," he reminded her, "so, no, it can't wait."

"Oh, that's right! I'm sorry, Ted! I hope you can get enough rest tonight." Jennifer was suddenly worried.

"I'll be fine," Ted brushed her concern aside as he pulled up to the house. Since he made no effort to get out, Jennifer followed his lead and stayed put.

After a few minutes of silence, she remarked, "It's chilly if you don't leave the heater running, Ted. We'd better go inside if you feel we need to have a conversation tonight."

Ted opened his door, and Jennifer did likewise before he could reach the passenger side. He quietly followed her inside. She turned on the entryway light while Ted headed straight for the sofa. She switched on a lamp before plopping down beside him.

"It was a lighthearted day, but now you seem somber about something, Ted," Jennifer observed. "Is anything wrong?"

"I don't know. I'm curious about a remark you made on the way home. You said that a guy at Tenger-Bio told you that young people choose to live in Rotan."

"Yes, that's what he said." Jennifer immediately caught her blunder. She should have refused that last glass of champagne. How perceptive of Ted to have picked up on the Tenger-Bio comment amid all of today's talk.

"I'd like a direct, honest answer to my next question," Ted continued. "Did you make a trip to Tenger-Bio after I asked you not to?"

Jennifer didn't recall Ted specifically asking her not to go to the research facility, but she did know he refused to accompany her and was against the idea of her visiting. Maybe she was mistaken. She chose her words carefully. "I did visit, and I was given a tour, Ted. I didn't learn much about Ruth because, as you pointed out, it's been too long ago."

"Why didn't you tell me? That's the part that bothers me. We talk practically daily." Ted didn't take his eyes off Jennifer, which made his comments cut deeper.

"I knew you wouldn't like it, Ted. I knew you were against me visiting Tenger. It's something I felt I needed to do, though, and it isn't like I didn't invite you to accompany me."

Ted lifted his hands, palms upward. "What specifically did you learn from your visit?"

"I learned that Tenger-Bio seems to be an excellent employer. I was treated very well, with respect. My aunt is honored with a large portrait in their entrance hallway. I got to see the area my aunt used to work in," Jennifer listed every point she could recall as if reciting for a test. "I met an old-timer named Hank who was a colleague of hers."

That sparked Ted's interest, as Jennifer suspected it would. "What did Hank have to say?" He eyed her closely.

"Hank knew Ruth when she had a young boarder, and Ruth was upset about having to ask him to leave," Jennifer told him bluntly. Why not be totally frank at this point? After all, he set this confrontation into motion. "Why did Ruth ask you to leave, Ted?"

His face registered shock as if Jennifer had just slapped him. He took a few seconds to compose his thoughts. "That hurts me, Jennifer! You assumed that Ruth asked me to leave. You didn't take into account that this ... Hank ... could be wrong. How do you even know that I'm the man Ruth referred to? What exactly do you think of me, Jennifer?"

"Hank recalled that the man was young and blonde. I did give you the benefit of the doubt, which is one of the reasons I didn't mention my Tenger trip to you."

"This whole thing feels like a lack of trust in me, Jennifer," Ted insisted. "I thought we were building a ... a partnership. Good God, Jennifer! I moved to Tilbrook to be nearer to you. I thought that we were doing things together now, such as when we packed my belongings and set up my apartment."

She was embarrassed. Ted had been awfully good to her. He earned praise from Teresa and Maria today, only to have Jennifer cast doubt his way. "It isn't that I don't trust you, Ted. I do like the partnership we're building. I want to make this better, so how about going with me to the antique shop in Bilmore after Thanksgiving? You wanted to be a part of the sorting and selling of my aunt's belongings. I want to make another trip to Carlson's Collectibles and Antiques, and now's a perfect time, right before the big holiday shopping season gets underway."

"I'm in Bilmore frequently on business, Jennifer," Ted said without enthusiasm. "I'm not interested in yet another trip to Bilmore, especially since I just moved from there."

Jennifer was stunned and spoke bluntly, "You told me you wanted to be a part of going through Ruth's possessions, at least the antiques. You do remember being angry with me when I made the first trip to the antique shop, don't you?"

"I apologized for that," Ted reminded her. "Yes, I'll gladly help you sort things and carry boxes, but it will be to Rotan. I'm sure you'll get better prices and a larger market."

"Carlson's in Bilmore was recommended to me, Ted, and I really like the elderly man and his son who own that shop," Jennifer held firm. "I feel I got a generous price, one I can live with, and both men welcomed me back at any time. I'd rather give my business to them than to an impersonal company in Rotan. Besides, that would be well over a two-hour roundtrip drive, hauling fragile antiques. Part of that roadway is bumpy."

"As I said, I'll help you with sorting, packing, and hauling boxes to your car, Jennifer." He stopped short of agreeing to accompany her to the Bilmore shop. "You have the right idea about selling before the holidays, and that's an example of the type of partnership I want us to have." His tone became more conciliatory. "That brings me to this." He stood to reach into his trouser pocket and handed her a key before seating himself again.

"What's this?" Jennifer narrowed her hazel eyes. "You're giving me a key?"

"A key to my apartment." Ted smiled. "I meant to do it earlier. It's only natural that we'd exchange keys. With you being gone for a few days over Thanksgiving, you'll want me to check on your house."

"Oh!" Jennifer paused for an awkward length of time. "Ted, I don't need you to check on my place. I don't have pets or houseplants, as you know. It's sweet that you want to give me your key, but there's an office at M. H., so I wouldn't actually need one."

"That's not the point," Ted said with transparent disappointment. "I want you to have this. I've already listed you as a key holder with the office. Naturally, I thought you'd want to exchange with me. That's what couples do, Jennifer. Are you so emotionally bruised by your ex-husband that you can't trust me?"

Jennifer knew that wasn't the case, but Ted's presumption could buy her time. She would never have thought of the angle of using Alex as an excuse. It wasn't ideal, yet it seemed better than telling Ted that he's too forward and tends to make himself too much at home. And then there's the issue of Ephraim. Jennifer knew she had to say something soon, so she went along with the "out" Ted unwittingly provided. "Perhaps. I guess you have a point about me being more guarded due to my experience with my former husband. You said you had an adjustment period when you got divorced, right?"

Ted put his arm around her and pulled her closer. "I heard you mention Alex to your friends today, Jennifer. That's why you all went silent when I got back into the vehicle. It was because you were having a frank discussion about your ex."

Although that wasn't exactly the case, Jennifer felt relief that Ted showed gentleness to her again and appeared to sympathize with the situation he had created in his mind. "Yes," she confirmed, "you did catch me discussing Alex." Since that part was true, Jennifer told herself she wasn't lying—only failing to clarify.

"Remember, I'm not Alex." Ted's tone became tender. "Someday, I hope you'll share more about him with me, but we'll leave it at that, especially since I have to be up early tomorrow and need some sleep. I'm someone you can trust, sweetheart. I insist that you keep my apartment key. Can I please have one to your home?"

"Teresa has my only spare," Jennifer said on impulse. Although she had asked Teresa to keep a house key for her, it was not true that this was the sole duplicate.

"Have one made," Ted instructed as he stood to make his way to the door. "I'll be gone two days. If I'm back in time on Tuesday evening, I'll swing past for the key. You don't leave until Wednesday, true?"

"Probably not," she agreed, unwilling to divulge specifics at this point.

"I'll see you off, either Tuesday night or early Wednesday before you go." Ted yawned several times in succession. "I'm more tired than I realized, so I'd better leave." He kissed her and suggested she get to bed herself.

"Ted, I had a fun day in Rotan, and I appreciate you allowing me to invite Teresa and Maria. I could tell they enjoyed themselves, too. Thank you," Jennifer said sincerely.

"It's what couples do," Ted took the opportunity to remind her. "Partnership," he added and, with that, bid her good-night.

She waited until Ted's SUV pulled away before turning off the outside light. Ted made a persuasive argument, but Jennifer still wasn't inclined to give him a key to her home, especially with her leaving town soon. She'd have to think of a diversion in the next few days.

Chapter 15

"YOU MEAN YOU SPENT the night in a motel?" Angie whispered as if they weren't alone in the Calberto kitchen. "Why didn't you come straight here? You're welcome no matter the time, Jen! You know that!"

"It was late, way too late for me to continue driving, plus you weren't expecting me until today," Jennifer explained to her closest friend. "I wanted to escape my problems, so I made a rather rash decision around lunchtime yesterday and took off."

"You could have called," Angie reprimanded. "You're by yourself. It's safer to keep your friends in the know."

"I can't argue with that, but I got increasingly nervous on Tuesday. Ted was either going to show up that night or early today expecting a spare key from me, and I didn't intend to give him one. I guess I panicked. Before I knew it, I had my bag in the Toyota and was en route."

"Okay, okay," Angie said soothingly. She stood to place her hands on Jennifer's shoulders. "Let me refill your cup. How about cider for a change?"

Jennifer nodded and pushed the empty mug to the edge of the kitchen table. She found the homey pattern of the vinyl tablecloth oddly comforting. It reminded her of past times when she had her mom, husband, and best friend close by. Jennifer set her elbows on the table, cupping her forehead in her palms. When Angie returned with a freshly warmed apple cider, she lifted her head and smiled at her dear friend.

"Thanks."

"Of course, Jen." Angie's voice was gentle. "We'll have several days to talk. Jolie has class today, and Mike's at work. Tomorrow, Thanksgiving, will be busy, but that's good. It will help take your mind off other things. Jolie's boyfriend, Sean, will be eating with us. She's crazy about him, and I like him, too. Of course, Mr. Dad, you can imagine he's not crazy about his baby dating, but I think he secretly approves of Sean. I'm getting off-track, Jen. Enough of the family stuff for now. I'm all ears if you'd like to talk."

"Ted's going to be upset that I left without at least telling him. All I wanted to do was escape the immediate situation. I didn't think of the consequences. Now, it's all hitting me, and I feel terrible about it." Jennifer buried her head in her palms again.

"I'm not going to sugarcoat it, kiddo. Ted has every right to be angry and hurt. What you need now is damage control, and I mean *now*. That is if you want to have Ted in your life. Do you? Or do you think you fled the scene because he's not the man for you?"

"I don't know, Angie. I honestly don't." Jennifer sighed. "Ted's great. He's been sweet, supportive, dependable, and patient for the most part. Granted, he can be pushy. He can also be a little nosy, but I guess that's because he wants to know more about me, and he wants our relationship to work."

"It sounds like you're not ready to lose him, huh?" Angie inquired softly.

"No. I'm not ready for that. All I wanted was the status quo, at least for another few months. I didn't want him to have a key to my home. I'd be spending Thanksgiving with you guys, wondering if he's looking through my closets, medicine cabinet, drawers—"

"Wow, Jen. Would you do that to him if he gave you a key to his place?"

"Remember, he did give me a key to his apartment, and the answer is no. I would respect his privacy," Jennifer answered adamantly.

"Okay. I'd be honest with Ted. Tell him he tends to snoop. I see the look you're giving me, Jen." Angie laughed. "And I know you'll be tactful. You're going to have to be direct with this guy, though. He acts as if he lives at your place when he's there, right? If you don't like that, you have to tell him. If he's who you think he is—a nice, sweetheart of a guy—he'll listen to you and respect your wishes. If not, you need to know so that you can make an informed decision. How do you like that term, Jen? Informed decision. Pretty good, huh?"

"Yeah, Angie." Jennifer managed a smile despite the anguish she was feeling. "You give good advice."

"Tell my daughter and husband that," Angie said teasingly.

"I'm going to have to confront Ted. He's pushing me too hard on the key issue. Ooh, I wish I hadn't fled to avoid dealing with Ted. My timing was horrible, too, right before Thanksgiving!" She lowered her head once again.

"Damage control, Jen. Did you at least text Ted today to let him know you arrived safely?"

"No, I haven't done a thing rather than drive here and pour my heart out to you." She choked back her tears. "What will I say?"

"Do you trust Ted enough to share your feelings with him?"

"Oh, gee, Angie, not you, too." Jennifer shook her head. "That's what Ted accused me of over the weekend. Lack of trust."

"It's something you need to consider seriously. If I didn't trust Mike, I wouldn't stay married to him. I don't care if he is the father of my child. The basis of a healthy relationship is trust and partnership."

"Ted mentioned partnership, too," Jennifer said softly. "I feel horrible, Ange. He hasn't given me any significant reason not to trust him. Maybe he's right, and I'm more messed up over Alex than I thought."

"I don't think you're messed up over Alex. I think Ted may be a little pushy and needs to slow down, but then I never met the man. You *do* need to call him soon, though, if you want him to remain in your life. You don't need to have all your issues sorted out before doing that. Call him now and tell him that I asked you to come a day early to help me with the Thanksgiving prep. Tell Ted it was a last-minute decision, and you simply forgot that he might be dropping by. Apologize for the inconvenience and leave it at that."

"You're advising me to say you asked me to come on Tuesday instead of today?" Jennifer lifted her head to look at Angie, making sure she understood.

"Yeah, Jen, it's no big deal. We're all here for you. I'll let Mike and Jolie know that you're going through a tough time with Ted and that if he ever asks, you came yesterday."

Jennifer hesitated. "That might be best." She suddenly felt some relief. "In the rush to get on the road, I forgot to leave him a message. Ted will still be hurt but not as much as he would if he knew I intentionally left early to avoid seeing him."

"Uh-huh. If you still want this man in your life, this is a chance to smooth things over. Let him have a nice Thanksgiving holiday. Then once you're back in town, you can make some decisions about the next step."

"I'd better hurry." Jennifer rose from her chair, feeling a sense of urgency. "Ted may call me any moment now, and it would be best if he heard from me first. I also need to phone Teresa, the one who has my spare key. I'll feel better if she knows what's going on." Jennifer started for the doorway, then turned to look back at her best friend.

"Take as much time as you need," Angie assured her. "I'll be here in the kitchen. When you're done, you'll find out that I was serious about you helping me prep for Thanksgiving. I have veggies to chop and two types of pies I want to make from scratch."

When Jennifer returned to the kitchen a half-hour later, her friend was rolling dough. "I'm sorry I left you for so long, Ange. It actually worked out quite well."

"Do tell!" Angie winked at Jennifer. "Don't mind me as I continue these pies. I left the radishes and green onions for you to prep." She motioned to the stack beside the refrigerator.

"I lucked out!" Jennifer enthusiastically announced as she rinsed the produce. "Ted had just returned from his business trip. He wasn't surprised that he'd missed seeing me off." She moved the cutting board, knife, and veggies to the kitchen table and sat down. "He assumed I left early this morning, and I didn't correct him. I let him presume that I'm still on the road heading for Reddington. He asked me to call him this evening to let him know I arrived safely."

"Okay." Angie frowned. "How was his mood? Did he seem like the same old Ted?"

"Yes, he did. He didn't sound suspicious. If anything, he sounded apologetic that he'd missed seeing me this morning."

"Did you reach your friend, Teresa?" Angie wanted to make sure Jennifer covered all bases.

"She didn't pick up, but I left her a detailed message on her cell." Jennifer sliced the end off another green onion before continuing, "Today's a workday for her. She'll probably call me back on her first break or between clients if she can. I'm not worried, though."

"How much did you tell Teresa, you know, in your message?" Angie probed.

"I didn't tell her that I'm already here with you now," Jennifer explained, knowing that was what Angie meant. "I only told her the basics. I said that I'm on my way to Angie's for Thanksgiving and will be back Saturday night. I also told her that Ted had insisted we do a key exchange, but I wasn't ready for that. I let her know that I fibbed and told him she has my only duplicate key."

"Well, good, it looks like it worked out fine." Angie turned to glance at Jennifer. "All it's done is bought you time, however, so you and Ted can both have a pleasant Thanksgiving holiday. You still need to deal with the reason behind not wanting to give him a key. Speaking of reasons to avoid giving your boyfriend a key to your house—how's Ephraim?"

Jennifer laughed and threw the smallest radish she could find at Angie. "How dare you," she kidded her friend.

Angie picked up the radish from the floor, rinsed it, and ate it. "Next time you throw produce at me, make it a green onion."

"I've been using the recorder I ordered from that paranormal shop. I can't report any fantastic results, but it's been interesting. I've gotten a couple of clear words," Jennifer said and coyly added, "spoken in a deep masculine voice."

"No, you didn't!" Angie sounded incredulous. "Why didn't you phone me? Immediately! I mean it, Jen! You should have phoned me."

"I just started the recording sessions recently, you know that," Jennifer said defensively. "Besides, I wanted us to have plenty to talk about over the holiday together," Jennifer teased, "and now we do."

“Was it Ephraim? What did he say?” Angie suddenly lost interest in her Thanksgiving pies and sat next to Jennifer at the table.

“Mostly just yes or no. I ask plenty of questions, and every so often, I'm rewarded with a male voice responding with yes or no.” Angie looked disappointed, so Jennifer quickly elaborated. “From this, however, I know that his name is Doctor Ephraim, and he is buried next to his son. He is the one who left the daisy on my journal.”

“Ooh,” Angie squealed with delight, “that is good information! Other than yes and no, which words has Ephraim said?”

“Caution or cautious. I haven't been able to clearly make out what he's said, but he's repeated this word or these words in several sessions. Nothing further, however. It's both exciting and frustrating! Maybe it means he's cautious or uses caution when communicating with me. Perhaps he's cautious because he doesn't want others to know he's around.”

“Yeah, Jen,” Angie kidded, “he wouldn't want someone coming in to clear his presence. If I were haunting a place, and I've told Mike this, I don't want any teams of experts brought in. Leave me alone.”

“And yet you were after me to hire paranormal investigators, buy equipment, and look for more of Aunt Ruth's diaries,” Jennifer reminded her.

“Well, now I have more sympathy for poor Doctor Ephraim,” Angie faked indignation. “I still want to meet him, you know. Between meeting Ted and Doctor Ephraim, if I only get one choice, I'd choose the good doctor." Angie burst out with a belly laugh.

"Ha, ha, Angie." Jennifer tossed a green onion her way.

Jolie plopped down on the sofa, adjacent to her boyfriend, Sean. When she placed her hand on the young man's knee, Mike cleared his throat and gave Jolie a look that caused her to shift her hand to her lap immediately.

"Sean, you like football, do you?" Mike asked in an attempt to make conversation.

"Not really, sir," the young man replied honestly, causing both Angie and Jennifer to stifle their sudden urge to laugh. Jolie shot a reproachful glance to all the adults in the room.

"Oh, okay, then," Mike said, obviously surprised since he loved football when he was Sean's age. "Any sports you do like?"

The teenager shrugged. "I like chess. I'm part of my school's chess club."

"That's not a sport, Sean," Mike corrected his daughter's boyfriend. "Basketball, soccer, hockey, baseball—now those are sports!"

"Dad!" Jolie exclaimed, blatantly mortified by her father's side of the conversation.

"Yeah, Dad," Angie chimed in, laughing. "So, Sean is in the chess club. Jolie tells me that you're quite the asset to the school's team."

"Mom!" Jolie reprimanded.

It was Mike's turn to laugh. "Yeah, Mom," he teased his wife. "Sean, on Thanksgiving Day, I traditionally watch football. If you'd care to join me, I welcome your company. I was on my high school football team back in the day, so if you have any questions about the game, ask away."

"Mom, can Sean and I leave for his house now?" Although Jolie asked in a calm voice, her eyes were pleading.

"Okay by me," Angie replied. "You see, Jen, Sean was on loan to us for the Thanksgiving meal. He has his own family, though, so Jolie and Sean will split their time between parents."

"You aren't going to eat another Thanksgiving turkey meal today, are you?" Mike directed his question to the two lovebirds with mock seriousness.

"I didn't eat a lot, sir," Sean answered honestly. "I knew my mom would be making dinner, but we have our meal later in the evening."

Jolie had already stood and was tugging at Sean's hand, urging him to rise from the sofa. Sean got the message and obeyed. She led him to the coat rack to retrieve their outerwear.

"It was nice having you join us today," Angie said and turned to wink at both Mike and Jennifer.

"Thank you for inviting me," Sean replied. "The meal was delicious," he added as an afterthought.

"When will you bring my daughter back?" Mike called out, still seated in his recliner.

"Right after dinner, so probably around eight. My dad will drive us because I'm not allowed to drive after dark yet."

"Aahh!" Jolie sighed with exasperation and shook her head vigorously. "TMI, Sean."

"Goodbye, Jolie. Goodbye, Sean," Jennifer called out to the couple, remaining seated herself.

Mike snickered when the door shut. "Well, that was jolly fun. I'd like my old daughter back, please."

Angie rejoined her husband and Jennifer in the living room. "How to embarrass your teenage daughter with just a few words," she said, laughing.

"What? Football? Asset? Sport?" Mike threw his hands into the air.

"I think all it takes is a hello." Angie slapped her thigh with a chuckle.

"You drove all that way, Jennifer, for this?" Mike kidded. "You must be a misogynist. Is that the word I'm looking for, Angie? Misogynist?"

"I don't think so, Mike. Doesn't that mean someone who doesn't like women?"

"Yes," Jennifer spoke up, glad to be able to contribute something to the conversation considering she had no kids. "I can't think of the word Mike wants, though. I guess he could call me a glutton for punishment, but in this case, being with all of you is a blessing."

"Maybe you're just a glutton," Mike teased and winked at Jennifer, knowing that would get a rise out of Angie.

Angie threw a pillow at Mike, hitting him on his lower leg. "What a way to treat our guest," she retorted. "You're a sadist. I'm pretty sure I'm using that word correctly—one who enjoys inflicting pain on others."

"When it comes to my daughter and her new boyfriend, that's pretty accurate," Mike agreed, nodding his head as if in serious contemplation. "Next time you choose to throw something my way, Ange, make it a beer. Better yet, just set it here on this nice table." Mike patted the adjacent stand.

Jennifer missed being around Mike and Angie. Tomorrow was already Jennifer's final day in Reddington. She'd head for home on Saturday, but she didn't want to think about that quite yet. Angie returned to the living room with a poured beer for her husband, who motioned for Angie to lean in for a kiss.

"Ah, my dear wife," Mike started, "if I haven't expressed my appreciation for that fine, fine meal you served, let me do it now." He patted his stomach, a huge grin on his face. "I might need to change into my Thanksgiving Day pants. Now that the kids are gone, no need to be so dressy."

"You still have company," Angie pointed her head in Jennifer's direction as she spoke. "Jen doesn't need to see you in your Thanksgiving pants. In fact, I don't need to see you in those things."

"Ah, it's just Jen," Mike said matter-of-factly. "She won't care. Football, beer, and my special pants, along with two of my three favorite girls. What could be better? Excuse me, ladies." Mike rose and gave a slight, formal bow as he made for the bedroom to change clothing.

Angie sighed and covered her eyes with her palms. "Agh! What am I to do? See? I have no control over anything in this household. Are you sure you don't want to move back here, Jen? Save me from this barbaric bunch?"

"Don't tempt me," Jennifer said, only partially joking. "You know you love it! You have a terrific family. You chose your husband well, Angie. You make a cute couple."

"Yeah, we do." Angie uncovered her eyes. "He's a keeper. So's the kid."

"I can't believe I'll be driving back home so soon. It seems like I just pulled up to your house!"

"That's always the way it goes. Before you know it, Christmas will be here, then the new year. It's Black Friday tomorrow, Jen! Want to go shopping? Maybe not for the whole day, but how about for the morning, and we'll have lunch at Caper's? Remember those huge chef salads? They still have them, and, yes, they're still wonderful."

"I'm game for whatever plans you have," Jennifer said sincerely. "Mike was certainly right about what a wonderful meal you prepared today, Ange. I am very appreciative that you invited me."

"You're always welcome, and you know that. You're family. We go way back. As you can tell," Angie suddenly paused and pointed towards the hallway, "Mike also thinks of you as family."

Mike made his entrance in red-plaid flannel pants held up by a drawstring. To emphasize his Thanksgiving pants, Mike began tucking his green sweatshirt into the waistband. He made quite the spectacle, which was the obvious intent. "This is my kick-off for the holiday season, ladies!" he proudly announced.

"I should kick you out for the holiday season!" Angie joked, but her voice betrayed how much she actually adored her husband.

⁂

"Are you sure you don't want to come back for Christmas, Jen?" Angie asked. "It's no trouble, you know. I enjoy having you here."

"Soon, the roads will be more difficult to travel," Jennifer reminded her friend. "Even if that weren't the case, I did promise Ted that he and I would spend Christmas together. I really won't stand a chance with him if I turn around and bail on him for another holiday."

"You're right. I got selfish. We can talk on the phone like we always do. Remind me to give you your birthday and Christmas presents before you go."

"Angie, you're so prepared! I'm going to have to mail you your gift. I hoped you might give me a hint about what you'd like on our shopping excursion, but it looks like you told Santa instead."

"Santa Mike, yes, I did. He's very good to me, and I'm very good to him." Angie hoisted her large shopping bag to shoulder height.

"Are you almost done with your gift buying for the holidays? You know, I don't have a clue what I'll get Ted. Maybe something for his apartment."

"I'm pretty much set now with the presents, even for Jolie because she's at the gift card stage," Angie explained. "I asked Jolie to pick up some small item for Sean from Mike and me. Since I only had a daughter, I'm not sure what a teenage boy might like."

Both women laughed at Angie's remark, the same thought entering their minds. "I think that was the sensible way to handle Sean's gift this year until you get to know his likes and dislikes better," Jennifer responded seriously. "He does seem like a nice kid."

"Yeah, he is. Jolie could do a lot worse. That's what I told Mike. You know romances at this age, right? Those two might break it off before we get to Christmas. In that case, I sure hope Jolie picks out a gift for Sean that either Mike or I will like."

Jennifer put her arm around her friend's waist and squeezed her. "I'm sure it will all work out for the best."

Jennifer thought she heard the familiar ringtone of her cell phone, but it was difficult to make out among the holiday music in the mall. She fumbled for her phone and saw that she had just missed a call from Teresa. "Oh, my friend back in Tilbrook called," Jennifer informed Angie. "Teresa Degra. She probably wants to know how Thanksgiving went. Remind me to phone her when we get to your place."

"Will do," Angie agreed and ducked into a shoe store to admire a pair of black leather boots she thought Jolie would love. Angie debated taking a chance on purchasing the boots, finally deciding that the worst that could happen was another trip to the mall for an exchange or refund.

Jennifer stepped out of the shoe store while Angie finished her transaction. Speaking of shoes, her feet were beginning to hurt. She took advantage of an opening on a bench diagonal from the store and rested her sore muscles. Jennifer surveyed the busy shoppers, noting how many had their cell phones in hand. That reminded her of Teresa's call, and Jennifer wondered if her friend had left a message. She pressed her voicemail number and code.

"Do you know I got an extra forty percent off those boots!" Angie exclaimed as she approached Jennifer. "Had I known that, I wouldn't have hesitated. Hey, if they don't work out for Jolie, it seems that they fit me well. She has a slightly narrower foot than I do, but on me, these boots are just a little tight. I think I could stretch them if needed, though, so I don't think that will be a problem. My guess is that Jolie can..."

Jennifer pulled her cell phone away from her ear. "I'm listening to Teresa's message. She wants me to call her but says there's no urgency. Teresa gave me a heads-up that Ted asked Maria, Teresa's partner and someone who lives in Ted's apartment building, to get my spare key from Teresa and give it to him. He told Maria that I meant to give it to him before I left, but he didn't get back into town in time for that to happen."

"Ooh!" Angie winced at the news. "Well, honest mistake, I guess. In his mind, you were going to give him your key that day. Did Teresa or this other lady give Ted your spare?"

"No. No, Teresa didn't go into further detail, but she specifically told me she has the key and not to worry."

"Are you worried, though?" Angie asked her friend bluntly. "Can you trust this Teresa and this other woman?"

"Yes, I can," Jennifer didn't hesitate to respond. "Teresa is smart and perceptive. I've already had conversations with her about liking my privacy and not being ready to have Ted move in with me. She's been totally supportive. As for Maria, she's a helpful sweetheart who likes Ted, but I can't envision Maria turning over my key to Ted without Teresa's permission."

"Makes sense." Angie nodded. "It's still kind of loud here. Do you want to listen to your message again someplace quieter?"

"I've listened three times already, so I think I'm good." Jennifer sighed. "Let's not have *this* change our plans for today, Ange. We only have a short time left, and I want it to be memorable in a good way. I *am* going to deal with the Ted situation when I get back home."

"On to Caper's then?" Angie asked hopefully. "Land of the super salad."

"Lead the way." Jennifer waved her arm in a polite gesture to Angie, who curtsied and motioned for her pal to follow.

Chapter 16

JENNIFER PULLED INTO HER driveway, thrilled to be home after twelve hours on the road. She left her headlights on to illuminate the walk to the front door. Jennifer shouted a greeting to Ephraim as she made her way to the living room to turn on another lamp. At first glance, everything seemed just as she had left it on Tuesday. She set down her purse and the shopping bag Angie had packed with gifts.

"Did you miss me, Ephraim?" Jennifer asked when she returned from the car with her luggage. "What? No flicker of the lamp?" she teased. "I'm tired but still wound up from the long drive. Oh, and I need to call Angie to let her know I made it home safely."

She pulled the cell phone from her purse and pressed the selected contact. Angie picked up at the same time Jennifer's doorbell chimed.

"Jen?" Angie greeted her friend eagerly from the other end of the connection. "Are you back home now?"

"Yeah, I just got in, and everything went well. Hey, Ange, someone's at the door." Jennifer turned on the porch light and squinted through the peephole. "Oh! It's Ted."

"I'll let you go, then, but I'm glad you got back safely. Call me later tonight if you need to talk. Bye!" Angie abruptly disconnected before Jennifer had a chance to respond.

She opened the door, phone still to her ear. "Ted! I'm surprised you're here! I was just on a call with Angie to let her know I made it home."

He held up a bottle of what Jennifer presumed to be some type of alcohol. Ted validated her guess. "Champagne. Since we last saw each other over a bottle of champagne, I thought it was fitting and romantic to toast the holiday and your return." He briefly kissed Jennifer before making his way to the china cabinet.

"Not those glasses, Ted," Jennifer cautioned. "Those are very fragile, and I already broke one. I've got sturdier glasses in the kitchen. I'll get them, but I don't plan to drink much. First of all, I'm exhausted from being on the road all day. Second, I got too tipsy the last time I drank, as I'm sure you recall."

He followed Jennifer into the kitchen and set the champagne bottle next to the two glasses she presented. "I just wanted to see you, Jennifer! I missed you, even though it's only been a week."

"I missed you, too." Jennifer put her arms around his waist. "Don't you want to take off your coat?"

"I do, I do," Ted replied. "Why don't we both get comfortable before I pour the beverages? I saw your suitcase just inside the door. Let me carry that upstairs for you, and you can unpack and freshen up. I'll make us a fire, too, if you'd like."

Jennifer was about to tell Ted that she'd prefer to unpack in the morning, but he already had her suitcase in hand and motioned for her to lead the way upstairs. She acquiesced since the thought of having time to clean up and change clothes appealed to her. When she came downstairs, Ted had a fire going and two poured glasses of champagne waiting on the table by the sofa.

"What's in the shopping bag?" he queried before Jennifer had a chance to sit down. He walked to the sack and peeked inside. Jennifer put her hands on Ted's and gently pulled him away from the bag.

"Angie's gifts for me for my birthday and Christmas. I can see that if I have a Christmas present for you, I'll have to hide it well."

If Ted picked up on Jennifer's slight annoyance, he chose to ignore it. "Birthday present? Is your birthday coming up soon?"

"Unfortunately. December 22. I came close to being a Christmas baby."

"Then we'll have two occasions to celebrate. Twice the fun." Ted moved his hands to Jennifer's shoulders. "You are going to be in town then, right? You aren't going to make another trip to see your friends?"

"I'm here to stay for now," Jennifer assured him with a smile. "When's your birthday, Ted? I hope you aren't going to tell me that I just missed it."

"No, my birthday was months ago, July 22. So, Jennifer's turning forty-three in a few weeks," he teased but quickly added, "You'll always be younger than me!"

"Yes, by two years, and don't forget that," she joked. "Is it time for a toast?" Jennifer motioned to the champagne behind Ted.

He turned to pick up both glasses, handing one to his sweetheart. "Here's to the kickoff of the holiday season, plus your birthday and the happiness I believe we'll find together in the future. I toast you, Jennifer." He clinked his glass gently against hers.

"That was a lovely toast," she said appreciatively as she raised the champagne to her lips. The rest was a blur, however. The glass went flying out of her grip. Simultaneously, the room chilled, and the lights flickered.

"What the...?" Ted cursed under his breath. "What is wrong with you, Jennifer? You did the same thing before! You're not usually this clumsy! And for God's sake, get an electrician over here! We've been through this before, and you've obviously done nothing about it!"

Jennifer managed to hold back her anger. Instead, she quickly surveyed the damage and located her dropped glass. It hadn't shattered, and it remarkably still retained some of its contents. Jennifer stooped to retrieve the glass and made her way to the kitchen to place it back in the cupboard before Ted noticed. She grabbed an identical one, and when Ted predictably entered the kitchen, Jennifer rinsed this clean glass under the faucet for Ted to observe. "Looks like I managed to spill it all," she informed him coolly. "Would you like me to pour us refills, or have I ruined your evening?"

"I'm sorry." Ted sounded sheepish. "You took me by surprise. All at once, we had a repeat of the other night."

"Yes," Jennifer agreed bluntly. She didn't bother to explain that the glass was slapped out of her hand. "It was like the other time you brought alcohol."

"Do you get muscle spasms at times, Jennifer? Are you on a medication that could cause something like muscle weakness?" He grasped at straws, trying to make sense of what he witnessed.

"No," Jennifer gave him a one-syllable answer, not in the mood for more.

"I don't mean to upset you," he said softly, hoping to get back into her good graces. "I'm sorry I lost my temper briefly."

Jennifer took the empty champagne glass from Ted's hand and poured him a refill. She watched him take a couple of sips before pouring an inch into her own glass. He kept a steady gaze on Jennifer.

"Ted, are you wearing cologne or aftershave? Something like that?" Jennifer suddenly asked.

"No," he responded, obviously puzzled by her question. "Do you smell something?"

"A light, musky cologne odor. It's a pleasant scent." She paused before adding, "I like it."

"Jennifer, I don't smell anything," Ted insisted, sounding a little worried. "Are you sure you're okay?"

"I'm fine," Jennifer said adamantly. "You obviously saw the lights flicker. Did you also notice that the temperature dropped in the room?"

"I don't know what you're getting at." Ted spread his hands in dismay. "Do you mean when we had our toast? You dropped your champagne, and the lights flickered. That's all I saw."

"Hmm." Jennifer took another small sip. "It seemed more dramatic than that to me." She chose to drop the subject, though. "Do you mind if we cut tonight short?" She glanced at the clock on the mantel. "It's almost ten. Angie's family saw me off around eight this morning, and I only stopped for about half an hour, except for a few bathroom breaks."

"Yes, of course, you're tired," Ted agreed and quickly turned to look for his coat. Jennifer was relieved he didn't try to change her mind. "Again, I'm sorry I lost my temper. I wasn't really mad at you, Jennifer. I was irritated by that damn short circuit or whatever it is you have going on with the wiring in here."

"And you were irritated that I spilled my champagne."

"Mildly annoyed," Ted countered. He pulled her in to kiss her gently on the temple, apparently leery about showing his usual amount of passion. "Get some sleep. Rest all day tomorrow if you'd like. It's Sunday, but I'll give you the full day to recuperate. Call me if you need anything."

Jennifer nodded and let Ted see himself to the door. She locked up and checked the peephole when she thought she heard his SUV pull away from the house.

"Ephraim," she called out when she returned to the living room, "were you trying to warn me of something?"

One flicker of the lamp.

"Ted?" Jennifer asked bluntly.

One flicker.

Jennifer retrieved the digital recorder from upstairs, where she had it hidden in a drawer. She practically flew down the steps, forgetting her earlier fatigue. She turned on the recording device.

"What were you trying to warn me about? Try to be specific." She repeated her question several times, allowing plenty of opportunities for Ephraim to attempt a response. Then she hit playback.

"Champagne. Do not."

Jennifer was stunned by the clarity of the male voice in the recording. "Champagne. Do not," she repeated slowly. "Do you think something was wrong with the champagne, Ephraim? I don't know. At first, I thought so, too, but Ted let me pour us refills from the same bottle. Ted drank a lot more than I did, and he was fine. I took a couple of tiny sips, and I'm okay." Jennifer switched the device to record again, allowing a full five minutes to elapse before selecting the playback mode.

"Yours," came a faint, concerned masculine voice, "first glass."

Jennifer replayed the full five minutes of recording several times, wondering if she'd missed something. No, that was all, but it was enough. "Ephraim, do you know for a fact that something was wrong with my first glass of champagne?" She paused. "Tonight?" she added for clarity.

The light flickered a single time before Jennifer had thought to turn on the recorder again.

"Do you have anything else you want to say?" Jennifer gave him a further opportunity to communicate. She waited an additional five minutes, but the recording device picked up nothing.

"Thank you, Ephraim. I'm grateful to you," she said and bid him goodnight. Suddenly, her earlier fatigue returned multifold.

"You're Ruth Gaitley's niece, I understand," an elderly woman in a wheelchair directed her comment to Jennifer.

Jennifer hit her shin on the church pew as she walked toward the older lady. "Ow!" she involuntarily gasped and rubbed her right leg. "Yes, I'm Jennifer Shemmer. Ruth Gaitley was my aunt."

"I'm so glad to meet you," the woman replied. "My name is Hannah Meyers. I was a friend of your aunt, but we lost touch after I moved to Rotan to be near my daughter." Hannah swiveled in her chair to point to a white-haired lady with a bob haircut who was speaking with the minister. "My daughter's name is Lois. She was kind enough to bring me to Tilbrook for a few days. I'm in assisted living now. I can't complain, but I do miss it here. Tilbrook was my home for ages. If it weren't for my daughter, I wouldn't have left." Hannah abruptly ended her monolog with a direct question. "When did Ruth pass?"

"This summer, the end of August," Jennifer replied. "Ruth died in her home, but she was well-cared for. She wasn't alone."

"You're living in the home now?" Hannah was apparently aware of the answer because she continued, "I think that's wonderful! Ruth had a lovely home, and she maintained it well. Ruth would be so happy to know that you decided to keep the house and make it yours."

"She left her entire estate to me since I'm her only surviving relative. Did she ever mention me to you?" Jennifer asked on a whim, "Did she mention her sister, Elizabeth?"

"No." Hannah shook her head. "I'm afraid not, dear. I didn't realize she had any family." Hannah laughed suddenly. "She kept herself occupied with her interests."

By now, Lois had spotted her mom talking with Jennifer and joined them with an outstretched hand. "Hello. I'm Hannah's daughter, Lois. It's nice to meet you." Jennifer shook the woman's hand, noticing her firmer-than-average grip.

"Lois, this is Ruth Gaitley's niece, Jennifer," Hannah informed her daughter. "Oh, I forgot your last name, dear."

"Shemmer. Jennifer Shemmer. It's nice to meet you both, Lois and Hannah. Lois, your mom was filling me in on how she knew my aunt."

"We stopped by your house the other day," the daughter told a surprised Jennifer. "No one was home. At that time, we thought Ruth might still be living."

"Oh, yes." Hannah nodded solemnly. "She was a year or so older than me, though, so her passing doesn't surprise me. We all have to go eventually." Hannah gave her daughter a comforting pat. Lois looked ill at ease, and Jennifer could empathize. Her own mom, Elizabeth, used to say the same phrase to Jennifer after Elizabeth's terminal cancer diagnosis.

"Would you like to come to my house, Ruth's house?" Jennifer extended the impromptu invitation.

"We're going back to Rotan shortly," Lois said, confirmed by Hannah's nod. "Mother wanted to attend Trinity before we left."

"Things have changed so much, but it was still good to see the church again," Hannah chimed in. "The minister is different now, and the music is modern. I miss the old hymnals of my childhood. Even the organ is gone." She shook her head in disappointment.

"Yes. I heard that the minister is new," Jennifer recalled from her initial visit to the Trinity Presbyterian office. "Since I'm new here myself, I'm oblivious to the changes that occurred. I like Trinity and attend fairly regularly now. I haven't met anyone who knows much about Ruth, though, other than you. I wish I'd been home when you came by, but I was out of town for the Thanksgiving holiday."

"If we come to Tilbrook again, we'll stop by to say hello," Hannah promised and reached out to touch Jennifer's hand. "But I don't know when we'll come again because I think this has been a challenge for my daughter. I'm old, you know." Hannah chuckled and patted her knee.

"I can tell you're still very sharp-minded, however," Jennifer assured her, and Lois concurred. "That's a huge factor."

"Ruth retained her memory, too," Hannah recalled, "but I don't know how she was at the end. I lost touch with whatever friends I had left after moving to Rotan." She made a face.

"Hannah, do you remember if my aunt had a young male guest living in her home for a while? It would be a long time ago, probably twenty years," Jennifer queried.

Hannah didn't need time to ponder the question. "Yes, I do remember. At first, Ruth thought highly of the young man and felt sorry for him. Eventually, she insisted he leave because the bugger was stealing from her!"

Jennifer was silent for a moment but, surprisingly, not stunned by the news. "Do you recall the man's name?"

Hannah shook her head. "Dear, it's been too long ago."

"Ted Filston? Does that name sound familiar?"

"Ted ... Ted Filston ...," Hannah slowly repeated, frowning in concentration. "Filston seems vaguely familiar. Ted doesn't sound right, though. I'd have to say no to that, I'm afraid. Let's say that it wouldn't hold up in a court of law." She giggled and patted herself on her knee again. Jennifer smiled. Hannah was endearing and reminded her of her own mother in some ways.

"No problem," Jennifer assured Hannah and thanked the two women for taking the time to speak with her. Both ladies insisted that it was their pleasure. As Jennifer left Trinity, she noticed that the mother-daughter pair were still chatting with a few stragglers from the congregation. She was glad they were making the most of their visit and sincerely hoped there would be a return trip to Tilbrook in the near future.

Jennifer walked around the periphery of the stone church. She paused under the large oak to phone Teresa.

"Hey, Jennifer," her friend answered brightly. "Are you back in town now?"

"Not only am I back, but I'm standing in front of your house. I thought I'd see if you were okay for company, and if you're not, really, that's fine. We'll make it another time."

"It's almost noon, Jennifer." Teresa laughed. "Even I don't sleep that late. Of course, come on over. I'm unlocking the door now."

She looked toward Teresa's home and saw her attractive dark-haired friend wave. "Thank you," she said, simultaneously returning Teresa's gesture and ending their call.

"Is Maria here?" Jennifer asked as she entered. "I hope I'm not interrupting any Sunday plans."

"Maria spent Thanksgiving with me and then went to be with a cousin over the weekend. Since she works tomorrow, she'll have to return by tonight. Speaking of Thanksgiving, how was yours? How is Reddington this time of year?"

"I had a great time," Jennifer answered with sincerity. "Angie has the greatest family. Her husband Mike is hilarious and so easygoing. Her daughter's a teenager with a new boyfriend, and he came for Thanksgiving. It was fun! Angie's a terrific cook, too. She enjoys doing that sort of thing, unlike me."

Teresa responded with a nod. "Cooking's not my thing, either. However, Maria and I roasted a turkey and made all the traditional stuff, although some of it was pre-made, frozen."

"Nothing wrong with that," Jennifer said as Hooligan jumped on her lap. She petted the purring black feline. Hooligan looked up with the most adorable green eyes.

"Guess who got a pretty fair share of t-u-r-k-e-y?" Teresa joked.

"Doesn't Hooligan spell?" Jennifer laughed as Hooligan turned to stare.

"Probably," Teresa said with a wink directed at her cat. "He knows more than he lets on, don't you, baby?" Teresa stood to reach over and pet Hooligan.

"Are you here on this lovely Sunday morning to find out more about Ted and your spare key?" Teresa asked bluntly and resumed her seat.

"Actually, it's Sunday afternoon," Jennifer corrected her friend with a smile. "I did want to catch up with you about your holiday, but I wouldn't be honest if I said I wasn't curious about what happened with Ted while I was gone."

"I'm glad you asked because I think it's a story worth telling. When we last left off with our soap opera, Ted asked Maria for Jennifer's spare key because she, for sure, planned to give it to Ted. It's too bad Jennifer forgot to give him the key before she left town." Teresa shook her head and clucked her tongue.

"Oh, tsk, tsk, yourself!" Jennifer laughed. "I didn't forget to give him the key, as you well know."

"Back to our story," Teresa continued, having difficulty keeping a straight face. "Teresa knew better, so she told Maria she wouldn't give Ted the key unless Jennifer directly asked her to do so. The wise Maria agreed, and to Maria's relief, Ted didn't ask Maria again."

"Well, good, then." Jennifer rubbed the area behind Hooligan's right ear. "I'm glad he gave up on the idea."

"Oh, but our story continues. Early Saturday morning, and I mean early, Ted rings the doorbell of Teresa's lovely home. Teresa has to quickly get dressed to receive visitors, although Teresa does not let Mr. Ted inside."

"Ted showed up at your house without calling first?" Jennifer blurted out, loud enough to disturb the napping Hooligan, who immediately jumped from her lap.

Teresa patted the sofa cushion next to her, and Hooligan sprang to his new resting spot. "Mr. Ted asked Teresa for Jennifer's key, saying that Jennifer meant to give it to Ted before Jennifer left town. Teresa said that it was odd Jennifer hadn't mentioned this to her. Ted told Teresa it was a last-minute decision and that he had promised to check on the place in Jennifer's absence."

"Actually, I told Ted it was unnecessary. I was only gone a few days, and there's really nothing to check," Jennifer objected.

"Teresa told Mr. Ted that Jennifer would be back home either that night or the next day. Surely, Ted could wait and talk to Jennifer about this situation when she returned. However, Ted didn't care for this idea, so Teresa devised a brilliant plan. Teresa retrieved an old key from a bag of miscellaneous keys that didn't fit anything. Teresa handed Ted one of those keys."

"That was quick thinking," Jennifer commended her friend. "But surely it didn't take Ted long to discover that the key didn't open the door to my house."

"Oh, no, it did not take long. Ted was back here at my place in a flash," Teresa said, dropping the third-person narration. "Ted told me I'd given him the wrong key, and I blamed the mistake on you. I told him that was the key Jennifer asked me to keep for her and that I'd never tried the key myself, so I had no idea there was a problem. I got back my fake key and told Ted to discuss it with you when you got home."

"Thank you so much, Teresa!" Jennifer responded with heartfelt appreciation. "I'm sorry you got caught in this mess."

"Don't worry about it." Teresa winked at her. "Truthfully, I kind of enjoyed it, watching Ted in action and thwarting him!" She chuckled while she petted Hooligan. "I don't envy you, though, Jennifer. He's pushy."

"Yes, he definitely overstepped. Ted showed up at my house last night. I'd only been home maybe ten or fifteen minutes. I was relieved that he never mentioned the key. It seemed like he was just there to welcome me back and tell me in person that he'd missed me. Unfortunately, he brought champagne to celebrate, and I accidentally spilled mine, which upset him. I can see why, though. I'd ruined his plans for a romantic evening."

Teresa shook her head emphatically. "No! Spilling something doesn't ruin an evening. If it did, Maria wouldn't have a thing to do with me by now. It's Ted's reaction that's the problem."

"I realize that." Jennifer rubbed her forehead. "I just found out something this morning at church. I met a woman there who was a friend of Ruth's. She told me that Ruth asked the young man who'd lived with her several decades ago to leave her home because he'd been stealing from Ruth."

"Wow!" Teresa's eyes widened. "Ted rubbed me the wrong way from the start, so I've always been a little guarded about him and his motives. Still, it surprises me that he was robbing Ruth."

"Unfortunately, Ruth's friend couldn't recall the young man's name. In fact, she didn't think Ted Filston sounded familiar." Jennifer wanted to give Ted the benefit of the doubt.

"What are the odds, though, that Ruth had two young male houseguests around that time? I think you should assume it was Ted unless you find out otherwise," Teresa advised.

"Well, I know what I have to do," Jennifer said, slowly rising. "Ted's probably working tomorrow, so I should approach him today."

Teresa rose from her seat on the sofa. "Do you need backup? I don't mind coming along."

"No, but thank you. I'll be fine. I'll be glad to get this over with. Then I'll be depressed and need to be home alone for a while to lick my wounds, so to speak." Jennifer sighed loudly. "I will miss Ted, the sweet, charming Ted I thought I knew."

"You've only dated a few months, not long enough to know the true person, Jennifer," her pal said soothingly. "Look, Ted has his good qualities, too. He's just overly pushy, and there's a little question about his past that he hasn't been forthcoming about."

Jennifer pulled her coat closer around her neck as she thanked Teresa again and set out to make the short walk to her car parked at Trinity. Something about the architecture of the old stone church increased her sense of peace, and she retained this tranquility as she drove to the Montgomery Haven Apartments. She pulled into the same space she'd occupied when she'd helped Ted move to his new home. Jennifer looked at the set of keys in her hand and removed the one to Ted's apartment. It was showtime.

Ted looked surprised when he opened the door but immediately broke into a broad grin. "Hey, there! I thought you were resting today." He quickly ushered her inside, startled that she stepped back when he attempted to kiss her. "What's wrong?"

"I'll make this brief, Ted. I'm giving you back your apartment key. This relationship isn't working for me." When he didn't accept the proffered key, she set it on the dinette.

"What? Jennifer!" He shook his head and motioned for her to move to the living room. Jennifer remained standing where she was. "Let's talk about this. I know I upset you last night over the champagne, but I didn't think I did anything that would put an end to our relationship!"

"It's not just that, Ted." She hesitated, not sure how much to tell him. She didn't want him to be angry with either Teresa or Maria, so she refrained from recounting the story she heard from Teresa.

"I think I should have given you space last night," Ted continued. "You were tired, of course, and I shouldn't have let my desire to be with you—"

Jennifer cut him off. "You're the self-confident, leadership type of person," she told him, not wanting to hurt his feelings. "I need someone who respects my boundaries even when they don't agree with them."

Ted shrugged. "I don't know what you mean. I do respect your boundaries. What have I done to make you feel otherwise?"

"Maybe I worded that poorly." Jennifer averted her eyes. "Ted, I'm just not ready for what you want, which is a partnership, your own wording. I don't want to exchange keys. I want my boyfriend to ask before he opens cupboards, looks into bags, and...," she trailed off. "Look, I'm not the woman you want, either. You're ready for someone who is emotionally available right now."

"I know what I want, Jennifer, and that is you. Can't we continue dating and see what happens? I'll try not to be so ... I don't know ... eager for the future."

"I'm asking for my space, Ted. I don't want to date anyone right now. I need to reassess what I want. I met you before I was settled into Tilbrook. I lost my husband, mom, and aunt and hadn't fully gotten past any of that. I left my closest friend behind and all that was familiar to me because I was blindsided by the inheritance of a large estate in another town. I didn't know what I wanted. You provided comfort, Ted, and you can be so endearing, but I wish now that I'd refrained from dating you until I had settled into my new life."

He said nothing and seemed to stare at a spot on the floor tiling. Jennifer patted his arm and backed away toward the door. She thought about saying a parting goodbye or waiting for him to comment but instead retreated, leaving Ted to shut the door when he was ready. To her relief, he didn't follow, and she was careful not to look back toward his apartment. It was better this way, she told herself.

Chapter 17

JENNIFER HAD NOTICED THE small police station multiple times but never thought she'd have cause to visit. The officer at the front desk was polite but didn't seem interested in Jennifer's query about having a substance analyzed. They seemed to be at a standstill, and Jennifer was about to let the matter drop when a middle-aged man dressed in street clothes came from an office space behind the front desk. He directed his inquiry to the police officer, who did a rather poor job of explaining why Jennifer was there.

"Follow me," the nicely dressed gentleman directed Jennifer, motioning her into a small office and pointing her to a chair behind what she assumed to be his desk. "How can we be of assistance?"

Jennifer felt intimidated and suddenly quite foolish. What had she gotten herself into? She stammered through her explanation of why she was suspicious of the amber liquid, the champagne, that she had brought in a glass jar to the police station. Jennifer sheepishly pushed the container toward the man and then pulled a bagged champagne glass from her purse, setting it next to the jar. She felt her face flush and imagined that she looked like a lobster at this point.

"Let me get you some water," the gentleman said, but Jennifer shook her head. "I think it would do you good." He left the room and returned quickly with a filled paper cup. Jennifer took a sip of the chilled water and realized he was wise to insist. He gave her time to drink and settle her nerves. "I'm Detective Kevin Blockard. I know I've seen you before," he informed her in a casual, small-talk tone.

"I don't remember seeing you," Jennifer responded bluntly. "I'm relatively new to Tilbrook." She finished the water, and the detective promptly brought a refill.

"You attend Trinity Presbyterian, don't you? I believe you were there yesterday."

"Oh!" Jennifer was surprised. "Yes, I was. I'm sorry, I don't recall seeing you." She searched the photographs displayed on his desk for clues. The detective wasn't the only one she didn't recognize. The woman and children in the photos were also unfamiliar. Jennifer blushed again when she became aware that the detective was observing her.

"Those are pictures of my wife and kids. My wife, Bonnie, died almost two years ago. My son's twenty-two now and lives in Rotan. My daughter is nineteen and attends college in Rotan. She's rooming with her brother," the detective explained. "Yesterday, I sat behind you in church. I've noticed you there on previous Sundays."

"I guess I don't pay attention to my surroundings like I should," Jennifer tried to cover, embarrassed that she honestly didn't recall seeing the detective prior to today.

"May I ask your name?" Detective Blockard asked politely.

"Oh, yes, of course, I'm Jennifer Shemmer." She was annoyed to feel the blood rushing to her head again. She felt like an idiot. Any degree of confidence she had when she entered the police station had vanished by now.

"I'm pleased to officially meet you, Ms. Shemmer, although I'm sure we would have met at church eventually. Are you feeling better after the water?"

Jennifer nodded and braced herself for the line of questioning she knew would come from the detective. Thankfully, the process wasn't as bad as she anticipated. The detective filled out the report, and she only had to sign in a couple of places. However, when Detective Blockard requested that she be fingerprinted, Jennifer balked. He patiently explained that her prints would be on the champagne glass.

Detective Blockard was reassuring and even fingerprinted Jennifer himself, something she gathered wasn't part of his usual job description. She began to relax. The detective was kind and respectful, and she felt more at ease with him than she did with the officer at the front desk.

"It will take at least a week to get the results back," Detective Blockard said apologetically. "It's considered a non-emergency, plus it goes to a lab in Rotan."

Jennifer chuckled and quickly explained that she hadn't heard of Rotan until relatively recently. Now the city's name came up in conversation almost daily. "I wasn't laughing about the police procedure," she added.

"It never occurred to me that you were," he assured her. "Rotan often comes up in conversation in my household because of both my children."

"You wouldn't prefer to live in Rotan?" Jennifer asked before she realized that was a somewhat personal question for someone here on business.

"No, Tilbrook is my home, and I prefer small towns. My wife and I raised our kids here, at least for the last decade. Rotan is an interesting place to visit, and it's handy for the smaller surrounding towns. As a father, I'm grateful that Rotan has a reputable college for my kids that is a relatively short distance from Tilbrook."

"Yes, that's nice," Jennifer responded politely but then bluntly added, "Am I free to go?" She blushed. What was wrong with her this morning? "I mean, is there anything else I need to fill out or do?"

"That wraps things up for today." He smiled. "Here's my business card, and don't hesitate to call me if you need anything." Suddenly, he removed the card from Jennifer's fingers. "I'm writing my personal cell phone number on the back. That way, you have access to help twenty-four seven. The station lobby is open nine until six, Monday through Saturday, and is closed on Sundays."

"Thank you." She accepted his card again and studied it. "That's kind of you, Detective Blockard."

"Not at all. I'll contact you personally when we have more information, Ms. Shemmer."

Jennifer left the station feeling that an emotional weight had been lifted, one that had gnawed at her. The detective had assured her that if the lab results of the champagne sample indicated no tampering or foul play, Ted would not be notified about the investigation. She was glad of that!

Jennifer had barely made it through her front door when her cell phone rang. She glanced at the screen and saw that it was Ted but wasn't even tempted to pick up. She wasn't surprised that he would try to speak with her again. If anything, Jennifer was astonished that he hadn't tried yesterday. She set her phone and purse on the table.

"Ephraim, I'm home. I just got done taking the champagne sample and glass to the police." She kicked off her shoes and reached for the pair of slippers she now kept downstairs. "I hope I didn't make a fool of myself in doing that. I'm going to feel like a complete moron if the report comes back that the champagne is simply champagne."

Jennifer returned to snatch her cell from the table and plopped down in her favorite chair, adjusting the pillow to fit her back. Time to listen to her messages, specifically, time to listen to what Ted had to say. Jennifer entered her voicemail PIN and put the phone on speaker. After all, she had no secrets to keep from Ephraim.

"Hey, it's me," Ted began. "Jennifer, please, please, give me another chance. I didn't sleep much last night, mainly thinking about you, about us, about what you said the other day at my apartment. If you want me to back off, I can do that, Jennifer. I realize I can be a little overbearing. I think I fell for you pretty early on and didn't take into account that you needed more time to, to, uh, process things. What I do know for certain is that I care about you, and I don't want to say a permanent goodbye. I know I pushed you too hard with that key business. I'm sure Teresa told you what happened. I'm sorry I rushed things between us, and I regret doing that. Again, please, give me another chance to prove myself to you. I think there's been a huge misunderstanding or probably several small misunderstandings that led up to this."

She listened through the long pause that followed, not sure if Ted hadn't already ended the call, but then his voice resumed. "I care about you, Jennifer. More than that, I'm falling in love with you. You're the loveliest, most special woman I've come across, and I don't want to lose you. I believe we can have a wonderful future together. Remember that I'm thinking about you, I'm here for you, and I'm not giving up hope. I'm begging you to return my call."

Jennifer's heart beat uncomfortably—rapidly and forcefully. Her hands trembled slightly as she replayed the message three times. Ted sounded so endearing and remorseful. She contemplated returning his call, but how could she do that after she had just given his name to Detective Blockard for a police report? What would Ted have to say about that if he knew?

"Oh, Ephraim!" she shouted to the empty room. "I don't know! I wish I could be sure that I did the right thing."

Jennifer remained silent and pensive for what seemed to her a long time. Of course, Ephraim hadn't answered or offered comfort, and she would have been shocked if he had. There was always Teresa, though. Jennifer scrolled through the contacts on her phone and selected Teresa Degra. It was a workday for her friend, but since she had freely offered support...

“Teresa?” Jennifer queried but didn’t allow time for a reply. “It’s me, Jennifer, and I’m upset over Ted. Can we meet sometime today? Lunch or after work?”

“Sure, Jennifer, sure,” Teresa’s usually chipper voice was remarkably silky and soothing. “Can you do lunch at Tito’s in about an hour?”

Jennifer thanked her and hung up promptly, respectful that Teresa was on the clock and a busy woman. With a little under an hour to kill, Jennifer phoned Angie but could only leave a message. She then turned her focus to Ephraim.

What if Ephraim was wrong about Ted? Jennifer began to have serious doubts about the night with the champagne. She got up from her chair and sought out the recording device, hitting playback as she resumed her seat. She listened carefully to the distinct, male voice, deeper and gentler than Ted’s in some respects, almost sorrowful, as it said only six words, “Champagne. Do not. Yours. First glass.” Jennifer replayed the recording several times, just as she had on the night when something or someone slapped that champagne glass from her hand.

Still, what if Ephraim was mistaken? He could have been. Was he overly suspicious of Ted, perhaps even a little jealous? Jennifer shivered, partially because of the chill in the house but primarily out of concern that she had acted hastily in doing something as drastic as going to the police. Ephraim was a ghost, a spirit. Had she given his words more credibility because of that? Had she assumed that Ephraim must somehow be more knowing and aware than she? Jennifer’s head began to pound mercilessly. She rose to find an aspirin and a cool glass of water.

What if Ephraim only existed in her mind? Jennifer gasped and rubbed her forehead nervously. Oh, my gosh, what if? However, thoughts of Ruth's diary reassured Jennifer that her aunt would not have journal entries about Ruth's friendship with Ephraim if he were only imaginary. Furthermore, there was the daisy placed on Jennifer's gratitude journal as a symbol of Ephraim's appreciation and proof of his presence in the house. She still had that flower, pressed to keep it preserved. Along with the recording of Ephraim's voice, she had sufficient proof that he was not a figment of either her or her aunt's wild imaginings.

Jennifer circled back to her initial nagging doubt. Had she sabotaged a fulfilling, loving relationship with Ted based on circumstantial evidence against him and an overactive imagination? Teresa was a savvy person and strongly supported Jennifer's decision to end things with Ted. On the other hand, Teresa had unfounded misgivings about him from the start and couldn't explain why. Maria was a sensitive, insightful soul, and she liked Ted. Angie seemed to like him, too, although Jennifer had never allowed her the opportunity to meet him.

Annoyed that she had nixed Angie's invitation for Ted to join them over the Thanksgiving holiday. Jennifer's head continued to throb beyond the relief of a single aspirin. She got up to retrieve an additional pill and refill her water.

She glanced at her watch, noting that she would need to leave in ten minutes to make it to Tito's for lunch. Jennifer considered phoning Teresa to cancel but couldn't off-hand come up with a convincing reason to do so, at least nothing that her perceptive friend would believe. It amazed her that she thought a visit with Teresa was a good idea an hour ago. Now, Jennifer felt like she was betraying Ted. In addition, Tito's was in his neighborhood, making the restaurant's location oddly unsettling.

Well, there was nothing to do but soldier on. Jennifer applied her lipstick and redid her ponytail. She looked at herself critically in the mirror, on the verge of tears. She grabbed a tissue from the box beside her, ready to blot her watery hazel eyes. But a male voice directly behind her, soft but distinct, caused her to jerk around with a start.

"Stand firm."

Jennifer froze on the spot, darting her eyes back and forth to detect the source of the voice. She saw nothing. Recovering slightly, she stepped into the hallway and loudly called out, "Where are you?"

There was nothing more than a soft, pleasant, musky cologne odor in the hallway, the same scent as the night of the champagne incident with Ted. Jennifer associated the cologne with Ephraim and felt more at ease and confident.

"Did you just say that I should stand firm?" Jennifer asked, turning her head left and right as if addressing a large audience. "Stand firm, as in don't give in? As in don't call Ted?"

She hoped for an audible reply but didn't get one. There was no time to spare for a recording session with Ephraim, something she truly regretted. She looked at her watch again and realized she'd be a few minutes late even if she left immediately.

Jennifer snatched up her coat and purse before rushing off. Whatever had just transpired between her and Ephraim served to bolster her outlook and soothe her nerves. Thank goodness she hadn't succumbed to Ted's pleas and caved to his voice message! Teresa had joked that Jennifer was better off adopting a cat than reconnecting with Ted. Jennifer happily anticipated what her pal would have to say over lunch at Tito's.

Unfortunately, the topic she most wished to discuss was off-limits with Teresa. Today was the first time Jennifer heard Ephraim's voice without the aid of a device. She hadn't dreamed that was possible, yet it had just happened! She smiled as she glanced at her reflection in the rearview mirror. Her connection to Ephraim was growing stronger.

Chapter 18

THE CHIME OF THE doorbell in the early evening sent Jennifer's heart thudding wildly. Could it be Ted? Her initial instinct was to ignore the bell, but whoever was at the door began to knock loudly and insistently. Jennifer slowly walked to the peephole.

The illumination wasn't ideal at dusk, yet she was reluctant to turn on the porch light and give away the fact that she was indeed home. On the other hand, her Toyota was visible, so any visitor would assume she wasn't out. Jennifer squinted to discern the figure on the other side of the door. A man, but to her relief, not Ted. Jennifer hesitantly switched on the light and loudly called, "Who is it, please?"

"Detective Blockard," a muffled voice answered. "I wanted to give you an update, Ms. Shemmer."

Jennifer scrutinized him through the peephole. He looked different than she recalled, yet she could see the resemblance between this person at her door and the one she'd talked with at the police station on Monday. Slowly, she cracked open the door, eyeing him with some uncertainty before saying, "Oh, Detective. Yes. I'm just surprised to see you."

"I'm sorry if I startled you, Ms. Shemmer," he began apologetically. "Usually, I'd telephone, but I live a few blocks from here and decided on the spur of the moment to stop by before heading home. Do you mind?"

Jennifer wasn't sure if she minded or not. In some ways, she found it disconcerting to see the detective standing there, but on the other hand, he had been very kind and helpful to her at the station.

"No, that's fine," Jennifer answered politely. "What did you have to tell me?"

Detective Blockard hesitated, waiting for Jennifer to invite him inside or come out onto the porch. When she did not attempt to undo the door's security chain, the detective said, "It's too early for the results from the chemical analysis. I don't expect to get that report until next week, possibly even the following week. I want to give you a heads-up that Edward Filston has a history with the police, but I'm not at liberty to discuss the details with you at this time."

Jennifer shook her head slowly. "I'm interested in Ted Filston, not Edward Filston, whoever that is." She wondered at the competence of this small-town detective.

"Edward Theodore Filston," Kevin Blockard elaborated, and when Jennifer said nothing, he added, "Theodore, his middle name shortened to Ted."

"My Ted was born on July 22," Jennifer countered, still not convinced.

"So was mine," the detective said and then looked slightly uncomfortable with his choice of wording. "The fingerprints on the glass you provided, Ms. Shemmer, match those of Edward Theodore Filston. Of course, your fingerprints were also on the glass, as we knew would be the case."

Jennifer paled slightly, the impact of the detective's words finally registering. She wondered what history Ted had with the police but simultaneously worried about the information Mr. Blockard might have gleaned about Jennifer from her own set of prints. Jennifer consoled herself that it couldn't be anything too embarrassing. Besides, she possessed a valid fingerprint clearance card needed to work with children. However, Detective Blockard might have found out about that one speeding ticket, but since she had paid it promptly—

"Ms. Shemmer?" The detective's voice cut through Jennifer's wandering thoughts. "Are you okay?"

"Yes, of course," Jennifer said, gaining her composure. "This has just caught me by surprise. Ted's not dangerous, though, right? I mean, lots of people have minor scuffs with the law and end up with a history, correct?" Jennifer looked at the detective for reassurance but found none.

"My advice is to be cautious, Ms. Shemmer. As I said, we haven't received the results from the champagne sample you provided. Maybe I'm premature in contacting you at this point, but I feel it's best to be proactive and armed with the information that Edward Filston, or Ted, does have some history to consider."

"Well," Jennifer half-laughed, even though she didn't think any of this was funny, "Detective Blockard, you have a way of not giving out much information while appearing to provide information." Jennifer immediately felt terrible for speaking to him in this manner. After all, none of this was his fault, and it actually was nice of him to swing past her place to warn her. "Forget I said that. Please forgive me," Jennifer recanted, breaking eye contact with the man standing before her.

"No need to apologize." The middle-aged detective smiled dutifully. "Do you have any questions I might answer?"

Jennifer bit her lip to repress the initial retort she had for him. She had just finished telling him she was sorry, so why tell him now that he wouldn't provide answers even if she did have questions? Instead, she gave a meek, "No."

"You've got my card and cell phone number if you need it. Might I suggest that you only meet with Edward Filston in public places? Don't invite him into your home, and don't go to his," Kevin Blockard advised in a fatherly fashion, or maybe it was a police-like manner. "Just as a precaution," he added with a smile.

"I broke it off with Ted," Jennifer told the detective. "He's called, but I haven't even picked up the phone or returned his messages." Jennifer wondered why she was telling Mr. Blockard this.

The detective smiled but said nothing in response. He tipped his head briefly and stepped back from the door. "Have a nice evening, Ms. Shemmer."

Jennifer finally unlatched the security chain to open the door wider, attempting to see where Detective Blockard had parked. She was curious as to what his vehicle looked like. Perhaps the station let him use a police car.

Detective Blockard suddenly turned in her direction. "I hope to see you this weekend."

"What?" That caught Jennifer by surprise. She was about to object, but fortunately, Kevin continued before she had a chance to rebuke him.

"Sunday? Won't you be attending Trinity on Sunday?" he asked matter-of-factly.

"Oh, yes, I guess. Probably. I might." What was wrong with her, she wondered? Was she intimidated because he was on the police force?

Kevin Blockard nodded and, this time, did retreat to his car, a vehicle that Jennifer couldn't quite make out in the darkness.

She absentmindedly shut the door and groaned, slapping her forehead with her palm. "What's wrong with me? I let him stand outside the entire time and didn't even think to let him in the house! He must think I'm really ungrateful and rather prickly!" She caught a faint whiff of musky cologne in the air. Ephraim. Maybe it was better that she hadn't asked the detective inside. If he smelled the masculine scent of cologne in her house, he might justifiably assume Ted had been there, and she did tell Mr. Blockard that she had broken it off with Ted.

Jennifer ruminated over the information the detective had given her. Edward Filston. Hmm. She wondered if Ted used to go by his first name, Edward. If he did, that might account for why the old-timers didn't recognize the name Ted Filston.

It was Friday evening, typically a date night for Jennifer when she had been seeing Ted. She thought she should do something, anything, to help take her mind off her current romantic woes. Jennifer went into the den and hauled several boxes labeled "Christmas" to the living room. She carefully removed the tape and white tissue paper from one of the boxes and slowly unwrapped its contents, mainly ornaments for the Christmas tree.

Alex had given her this one, she reflected, as she held a delicate glass angel up to the light. It was one of his rare romantic gestures early in their marriage. Alex said this was an angel for his special angel, Jennifer. She picked up the next ornament, a small hanging gold photo frame, a portrait of the two of them just prior to their marriage. Oh, and here was a rather expensive crystal apple that Alex bought for Jennifer despite her objection to spending that much money on a single ornament. He wanted her to have this crystal apple, he said, because Jennifer was an exceptional teacher and deserved the best. Jennifer plopped down on the floor and studied more of the box's contents.

Well, if Jennifer drank, this would certainly cause her to go looking for alcohol. Her attempt to cheer herself up over Ted only served to depress her over the dissolution of her marriage to Alex. How could Alex have cheated on her? How could he have chosen Charlotte over her after sixteen years of marriage, especially when he knew that Jennifer's mom was in failing health?

Quickly, Jennifer rewrapped each ornament in crumpled tissue paper and repacked them haphazardly. She lifted the box and returned it to the den, along with the other Christmas boxes she had intended to open. Jennifer glanced up at the wall portraits of Aunt Ruth, both of which seemed intent on watching Jennifer tonight. She smiled at her aunt's images and gave a slight wave.

Still in the mood to decorate for Christmas but not willing to do so with her own nostalgia, Jennifer went upstairs to the mystery room. There were only two cardboard boxes Jennifer recalled seeing that had been marked "Christmas" by Aunt Ruth. It might be fun to go through them tonight. Perhaps she could go through the contents with Ephraim. He and Aunt Ruth had likely done the same thing together over the years.

Jennifer's back lightly spasmed when she attempted to lift the heavier of the cartons, warning her against her initial plan to bring them downstairs. Instead, she opted to move the larger of the two to her bedroom. With the box at her feet, she positioned herself on the bed and gently stooped to retrieve one object at a time. She invited Ephraim to join her in looking through the contents, holding each item up for him to observe—wherever he was.

"Do you remember this one, Ephraim?" she asked, not expecting an answer. Jennifer studied the tiny carolers dressed in brightly colored winter clothing. "I'll have to set up a tree tomorrow, but downstairs, of course. This will look nice hanging on the tree, don't you agree? I don't know what Aunt Ruth liked best, but I believe my favorites so far are these odd-shaped but cute hand-painted ornaments. They look early-twentieth century. Maybe not. I wish you could point out your favorites, Ephraim."

Jennifer sighed. She could sense his presence, but she was unable to hear his voice. "I'm going to separate what we'll use tomorrow from what we'll leave in the box for another year. I only have a small Christmas tree that my mom and I used. After my divorce, I didn't keep the big tree that Alex and I had. Maybe next year, I'll feel like getting a larger one. Did Ruth buy a live Christmas tree? I haven't seen—" Jennifer abruptly stopped, listening carefully. She thought she heard a noise downstairs. She instinctively rose to her feet and hurried to the top of the staircase.

Ted stood between the entryway and the living room. A shocked Jennifer wondered how he'd gotten inside. She swore under her breath when she realized that she'd forgotten to lock up after Detective Blockard left. Of all the times to have forgotten.

"W-what are you doing here, Ted? You need to go," Jennifer commanded, standing frozen at the top of the stairs.

"Why aren't you answering my calls?" Ted countered. "I think I have a right to talk with you. I have a right to have my calls answered." He stumbled a little as he made his way into her living room.

"Ted, you've been drinking," Jennifer inferred as she rapidly descended the stairs. "I'll talk with you on the phone tomorrow but not here tonight. Go home and sleep. You'll feel better in the morning."

"Don't tell me how I'll feel," slurred Ted. "I'll talk to you now, right here. I'm here, you're here, we're here. Here is where we talk."

"No, Ted. No. You're going to leave. I'll call for a ride for you since you're not in a position to drive yourself home." Jennifer hated the idea of leaving his SUV at her house, but the alternative was worse. She reached for her cell on the table.

"Oh, no, you don't," he retorted and sprang toward Jennifer, knocking the phone from her hand. "You're going to listen."

Jennifer bent to retrieve her phone, but he blocked her. "Ted, get out of my way. I told you I'd talk with you in the morning. Now's not the time."

"Why are you acting this way, Jennifer?" He grabbed her by the shoulders and shook her with increasing force. "Why couldn't you be different?"

"Ted, let go!" Jennifer ordered loudly. "I want you to leave now!"

"Oh, I don't think so, Jen," he said softly with a smirk. "I'm done with all your rules. All your rules, Jen. No, I don't think so. Now, I think we'll play by mine." He gripped her blouse and yanked until the material tore.

Jennifer slapped his face with a force that made her hand burn. "Get out, Ted!" she screamed just before he landed a solid punch to her jaw. She fell backward, hitting her head against what she thought to be an edge of a table. Ted took the opportunity to leap on top of her, unzipping her jeans. Jennifer was crushed under his weight, unable to defend herself.

In an instant, Ted was propelled upward, away from Jennifer. He slammed headlong into the wall, causing a heavy, framed picture to fall and crash beside him. "You little bitch," he seethed and returned to throw his body unmercifully on top of Jennifer's.

"Stop, Ted! Please, no! I didn't push you!" she pleaded, but with little breath available.

Everything in that moment seemed surreal. Jennifer's head throbbed from the blow against the table, and the room spun with increasing speed. She could barely breathe with the weight of Ted on top of her. She could have sworn that the two of them were outside in a ferocious windstorm, lightning flashing around them. Despite Ted's hot, alcohol-tinged breath against her skin, she felt the chill of the air. It was impossible to know what was real and what was not. Was this all simply a dream, an awful nightmare? Her body ached with head-to-toe pain, bringing with it the uneasy awareness that this was reality.

"Freeze! Don't move!" ordered a vaguely familiar male voice from the doorway.

Jennifer was in no state to make sense of what was happening. Ted still lay heavily against her, but at least the room had stopped spinning, and the fierce storm appeared to be over. She lay there helplessly in agony.

Suddenly, the full weight of Ted was off of her. Jennifer heard a masculine voice but couldn't make out what it said. She heard clinking, some kind of metallic sound, then there appeared to be more muffled voices, all male. Jennifer closed her eyes. She could feel her head being lifted and gently examined. She was cradled while someone placed a blanket or other piece of fabric over her.

"Can you hear me, Jennifer?" Again, the voice was vaguely familiar, but no one she could place at the moment. "Jennifer, try to open your eyes. Open your eyes, Jennifer!"

She did as the voice commanded, finding that her gaze met that of Detective Blockard. If she had any pride left at this moment, she would have blushed solidly.

"I'm going to take her to Bilmore Hospital," Detective Blockard said, apparently speaking to someone behind him as he turned his head away from Jennifer. "I think she needs to have her head imaged, and Tilbrook doesn't have the equipment." Jennifer couldn't make out the other's response. "No," Detective Blockard continued. "It would take longer to get non-emergency medical transportation, and Ms. Shemmer should have someone accompany her."

Jennifer attempted to sit up, and the detective cautiously helped her while keeping his grip firm. "I'll be okay," she managed to say. "I don't need a hospital. I think I just need some sleep."

"I think you're going to be all right, too, but you do need to be checked over," Detective Blockard said flatly. "The guys are taking care of your Mr. Filston, and I'll run you to Bilmore. Let's get your coat on."

Jennifer became acutely aware of her ripped blouse and her partially pulled-down jeans. She felt mortified, but the detective acted matter-of-factly and simply helped her with her coat. "I should change clothes," Jennifer told him, although she didn't relish climbing the stairs to the bedroom.

"No, you shouldn't." Detective Blockard gently spun her around toward the door. "Where's your purse? Do you mind if I get your keys out?"

Jennifer slowly shook her head, realizing that it was painful to do so. At least the detective asked permission before rummaging through her purse. Before Jennifer knew it, she was inside Detective Blockard's car, a practical family sedan with comfortable seating. He reached around to buckle her in securely before taking his place on the driver's side. He fastened his own seatbelt before again asking Jennifer if she was all right and ready to go.

She made one final protest, even though she knew it was futile. "Detective Blockard, I appreciate all you've done for me, but I honestly think it's unnecessary for you to drive me all the way to Bilmore." She paused before adding, "On a Friday night, too."

He chuckled very softly, and Jennifer realized how ridiculous it sounded to add that last part. "When it comes to head injuries, it's best to err on the side of caution."

"Caution! You use that word a lot, you know, Detective," Jennifer was feeling achy, and her mood matched. It didn't help that one of the few words Ephraim voiced to her also dealt with being cautious.

"Kevin," he replied in an even tone. "I've been calling you Jennifer tonight, and I think it's fair that you address me by my first name. It's Kevin." When she didn't answer, he added lightly, "We go to the same church, too. Don't you think that sooner or later, we'd call one another by our first names?"

Jennifer still didn't reply. She was upset by Ted, knowing that if this Detective Blockard hadn't arrived when he did, her fate would have been much worse than several blows to the head, scrapes, and severely bruised pride. Come to think of it, why had Detective Blockard shown up in her living room at just the right time?

Chapter 19

JENNIFER WAS GLAD WHEN the hospital doctor finally gave her clearance to return home. She had spent hours in the emergency area and was very displeased to be subjected to what she regarded as an unnecessarily thorough examination, plus photographs of her injuries. The wait for the CAT scan of her head and the results took the longest, pushing the time into the early waking hours of the morning. At least she hadn't been admitted to the hospital. Jennifer looked at the clock in the emergency ward and wondered how easy it would be to get transportation to Tilbrook at six in the morning on a Saturday. She'd ask at the front desk.

"I bet you're anxious to get home," Detective Blockard greeted Jennifer immediately as she exited the swinging emergency doors.

"Oh, you're here," Jennifer said in surprise. "Are you going to drive me back?"

"Of course, I am," he replied evenly. "I brought you here. I wouldn't go off and leave you stranded."

Jennifer was pleased to see him but puzzled. The detective looked like he could use a cup of coffee and a shave, not necessarily in that order. "Did you drive back to Bilmore Hospital this morning?" She hoped that was the case and that he hadn't spent the entire night stuck in the lobby waiting for her release.

"No, I've been here as long as you have." He smiled slightly. "I bet I got more sleep than you did, though. I managed to doze off and on."

"You didn't have to stay." She felt guilty that she hadn't thought to tell him to go home when they entered the hospital last night. "I wouldn't have expected you to. That's going way beyond your job description."

"I wasn't going to leave you in the hospital with no friends or family present," Detective Blockard replied blandly. "Do you have all the paperwork you need for discharge?" Although he asked, he checked at the ER desk without waiting for her response. Apparently, Jennifer was given the green light because he smiled at her and motioned for her to walk ahead of him.

"I'm sorry to have been such a nuisance," Jennifer started to apologize as he opened the passenger door of his sedan. "I bet you weren't expecting all that to happen after you left my house the first time last night, Detective," she said, referring to the visit he had made to warn her about Ted.

"Kevin," he corrected. "Do you mind if we stop for a bite to eat here in Bilmore? We're close by to a mom-and-pop place that makes great homemade breakfasts. I used to bring my kids here on Saturdays before they moved to Rotan."

Jennifer preferred to go home, but how could she refuse a guy who had just spent the entire night sitting in a hospital lobby waiting for her, a woman he barely knew? She hesitated, though, when it dawned on her that she was wearing what little remained of a ripped blouse underneath her coat. "I'm not suitable," she began and then added, "Kevin," to soften her refusal.

"You mean your clothes?" He glanced at her from the driver's seat. "We'll sit by the door where it's coolest, and you can leave your coat on. You look fine."

Jennifer doubted very much that she looked fine, especially with her facial bruising beginning to darken, but realized that her protests were in vain. The detective obviously was hungry and wanted to eat. It was possible he hadn't had dinner last night. "Were you on duty?" she suddenly asked.

"What?" Kevin asked blankly, already turning into Bria's Eatery. "Do you mean today?"

"Last night. I thought you said yesterday, around dusk, that you were on your way home and decided to drop by my place to give me information about Ted. Did you have to go back to work afterward?"

"No, I didn't," he answered and quickly got out of the car to meet Jennifer on the passenger side. He held the door open for her. "I was off-duty both times when I came to your home. I got a call on my cell telling me that you were in danger. I don't live far from you, so I immediately went to your house and saw an SUV parked there. I figured that would belong to Filston, so I called the station as a precaution."

Jennifer forgot her awkwardness about her appearance as she slid into the booth across from Detective Blockard and digested the information. "You got a call on your personal phone about me?" She could hear her voice rising and hoped it wasn't noticeable to the customers in the small café.

Kevin nodded, briefly thanking the waiter who brought two menus and glasses of water. "Yes. A man phoned and said that Jennifer Shemmer was currently in danger. I asked who was calling, and he told me a concerned doctor. Of course, I shot over to your place as quickly as possible, and we know the rest. It's odd that my phone didn't register any caller identification for this ... concerned doctor. No name and no number. I don't recall that ever happening on this phone before." She shivered involuntarily. "Are you chilly, Jennifer? We could move further from the door if you'd like."

"No, I'm fine. Are you sure that's all the man said?" she pursued. "He only said that I was in danger and that he was a concerned doctor? What were his exact words?"

Kevin smiled, and Jennifer realized she sounded like a police officer interrogating him. "I'm paraphrasing, Jennifer, because his words were fragmented. He said your name. When I heard 'current danger,' I rushed to your house. Do you have a friend who's a doctor?"

"No," she said adamantly and then felt disloyal to Ephraim. "I have few friends here since I'm so new to town, and my only male friend was Ted, and he certainly didn't make the phone call to you." Jennifer knew that her tone was slightly crabby. "I don't even have a doctor in Tilbrook."

Kevin nodded. "It is a mystery, but one that brought you help, so I'm glad whoever it was called me." He passed a menu to Jennifer and signaled for the waiter to bring two coffees. As an afterthought, he asked, "Do you like coffee?"

"Not really," Jennifer confessed, "but I'll drink it with lots of sugar and cream or milk." She quickly and profusely assured Kevin that he didn't need to order a different beverage for her. It was nice that he seemed to care, and Jennifer was aware that she had initially treated the detective a little coolly. He deserved better, she mused.

When their hardy breakfasts arrived, she thanked Kevin for suggesting they eat at this quaint café before heading home. He asked Jennifer to pass the pepper, and she, in turn, asked for the cream.

"I told you so," Kevin said with a twinkle in his deep brown eyes.

When he didn't elaborate, Jennifer looked up from her breakfast plate and studied his face. He was relatively nice-looking, probably even more so when he was clean-shaven and given a chance to have a full night's sleep in his own bed. His salt-and-pepper hair, although cut short, was in need of a quick combing. Jennifer could tell that Kevin worked out. Perhaps he had to for his job on the police force. Physical strength was an asset when pulling people such as Ted off of people such as Jennifer. Again, she gave an involuntary shiver.

"I think you're still suffering a little shock from last night," Kevin said quietly, almost to himself.

"No, I'm fine, really. What did you mean when you said that you told me so?"

"That we'd see each other over the weekend." He grinned and laughed softly at her expression.

"Yes, you were absolutely correct." Although Jennifer agreed, she didn't feel like joining in the amusement. "What will be the next step with Ted?"

Detective Blockard knew exactly what she was referring to. "Unfortunately, Jennifer, he'll be released on bail. It won't surprise me if that's not already happened. You'll have to be extra careful, and I'll check on you often and have officers swing past regularly. It's a small town, so I doubt he'll try anything, but," Kevin hesitated, "it pays to be cautious. Yes, there's that word again. I know how much you like to hear it," he teased. "We'll get a restraining order in place, A.S.A.P."

"I hadn't thought about bail that quickly." Jennifer was a little shaken.

"Yes. How did Filston get into your place? The door didn't appear forced. Does he have a key?"

"I stupidly forgot to lock up after you left last night," Jennifer admitted after a few seconds of hesitation. "I was upstairs going through my aunt's Christmas decorations when I heard a noise downstairs. When I went to check, there was Ted, already inside. No, he doesn't have a key."

"Always lock your doors, even in a small town," Kevin advised but was kind not to remind Jennifer that she had kept the safety chain on her door throughout the detective's visit, not inviting him inside despite the cold. It was ironic that Filston managed to walk in unimpeded.

Jennifer nodded and took some cash from her purse when the waiter brought the bill. Kevin pushed her money back across the table. "I should pay for breakfast," she insisted.

"It's the very least I can do, considering that you came to my rescue and didn't get a chance to return to your own home until the next morning."

Kevin shoved the money across the table to Jennifer a second time. "Nope, forget it. It's on me. After what you've been through, you deserve to be treated to something nice. Anyway, I have wanted to come here again but have difficulty getting up the motivation to drive to Bilmore on my own. Next time we come, though, I'm hoping we can skip the hospital."

Jennifer wanted to ask if he genuinely intended that there would be a future visit, but she didn't have the nerve. Besides, she wasn't sure she wanted a second time. Kevin was kind and had been there for her when she was in need, but she was still reeling from her relationship with Ted.

Kevin was mainly quiet during the drive back to Tilbrook, and Jennifer wondered if he had misgivings about his casual friendliness over breakfast. He resumed his role as detective and brought up the delicate matter of police access to Jennifer's hospital records for the case against Filston. Jennifer shuddered. She'd love to forget the whole affair, but Ted did need to be reined in so he wouldn't hurt anyone else. Jennifer knew that Kevin took it for granted that she would press charges and fill out every form the detective presented without question.

When Kevin eventually pulled up to Jennifer's home, he ordered her to stay in the car and give him her house key. She was silently obedient because protesting would be a waste of time. Clearly, he wanted to make sure the so-called crime scene was safe. Jennifer knew it would be because, after all, Doctor Ephraim was in the house, probably anticipating her return. But Kevin didn't know that. He needed to fulfill his role as protector and make sure the house was free of Ted and any other possible intruder. Jennifer watched as the good detective made his way back to the sedan, approaching her on the passenger side.

"Coast is clear," he announced. "The place is as you left it. I turned the lights out, including the one in the bedroom. You don't need them at this time of day." He smiled. "Lovely Christmas ornaments, by the way."

"My aunt's. Ruth Gaitley's," Jennifer emphasized. "Did you know her? She also attended Trinity, but probably a while ago."

"I didn't know her." Kevin shook his head. "Her name sounds familiar, however, and I know I've heard your home referred to as the Gaitley house."

"I guess if you didn't know her, that means she didn't have a police record," she joked.

Kevin laughed softly, a gentle, easy laugh that made Jennifer like him just a little bit more. "I guess she didn't have a record. I'll walk you inside before I take off. I'm sure the doctor's orders were to rest today and probably for the next few days. You did have several nasty blows to your head." He observed her bruising but decided not to comment on it.

"I'm not going to do anything strenuous," Jennifer agreed, already thinking it was time for another aspirin. "Thank you again, Kevin, for all you've done for me. I truly appreciate it!"

"I'm just glad I got that call. I'm going to listen for you to lock the front door and secure the safety chain, Jennifer.

Please don't, and I repeat, don't let anyone in the house unless you are one hundred percent certain who it is. Whatever you do, don't let Filston talk to you. If he even attempts a phone call, let me know. Do you still have my card with my number?"

"Yes, it's on the table next to the landline. I'll make sure I also enter your number into my cell." She had no problem agreeing to all of the detective's requests.

Jennifer opened the blinds to watch Kevin climb into his sedan and subsequently drive off toward the west. She backed away from the window and walked toward the phone. To her relief, she had no messages. At this point, she didn't even feel like talking to Angie. Gingerly, Jennifer climbed the staircase, looking forward to the softness and comfort of her bed. However, the ornaments still sprawled over the bedspread reminded her of Ephraim and her unfinished business with him. Jennifer had profusely thanked Detective Blockard for coming to her rescue Friday night, but the one who made that possible was Ephraim. Ephraim, the concerned doctor, who somehow managed to call Kevin's cell phone.

"Ephraim, I know you're the one who got help for me," Jennifer spoke out loud. "You're also the one who slammed Ted into the wall after he jumped me the first time. Thank you!"

She continued moving her aunt's Christmas ornaments until the bed was cleared. As tempting as it was to lie down against the soft sheets, Jennifer felt dirty from Ted's attack and her stint in the emergency ward. She removed her badly-torn blouse but kept it as Kevin had instructed.

She started to draw a warm bubble bath but turned off the faucet within minutes. First, she wanted to do something for Ephraim to express her appreciation, something more concrete than words.

Jennifer put on a clean pair of jeans and a pullover sweater. As much as she knew it would upset Detective Blockard if she were to leave her home today, Jennifer had an insatiable impulse to drive to the old cemetery and visit Ephraim's grave. She reasoned with herself that the trip could wait a few days, but her emotions got the final say. She carefully made her way down the stairs to grab her purse and a warm coat. There was no time like the present, and if she went to the cemetery now, she'd be free to spend the rest of the day relaxing as ordered.

She hoped the small grocery where she purchased the daisies for Ephraim's grave would be open today. Well, it was Saturday, not Sunday, so the odds were good. When she arrived, she was pleased to see that the store was indeed doing business. Jennifer browsed the floral selection, but there wasn't much to choose from save a cluster of four red roses. She went ahead and bought it, along with a boxed chef salad for dinner. With her purchase complete, she wound her Toyota toward the old cemetery, anxious to see the gravesite again.

Usually, Jennifer felt sorrow or discomfort visiting a cemetery. She hadn't been to Aunt Ruth's grave since the burial service, yet she had already returned to this old cemetery several times. It was as if she were visiting a friend, greeting him with lovely roses to brighten his day.

Jennifer walked directly to Ephraim's tombstone. She placed the flowers as she read the inscription on the marker, sad that he had been fatally shot, cutting his life short. Then Jennifer remembered his son, Ephraim Walson, Jr., and carefully removed a single rose to place on this man's grave. "Died in 1938," she read. So sad that he passed before his dad, way too young.

"I'm so sorry that happened to you, Ephraim," Jennifer spoke directly to the son's tombstone. As she stood there viewing the graveyard, the complexity of there being two Ephraims finally hit her. She had just finished addressing the son as Ephraim. She didn't call him Junior. She didn't call him Ephraim Junior. Hmm. When her aunt wrote about Ephraim in her diary, was she actually referencing the senior man, Doctor Ephraim? Why hadn't Jennifer thought about this earlier since there clearly were two men named Ephraim Walson? Jennifer knew for certain that it was Doctor Ephraim's spirit she spoke with on a regular basis. So, the senior man still occupied the house, but what about the son? Was he there, too, also answering to the name of Ephraim? Which Ephraim was Ruth so attached to? Father or son?

Jennifer frowned as her eyes slowly moved from one tombstone to the next. She'd accomplished her main task today, bringing flowers to express her gratitude to Doctor Ephraim for rescuing her from Ted. Now it was time for her to take care of herself. She longed to get cleaned up, dress in her coziest fleece, and relax in bed.

Upon returning home, it didn't take Jennifer more than thirty minutes to ready herself for her inviting bed. She pulled the soft comforter over her freshly bathed but still aching body and rested her head on the feather pillow. The back of her skull began to throb again, and she looked at the clock to see if enough time had elapsed for her to take another pain pill safely. It had, so she willed herself to get up for the sake of soothing her headache.

Jennifer was about to get back in bed when she noticed the single red rose resting on top of her journal. Her mouth flew open, but no words came. She quickly reached for the flower and touched the satiny edges tenderly with her other hand. This was definitely the same type of rose she had put on Ephraim's grave less than an hour ago. Same color, same length, same everything.

"Oh, Ephraim," she whispered and, despite her throbbing head, went to get the digital recorder. Jennifer returned to the bedroom and pushed back the comforter to sit directly on the sheets.

She turned on the device and asked if the red rose was from Doctor Ephraim. She was rewarded with an answer in the affirmative. Tears slowly trickled down her face.

"Ephraim, I have some important questions for you. At least important to me," Jennifer started, not quite sure if she was up to tackling this now but bent on getting answers to questions that pounded in her head as much as the pain from the injuries Ted caused last night. "Aunt Ruth referred to Ephraim as her friend. She mentions the name repeatedly in her diary. Are you that Ephraim, or was it your son?"

Jennifer stopped to replay the conversation. "My son," said the male voice on the recording.

Again, Jennifer readied the digital device for another question. "Is your son, Ephraim Junior, here with you now?"

After allowing sufficient time for a response, she switched to playback mode.

"No. He left."

It was tedious manipulating the recorder, especially with a throbbing head, but Jennifer didn't want to miss this opportunity. Doctor Ephraim was coming through clearer today than she'd yet experienced. "When did your son leave?"

"When Ruth died."

Jennifer was too busy switching between record and replay to process fully what Doctor Ephraim was telling her, but she recognized the significance. "Why did he leave when Ruth died?"

"Love," the masculine voice answered.

"Love?" Jennifer repeated, at this point forgetting her head pain. "Are you saying that your son loved my aunt?"

"Yes."

"He loved her? Do you mean like friendship? Aunt Ruth was ninety-six, and your son was thirty-one when he died."

She played back the recording, but there was silence. Jennifer tried to think of how to rephrase her question to Doctor Ephraim. Then it finally dawned on her that Ephraim Junior was a young man when he died. Her aunt would have been ... thirteen. Ruth spent a great deal of time outdoors, appreciating and studying nature. Ephraim Junior rented the adjacent guesthouse and was fatally shot with an arrow while on that property. The teenage Ruth walked that area frequently. Suddenly, Jennifer saw things from a different perspective.

"In love with Ruth," a male voice said. Jennifer jumped when she realized that this voice didn't come from the digital recorder. In fact, she hadn't hit either the record or the replay.

"Ruth loved Ephraim, too, didn't she?" Jennifer asked softly, setting the device aside absentmindedly. "She grew up in front of him, so to speak, didn't she?"

"Yes. Both in love."

"I know this is a painful subject, Ephraim. You may not know the answer, but was your son accidentally hit with that arrow, or do you believe he was intentionally killed?" Jennifer regretted asking the question as soon as it left her lips, but it was too late to retract.

"Intentional. My belief."

Jennifer hesitated. It was difficult to know what to say to that. "I am very sorry. Did you and your son stay behind on Earth because of that?"

"Initially."

"It got complicated, huh," Jennifer gently stated more than questioned. "Your son loved Ruth, and she loved him, and you loved your son."

"Complicated," he agreed.

"I like that we can now communicate without this." She picked up the recording device and held it up briefly before placing it on the nightstand.

"Yes."

Jennifer sighed. "What about my aunt? Did she go with your son when she died? I mean, did you see them leave together?" Jennifer was a little afraid to hear his answer, in case it went against her hopes.

"Yes. Together." The male voice was incredibly gentle.

With this information, she let out an audible sob and reached for a tissue. She was happy for her aunt. Ruth was very much loved and reunited with Ephraim's son on a nonphysical level. Jennifer briefly pictured her aunt, much younger in her newly-found form, joined hand in hand with the young Ephraim.

She positioned herself under the comforter again, resting her increasingly sore head, daubing her eyes with the already saturated tissue. "I'm tired and not feeling well," Jennifer told Doctor Ephraim. "As you know, it was a rough night, and I hated going to the hospital," she said with emphasis, like an upset child. She closed her eyes and then as an afterthought, added, "If your son stayed for Ruth and then left when Ruth died, why didn't you go, too?"

At first, Jennifer thought that Doctor Ephraim must have left the room, for there was no immediate response. She grimaced as she daubed at her tears again.

"You," he finally replied.

Jennifer opened her eyes but kept her head resting on the pillow. "You mean you stayed because of me?"

"Yes," he answered without hesitation.

She had no idea how to respond to that and started crying harder, grabbing a handful of tissues at this point. Jennifer felt a light stroking of her hair and a brush against her temple. The sensation was comforting, and soon the bedroom held the slightest hint of cologne. His touch was soothing and did more to curb her headache than any pain medication. Jennifer slept soundly in this lulled state. When she finally awoke hours later, the cologne scent had vanished, but the red rose was on the bed beside her.

Chapter 20

JENNIFER TILTED HER HEAD to the left, studying her face in the bathroom mirror. She felt she looked rather like a lopsided raccoon, the punch she took from Ted now making its mark intensely visible. It went well with the lump on the back of her tender head. Jennifer didn't have makeup that would conceal this much discoloration. She was embarrassed to leave the house to run errands, but fortunately, she had Teresa and, much to her surprise, Detective Kevin Blockard, who, true to his word, regularly checked on Jennifer. Sunday, it was chicken noodle soup, which he brought to her home after noticing her absence at church. Monday, it was Chinese take-out, three different dishes to make sure he got something she'd find appetizing. On Tuesday, he dropped by after work and insisted on making scrambled eggs and toast for both of them. Today was Wednesday, and Jennifer wondered if the good detective would show up bearing food once again. He'd have to bring this to a halt sooner or later.

If he didn't, Jennifer intended to be more insistent than her current, "You really don't have to do this, Kevin! I'm fine."

Angie, Teresa, and Maria had all been equally solicitous in their own ways. As expected, Angie worried over Jennifer in a maternal fashion, despite being several months younger than Jennifer. She offered to come and stay for a week, but Jennifer would have nothing of that. Angie had Jolie and Mike to consider, especially during this busy holiday season. Besides, Jennifer didn't like the idea of her best friend making that twelve-hour or so drive between Reddington and Tilbrook at this time of year. In an emergency, Mike would gladly drive his wife, but this wasn't urgent per Jennifer, so she advised Angie to stay put.

Even with miles separating them, Angie was uniquely able to provide Jennifer with what she most wanted—someone to confide in about the latest communication with Doctor Ephraim. As anticipated, Angie squealed with delight when Jennifer told her about the rose and Ephraim's choice to remain behind for Jennifer rather than leave with his son and Ruth. Ever the romantic, Angie now inquired about Ephraim as if he were an in-the-flesh person with whom Jennifer hung out on a regular basis.

Teresa and Maria were also dears, visiting Jennifer within hours of hearing the news about Ted. Teresa refrained from pointing out that she had reservations about Ted from the start. Maria, who actually had been charmed by Ted, now recalled that she had also distrusted him from the beginning. Teresa winked at Jennifer but said nothing to refute her partner.

Jennifer asked Maria if she'd seen Ted around the Montgomery Haven Apartments. Although his SUV was in the lot, Maria said she saw nothing of him and didn't even know if Ted was still in town. Teresa pointed out that he'd have to be, meaning it would be a court-ordered stipulation. Jennifer had a newfound appreciation for restraining orders.

She made herself a hot cup of ginger green tea and settled in her favorite chair with a book she'd intended to read about six months ago. It was a captivating story, and Jennifer was amazed at how the day flew by. She only had about fifty pages left, and Jennifer weighed the option of finishing the book now or having an early dinner. The doorbell rang just as she located the bookmark she intended to use.

"Aren't you trusting," Detective Blockard said dryly, apparently not pleased when Jennifer opened the door swiftly and willingly.

Jennifer silently pointed to the peephole and shrugged. "Too trusting of you? Is that what you mean?"

Kevin laughed, and Jennifer smiled at the soft tone of it. "You'd better be using that peephole, Ms. Shemmer," he replied, obviously referencing Ted.

"I do, Detective," Jennifer agreed, unknowingly tilting the badly bruised side of her pretty face toward him. "You don't have to worry about me." When Kevin revealed the take-out bag he had been holding behind his back, she added, "And you don't have to feed me every day either. I do thank you, though. It's been great for these past days, but you can't keep it up forever."

"Do you mind if I come in?" Kevin dismissed her comment. "I brought food for both of us."

"Please do." Jennifer stepped aside and let the tall, athletic man enter. He still wore his more formal clothes. Apparently, Kevin had gone directly from work to pick up dinner to bring to her place.

"Chicken or fish?" Kevin presented two plated dinners, both of which looked delicious.

"Either's fine by me, and both look great. You get first dibs since you went to the trouble of getting them," Jennifer said firmly since he'd also paid for the food.

"I wouldn't have ordered something I didn't like." Kevin shrugged and pushed both plates toward her across the dining room table.

"Okay. Fish, then," Jennifer said, knowing that this back-and-forth could go on for a while. Kevin was a very accommodating person. She got silverware and napkins from the kitchen and joined Kevin, who was already seated in front of his chicken dinner.

They ate in silence initially, both hungrier than they originally thought. Eventually, Jennifer made small talk about the food, Kevin nodding agreeably but not adding much to the conversation. Still, she felt at ease with him, and evidently, he did with her, too.

When they finished eating, Jennifer cleared the table and invited Kevin to the living room. He willingly obliged, choosing a chair opposite her favorite floral one. Jennifer switched on two of the lamps, hoping Ephraim wouldn't make them flicker. So far, there hadn't been any "incidences" with Kevin in the house—no icy cold spots, no trickery with the lamps, no indoor wind gusts, and no musky cologne. Kevin must be on Ephraim's "nice" list, Jennifer thought as she glanced across the room at the detective sitting in the vicinity of her small-but-pretty Christmas tree adorned with Ruth's old-time ornaments.

Kevin must have followed her gaze as he remarked, "Lovely tree. I like vintage decorations. My daughter would approve."

Jennifer had forgotten about his two children. "What are your kids' names again?" she asked, frankly not sure if he had ever told her.

"Laura, who's nineteen, and Matthew, who's twenty-two. He goes by Matt, for the most part. Laura's on winter break after finals. I believe they end next week. She's staying with her old man for all six weeks."

Jennifer noticed how proud Kevin looked, like a doting father. Obviously, Kevin felt honored and possibly a little surprised that his college-aged daughter would agree to spend her entire vacation with him.

"That's so nice," Jennifer responded. "I remember being ecstatic about winter and summer breaks when I was in school." That segued into a discussion of college days, and Jennifer was just about to ask Kevin how he went from being an English literature major to having a career in law enforcement when he abruptly changed the topic.

"Jennifer, another reason for my visit tonight is to talk with you about the results of the chemical analysis," he stated bluntly.

"Oh, you got back the report?" Jennifer realized it was a silly question but was surprised that the highly professional detective hadn't led with this piece of information, perhaps before sitting down to dinner.

"Today," he agreed with a nod. For the next few minutes, Jennifer felt like she was sitting across from Detective Blockard in his small office at the police station, an image made even easier by the polished shoes, dress pants, and crisp button-down shirt he sported.

"So that ... whatever drug you said ... would make me lose consciousness?" Jennifer finally cut in. "Why would Ted use that on me?"

Kevin repeated the chemical name and classified it broadly as a rape drug. Jennifer shook her head, finding it difficult to believe the lab report yet simultaneously reminding herself that Ephraim had warned her about the champagne. Plus, she'd been suspicious enough to work up the nerve to take the sample to the police.

"I don't see why Ted would have used drugs on me, though, considering—" she stopped short. Her private life wasn't any business of the detective. Besides, Ted had been obsessed with getting a key to Jennifer's home, giving him access to all possessions when she wasn't in the house. There was the possibility that Ted wasn't thinking of rape when he slipped the drug into her glass that night.

"You do want to press charges against Filston, don't you?" Kevin asked in a serious tone that Jennifer would not have dared oppose.

"Yes," Jennifer replied with sincerity, although she dreaded the legal proceedings and probable testimony she'd have to give. "Ted shouldn't get away with this, too. Apparently, he stole from my aunt about twenty years ago. He seemed overly interested in her antiques, the things locked away in a room upstairs. The more I think about it, the more I believe he was using me to get to them."

"Possibly. Filston has a record, Jennifer. He embezzled from Tenger-Bio when he worked in finances, but fortunately for him, the company didn't pursue charges. He has been involved in domestic violence allegations, although charges were dropped in those cases, as well." Kevin sounded annoyed, breaking from his even, professional tone.

Jennifer let the information sink in. Domestic violence? Ted? Up until Friday evening, she would have thought that impossible. She decided to address only the Tenger-Bio portion of what the detective told her. For some reason, the embezzlement allegation didn't shock her as much.

"I wonder if my aunt had some influence in regards to Tenger not going after Ted legally. She was highly respected there and seemed to have sympathy for Ted at the time. He was only about twenty-five, not much older than your son, come to think of it, and recently divorced."

"Hmm," was all that Kevin said.

"Did I tell you that I met a lady at Trinity, well, a lady who was visiting Trinity but knew my aunt? She said Ted was stealing from Ruth, and when Ruth found out, she asked him to leave. I'm highly paraphrasing because she couldn't recall the guy's name, but it fits that it was Ted. I bet he was the only boarder Ruth ever had." The thought of both Ephraims as boarders rushed into Jennifer's mind, and she blushed.

Kevin noticed her flushness but misinterpreted the cause. "Kind-hearted, honest people often have difficulty recognizing dishonesty in others. It's nothing to be embarrassed about. Your aunt sounds like she had a soft spot for the underdog." He then added as an afterthought, "Filston knows how to con and capitalize on his good looks."

This time Jennifer blushed because she knew Kevin was referring to the reason Jennifer fell for Ted's charm, or con, as Kevin bluntly put it. Yes, Ted's handsome looks indeed held appeal. Detective Blockard looked grim, Jennifer observed. She wondered if he was contrasting his own appearance to Ted's and judging himself as lacking. Jennifer smiled slightly. Kevin wasn't handsome like Ted, but he was nice-enough looking. She laughed, wondering how Kevin would feel to be deemed just "nice-enough looking."

Kevin momentarily stopped talking at the sound of Jennifer's laughter. He then directly addressed it with, "Did I say something that amused you, or are you lost in thought somewhere?"

Frankly, Jennifer was unaware that Kevin had been speaking and felt embarrassed that she was clueless about what she missed in this one-sided conversation. "Lost in my thoughts, I'm afraid," she said but wisely chose not to expound.

"Mm," Kevin said and then, with some reluctance, added, "I should be going. I've got a dog I need to see about, actually Laura's dog. A beautiful black Lab."

"Oh, I didn't know you had pets." Jennifer couldn't recall any animal photos in the detective's office.

"Only Nora, and she's my daughter's dog," he emphasized. "Good company, though."

That reminded Jennifer that Kevin was widowed, relatively recently, too, judging by the photo on his desk of his wife embracing two teenage or young adult kids. Had he said a couple of years? Jennifer couldn't remember. She had been nervous at the police station and certainly not there for social reasons.

Jennifer rose to escort Kevin to the door. As she led the way, she thanked him again for his kindness in providing dinner. She then turned to face Kevin and let out a stifled but somewhat shrill scream.

Kevin immediately did an about-face, solidly standing his ground, positioned to tackle any intruder coming his way. There was nothing behind him, however. After slowly taking in the living room, entry, and what could be seen of the dining room, Kevin returned his attention to Jennifer, who still appeared stunned. She had gone white, causing her bruising to stand out all the more by contrast.

"What do you think you saw, Jennifer? Filston?" he asked gently, with sincere concern in his brown eyes.

"I-I don't know." She tried to gain her composure. "Maybe I'm having flashbacks about Friday night. It really hasn't been that long ago."

Kevin nodded, seeming to accept Jennifer's explanation, yet he walked into the dining area and kitchen, checking the side door and windows. She followed silently. When he asked if it was all right to open the closets, Jennifer gave him permission. Kevin then made his way to the den while an embarrassed Jennifer apologized for all the cartons, explaining that she still had boxes to unpack from her move. Kevin's brief gesture brushed her misgivings aside. He appeared to take in every detail of the den, and Jennifer noticed that his gaze rested briefly on the portraits on the wall.

Finally, when they had returned to the living room, Kevin said, "I don't see any signs of an intruder. I'm pretty observant, and I didn't hear anything behind me or see any movement from my peripheral vision. I believe I would have if someone had been behind me or fleeing. Would you like me to check upstairs, though? I'd be glad to do so to put your mind at ease."

Jennifer quickly turned him down. "I've wasted enough of your time. I'm sorry that I shrieked like that. I'm more on edge than I realized. I'm not even sure what I think I saw—just a flash of something. Again, I'm so sorry."

"No apology needed or wanted. I'm glad I was here when you screamed, though. Why don't you have something warm to drink and get to bed early? I bet you need additional rest," he said graciously, then added, "You have my number if you need it. Call any time, no matter what the hour."

Jennifer agreed, carefully locking the door and placing the security chain once Kevin left. She parted the blinds slightly to watch as his sedan passed out of view. Then she turned off the porch light and walked back to the living room.

"Ephraim!" she urgently and rather loudly called. "I saw you! I saw you standing behind Kevin."

Chapter 21

TWO GIFTS SAT UNDER Jennifer's small Christmas tree, both from Angie. Jennifer stooped to pick up the one wrapped with birthday cake images. Today was her big day. Jennifer couldn't believe she was already forty-three, not that she considered that old, but still. The years had flown by. She tore the gift paper from the box and pulled out what she figured to be some type of clothing. Jennifer unfurled the item and held it up before her. Yes, a lovely deep violet pullover top with a particularly attractive V-neckline adorned with a partial collar and a small amount of lace trim. Angie was the one person who could successfully pick out clothing for Jennifer. Even Jennifer's own mom had difficulty getting sizes and styles to match Jennifer's frame and taste.

She quickly removed her current top and pulled Angie's gift over her head. It felt comfy, and she smiled when she studied her reflection in the mirror. Angie had done well. Jennifer picked up the phone to give her pal the news directly. She was sure Angie anticipated her call this morning to thank her for the pullover.

"Happy Birthday, Jen!" she blurted out before Jennifer had a chance to say hello. Angie began singing the birthday song and added at the end, "And many, many more!"

"Thank you," Jennifer responded sweetly. "Guess what I'm wearing today? A beautiful purple sweater top that fits perfectly and looks classy with the black slacks I have on."

"I'm so glad you like it and that it fits. As soon as I saw the sweater at the mall, I thought of you, and they had it in your size. So, what are you up to on your special day, girl?"

"Not much," Jennifer confessed but tried not to sound gloomy. The truth was she was slightly depressed and homesick for her previous life before Tilbrook. Birthdays made her nostalgic for her mom, dad, marriage, past career...

"Well, you can change that, can't you?" Angie cheerfully stated more than asked. "You have a few friends in town. Call them. If they know it's your birthday, they'll do something to celebrate."

Jennifer hesitated, and Angie was perceptive enough to allow her friend time to gather her thoughts. "Can I speak openly and honestly to you, Ange, without having to put on a happy birthday front?"

"Of course, you can, Jen. What's up?"

"I don't feel like celebrating. Actually, I feel kind of crabby. Not long ago, I thought I'd be spending today with Ted. He was already making a big deal out of my birthday. I miss his arms around me and his kisses and," her voice trailed off. "I'm not saying I want him back. I realize Ted is bad news, yet I miss what I thought I had."

"Sure you do, Jen," Angie sympathized in a soothing voice. "I hoped he'd be the right one for you, also, but you two were early on in your relationship. It takes a lot more time than you had to find out what the other person's really like. I think you got off lucky. A lot of women, especially with all the stressful situations you had going on, would have jumped at a charming, handsome guy like Ted. You took it slowly, and it paid off big time. He never got his foot in the door the way he hoped. He didn't get to move into your house or otherwise take over your life and, frankly, your possessions."

"Still, I was a fool." Jennifer felt deflated. "I saw red flags and ignored them."

"You gave him the benefit of the doubt," Angie rephrased Jennifer's statement. "Heck, I gave him the benefit of the doubt, too. It's a good thing you didn't bring him to my house over Thanksgiving, or I might have given him a key to my house!"

Jennifer chuckled. "Yeah, Mike might have been slightly annoyed if you had."

"Oh, I don't know. If Ted was as charming as you thought, Mike might have given Ted a key himself."

"It's nice to talk to you, Ange," Jennifer said with sincerity, now smiling broadly. "I do have friends in Tilbrook, but it's not the same."

"That's because you and I go way back, way, way back. Speaking of friends, what about that nice detective who helped you out so much? How's he doing? More specifically, what's he doing tonight, on your birthday, hint, hint."

If Angie had expected her to laugh, she was disappointed. Jennifer took a deep breath. "The detective, Kevin, seems to have distanced himself from me, not that that's a problem. His daughter's staying with him for now, over her winter break from college in Rotan. Kevin invited me to dinner one night, and Laura, that's the daughter's name, took an instant dislike to me. I mean instant dislike. I couldn't say or do anything right in her eyes. It was so noticeable, and I'm sure the observant, keen-witted detective picked up on it. Anyway, there have been no further invitations, and Kevin certainly doesn't stop by my place anymore. There's no need to, though, either professionally or personally. I'm pretty much healed, although the bruising on my face hasn't completely faded. Let's just say the yellowish coloring locks lovely with the purple of the new sweater you've just given me."

Angie chortled at that and then commented, "Getting back to the daughter, it's natural that she wouldn't like you, Jen, and that has nothing to do with you personally. Zilch. How old is she? A college student, so somewhere around eighteen to twenty? Her mother died recently, and now she suspects that her dad might like another woman, even a little, enough to invite this woman over to dinner. Of course, she doesn't like you. Few people are honestly happy to see their parents date again, whether it's due to divorce or death."

Jennifer couldn't disagree with that. "I'd feel the same as Laura, I'm sure, at least at nineteen. I'm used to being liked by young people, though—people in general. It's not that Kevin and I were dating, either. We were on our way to becoming friends, I think, because of the ... Ted situation. It's kind of hard not to be friendly when someone drives you to the hospital, spends the entire night in the waiting room, and makes sure you're well-fed every day afterward."

"He sounds like a stand-up guy," Angie agreed, "like my Mike. Jen, if God forbid something happened to me, I don't think Jolie would be happy about Mike dating anyone."

"Jolie's exceptionally mature," Jennifer defended Angie's daughter in this hypothetical situation. "Maybe not right away, but I think she'd want her parents to be happy in the end."

"Okay. Notice that you said 'not right away,' and that's what I'm saying about Kevin's daughter. Give her time. Don't write Kevin off because of her."

"I'm not writing him off, Angie, but I'm also not thinking of him as a romantic partner. It's too soon after Ted, and frankly, it was too soon for Ted, which is why I slowed our relationship. Anyway, it's a moot point."

"Moot," Angie repeated and laughed. "I like that word. What exactly does that mean, a moot point?"

"Kevin used to sit behind me at Trinity Church, or so he told me. Honestly, I don't remember that. However, after Ted, he started to sit beside me but only for a few Sundays because Laura soon came back to stay with him."

Angie tried to follow along, but it was getting a little confusing. "So, you're telling me that Kevin sat next to you at church for a couple of Sundays, and now he ... what? Doesn't attend? Sits somewhere else?"

"He sits in the back with his daughter, Laura. I wave at them, and Kevin lifts his hand and nods. Laura doesn't acknowledge me. He doesn't make an effort to walk over and say hello to me, but on the other hand, I don't do that either."

"Okay. The daughter doesn't want you with her dad. Personally, I think she's old enough that Kevin could excuse himself and do what he wants, but—" Angie cut the sentence short, and Jennifer could visualize her friend shrugging her shoulders.

"So, the moot point is that Kevin has gone back to a strictly professional relationship, not a budding friendship or whatever you'd call it," Jennifer stated firmly.

"The kid will go back to college next month, Jen. When?"

"I don't know. I think she's off for at least six weeks. Later in January," Jennifer estimated. "I get your point, Ange. Once Laura's left Tilbrook, perhaps Kevin will come around again. I'm just not sure I would want that, you know?"

"Yes," Angie said empathetically. "I do know. I'm inclined to agree with you that you need time to heal. Maybe it's a good thing that the daughter is staying with her dad for the time being."

"I think so." Jennifer paused. "Can I tell you something about Ephraim?"

"Oh, please do," Angie crooned. "Now, we're talking Doctor Ephraim, right? Not his kid, also named Ephraim."

"The son, Ephraim Junior, left the house when Aunt Ruth departed. They left together," Jennifer reminded Angie and heard her friend let out a romantic sigh about the two lovers departing for the heavens hand in hand. "I think I've developed feelings for Doctor Ephraim," Jennifer confided in almost a whisper.

"Ooh!" Angie hesitated. Jennifer hoped she hadn't stunned her friend with her frank admission. "I can understand that." Angie took a long pause again, obviously searching for words. What exactly does one say when your best friend begins to fall for a ghost? "You're in the house with him every day. He's rescued you several times from Ted, so he's been your protector. You have a copy of a photo of him, so you know what he looks like. Now you're able to talk with him and even see him on occasion. So, yeah, Jen, I guess I can see how you may have fallen for Ephraim."

Jennifer felt relieved to have Angie validate her emotions rather than ridicule or argue against them. "Thanks, Ange. I realized how I felt about him the day I saw the rose lying on my journal. He's always there, and I don't mean always around because I'm not sure he is, but he's there for me for support. He's kind and gentle, and I just like him. I strongly like him."

"You're also reeling from Ted," Angie reminded her friend. "You're also a little hurt that Kevin backed off due to his kid. Ephraim's the one constant in this picture."

"Yes, Ephraim is," Jennifer readily agreed. "I realize I don't know a lot about him, but he has to have been an exceptional person. He suffered the death of his son, believing that the arrow was no accident, even though the police treated the case as a mere hunting incident. Doctor Ephraim was murdered right outside this very home, coming as a physician to care for Aunt Ruth when she was a girl. He chose not to cross over to the other side because his son had stayed behind to be with Ruth. The tragic, unexpected circumstances surrounding their deaths probably had something to do with it, but the point is that Doctor Ephraim wanted to be with his son. And once Ruth and the son departed, he chose to remain in this home because of me."

"Yeah, that's sweet, Jen, and you know I'm a sucker for romantic notions, but—" Angie stopped short of stating the obvious.

Jennifer finished the sentence for her. "But Ephraim is a spirit. What's the future in loving a ghost?"

"I don't know, Jen, I don't know. You can't help how you feel. It looks like Ephraim is part of the parcel, part of your inheritance." Both Angie and Jennifer laughed at the thought. "I'm not in your shoes, and I have no way of actually knowing how I'd react. I guess if Mike died and still inhabited the house, I'd be committed to him. No one would be able to convince me to walk away from him, stop loving him, or move on to a new relationship. On the other hand, Mike and I met in the physical world. You're just meeting Ephraim now, and you're in the flesh, but he isn't."

"Tell me about it," Jennifer said dryly. "I don't intend to give up this house. Ephraim might leave if I asked him to, but I honestly don't want that. I'd be devastated." And with that revelation, Jennifer began to cry.

"Oh, I know, Jen. Gee, don't cry. It's your birthday, too. You should be happy. No one said anything about selling your home or asking Ephraim to leave. Why don't you just play it out? Let things unfold naturally. You don't know how you'll feel about Ephraim months from now, especially if a special man comes into your life who can offer you more than a ghost can. On the other hand, if it's Ephraim who makes you happy, I'm going to support you in that, too. Your aunt clearly was happy with the son. Some people go their entire lives without finding someone to truly love. Maybe you'll always have Ephraim, and in addition, you'll have a guy here in this physical world, you know, with some meat on his bones."

Jennifer giggled. "Angie, the things you say."

"Hey, I'm not the one telling her best friend about falling for a handsome doctor who's been dead for over a hundred years."

"It hasn't been a hundred years," Jennifer corrected, "but he was born over a hundred years ago."

"Well, there you go!" Angie teased. "Of all the life experiences I thought we'd share, you falling for a ghost wasn't one of them. I think it's better than you falling for an embezzler-rapist jerk, however."

"Yeah, I'd say he's a step above Ted." Jennifer smiled, still daubing the tears from her eyes. "I'm going to have to stock up on tissues. It seems I've been crying a lot lately."

"What's the word for that? Cathartic? Did I say that right? After all you've been through, not only this year but last year, I should send you several crates of tissues."

"Mm," Jennifer agreed and took the opportunity to blow her nose before resuming the conversation. "I'm really very fortunate, yet I'm allowing myself to wallow in a little self-pity today. I know, though, that I'm set up financially, and I was well-loved by my parents. I had the experience of what I thought was a good marriage up until Alex cheated on me. My career was fulfilling. I'm making new friends, I have my health, and I enjoy my new home in a new town. Ephraim keeps me company or gives me the illusion of not being alone, and," Jennifer paused for emphasis, "I've got the best friend in the world, and her name is Angie Calberto."

"I was waiting for that," her friend agreed. "Me, too, Jen. We should count our blessings. You're sentimental today, more so because it's your birthday and the holidays, but a new year is rapidly approaching with new adventures. I think you're past the worst, and things will improve."

"I'd like to believe that," Jennifer concurred, aware of a fresh headache beginning, probably due to all the tears she'd shed.

"Why don't you call one of your friends and see if they're free tonight or tomorrow? Go out for lunch or dinner. Go shopping and buy yourself something for your birthday. Get a cake and eat as much as you want."

"I'll think about it," Jennifer replied. "I definitely feel better now that I've talked to you. I believe I can manage through the day. Thank you again for the beautiful sweater. I love it! You know my tastes."

"Yes, I do. Sometimes, I think I know you better than you know yourself."

"I'm going to say goodbye now, Ange," Jennifer said reluctantly. "I've got a slight headache, and I want to take a pill before it becomes major. Thanks again."

"You bet! Happy birthday, girl! Hang in there."

Jennifer sighed and went upstairs to get the aspirin. She swallowed a tablet with a little water and set the glass on the countertop.

"Happy birthday, Jennifer," a male voice, Ephraim's, said from behind her. She glanced up at the mirror over the sink and saw not only her reflection but his. Abruptly, she swung around, knocking the water glass to the floor. She looked down briefly to see if it had shattered. It hadn't. She fully expected Ephraim to have vanished by this time, but to her delight, he stood before her, faint but still visible. His face showed tenderness.

"Thank you," Jennifer voiced softly. "Oh, Ephraim, I can see you."

"Yes." He smiled and walked towards her bedroom, stopping outside the doorway.

Ephraim motioned toward something in the room but disappeared before Jennifer could make out what he was communicating. She stepped into her bedroom and looked around. Since, in the past, Ephraim had used her gratitude journal as a pedestal for placing flowers, Jennifer quickly walked to the book. To her amazement, a beautiful gold filigree heart pendant rested atop the journal. Jennifer picked it up gently. It looked vintage, probably something that belonged to her aunt. However, Jennifer had never seen this pendant, with its reddish violet heart delicately wrapped in gold swirls. It was a gift from Ephraim, a birthday gift. She placed the dainty pendant around her neck and had no difficulty with the clasp. It hung at the perfect length for the new sweater top Angie had given her, right above the graceful V-neck, the shade of the heart going nicely with the purple hue of the pullover.

Jennifer walked to the dresser mirror to get a better view. She was still touching the filigreed heart when she turned around and found herself facing Ephraim.

She intended to thank him, but strangely, no words came. Doctor Ephraim looked pensive, which surprised Jennifer that, in the nonphysical, he could have that much expression.

Finally, Jennifer managed to find her voice, albeit a whisper. "It's beautiful, Ephraim. Thank you. Thank you so much."

With that, she felt the soft brush of his fingers against her arms and was aware of her head being gently tilted to receive one of the most pleasant kisses she'd ever experienced.

"Oh, Ephraim," she said when he released her. His smile was as tender as his kiss.

When he disappeared, she wasn't upset. Her head no longer hurt, and her depression had dissipated. It no longer bothered her to be another year older, to have lost Ted, nor to have Kevin distance himself. Jennifer felt this to be one of her happiest birthdays yet, and suddenly, she looked forward to the new year.

The End of Book 1

Be sure to check out Book 2 of the Familiar Hauntings Series, *The Past Present*, when Jennifer's already complicated love life gets jolted by the arrival of her ex-husband.

Also By

Kathy Madsen

Familiar Hauntings Series:
Jennifer's Secret (Book 1)
The Past Present (Book 2)
Through Many Eyes (Book 3)
Look for more titles to come...

Gratitude and Dreams Monthly Journal

About Author

Kathy Madsen is the author of the fiction series *Familiar Hauntings*, which follows the character Jennifer Shemmer as she rebuilds her life, coping with unique challenges and complicated love relationships along the way. Kathy currently resides in Arizona.

If you enjoyed this book, please consider posting a short review on the store page you used to make your purchase. Reviews make a book discoverable by others and are greatly appreciated.

www.ingramcontent.com/pod-product-compliance
Lightning Source LLC
Chambersburg PA
CBHW031336020726
47499CB00005B/1283

9781953675088

A Mayfair Christmas

Two Scintillating Regency Romances

ANNA CAMPBELL

ISBN: 978-1-925980-34-9

Publisher's Note: This is a work of fiction. Names, characters, places, and incidents are a product of the author's imagination. Locales and public names are sometimes used for atmospheric purposes. Any resemblance to actual people, living or dead, or to businesses, companies, events, institutions, or locales is completely coincidental.

Cover Design: Hang Le

Lady Elizabeth's Winter Stranger

A Mayfair Christmas Romance

ANNA CAMPBELL

A father's ultimatum...

On Christmas Day, Lady Elizabeth Tierney is aghast when her father tells her he's found her a bridegroom. She'll meet her suitor, Viscount Fairchild, at tonight's festivities, and Elizabeth had better charm him – or else!

A daughter's defiance.

The spirited beauty has danced her way through four seasons and sees no reason why her life needs to change. At least until she falls in love with one of her admirers – and that shows no sign of happening. In a fit of temper, Elizabeth escapes to Hyde Park where she stumbles upon an intriguing gentleman who steals her heart.

Lady Elizabeth's choice?

Which suitor will win her hand? Or has fate got another trick up its sleeve for Lady Elizabeth and her winter stranger?

CHAPTER ONE

Lorimer Square, London, Christmas Day, 1819

Sander Hall, Cumbria

Monday, 20th December, 1819

My dearest daughter Elizabeth,

I'm writing to you with the expectation that this letter will reach you after your return from the Wetherbys' house party and before the family arrive back in London for our usual Christmas celebrations on the evening of the 25th.

My intention is that you have time to mull over what I say and accept that I'm acting in your best interests. Nothing I tell you here is new, but I'm hoping that now you see it in writing, you'll understand this time, I'm in deadly earnest. I will not be swayed, as you've managed to sway me upon every other occasion that this subject has arisen.

You're twenty-four, Elizabeth, and it's time you married. So far, I've allowed you your choice of a husband, because I'm very fond of you and I don't want you tied to a man you can neither respect nor love.

But enough is enough. As you've seen fit to refuse every one of the many eligible gentlemen who have requested your hand in marriage, I've decided that it's time to step in and accept a young man's proposal on your behalf.

Stanton Morley-Bridges, Viscount Fairchild, comes from excellent stock. He is heir to the Earl of Blaydon, a gentleman I've long admired for his political acumen. Fairchild is twenty-eight, the perfect age to settle down and establish himself as a family man. To date, he has been working on the Continent as a diplomat and I gather doing a brilliant job. Your brother met him in Paris a month ago and Guy speaks most highly of his principles and intelligence. As his father's health is deteriorating, Fairchild has resigned from the service and is returning to England where he intends to seek a wife. Guy suggested that he joins us for Christmas to meet you, with a view to making you an offer of marriage. This plan has my full support.

At this stage, I'm sure you're bristling, Elizabeth, but I will not be gainsaid on this matter. From all reports, Fairchild is a sensible man of generous fortune and commendable character. He will make you an ideal husband. Should the young man decide you are a suitable bride, the marriage will take place early in the new year.

You've been out in London since you were twenty and you played your part in local society for several years before that. From the first, you were much sought after and the ton has acclaimed you as a diamond of the first water. If you haven't settled your mind on a match by now, you're not going to, unless some well-meaning person applies pressure.

Well, I am your father and I am well-meaning and I'm applying pressure. So far, I have tolerated your feminine whims, even if I haven't approved of them. I will not accept your defiance on this issue.

Should Viscount Fairchild decide you'll make a good wife, you will accept his offer. If you kick up a fuss, as no doubt right now, you intend to do, I will immediately stop your allowance and remove you from London. Your Great-Aunt Agatha in Caithness requires a companion. You will fill that role until you think better of your imprudent choices and agree to wed Lord Fairchild. I imagine you won't last long in her ramshackle, waterlogged castle in the coldest part of Scotland with no other company to distract you.

Elizabeth, I repeat that I'm taking this step out of love. Guy speaks in glowing terms of young Morley-Bridges and says he will make you a fine husband. I hope you agree when you meet him. If you don't, I wish you well of Aunt Agatha and her twenty incontinent pugs.

Your mother and I will see you tonight at our family dinner to mark the festive season. Wear your prettiest dress and prepare to smile for your new suitor, or bear the consequences.

Your loving but very determined Papa.

"My loving Papa!" Elizabeth spat out, screwing up the letter and pitching it into the library fire. "I don't think so."

She was so angry that she felt sick with it. As she began to pace across the Turkey carpet, the dark green skirts of her fashionable traveling ensemble swished about her long legs. If she had a tail, it would be lashing.

"How dare he?" she muttered, clenching her fists

at her sides. "How dare Guy?"

She and her brother had always been co-conspirators. Knowing that he'd betrayed her like this rubbed salt in the wound. She was almost more upset about Guy's involvement in this vile scheme than she was with her father.

"Feminine whims? Great-Aunt Agatha? Caithness? I'll set fire to damned Caithness before I move there."

She stopped in the middle of the room, gasping for breath as an ocean of rage seethed in her stomach. Rage and, much as she hated to admit it, fear.

Because while her father had made noises before about her taking a husband, something about the implacable tone of that odious letter told her that this time, he wouldn't relent. She couldn't distract him with her usual excuses about wanting a love match like her parents'.

Not that that was a lie. But as her father said, she'd enjoyed four seasons that had left her heart resolutely untouched. She'd reached the conclusion that she was immune to romance. As an adult, the closest she'd come to a *tendre* was her penchant for her father's handsome American gardener, Caleb Black, three years ago. Even at the time, she'd known it was all a silly fancy. Which turned out to be a good thing when he eloped with her friend, Lady Imogen Ridley.

Assured of her immunity to masculine wiles, she'd continued to dance and flirt and gossip and glitter her way through London's social whirl. As far as she was concerned, that happy state of affairs could go on forever.

Her father clearly harbored other ideas. Ideas that he'd outlined in writing for the first time, as if he knew that she'd try and wheedle her way out of his ultimatum if they were face-to-face.

She growled low in her throat and resumed pacing. This Stanton Morley-Bridges sounded like a complete pillock. Even his name was enough to make her bile rise.

Elizabeth could already imagine him. Tall and weedy and shortsighted and convinced of his intellectual superiority. A bore who never let anyone else get a word in. There had to be something wrong with him, or else he'd be able to find a wife for himself and woo her in the customary manner.

If her father thought that she was going to accept a prosy windbag as her life partner, he could think again.

Except through all her brave words, that niggle of fear persisted. A niggle that rendered her defiance unconvincing.

Because unlike lucky Imogen, Elizabeth didn't come into a huge fortune at twenty-five. While she'd bring her husband a generous dowry, that was at her father's discretion. There was a small inheritance from her grandfather, but she couldn't get her hands on that until she was thirty. Unless she married first.

What an irony.

Her present delightful existence relied on her father funding her activities and buying her gowns and offering her a luxurious place to live in London. He'd never before threatened to take his support away. If he really was serious about exiling her to the windswept desolation of Caithness, she supposed she could stay with friends here in London, but she was wise enough to know that offered no long-term solution.

So if she didn't marry Stanton Morley-Bridges – and that wasn't an option – she was stuck with moving in with Great-Aunt Agatha. Who was sour-natured and demanding and never bathed unless there was an emergency. And there never seemed to be an emergency.

Ugh. It was enough to make Elizabeth want to pick up the Meissen shepherdesses from the mantelpiece and hurl them at the wall. Their smug smiles hinted that on this occasion, she was going to lose the battle.

She sucked in a shuddering breath and told herself not to panic. Even as panic surged in her throat like vomit.

Because her father had her trapped between two unacceptable choices. And he knew it. He generally wasn't a bully, although like most men, he preferred his own way. But right now, Elizabeth felt bullied.

She loathed feeling so powerless.

She loathed recognizing that right now she *was* powerless.

Gritting her teeth, she resisted the sensation of the walls closing in on her. The way an unappealing fate closed in on her.

Elizabeth refused to cry. She didn't want to cry. She wanted to fight. But there was nobody to fight with on this day of goodwill to all and peace on earth. And she had a horrid presentiment that if she started to cry, it was the first inevitable step toward caving in to her father's orders.

She would not countenance that.

Desperate to release her frustrated rage, she slammed out of the library and into the empty hall. Usually this opulent house in Lorimer Square bustled with family and servants and callers. But at this hour on Christmas morning, the rooms around her were unnaturally silent.

With a shock, she realized that for the first time in her life, she was completely alone in the house. In any house. The principal servants had traveled to Cumbria with Lord and Lady Tierney and would return with them. Any London-based staff had been released from their duties to visit their families for the holiday, although they would have worked this week, preparing for the opulent Tierney Christmas dinner tonight.

Elizabeth hadn't been expected back until this afternoon, but in Surrey, her maid Flossie had come down with a bad head cold. Worried for Flossie's health, Elizabeth had ordered the carriage for dawn. On the way home from the Wetherbys' house party, Elizabeth had dropped Flossie in Stepney where the girl's large, noisy family lived.

Even her coachman had gone for the day to visit his brother's family in Essex. He'd suggested staying so someone remained in attendance, but Elizabeth sent him on his way once he'd brought her home The other servants would trickle back later in the afternoon and her parents would arrive before five, if all went to plan.

Well-bred young women were granted many privileges. The chance to bask in their own company wasn't one of them. In London, well-bred young women never left their homes without an escort either. A relative or a female friend or a chaperone or a servant. Her reputation would suffer, if she took to wandering the streets of London unaccompanied.

Right now, she was furious enough not to give a fig for her reputation. She just had to get out of this house and find somewhere where she could breathe. Because if she stayed inside, she'd start screaming, and she wasn't sure she'd stop.

Elizabeth was still dressed for travel. She hadn't even been upstairs yet. She'd come through the front door and found the mail set out on the hall table. A pile of invitations for her, as befitted one of London's fashionable belles, even at this quiet time of year. A couple of letters from friends who were celebrating

Christmas in the country. And her father's unwelcome ultimatum. She'd brought the pile of correspondence straight into the library where Jones, her coachman, was lighting the fire. Because Elizabeth was home so much earlier than planned, the house hadn't been ready for immediate occupation.

She didn't mind. Under her London polish, she was a practical creature. Fending for herself for a few hours wouldn't be too onerous. What she did mind was her father disposing of her like a book overdue at the circulating library.

The house came with a large garden, but right now, something about walking within her family's domain only stoked her temper. She strode across to collect her bonnet and gloves. With shaking hands, she jammed the hat on her head and tugged on her gloves. She slipped her house key into her reticule and for the first time in London, she set foot outside all alone.

Elizabeth paused on the top step of the short flight leading down to the icy pavement. She sucked in what felt like the first free air that she'd enjoyed since opening her father's letter.

Lorimer Square was as empty as the house, although churned-up snow on the road showed that the few residents who hadn't left Town had ridden to church in their carriages early this morning. Pristine white covered the garden in the middle of the square. With the cold, nobody was hanging around outside to admire the greenery.

And if she didn't move, she was likely to become as frozen as the trees and bushes that she stared at without really seeing them. Her mind was on the horrors of Great-Aunt Agatha's drafty, leaky castle on the clifftop facing a gray, stormy Pentland Firth. Great-Aunt Agatha who never had a caller under eighty, and not many of those either. Elizabeth would just die, if she was exiled to that gusty, dreary outpost.

Rancid nausea heaved once more in her stomach and those pesky tears threatened again. To outrun the danger of crumpling into a sobbing heap, Elizabeth descended the steps and started to tramp around the square. Her dark green half boots crunched across the dry snow, and chilled air filled her lungs. There was a faint aroma of coal smoke, but with so many people away, the air was fresher than usual.

Most of the houses had taken their door knockers down to signal that the residents were away. The square, always full of activity, was rather eerie, covered in snow and without any signs of life. She didn't see so much as a stray cat. Which given the cold was lucky for the cats.

Elizabeth felt rather like a stray cat herself. Cast out in the wilderness to make her own way.

Even in the depths of her tantrum, she couldn't contain a snort of contempt for that idea. If she was a stray cat, she was an expensively dressed one. Like most of her clothes, the ensemble that she wore had cost a fortune and the cut was right up to the minute.

Elizabeth loved clothes. During her London seasons, she'd become something of a style leader. She'd been very pleased with how the color of her traveling ensemble contrasted with her blond hair and dark blue eyes. But that was part of the problem. She'd dressed to be noticed when, right now, that was the last thing she wanted.

Her urge to smile ebbed, as she pictured all those extravagant garments going to waste in Caithness.

No, she couldn't go to Scotland to squander her youth and spirit tending to Great-Aunt Agatha and her pack of panting, slavering, piddling pugs, almost as smelly as their mistress. But that meant marrying Stanton Morley-Bridges. Which meant signing up for a lifetime of misery.

Could she make herself so unpleasant tonight that her unwelcome suitor decided he'd rather have teeth pulled than marry her? Except her father would interpret that as breaking faith, and he'd send her to Caithness anyway.

Whatever she did, she couldn't stand out here in Lorimer Square until she turned into a block of ice. Every cell in her body rebeled at the thought of waiting meekly in the house for her parents to return, as each second ticked closer to her meeting with the man her father wanted her to marry.

But if she intended to roam, she needed to wear something that hid her rank. The green outfit announced far too loudly that she was from a rich family and she shouldn't be out and about on her own. She let herself back into the house and ventured down into the kitchens. The benches were crowded with various showpieces that would be served at the dinner tonight. On the coat stand near the door, she found what she wanted.

The voluminous cape belonged to the housekeeper, Mrs. Dawkins. It was warm and practical and made from a serviceable gray wool that would arouse no curiosity. Even better, it had a generous hood that would conceal her face.

The horrible choices awaiting Elizabeth had her stewing so hard that she was out the front door and down the steps again and on the short street leading out of the square without realizing it. Before she understood the risk she took, she was halfway to Piccadilly.

She stopped in confusion. She couldn't march down one of the capital's major thoroughfares without an escort. Even in her snit, she remained aware of that.

But the prospect of slinking back to the house made her gorge rise.

She wanted space. She wanted growing things around her. In built-up London, Hyde Park was the nearest that she was going to get to that. Green Park was nearer, but it was too open and too close to home for her to escape notice.

It was dangerous for unaccompanied women to wander around Town. She might be in the better part of London, but Seven Dials wasn't a million miles away. On the other hand, she was yet to see a soul and she could make her way to Hyde Park via backstreets. She'd have to cross Piccadilly at some stage, but her cloak should ensure that she remained inconspicuous.

It was Christmas Day. Surely any footpads would be with their families, the way honest men were. In frigid weather like this, a footpad would have to be desperate indeed to lie in wait for a potential victim.

On a normal day, she'd never chance gallivanting around Town on her own. But Christmas wasn't a normal day. With sudden purpose, she tugged the hood further forward and turned onto a side street that took her in the direction that she wanted to go.

CHAPTER TWO

The park was mercifully empty. Or at least the part of it that Elizabeth was in. She drew a deep breath to settle her pinging nerves and strode down a path between the huge plane trees, leafless at this time of year. Hoofprints and bootprints in the snow provided evidence of earlier traffic. In the distance, she saw a few couples walking together, but nobody looked in her direction.

The next breath that she took went some way toward easing her roiling anxiety. While she was still angry with her father, being outside settled her. She started to think, instead of wallow in a morass of horror.

There must be some alternative to the unacceptable options of Caithness or Stanton Morley-Bridges. Perhaps the spirit of Christmas had softened her father's attitude and he'd already thought better of his decision. She could perhaps negotiate another season in London, with the promise that she'd accept one of her long-term suitors before summer. She didn't love any of the men who pursued her, but there were one or two she liked as friends. Or a miracle might take place: some gentleman might claim her heart at last and she'd gladly agree to a wedding.

No, all was not lost.

She slowed her furious pace and started to pay attention to her surroundings. She'd emerged into a clearing with a marble statue of a faun. The sky was gray, but showed no sign of sending down any more snow.

Her walk had done more good than she'd expected, but she'd tempted fate long enough. It was time to return to Lorimer Square to prepare to convince her father that he was being unreasonable. She needed to be safely back before anyone discovered that she'd dared to walk about unchaperoned. Or else Papa would hit the roof, and any chance of persuading him out of his decision would go up in smoke.

She turned to find a man studying her from under the trees.

Her heart slammed to a stop, as alarm turned her blood colder than the winter air. All the warnings about never going out unaccompanied in the capital clamored in her ears. She cast a frantic glance across to where she'd seen the other people, but they were no longer there.

"Please don't be frightened, miss." The man spread his hands palm upwards in a conciliatory gesture. "I didn't mean to startle you."

He had a pleasant voice. Deep and musical and with a clipped upper-class accent like her own. He was dressed like a wealthy man, too. His low-crowned hat was all the fashion, and his greatcoat had more than enough capes to impress the dandyish set.

None of that meant she wasn't in danger. She studied him for a tense second, wondering if she could outrun him on the snow. He was tall and broad-shouldered, and she had a grim feeling that he'd catch up with her before she got halfway across the clearing. Even standing still, he gave the impression of loose-limbed athleticism.

Elizabeth cursed her stupidity. And her temper fit. And her father for making her so angry in the first place. Despite knowing that it wouldn't make a scrap of difference if the stranger decided to assault her, she backed away.

To her relief, he didn't shift any closer. "May I escort you back to your family? Ladies shouldn't be out alone in the middle of London, even on Christmas Day."

She didn't answer. Instead, she studied him, noting that he looked sincere. While he wasn't conventionally handsome, he had an interesting face. Prominent bone structure with hollows under his cheekbones. A long nose, a high forehead, dark winged eyebrows over deep-set eyes. Right now, he looked troubled, but something about the set of his mouth told her that he was more accustomed to smiling than frowning.

As if to prove that, he ventured a smile that set all sorts of interesting creases into his face. He kept his tone light. "I'm completely harmless, I swear."

"So you say," she bit out, then had cause to regret speaking, because his gaze sharpened on her. He'd notice her accent, just as she'd noticed his. He'd pick up that she was a woman of rank.

She braced for a barrage of questions, but he must have guessed that she was on the verge of scarpering. "My name is Tom."

"I don't need to know your name."

"No, you don't. But you might feel safer if I tell you."

"The only thing that isn't making me feel safe is

you." Perhaps not polite, but despite his assurances, she was rattled. No amount of smooth talking and lack of immediate attack made her forget how vulnerable she was. Nobody even knew where she was.

"I apologize for frightening you." Regret turned his mouth down. The odd combination of features – chiseled jaw, beaky nose, prominent cheekbones – all made for an unusually expressive face. "But when I saw you all alone over here, I feared you were in trouble. I wondered if perhaps I could help."

He was right about one thing, at least. Elizabeth was in trouble. Unfortunately not the sort of trouble that a passing stranger could solve.

She adopted a dismissive tone. "I appreciate your concern." Which they both knew was a lie. "But I'm perfectly fine. You may go on your way, sir."

"Tom."

"Tom," she said with a hint of a snap, although Christian names generally weren't used outside one's closest circles.

He didn't shift. She'd had a feeling that he wouldn't. That square jaw conveyed stubbornness, just as his mouth conveyed humor. "A gentleman likes to oblige a lady, but I'm afraid I can't leave you at the mercy of the elements and any stray ruffian."

"No, just at your mercy."

Another smile. Despite her peril, she couldn't help noticing that it was a nice smile. The sort of smile that invited a person to smile back. She didn't.

"Yes, but I only harbor the most innocent intentions toward you."

She still didn't smile. "Words are cheap."

His lips twitched. "Undoubtedly, and there's nobody around to vouch for me. Where I come from, I could probably rustle up a respectable squirrel to confirm I'm a capital fellow, but I'm new to London and a stranger to the local wildlife."

Despite everything, some of Elizabeth's tension drained away. This time, it was an effort to fight a smile. He was charming. But that didn't mean he was safe. She injected more determination than she felt into her voice. "I'm perfectly all right. There's no need to concern yourself."

He waved away her answer. "But you see, there really is. I know hardly anyone is around, but that's the issue. Should anyone offer you insult, there's no rescue at hand. If I arrange to stay ten paces behind you, can I at least see you back to where you live? On my solemn oath, I'm really no danger to you. You shouldn't be out here with no protection. No man of conscience would allow it."

"It's really none of your business. You could pretend you never saw me."

"No, I couldn't."

A long-suffering sigh escaped her. "Because you're a man of conscience."

Somewhere in the last few seconds, she'd accepted his good intentions. Perhaps because he made no attempt to threaten her physically.

He must have heard surrender in her tone, because those impressive shoulders relaxed. "Precisely. Chivalry forbids me to abandon you."

"Then by all means, we must obey chivalry's call," she said drily.

He smiled at her again, with a touch of approval this time. "So you'll let me see you home?"

Did she want to go home? For a few precious moments, she'd tasted freedom. She'd received a nasty fright when this man accosted her. But the suffocating feeling that had overwhelmed her when she read her father's letter had faded once she was outdoors.

Elizabeth wasn't ready to retreat to Lorimer

Square and hide away inside until her family arrived later this afternoon. Slinking home and forsaking this brief liberty would only remind her of her restricted choices. She'd fret herself back into a complete state.

That queasy, trapped feeling stirred once more and made her stomach clench. What on earth could she do, if her father refused to compromise? "I…"

Tom's fixed attention should make her uncomfortable, but somehow it didn't. Perhaps because his expression conveyed no judgment, just friendly interest. It was a clever face. But now that her initial suspicion faded, she couldn't help thinking that it was a kind face, too.

"I know I'm a stranger, but I'd love to help. You can trust me, you know."

The strange truth was that she did trust him, which seemed mad when she didn't know him from Adam. Heavens, she didn't even know his last name. Probably better that she never did. For the sake of her reputation, they shouldn't meet again after today.

Even more bizarre that the thought stirred a vague regret. She knew nothing about him, but she could already tell that he was among the nicest men she'd ever met.

"Will you please escort me back to Piccadilly? I can find my way from there, thank you."

She didn't want him to know who she was and where she lived. The story of Lady Elizabeth Tierney traipsing around Hyde Park and chatting to strangers without a chaperone would make for delicious gossip. While she'd undoubtedly been rash to leave home alone, she'd rather avoid a scandal if she could.

"It would be my pleasure."

She took a step in his direction. Her half boots

were designed for a winter's day, but when she stood still so long on the snow, the cold seeped up through the stout soles. She was grateful that she wore Mrs. Dawkins's thick cape, for the warmth it provided as much as the concealment.

"Would you like me to walk behind you?"

This time, she couldn't stop herself from smiling. "That would be more likely to draw attention than if you walked beside me."

He looked arrested. Those deep-set eyes sharpened on her features. It was the most male expression she'd seen on his face. As if within a flaring instant, the quality of his interest changed.

Elizabeth gave a shiver, not because of the bitter cold. Nor was she frightened, although perhaps she should be. Instead, something deeply feminine inside her responded to that sudden masculine reaction.

When he approached and extended his arm, she curled her gloved fingers around his elbow with a willingness that surprised her. Warmth radiated through her. She'd been feeling so hideously lonely. Accepting the company of a tall, protective stranger made her heart expand in a way that was almost as disturbing as her initial fear of him.

Settle down, my girl. She wasn't a wide-eyed debutante of seventeen. She was a sophisticated woman who had danced with a hundred men much more handsome than this one. For season after season, she'd held her own in society. As her father had pointed out in his infuriating letter, she'd refused a long list of requests for her hand.

"I appreciate your trust," he said softly. This close, the deep voice vibrated in her bones in a pleasant if unfamiliar fashion.

"I appreciate your offer of assistance."

"I hope you won't feel I'm prying, but would it

help to talk about whatever is worrying you?" He began to retrace the path that she'd tracked across the snow. Although he shortened his stride to match hers, she'd been right about his ease of movement.

"No, thank you." For a moment there, Tom's subtle but increasingly powerful attractions had distracted her from her dilemma. His question reminded her that this glimpse of freedom, however fleeting, might become a poignant memory when she was running herself ragged at Great-Aunt Agatha's beck and call. "It's a family matter."

She cast him a sideways glance. When their eyes met, heat flushed her face as if she'd never met a man before. With his coal-black hair, she'd imagined that he'd have brown eyes. But the irises between the thick black lashes were a clear gray, the color of a calm sea just before sunrise.

Hoping Tom wouldn't notice her fluster, she looked away quickly and lowered her chin. What on earth was wrong with her? She was acting like a fluttering little fool, when she prided herself on her composure in social settings.

"I hope something you can sort out." His easy response went a little way toward restoring her customary optimism. He spoke as if he couldn't imagine her failing to achieve her aims in any sphere.

"I do, too," she responded with a bitter edge.

They turned onto the path that wound between the trees. "Well, if you feel the need to confide, your secrets are safe with me. You have my word on it."

While he spoke lightly, something in his tone suggested that he was in earnest. Perhaps it was just more madness, but Elizabeth was tempted to pour out all her troubles. She didn't. She preserved just enough caution to control the impulse.

They were two chance-met strangers. This would

be their only encounter. Even that reached an end. They weren't far from the park gates. Then it was a stroll to Piccadilly and the place where she and Tom would say their farewells. Another twinge of inexplicable regret.

She'd like to know him better. Because he'd been kind, and he hadn't taken liberties, and he'd stepped up to offer aid when she was at risk of getting into very hot water indeed. And despite all her turmoil, it was pleasant to amble around Hyde Park in the presence of a charming gentleman who she could tell admired her. All those eventful seasons hadn't gone to waste. She knew enough to recognize that Tom responded to her the way a man responded to a woman he found of interest.

What was more unusual was that Elizabeth just might be a little interested in him in return. Not that she intended to do anything about it. But the frisson in the air had nothing to do with the frigid temperatures and everything to do with her intriguing companion.

So when they approached the gates, she couldn't stem a pang of disappointment. And gratitude. "Thank you for coming to my rescue."

He stopped and she waited for him to reply, but then she, too, heard the faint cries.

"I think someone else is in trouble." Tom released her to run in the direction of the high-pitched shrieks.

Nonplussed, Elizabeth stared after him. She'd been right about his athleticism. He moved as smoothly as a jungle cat. And as fast.

She refused to be left behind, even if she was only a few hundred yards from the park's entrance. Picking up her skirts, she rushed after Tom, who remained visible amongst the sparse winter vegetation, despite how far ahead he was now.

CHAPTER THREE

"Help! Help!"

A towheaded boy of about six was stuck up a tree. He'd climbed so far that the thought of falling now gripped him with paralyzing terror. His earsplitting shrieks echoed around the almost empty park.

When Elizabeth caught up with Tom, he was standing beneath the oak and staring up at the child. "What's all this noise, my good fellow?"

"Help! Help!" The boy was so hysterical, he didn't seem to notice that rescue had arrived.

"Stop that now," Tom said in a tone of such authority that Elizabeth was startled. So far, he'd come across as an amiable stranger, but that voice could command armies.

It worked with the child. There was an audible sob, but the pleas for assistance stopped. His face red and shiny with tears, the boy stared down at Tom. "Who are you?"

"I'm the man who's going to climb this tree and get you back onto the ground, if you promise you won't yell anymore."

To Elizabeth's relief, the boy took the instructions to heart. "I'm very high."

The lad perched on a thick branch, and he seemed to have a firm grasp. As long as he didn't do anything rash, he seemed safe enough where he was. But he was right. It was very high.

"Yes, you are. But I'm an excellent climber, and this lady is going to help me."

"I haven't climbed a tree since I was twelve," she muttered at a volume that wouldn't reach the child.

Tom muffled a laugh. "I'd like to have seen that. Don't worry. I'll do the climbing. But I'd like you to be ready to catch him when I get him within reach. God knows how he got all that way up. That's not an easy ascent."

Elizabeth considered the tree and couldn't help agreeing. "Do you think you can manage it?" She wished she didn't sound so doubtful.

He reacted to her question with amusement, not a fit of male pique, she was pleased to note. "We'll have to see."

Tom took off his hat to reveal a thick head of disheveled black curls. He set his hat on a bench that was close but unfortunately not close enough to help him scale the tree. He tugged off his gloves to bare long-fingered, capable-looking hands. Quickly he unbuttoned his greatcoat and draped it over the seat.

"Hurry up. I'm getting cold," the lad said in peremptory tones. Elizabeth couldn't resist a pang of sympathy for whoever his mother was. This boy was clearly a handful, and Elizabeth had only known him for a few minutes.

"I'm doing my best," Tom said with commendable mildness. "My name's Tom. What's yours?"

"Cyril. Cyril Polkinghorne."

Tom's lips twitched. "That's a big name for such a young man."

"I'm not a young man. I'm six."

"My apologies." A scatter of snow descended onto

Tom's head. "Are you wriggling up there like a worm, Cyril?"

"No-o." He didn't sound sure. "Not like a worm."

"I don't want you wriggling at all," Tom said crisply. "I'll be most displeased if I go to the trouble of climbing this tree and you fall out of it before I get to you."

He shrugged out of his snug-fitting dark blue coat to expose a cream silk waistcoat and white shirtsleeves. The generous greatcoat had revealed his height but not his impressive physique. She'd never been so conscious of a man's sheer physical presence. She hadn't known she could be.

"My bum's cold," Cyril said with a hint of a whine.

Tom's eyes, bright silver with repressed laughter, met Elizabeth's. Warmth flooded her, despite the cold air, and made her fingers and toes tingle. She couldn't help smiling back, while deep inside her, something bloomed like a rose. The sensation was extraordinary. She didn't know what all this inner disturbance meant, but she was sure that she'd remember this moment when she was old and gray and reviewing her life's significant events.

"I'm sure you know better than to use crude language in front of a lady, Cyril," Tom said.

"But I'm freezing my arse off up here," Cyril said. "Hurry up."

Elizabeth couldn't contain a muffled snort of amusement. "Say please, Cyril. A gentleman shows his quality by demonstrating grace under pressure."

As she raised her head to address Cyril, her hood fell back. When she glanced at Tom, he was regarding her with an arrested expression that made that core of heat in her middle expand in a most disconcerting manner. "What is it?"

He blinked as if he came back from somewhere far away, and a tinge of color edged those spectacular cheekbones. "You have golden hair," he said softly. "I wondered."

Elizabeth had played a part in Cumbria's local society since she was seventeen, and she'd enjoyed a string of London seasons. Through those years, she'd received a thousand compliments, most of them considerably more flowery than this. In fact, it wasn't even a compliment. Not really. More a statement of fact. Perhaps it felt like a compliment because of Tom's rapt expression. Nonetheless, he wasn't the only person blushing.

"I..." she started, at a loss for an answer.

"Come on!" Cyril said from above, breaking the spell.

"You should start climbing before you freeze to death," she said.

"And before Cyril writes a letter to the *Times* complaining about the poor standard of rescuer in this day and age." Tom turned toward the tree. Elizabeth's heart, that had shown a lamentable urge to stop altogether, started up again.

Only to begin racing when her gaze dropped to the narrow hips under the tight buckram breeches. That arse – or bum, as Cyril would put it – was fascinating. Tight buttocks that flexed with every step. Her hands closed to fists at her sides, as if they curved around that taut flesh.

Good heavens, she'd had no idea that a man's body was quite so interesting.

What the devil was her problem? She was a sophisticated woman. She didn't go around ogling attractive men and their rippling hindquarters. Except it seemed that she did.

Without warning, Tom glanced back at her and her color surged once more, as she hurriedly fixed her gaze on Cyril. Had Tom noticed her wanton attentions to his rear? How humiliating if he had.

"Will you be ready to take him once I get him down far enough?" The question was serious, the tone wasn't. It reminded her how much she liked that warmly amused baritone. Although perhaps not just after he'd caught her leering at him. "Miss?"

She started and made herself look at him. "Of course."

At least he didn't know her name or anything about her. With a bit of luck, he was only passing through London and she'd never have to see him again. That was altogether the best outcome for today and its adventures.

She needed to tell herself that again and mean it this time.

"Come on!" Another fall of snow hinted that Cyril was getting impatient.

"You need to get him before he breaks his neck," she said, hoping that concentrating on the matter at hand would divert Tom from her *faux pas*.

"I think that's a good idea."

If she was trying to distract Tom from her gaffe, and she was, even she could tell it was an abject failure. Laughter sparkled in his gray eyes. He'd definitely noted her curiosity about his body.

Her voice emerged high and breathy. "What do you want me to do?"

She ventured nearer, near enough to catch the scent of his skin in the sharp air. She'd been close to men before, dancing or in carriages or walking arm in arm. She might be yet to choose a husband, but she'd thoroughly enjoyed a few flirtations.

Standing just behind Tom, she shouldn't be bowled over by the spicy scent teasing her nostrils. It wasn't as if he didn't smell like most other men she knew. At least the ones who took care about bathing regularly and wearing fresh linen.

There was the smell of leather and clean male

skin and a tinge of the outdoors. It was a mystery that in Tom, this banal mixture should combine to create a perfume as heady as any priceless blend from the Orient.

He turned to her with another smile. “Wish me luck.”

The smile started up the flutters inside her again. “Good luck.”

His attention narrowed onto her face. She noted his sudden tension. The air gave an odd shimmer, as if the world held its breath. Elizabeth even had time to move away.

She didn’t want to move away.

So she remained just where she was. She might even have leaned forward when he bent his tousled head and brushed his lips across hers.

There was a surge of tempting heat. Then the contact was over.

She released a soft sigh as he drew away, sorry it ended so soon. It seemed she was a hussy. It wasn’t her first kiss. But it was the first kiss in a long time that left her hungry for more.

“Hurry up!” Cyril insisted from above them. “There’s no time for all that slop.”

Tom’s brief smile conveyed regret that the kiss had ended. He peered at her with a concentrated focus that made her pulses rush. When she read approval in his eyes, another wave of warmth washed through her. “If I’m about to break my neck, I’ll die a happy man, at least.”

She responded with a throaty giggle, when she should be telling him off in no uncertain terms. Or running for her life.

Cyril released an audible sigh from above. “A fellow has better things to do than watch you two bill and coo.”

Tom tilted his head. “If you expect me to risk life

and limb to come to your aid, I'd stick a sock in it, you troublesome brat."

"I told you about my arse." It was clear Cyril found the word extremely pleasing to say. Elizabeth supposed he was that age to find pleasure in shocking the grown-ups. Although her experience indicated that some men were always that age.

"You did indeed."

"Then come and get me."

Tom sighed and made a jump for the lowest branch, which to Elizabeth's worried eyes seemed a long way from the ground. His hands failed to find purchase on the damp wood, and he dropped back to earth with a muttered curse.

So far, Elizabeth had been so distracted by her interest in a compelling stranger that she hadn't thought much about the genuine dangers involved in climbing a lofty oak on a snowy day. Her stomach which had been full of pleasurable, if socially unacceptable butterflies knotted in sudden worry. "Be careful, Tom."

He sent her one of those laughing glances that made her feel all shaky and enchanted. "I'll be fine. I have important things to do today."

She smiled back, even as she took in his tacit message that kissing her again was on his list. Any girl of sense who had been out in society knew how to quash unwanted male attention. Despite chaperones and the rules of propriety, not to mention basic human decency, there was too much of it. But the idea of giving Tom a cutting setdown didn't occur to her. It seemed that somewhere in the last hour, his attentions had become wanted.

How astonishing. How...troubling.

He jumped again. This time, his grip held. With the athleticism that she'd noticed straightaway, he dragged himself up onto the branch and began to scale the tree with impressive skill.

Her heart in her throat, Elizabeth watched him rise higher and higher.

Cyril's expression filled with wonder. "Cor, you're like a blinking monkey."

Perhaps it wasn't quite how Elizabeth would have phrased it, but Tom's expertise as a tree climber flooded her with admiration. He went up quickly and cleanly, and now he was within reach of the boy.

"I'm concentrating. Don't distract me," Tom said breathlessly, as he stretched for the branch just below Cyril. "The branch you're sitting on won't hold my weight. Can you lower yourself down and I'll catch you?"

"I think so." But the child didn't move.

It was the first sign of uncertainty that Cyril had shown since his shrieks for help. Elizabeth couldn't help thinking that both boy and man were awfully high up in the sky. A fall now would mean serious injury or even death.

While she didn't wish harm to anyone, it was disconcerting quite how much she wanted Tom to emerge unscathed from his heroics. This time, when her hands curled into fists, it was because she was strung tight with fear.

"Cyril, your arse is only going to get colder if you stay there. Come on, young man, move. I'm sure you've got a Christmas dinner waiting. You don't want to miss out on that, do you?"

"No." Cyril's doubt was audible in the drawn-out syllable.

"Come on. You were brave enough to get up there. You're brave enough to climb down one branch."

Feeling sick, Elizabeth watched the boy gingerly shift closer to the trunk.

"That's it. Slide down and I'll catch you." Tom slung his arm around another branch and held his hand out to Cyril.

Cyril came to a trembling stop. "I'm afraid."

Elizabeth hadn't been particularly impressed with Cyril so far, but right now, he sounded like a frightened child and her heart ached for him. Having two brothers, she was well aware what that small admission had cost him.

"Not you." Tom's laugh was encouraging. "You're a hero. Don't you forget it, Cyril."

The voice conveyed a confidence that made Cyril sit a little straighter. He still didn't budge, but even from the ground, she saw the tension seep from the taut little body. "Do you think so?"

"I know so." Tom stretched out further. "Let's get you down."

Cyril made a jerky movement and suddenly slipped from the branch. For a giddy moment, he plummeted through midair. Elizabeth muffled a horrified gasp, not wanting to distract them.

Tom lunged as far as he could and caught the boy before he lost his balance entirely. Cyril's feet struck the branch Tom stood on and for a sickening moment, Elizabeth feared that the lad might slip, taking his rescuer with him.

But Tom managed to bring the boy close. When Cyril's arms wrapped around the man, she heard him sob. She felt rather like crying herself.

"We'll get him safely down now." Tom smiled down at her with unconcealed relief.

"Thank heaven." She clasped her hands in front of her chest. "Thank *you.*"

Tom turned his attention to Cyril. "Let me go now and hold onto this branch. I'll turn around and get you down. If you climb onto my back, we'll get to the ground as easy as can be."

It took a little while for Cyril to obey the instructions, but eventually he clambered around to find a safe perch on Tom's back. The two came down the tree as effortlessly as Tom had scaled it in the first place.

On the bottom branch, Tom paused to let Cyril climb off his back. "I'll let you down from here. It's a bit of a drop."

Elizabeth stepped up to stand below them. "I can take him."

"Thank you," Tom said.

She reached out and accepted Cyril's weight, when Tom lowered him toward the ground. As she staggered, Tom jumped down beside her.

The lad was cold and shivering with fear as well. No doubt his arse *had* been freezing up there.

"Cyril Polkinghorne, I'll tan your hide when we get home, you imp of Satan!" A stout woman in a red and green striped pelisse bustled up toward them. "Your mother will have my guts for garters if she finds out you ran away from me like that. I've got a good mind to send you back to Slough with no Christmas dinner at all."

Cyril struggled out of Elizabeth's arms and regarded the middle-aged lady with a gleeful smile. The moments of appealing vulnerability hadn't lasted long. "Grandmamma, I've been having adventures. It's been ever so exciting. I climbed the tree and—"

"And needed this kind gentleman and lady to help you down. Lawks a-mercy, I nearly had kittens when I saw you stuck up there."

"I wasn't in any trouble," Cyril said with a worrying disregard for the truth.

His grandmother eyed him without favor. "That's what you think, young man." She opened her arms. "Now give me a hug. You've given your old gran a nasty fright."

Cyril went readily into her arms and suffered

through a suffocating cuddle with reasonably good grace. Behind them, Tom stepped aside to pull both his coats back on. He finished by putting on his hat and gloves. He must be freezing. The sun struggling to shine through the clouds shed no warmth.

"I'm Dora Polkinghorne. Thank you for your kindness in saving Cyril. He's a young devil, but I'd hate him to break his neck."

Tom smiled and took Elizabeth's arm with a proprietary air that would have annoyed her in any other man, particularly one she hardly knew. She was perturbed that right now, all she felt was pleasure in the contact. "My wife and I were happy to help."

Wife? Elizabeth cast him a quick, questioning glance, but he was smiling at Mrs. Polkinghorne with more of the easy charm that had already beguiled Elizabeth.

"I'm just so glad you were here. The park is nearly empty." Mrs. Polkinghorne released a ruffled Cyril from the enthusiastic hug and regarded him with a frown. "If he'd fallen and hurt himself, my daughter-in-law would never forgive me. He's her only child, and I'm afraid she spoils him."

"Not to mention that if something had happened to him, it would ruin Christmas," Elizabeth said lightly.

"I could have got down," Cyril said belligerently.

"No, you could not," his grandmother said. "Now thank this nice gentleman and his lady for helping you and I'll take you home. Mary's got dinner nearly ready and she'll sulk for a month if it's burned."

Cyril turned to Tom and Elizabeth. "Thank you for getting me down out of the tree."

"You're welcome, Cyril." Tom reached forward and shook his hand.

"And thank you for catching me," he said to

Elizabeth with a surprisingly deft bow.

"That was very neatly done," Mrs. Polkinghorne said. "Now, let's get you back to Paddington. I'm too old for all this excitement and it's too cold to stand around in the snow."

"I know. When I was up the tree, my arse nearly froze off."

Mrs. Polkinghorne went red in the face and caught him by the collar. "That's enough of that, you little horror. I'm so sorry, sir and madam."

"He's only trying to shock," Tom said. "Would you like us to come with you through the park?"

"No, thank you. I'm only a few minutes from home." She paused. "Unless you'd like to join us for Christmas dinner? There's plenty, and I'd love to thank you properly for saving my grandson."

"That's very kind, but we have another obligation," Tom said smoothly.

"But my arse *was* frozen," Cyril protested.

"We've heard quite enough about your rear end," his grandmother scolded. "Happy Christmas to both of you."

"And merry Christmas to you," Tom said, tipping his hat to her. "Be good, Cyril."

He didn't sound very certain. Elizabeth couldn't blame him. "Goodbye, Cyril. Goodbye, Mrs. Polkinghorne. Happy Christmas."

With a wave, Mrs. Polkinghorne hauled a reluctant Cyril away. It was clear that she had no intention of letting the boy run off again.

"If Cyril's good, it will be a Christmas miracle," Elizabeth muttered, as Tom drew her back to the path.

"O, ye of little faith, wife," he said in a laughing voice.

"That was quick thinking," she said.

Still holding her arm, he began to retrace their

path toward the gates. "It gave us a reason to be together without a chaperone. With your gloves on, she wouldn't notice the lack of a wedding ring." He paused. "Actually I have no idea if you're married Are you?"

"No," she said, although his question reminded her that she might be soon. The events of the last hour had eclipsed her quandary, but now her dilemma slammed back into her with all its previous impact.

"Well, that's a relief." He sounded as if he meant it.

She glanced at him. "Are we going to talk about the kiss?"

CHAPTER FOUR

Tom stopped and regarded Elizabeth with a searching attention that she felt to the soles of her feet. "I don't know. Are we?"

"Would you rather ignore it?"

"That depends." He continued to eye her uncertainly. "Are you in a mood to slap my face or have hysterics?"

"I'm not the hysterical sort."

"No, I've noticed that. But that doesn't mean you don't want to tear a strip off my hide for taking such a liberty."

"I'm not angry," she said in a neutral tone. She wasn't, although perhaps she should be. Instead she was curious, intrigued, beguiled. Edgy with suspense about what might happen next.

Nor was she afraid. She'd believed almost from the first that she could trust him. His manner reeked of benevolence. Cyril had clearly felt the same.

"That's good." He subjected her to another of those disturbing surveys that seemed to pierce through to her soul. "I hope you're not frightened. I did promise to keep you safe, after all. Please believe me when I say my intentions were only of the purest.

For the first five minutes of our acquaintance anyway."

She told herself that if she laughed, it would just deliver her over to his attractions. She wasn't quite there yet. Nor did she want him making assumptions about her willingness to surrender her virtue.

Elizabeth liked Tom. She liked him as much as she'd liked any man she'd ever met. But she didn't intend for her uncharacteristic recklessness today to have drastic consequences.

"I don't in general kiss strangers," she said.

"I don't either."

"Then?"

When he looked abashed, the impression charmed her. Society was full of dominant, endlessly confident men. It was nice to be in the company of someone who wasn't convinced that he had all the answers. "That was a deuced tall oak tree and Cyril was a long way up."

"Yes," she said, not sure where Tom was going with this.

His shrug was equally charming. "I didn't want to break my neck without kissing you first."

"Oh," she said, taken aback and captivated at the same time. Something melted inside her. The same something that had become all hot and confused when Tom had remarked on the color of her hair, as if he'd discovered a treasure at the bottom of a deep well.

A self-deprecating smile curled his lips. "When a man's just met the prettiest girl he's ever seen, it would be a cruel fate indeed that decreed he die without kissing her."

"That's..." She was definitely blushing now. "Thank you."

"No, thank *you*. I have a feeling that when I'm an old man breathing his last, I'll smile to remember the snowy Christmas Day when I kissed a beautiful stranger in Hyde Park."

Elizabeth goggled at him, as she struggled to come up with some adequate response to the extravagant compliment. It wasn't as if men had never said ridiculous things to her before. At the recent house party, her most persistent admirer had likened her eyes to sapphires and her lips to rubies and claimed that angels sang when they danced together.

Elizabeth had had trouble holding in her laughter.

She didn't feel like laughing now. When she studied Tom's face, what she really wanted to do was fling herself into his arms and beg him to kiss her again. And take his time on this occasion. That last kiss had ended before she had a chance to settle in and enjoy it.

She couldn't do that. Despite today's larks, she retained that much awareness of propriety.

He smiled at her with such sweetness that her innards turned to syrup. "I've shocked you."

"Yes." They started to stroll toward the gates that she could see in the distance.

"I can't believe nobody's told you you're beautiful before. That would mean every man in London needs new spectacles."

"The difference is that you sound like you mean it." She only realized how vain that sounded, once the words had left her mouth. "I mean..."

His smile broadened. That smile was jollier than puppies and dancing a waltz and Christmas. That smile made her realize that she was on the verge of more trouble than she could handle. "There's no need for false modesty. If the gentlemen of Britain don't shower you with praise, I despair of them."

In what had been an awful day full of

inconvenient travel, starting in the cold predawn hours with a cranky, ill maid, and crowned with her father's humiliating letter, this time with Tom stood out as remarkably pleasant. Elizabeth wished she hadn't been so insistent on leaving, although every rule asserted that she bring the encounter to a close as soon as she could.

Tom's mind must work along similar lines because his footsteps slowed. When he bent his head to her, his soft purr made every hair on her body stand up with awareness. "Do you really have to go so soon? I feel Cyril has dominated our time together, and I'd love the chance to get to know you better."

Elizabeth couldn't help thinking that if she dallied a little longer, he might kiss her again. She liked that idea. She was caught between the Scylla and Charybdis of Stanton Morley-Bridges and Great-Aunt Agatha. The prospect of this handsome hero seizing her in his arms and taking her mind off her dilemma was dangerously appealing.

"I could probably stay for a little while." The family weren't due back for ages yet, even without the heavy snow that was likely to delay them. Another hour with Tom wouldn't make much difference to the risks that she'd already taken, although it would make a difference to her.

He rested his gloved hand on hers where it curled around his elbow. Through two layers of leather and with the air so sharp, heat shouldn't flood her. But his touch filled her with summer.

"However..." she said, not sure how to explain that this concession didn't mean she conceded altogether.

Another sweet smile that made Elizabeth wish she could stay out here with Tom forever. In his company, she forgot her troubles. Instead she found endless understanding and kindness and admiration.

But of course, a life in Hyde Park wasn't practical. For a start, it was too cold in December to set up residence. Not to mention that she knew nothing about him. That was part of the appeal: they were true strangers, owing each other nothing. But presumably like her, Tom had a family and obligations and a life beyond rescuing small boys and flirting with random damsels.

"I assure you, I'll continue to treat you with all due respect." A glint of devilry entered his eyes, turning them bright silver. "Unless you're interested in more kisses. I wouldn't be averse to those."

Wry humor turned her mouth down. "In the most respectful fashion, of course."

"Of course." He regarded her with a question in his eyes. "So you're not going to rush off and abandon me to the icy wilderness?"

"Like the ending of *Frankenstein?*"

Pleasure lit his expression. "I couldn't put that story down."

"Neither could I. I felt the most delicious shivers when I read it. And I couldn't sleep afterward." She'd read the novel shortly after it came out last year. It had been published anonymously, but society was abuzz with rumors about the author's identity. Most people she knew assumed it was the scandalous Lord Byron.

"I'm all for delicious shivers," Tom said and much to her dismay – and reluctant delight – a delicious shiver ran through her at his suggestive tone. "Although speaking of shivers, perhaps it's time I tried to warm you up."

She'd been blushing on and off since she met him. Now her cheeks stung with heat, partly because a wicked part of her responded to that idea with a resounding *yes*. “Tom...”

He gave a soft laugh. “I meant I know a man who sells hot chestnuts at one of the gates a little further on. I know it’s Christmas Day, but let’s see if he’s there. One of life’s luxuries is a hot chestnut on a cold day. May I treat you?”

The tension flowed out of Elizabeth, even as she felt a shameful pang of disappointment. “Thank you. I’d like that.”

He turned away from the path that led back to Piccadilly and Lorimer Square and all her problems and set off across the snow. The fitful sun chose that moment to emerge and transform the park into a sparkling fairyland. In this man’s company, Elizabeth couldn’t help feeling that her vexing day turned enchanted as well.

“After that, I should come up with some entertainment for you. What on earth does one do on a snowy day in London?”

“Stay inside and toast one’s toes at the fire?”

Another grunt of amusement. “I’m happy to take you back to my rooms, if that’s what you’re suggesting.”

She rolled her eyes at him, which made him laugh again. “On second thoughts, perhaps we should stay in the open.”

“Perhaps we should.” He looked around. “We could have a snowball fight.”

“That would attract too much attention. And anyway, I don’t fancy getting wet and cold.” And drenching Mrs. Dawkins’s cape so she’d know someone had borrowed it. “Call me horridly unadventurous.”

“Never,” he said with theatrical emphasis. “So making angels in the snow is out, too?”

She gave an exaggerated shiver to match his tone. “Even wetter and colder.”

"We could build a snowman?"

Elizabeth wrinkled her nose. "That also sounds rather cold and wet."

"That's the problem with snow." Tom tucked her hand more firmly into his crooked elbow. "In that case, it's chestnuts and conversation."

She cast him a quick sideways smile. "That sounds perfect."

"Doesn't it just?" The warmth in his voice set up a corresponding warmth in her heart, despite the frosty weather.

When they crossed an open area that in summer would be smooth green lawn, a large dog, some kind of retriever, lolloped towards them with a bark of delight. As the huge black beast hurtled at them, Elizabeth braced for it to jump up and knock her over. Instead, it skidded to a stop at Tom's feet to ogle him with patent adoration. Elizabeth hid a wince. She feared that she might look at Tom in exactly the same way.

Tom released her and went down on his haunches to rub the dog's floppy ears. The attention made the shaggy creature whimper with delight. "You're a handsome fellow, aren't you?"

"Do you know this dog?" she asked.

Tom cast her a glittering glance. "Never met him before in my life."

"He clearly likes you." Who could blame him? Elizabeth liked Tom, too. More than anyone she'd met in London. More than anyone she could ever remember meeting anywhere.

"I suspect he just wants some attention." Tom continued to fondle the dog, as he surveyed the park. "I wonder where his master is."

The dog wasn't a stray. He wore a fine leather collar with silver chasing and trailed a lead, hinting that he'd got away from the person walking him.

When Elizabeth scoured their surroundings, she spied a liveried footman rushing toward them. "My bet is his master is warm at home and a servant is responsible for the dog."

"Bruno! Bruno, you rotten sod, come here!" As the footman, little more than a gangling boy, careered up to them, Elizabeth pulled her hood forward to shadow her face. "Come here, I say."

When Tom rubbed his face and patted his flanks, Bruno's eyes closed in bliss. He paid no attention to his guardian's arrival, until Tom picked up the lead and stood. Tom passed the lead across to the boy. "Just Christmas high spirits, I think."

"No, he's always causing trouble," the boy said taking the leash before he performed a belated bow "My lord, my lady."

Bruno observed Tom with a disappointed expression and settled on his rump, clearly in no rush to resume his walk. Elizabeth smothered a giggle. It seemed she wasn't the only one susceptible to Tom's fatal charm. So far, he'd proven irresistible to children and dogs. What better recommendation could she have for his character?

"He's a champ," Tom said with that easy smile that always gave her far too much pleasure. "When he grows up, he'll make a capital companion."

Now that Elizabeth looked closer, she saw that Bruno, like his guardian, wasn't fully mature yet.

"I'll believe it when I see it," the lad muttered, tugging at the lead. "Come on, Bruno. There's a nice warm kennel waiting for you. Stop annoying this lady and gentleman."

"He's not annoying us, but I imagine you want to get back home yourself."

"Aye, I do. It's perishing out here."

"Invigorating," Tom said.

The footman regarded Tom as if he was mad. He

clutched the leash tighter, as Bruno strained to get closer to Tom. "If you say so, sir." He returned his attention to the dog. "Bruno, stop pulling."

"Sit," Tom said in the voice that had evinced instant obedience from the rambunctious Cyril. In comparison, Bruno presented no challenge at all. He sat and directed a mournful brown gaze at Tom.

"I'll hold him here while you move on, if you don't mind, sir?" the boy said, reaching forward to clutch Bruno's collar as well. He obviously expected the dog to take off after his new idol, once Elizabeth and Tom walked away.

"Splendid idea." Tom leaned forward to give Bruno a final pat. "Goodbye, old man. And be a bit kinder to your keeper. It's Christmas after all."

Whether Bruno understood the command or not, he remained with the footman as Tom and Elizabeth continued arm in arm toward the chestnut seller. Although she couldn't contain another laugh when she saw the animal's unhidden regret that in life's lottery, he was left with the boy and didn't get to go with the man who knew exactly how to treat a dog.

"Are you ready to tell me your name yet?" Tom asked, as their boots crunched over the snow. Behind them, Bruno gave a long whimper of sorrow as if saying a wistful farewell.

Caution made her shake her head. "It's better I don't say."

She waited for him to push, but he nodded. "Very well. But I want you to know that I can keep my mouth shut."

She believed him, but something about performing introductions would force her back into the real world, where her once-tolerant father acted with such uncharacteristic tyranny. "I appreciate that, but I'd rather that we remain strangers."

"You don't feel like a stranger."

She tried to resist liking that too much. "You don't either, but I think that's just Christmas stardust."

"I like stardust."

"So do I." The smile they shared made her unruly heart break into a jubilant jig.

"But what shall I call you?"

Her lips twitched. "Flossie."

She was fond of her maid, who was diligent and clever and uncomplaining. When she wasn't suffering the mother of all head colds. And after all, it was thanks to Flossie and her illness that Elizabeth had met Tom in the first place.

His laugh rang with surprise. "You're never called Flossie."

"It suits as well as anything else." The other pet names people used for her – Bess, Eliza, Beth, Lizzie – all led back too easily to Elizabeth.

"I beg to differ. A woman like you should go by Ariadne or Andromeda."

It was her turn for a giggle. "All too much of a mouthful."

"Then Flossie you shall be."

"Thank you." She frowned. "I know I said I don't want to learn your full name—"

"Actually you said you didn't want me to learn your name."

She ignored that. "But are you married?"

He stopped and regarded her with displeasure. "I kissed you."

As if she could forget. "Yes."

"A man of honor doesn't run around kissing unfamiliar women if he's got a wife at home."

Elizabeth knew nothing about Tom. Not really. Except that he'd put himself at her disposal to save her from getting into trouble and he was willing to risk injury to rescue a less than winsome child. And he was funny and kind and clearly taken with her.

Apart from his claims about himself, she was in no position to conclude that he was a man of honor.

"No wife at home?"

"Or gadding about either. I'm as free as a bird."

How she wished that she could describe herself in those terms. This morning when she'd left the Wetherbys' charming country house, she'd had no idea of the restrictions about to close in around her life.

"I'm glad," she said, then felt that cursed blush rise again.

Tom stopped and arched an eyebrow at her. "Are you indeed?"

"I'd hate to think you were playing a wife false."

"That's very admirable." He paused. "I'd hoped you were glad because it meant I could kiss you with a clear conscience."

She should put him in his place, but the truth was that she also thought about kisses. It would be the height of hypocrisy to berate him for letting his mind follow the same path. Lady Elizabeth Tierney might be a bit of a flirt, but she was never coy. "First, you promised to feed me."

When he started walking again, his expression indicated satisfaction. Elizabeth suffered a nervous wobble, but that uncertainty came with an undeniable charge of anticipation as well.

CHAPTER FIVE

The hot chestnuts were welcome. Elizabeth hadn't stopped to eat before she left the Lorimer Square house in such a temper. And it was a long time since her bread and cheese in the coach early this morning. Even more welcome was the heat radiating from the chestnut seller's cart. Elizabeth was dressed for the weather, but that didn't mean she said no to extending her hands toward a nice warm brazier.

"That was lovely. Thank you." She stretched her booted feet out on the snow in front of her, appreciating her thick woolen stockings. They'd finished their chestnuts sitting on a bench in a sheltered corner of the park. Tom had cleared the snow from the seat and dried it off with his handkerchief. Elizabeth's cape, gown and petticoats saved her from feeling the chill of the wood beneath her.

"I've become a regular customer since I came back to London a few days ago." Tom plucked the crumpled paper from her fingers and crushed it into the pocket of his greatcoat. He took off his hat and set it on the bench beside him. The gesture expressed a purposefulness that she couldn't mistake. A thrill coiled down her backbone.

"You've been away?" she asked, before she remembered that if she refused to tell him about herself, it hardly seemed fair to interrogate him.

"Yes," he said with a contented sigh, sliding his arm around her as if he'd been doing it for years. "I'd forgotten how charming old England can be. Or at least some of its citizens."

Elizabeth tried to tell herself that she relaxed back into his embrace because it was cold and he was alluringly warm. But that explanation smacked of odious coyness. She snuggled up to Tom because she wanted to be close to him. Odd that a stranger should make her feel so safe and cherished.

"This has turned out to be a lovely Christmas," he murmured.

"Yes, it has." Which was something that she hadn't expected to be saying a couple of hours ago.

For a delightful interval, they sat in silence. This secluded bower provided appealing privacy, as if they inhabited a magic bubble separate from the world and its concerns. While that might be an illusion, it was a devilish appealing one. Every so often, people passed behind the holly hedge that concealed them from the rest of the park. A robin in search of lunch fluttered around them.

She released a sigh even more extended than Tom's. Was her situation quite as dire as her initial panic made it seem? She wasn't beaten yet. Life offered Elizabeth Tierney more than inept suitors and temperamental great-aunts. In fact, right now, life was overflowing with tantalizing possibilities.

"Feeling better?" Tom asked softly.

She turned to regard him. When they'd met, he'd noticed how upset she was, but he'd been tactful enough not to pry after she'd brushed off his questions. "Yes, I do."

He ran one gloved finger down the side of her face. The gesture conveyed tenderness rather than predatory intentions. That vulnerable place inside her went squidgy with delight. He really had the most bizarre effect on her internal organs.

"When we met, you looked ready to pitch yourself headfirst into the Serpentine."

So far, they hadn't ventured toward the lake in that part of the park. "I suspect it's frozen over."

"You know what I mean."

"I'd just had some unwelcome news." What a wishy-washy way to describe a letter that threatened to turn her life upside down.

"I'm sorry. That's tough at Christmas."

Her lips tightened. "It would be tough whenever it arrived."

"Can I help?"

"You have already." She summoned up a smile. "I'm glad you came to my rescue."

"So am I."

For a long moment, she stared into silvery eyes that held a whole world of feeling. Warmth. Empathy. Interest. Interest that sharpened into sudden intent in the time it took him to blink.

Without rushing, he angled toward her and his hold around her shoulders firmed. In spite of his unmistakable desire, he remained tactful. He gave her time to pull away if she wanted to. She appreciated his consideration, but right now, she hungered for the touch of his lips.

Anyway, another, more thorough kiss had loomed ever since that unsatisfying peck before he'd rescued Cyril. It was as inevitable as tomorrow's sunrise.

So Elizabeth tilted her head up and closed her eyes, as she leaned into that powerful chest.

On a hum of approval, he brushed his lips across hers. It was akin to the chaste kiss that he'd given her under the oak tree. Over in a second. The difference was that this time, the kiss asked a question. An inquiry as to whether she wanted more.

She did.

When he shifted away far too soon, a muffled murmur of frustration escaped her. Tom reached out to cradle the side of her face in one gloved hand.

Before his head descended once more, she had a chance to snatch a breath. At last his lips clung, summoning the most glorious sensations. When his mouth touched hers, her whole body dissolved into a puddle of delight.

He sucked gently at her upper lip and grazed his teeth against the lower one. A shiver of pleasure rippled through her. That delicious masculine scent overwhelmed her senses. A smoky trace of roast chestnuts flavored his kiss. Chestnuts and something that was all Tom. Heat pooled in the pit of her stomach, set up a restless swirl in her blood.

Elizabeth murmured encouragement as the pressure deepened. Wanting more, she slid one hand up his woolen greatcoat to clasp his shoulder. She moved her lips against his, pursing them to intensify the contact.

When he pulled away, she released a sigh of disappointment and opened her eyes. "Why did you stop?"

His lips, sleek from the contact with hers, curved in a smile that conveyed endless pleasure in her. "I don't want to make assumptions."

"You may assume that I want to kiss you."

His gaze narrowed on her lips. "Then I'm blessed among men."

His dry remark evoked a huff of amusement that faded against his lips. This time, he kissed her with more intent. Nibbling along the seam of her lips, using his tongue to tease the corners. When his teeth grazed her again, she gasped and his tongue slipped into her mouth on a foray that felt like another question.

Arousal stirred her blood and made her nestle closer. The second time his tongue slid between her lips, he lingered to luxuriate in her taste.

She took longer to come back to reality from that kiss. Her eyelids felt weighted down, as she slowly opened them and pulled away far enough to focus on his features. He, too, looked lost in wonder, as if during the last few minutes, the earth beneath them had moved on its axis.

"That was...nice," she said. The scale of that understatement was farcical. "Nice" was a word one used for a tasty lunch or a sunny day. Tom's kiss had shaken her world.

"It was indeed." The corners of Tom's lips deepened in amusement. "Can I do more to keep you from the cold, cold snow?"

She stiffened. "I don't—"

Fondness braided his laugh in a way that made her pulses dance. "I know you aren't committing to more than kisses." He paused. "Anyway it's too cold for seduction."

Her brief spurt of fear drained away. "I don't feel cold when you kiss me," she admitted.

His eyes brightened as he stroked her hair. "Then it's my Christian duty to kiss you again."

This time, she laughed. "And it's Christmas as well."

"Yes, by all means, let's blame Christmas."

This time, his kiss was more commanding. He held her closer and after her lips opened to his, the kiss caught fire. When his tongue tangled with hers, she responded. For an immeasurable interval, the sensual duel continued.

Elizabeth was breathless when he raised his head to pepper her face with a rain of little kisses. Kisses across her chin and cheeks and brow and nose. Each sparking a delight that stoked the heat flaring inside her. Her heart was pounding, and she'd never felt so alive. Every sense worked at full stretch to capture this extraordinary experience.

She'd been kissed before. When she was sixteen, she and Alexander Comerford had conducted a secret flirtation that involved far too many torrid embraces in the woods at Sander Hall. But once that summer was done, her ardor for the future Lord Lumsden was done as well. Her adolescent passion left only a friendly interest behind. A good thing, given Alexander was now married to one of her best friends.

In the years since, a couple of men had defied propriety and kissed her. Some with her cooperation, some without. When she'd cooperated, she found the experience pleasant, but nothing more. None of those kisses came near to igniting the heat that Alexander had. Until now. Until Tom.

Tom's kisses swept her into a new universe, conjured up sensations that she had no idea existed. When his lips touched hers, her soul took flight.

The moment that his lips returned to hers, she melted against him and her hands raked through his thick, black hair. Her bosom swelled against her bodice, while a heavy weight settled in the pit of her stomach. An aching, longing, hungry weight.

It was a huge, unprecedented reaction to a kiss. Goodness, imagine if he set out to seduce her. She'd be helpless against his attractions.

He shifted along the seat away from her. In visible torment, he shut his eyes and ran a shaking hand through his messy hair. "Don't look at me like that."

Elizabeth blushed, guessing that her expression must betray the wanton direction of her thoughts "We should stop."

At her deepest level, she didn't mean that at all But voices on the other side of the hedge signaled that a family passed by. She was painfully conscious that someone just had to take the narrow path between the holly bushes to stumble upon her entangled in Tom's arms. Despite those heady kisses, she wasn't entirely lost to prudence. Although if Tom kept kissing her, she wasn't sure that her caution would persist.

"We should." He sounded as reluctant as she did.

She wasn't sure who shifted, her or Tom. But they were kissing again with a fervor that made her head spin. This time, breaking free of his embrace was so difficult that it verged on the impossible.

He groaned when at last she found the willpower to end the kiss. "We need to get back into the open," he rasped out.

Her hands tightened on his shoulders, as if her body resisted that idea, even while her mind recognized its necessity. "Yes."

Another kiss, but Elizabeth couldn't forget the danger. This time, when Tom lifted his head, she struggled onto her feet and held out her hand. Standing presented a challenge. Those thrilling kisses had transformed her once perfectly functional knees to jelly. "Come on, Tom. Let's see if we can find some more winsome tots to rescue."

Heavy-lidded eyes dwelled on her. He looked like he hadn't yet returned to the snowy reality of Hyde Park on Christmas Day. Her kisses had transported him as thoroughly as his had transported her. She stifled a surge of pleasure at the thought.

His face was flushed, and his lips were full and dark. Dear heaven, what delight those lips could deliver. For a prickling moment, Elizabeth considered returning to his arms. Then she straightened her backbone and stiffened her wobbly knees and told herself to be strong.

She watched him suck in a deep breath, as the dazed pleasure seeped from his face. The ardent lover faded from view. He became again the debonair stranger she'd met mere hours ago.

Although after those kisses, he'd never be a stranger again.

"I wouldn't describe Cyril as winsome."

Her laugh cracked. Despite her best efforts to appear calm, she was still shaky. Tom's kisses made her blood churn, and his taste lingered on her lips. "I'm not sure I would either."

With visible regret, he picked up his hat and placed it on his head. She shared his regret, but she could no longer forget that they were in a public place.

Would she find a chance to kiss Tom again, free from the fear of discovery? The idea made her heart leap with forbidden elation. Perhaps if they had privacy, he'd do more than kiss her. The shocking idea made her breath catch in her throat. The need to avoid a trip to Scotland became even more urgent.

To her relief, Tom rose and took her hand. The contact went a little way toward making up for her self-sacrifice in abandoning his kisses. She curled her fingers around his, as if making a silent vow of allegiance.

They emerged from the hedge to discover that the brighter weather had enticed more people into the park. Tom paused beside the holly hedge to pull up the hood of her cape. His care for her reputation warmed her heart in a different way from that passionate embrace.

To her dismay, the short winter's day closed in,

bringing an end to her freedom. Tom must have noticed, too, because he frowned and spoke with uncharacteristic force. "Damn it, I want you to stay. But you're about to tell me that you have to go, aren't you?"

Elizabeth was just as torn. She felt like she'd gained a friend and a lover, although their acquaintance was too short for him to qualify as the first and every rule of society barred him from becoming the second.

"And this time, I'll mean it," she said ruefully. If she was to have a hope of bringing her father around from his draconian plans, she needed to mind her manners for the next little while.

Should Lord Tierney discover that his oldest daughter had been romping around Hyde Park like an amorous milkmaid, he wouldn't even give her the option of marrying the man of his choice. He'd pack her off to Great-Aunt Agatha before Elizabeth could say "I do" to her imposed bridegroom.

"Let me take you home."

"Across Piccadilly at least."

It would be bad enough if she was caught alone out on the streets of London. If someone saw her with a man, her goose would be cooked.

But Elizabeth wasn't yet ready to relinquish Tom's company. Goodness, given a choice, she'd never leave him. Which was mad. Through four seasons, no swain had made her heart skip a beat. After one snowy afternoon in Hyde Park, a stranger had enthralled her so completely that she had difficulty imagining they would never meet again.

"Thank you," she said, pulling her hood further forward and slipping her hand around his elbow. Already the act of walking at his side seemed natural, something she could happily do for the rest of her life.

She waited for him to resume their playful banter, but he remained quiet as they walked toward the gates that she'd used to enter the park. She didn't say much either. It was one of those awkward occasions when one said absolutely everything lurking in one's heart or nothing at all.

To her relief, nobody spared the tall man and the caped woman at his side a second glance. Right now, being in Tom's company made her less noticeable than if she was unescorted.

They wended their way through the streets to Piccadilly, crossed the road, and paused in the recessed doorway of a closed glove shop. A few feet away, the world and his wife went on their merry way. Traffic clattered past, and people hurried home out of the cold, looking forward to their Christmas revels.

Lucky them. Most years, Elizabeth enjoyed the Tierney family Christmas. Not this year. And not just because at the very least, she'd have to be civil to Stanton Morley-Bridges tonight.

In the shadows of the doorway, she could barely see Tom's face. He was just a warm, solid presence in the gloom. Now that she couldn't see him, that alluring, spicy scent flooded her nostrils in a most intoxicating way. She was more aware than ever of his imposing height.

"Can you get home without consequences?" His velvety baritone stroked her senses as powerfully as if he touched her.

"I should be able to sneak in through the kitchens." As long as the servants weren't back already. She really was taking a risk, lingering now. The timing grew dangerously tight.

Out of sight of the street, Tom rested one hand on her hip where it pressed against the shop's wooden door. The heat that radiated from his touch vied with the creeping chill in her heart at having to forsake him.

"I don't want you to go." His voice turned low and savage. "These hours with you have been magic. I can't even kiss you goodbye."

She tipped her face toward him. "We should have gone back to our hidden place in the holly."

When he shook his head, she knew he smiled. "No, we shouldn't."

"Oh?"

"Because we'd still be there."

They would. "You can't take me all the way home. If anyone sees us together, there will be the devil to pay."

"I'm not leaving you alone in the middle of this crowd."

From the start, she'd recognized his strong protective streak. He'd demonstrated it when he climbed an oak to save the presumptuous Cyril. It had made him offer Elizabeth his company when he saw her.

"I live in a square off Piccadilly." That was an admission of her status. He'd know even more about her, if he accompanied her to the short side street leading to Lorimer Square. But she'd decided that she didn't want to be a mystery to Tom. She wanted him to be able to find her again.

"Then I'll take you that far."

"Thank you." She rested her hands on his chest, wishing several layers of fine English wool didn't muffle his heartbeat. A winter meeting involved far too much heavy clothing. She wished to heaven that they'd met in summer, so when she touched him, she could feel the warmth of his skin.

Although in summer, the park would be so crowded, she'd never risk a solitary walk.

Their kisses had sparked a craving for more than

his conversation. She loved talking to him. She loved his sense of humor. She loved his transparent interest in what she said. Pretty girls were used to men admiring their looks, but less used to men being curious about their thoughts and feelings.

But Tom had awoken her animal impulses. Now above all, she wanted physical contact. Kisses. Touches. His breath on her skin. His heart thundering beneath her palms.

"Damn it, I want to see you again." His Adam's apple bobbed as he swallowed. Could her hands on him have the same incendiary effect as his on her? "Can you get away tomorrow?"

While hearing that he didn't want things to end was no surprise, it made her happy. "I don't know."

How dictatorial was Papa likely to be? Would he forbid her from leaving the house?

A faint frown drew those expressive brows together. "Do you want to see me again?"

"Of course I do," she said, before she thought of playing flirtatious games.

He smiled at her. One of those lovely smiles that made her silly heart turn cartwheels. "I hoped you would."

"I kissed you." She was grateful that her hood and the unreliable light hid her blush. "It's a sign that I like you."

"I could say the same."

She smiled back, enraptured despite the looming disaster of tonight's Christmas party. Because chance or fate or providence had tossed this marvelous man in her path when under normal circumstances, it was likely that they'd never have met.

"If I can, I'll come out riding at dawn. If not, I'll do my best to get you a message." It was a pity Flossie was with her family. Elizabeth could trust her with a note.

"I'll wait near the gates."

"I'll look for you."

"I won't be able to steal you away for a kiss."

Her dour groom Stubbs would have a fit if she ran off into the bushes to kiss Tom. He'd make sure that Papa heard about her sins, the minute she got home "No. But perhaps—"

"We could talk about future meetings?"

"I'd like that." In the restricted space, she made herself shift away from him. "Now I really must go."

She prayed that the servants hadn't come back early. She prayed that her parents hadn't had a quick trip south. The idea of being sent away to Scotland now, when life in London turned so intriguing, was too awful to contemplate.

Tom took her arm, and they stepped out of the doorway together. She kept her head down so the loose hood concealed her face. She'd managed to escape discovery so far, but this close to home, the risk became more immediate.

Elizabeth was glad of Tom's arm, and not just because she liked touching him. The crowd on the street was rowdy with Christmas cheer. Carol singers stood in front of Hatchards, and a host of vendors had set up on the footpath, hawking mulled wine and sweets and decorative sprigs of holly. Their old friend, the chestnut seller, had even found himself a new patch, although he was busy with customers and didn't notice Tom and Elizabeth passing.

"This is where I turn off," she said when they reached her corner.

"This leads to Lorimer Square," Tom said with audible surprise. While he must have already guessed that she was a lady, Lorimer Square was one of the most exclusive addresses in London.

"Yes, it's where I live." She tugged free of his arm.

Whatever she might prefer, she couldn't linger for a long farewell. "I should be safe going on from here. Even if someone sees me in the square, I can make some excuse that I slipped out for a breath of air."

"I'll wait here. I can watch until you turn off into the square. Call out if you run into trouble."

"I doubt you'd hear me over the din."

"I'll always hear you, Flossie."

She paused to look deep into his eyes. "My name isn't Flossie."

Elizabeth was acutely aware of this moment's significance. So far, they'd played an enjoyable game, but once Tom knew who she was and where she lived, the game ended and real life took over. This budding attraction between them might blossom into something very significant indeed.

His lips turned down with the humor that she'd liked from the first. "You don't say."

"It's Elizabeth."

"Elizabeth?" He looked ridiculously pleased. She supposed he recognized that she was ready to put an end to the mysteries between them. Next time they were alone together – and she was sure that time would come – they'd learn everything they needed to know about each other. Although they'd already learned the most important thing: that a raging fire of desire burned between them.

"Goodbye, Tom. And happy Christmas."

He caught her hand and squeezed it in a way that somehow translated to her heart cramping with yearning. "Happy Christmas, Elizabeth. It's been marvelous."

"Yes, it has." She mustered a mighty effort to tug her hand free and rush down the snowy street toward her house. She didn't look back. But all the way, she could feel his gaze on her.

CHAPTER SIX

Elizabeth looked her best when she ventured downstairs for the family Christmas celebrations. If she'd had the faithful Flossie helping her dress, she might have been able to contrive an unflattering appearance. But her mother had sent her daunting lady's maid Josette in to ensure that no curl remained unarranged and that Elizabeth wore her prettiest gown. If she'd hoped to look like a total fright to deter Stanton Morley-Bridges from pursuing her, those hopes died the moment Josette appeared.

As Elizabeth approached the drawing room, she felt queasy. Gales of laughter and the buzz of happy conversation emerged from behind the closed door. It seemed that everybody except her was getting into the festive spirit.

Things had been bad enough when she'd learned that her father intended to foist her off onto an unknown and unappealing suitor. They were worse, now that she'd met Tom and had a very different beau in mind as a potential husband.

At least she'd managed to slip back into the house unnoticed. Although only by the skin of her teeth.

She'd just hung up Mrs. Dawkins's cape when the housekeeper herself bustled into the kitchens. Thank heavens, the woman was too focused on getting the extravagant meal started to notice the garment's damp hem.

Not long after that, the family had arrived. If Elizabeth had succumbed to temptation and lingered even a few minutes longer with Tom, she'd have come undone.

Before dressing for dinner, all the Tierneys had congregated in front of the drawing room fire for spiced wine and mince pies and the exchange of gifts. Guy was there, and her mother and father, and her two younger sisters and little brother.

Elizabeth had tried to corner her father to talk about his absurd ultimatum, but he was canny enough to avoid a tête-à-tête. Not for nothing was he known as one of Westminster's slipperiest politicians. Amidst the uproarious chaos, there was little chance for a serious discussion anyway. Which wouldn't have irked her nearly so much, if she wasn't sure that her father had arranged the timing of his letter precisely to match all the distracting activity.

When she gave him a gift and a dutiful kiss – Elizabeth wasn't feeling particularly fond of her papa right now – he'd asked if she'd received his letter. Her cold response hadn't dampened his mood at all. Nor had he lingered with her. Instead, he'd patted her cheek and turned away to give a present to her sister Susannah. Elizabeth could see that it would be Boxing Day before she found an opportunity to beg him to relent.

She'd tried to waylay her mother, once everyone went upstairs to prepare for the evening's festivities. Lady Tierney could generally bring her husband around. But Mamma had chased her away, saying time was too short for a coze when visitors were due in an hour.

So now when Will the footman opened the door to the crowded drawing room, Elizabeth felt frustrated and trapped and ignored, and very sorry for herself indeed. She was so upset that it took her a few seconds to see the people inside as individuals and not just a solid wall of humanity. Humanity amidst masses of holly and mistletoe, hauled down from Cumbria to adorn the house.

Apart from her little brother Peregrine, everyone was drinking champagne. Her mother and father stood in front of the hearth, looking very pleased with themselves. Her sisters, Susannah and Marianne, were talking to Lord and Lady Shelburn who had stayed in Town for Christmas this year. As had the Colvilles, and Lord Denton and his new bride Anthea, all of whom were deep in conversation in front of the tall window with its amber velvet curtains. Her father's two widowed sisters, who lived at opposite ends of the country, sat exchanging gossip on the brocade sofa near the fire.

A peal of masculine laughter made her glance toward the far corner, where Guy was talking to Ivor Bilson and another man who had his back to her. Her heart surged up to lodge in her throat, as she took in broad shoulders and glossy black curls. The stranger was very tall, a few inches over Guy's six feet.

This must be the dreaded Stanton Morley-Bridges. The urge to turn on her heel and flee back to her bedroom rose, but she knew that wouldn't help her. Let her at least meet her nemesis and work out how best to discourage any interest he showed.

Whatever happened, she refused to buckle under her father's tyranny. She was braver than that. She leveled her shoulders and raised her chin and told herself that she'd come out of this somehow.

Her father looked toward her and had the nerve to send her a beaming smile. Very pointedly, she didn't smile back. "Elizabeth, we wondered where you'd got to."

No, he hadn't wondered, the lying snake. He knew that she'd stayed upstairs as long as she could to put off the promised introduction.

Her father's greeting created a lull in the conversation. All attention fixed on her, and the unknown young man turned slowly in her direction.

When she met a familiar pair of silver eyes, a haze descended over her and her heart stuttered to a stop. She felt like someone had punched her in the stomach.

Through her speechless bafflement, she saw Tom smiling at her as if she was exactly what he wanted for Christmas. What on earth was going on? How could this be? Was Stanton Morley-Bridges yet to arrive? And what in blazes was Tom doing here? Her heart thudded in her ears, as she struggled to make sense of what she saw.

Tom noted her appalled reaction. His spontaneous joy at seeing her faded, replaced by concern. She was too shocked to know what she felt. Or to hide it. The haze around her thickened. The room receded down a long tunnel, and she reached out with a shaking hand to clutch the bronze doorknob behind her.

"Elizabeth, I've been dying to introduce you to my friend, Tom." Guy clapped Tom on the shoulder and urged him toward her. "Tom, this is my sister, Elizabeth. I've told you all about her."

"Yes, you have." Tom approached with a worried frown and an audible note of caution. "Lady Elizabeth, I'm delighted to make your acquaintance."

Without thinking, she extended her hand and he

caught it. Rather than a polite gesture, his grip felt like the only thing keeping her upright. It was the first time that they'd touched each other without gloves. Even through her turmoil, she felt a wave of heat wash over her.

"I don't..." What could she call him? She couldn't call him Tom when everyone here thought they were meeting for the first time. While all the time, the horrifying truth pounded through her over and over. *He knew who you were. He knew who you were.* He'd deceived her from the first.

Tom bent over her hand and glanced up. "Breathe," his lips formed soundlessly.

She blinked and realized at last that she was making an exhibition of herself. Her hand clenched on his, as she sucked in a shaky breath. Straightaway the room's details sharpened, including the curious gazes aimed her way. Still grasping Tom's hand, she stepped away from the door on shaky legs.

Guy was talking about something. Through the rush of blood in her ears, she heard him say the impossible. "This is Stanton Morley-Bridges, Viscount Fairchild. We met while I was in Paris last year. I saw at once that he's a thoroughly good chap."

"Good chap" was the highest praise in her brother's vocabulary. Elizabeth however remained bewildered. "But isn't your name Tom?"

Tom had straightened. Now he cast her a faintly apologetic look. "When I was born, my older sister couldn't manage Stanton, so she used to call me Tom. It stuck."

Elizabeth supposed it made sense, if anything about this farcical encounter made sense. When Tom's hand tightened on hers, she realized that she still clutched at him. On a surge of anger, she snatched her hand back.

"How charming," she said in a tone conveying

that it was anything but.

Guy regarded her in startled dismay. "Tom's in London for Christmas, sis. I thought it would be just the thing if he celebrated the season with us."

"Yes, I only arrived a few days ago. It's a long time since I've been home, so I've been exploring old haunts."

And making fools of gullible girls who should know better.

"I can imagine." With jerky movements, Elizabeth stepped further into the room. She wished that everyone wasn't looking at her. She wished that the floor below her feet would open up and swallow her. She hated to think that the man she so liked – who had kissed her, for heaven's sake – had taken her for such a dunce. Coming downstairs to meet an unknown suitor, she'd felt sick. She felt sicker now. Humiliation had that effect on a person.

"May I get you some champagne, Lady Elizabeth?" Tom sounded urbane, like the international sophisticate that she now knew him to be. But she couldn't help noticing the muscle that danced in his cheek. He was feeling uncomfortable.

So he jolly well should.

"That would be very nice, thank you, Lord Fairchild." Her tone remained wooden.

Tom reached to grab a glass from the tray that a passing footman was carrying. He passed it to her with a meaningful look that she refused to return. Instead, she raised her glass and drained half of the wine in a single draft.

The wine helped to clear her head. "Thank you," she said without a trace of genuine gratitude.

Tom looked even more troubled. "My lady, I'm truly glad to meet you." Looking hunted, he glanced to either side and lowered his voice. "It's not what you think."

She plastered an insincere smile to her face. It was a nightmare, trying to conceal her devastation. "Isn't it?"

Her father strode across with a thunderous expression. The softness in his voice in no way hid his rising temper. "Elizabeth, I hope you're aware of the courtesies due to a guest in this house."

Her mother followed and spoke in a carrying pitch. Lifting her glass, she addressed everyone in the room. "What fun to have you all here for Christmas. Old friends. And new friends we hope will become old friends. To the Christmas season."

Everyone raised their glasses, although Elizabeth couldn't ignore the sidelong glances directed toward the Tierney family group.

"Mamma..." she began, not sure what she could say. She could hardly fling her champagne in Tom's face and tell him that he'd broken her heart.

Anyway, she refused to accept that was what had happened. One eventful day in Hyde Park couldn't change a person's life. Even if it might feel that way. Even if it had involved kisses that had promised to steal her soul.

Well, her soul remained her own. And also her kisses. Right now, servitude with Great-Aunt Agatha seemed preferable to any further contact with the loathsome Viscount Fairchild.

Her mother sent her a lowering glance, even as she kept her smile in place. She spoke in an undertone. "Behave yourself, Elizabeth Isabel. We're not going to spoil Christmas just because you're having a tantrum."

"That's right," her father growled. "I expect you to behave as befits a lady."

The countess shot her beloved husband an inimical look. "I'd err on the side of discretion, my darling. The least said, the soonest mended. I told you that letter was only going to get Elizabeth's back up. And she's as stubborn as you are when someone tries to push her in a direction she doesn't want to go."

"What letter?" Guy asked with a frown, his blue gaze moving from his parents to Elizabeth and back again.

A low growl escaped Mamma. "We can't talk here."

"Perhaps I should make the acquaintance of some of your other guests," Tom said, a reminder that he'd been in the diplomatic service.

"No, I think you should be part of this discussion," Elizabeth said. If her tone wasn't exactly one that a lady would use to address a stranger, she was past caring.

Plaisted, the butler, opened the door. "The carolers are here, my lord."

Her father looked like he wanted to explode. Her mother shot him another worried glance and turned to Plaisted. "Please ask the singers to line up on the staircase. Our guests can stand in the hall and listen."

Plaisted bowed. "Very good, my lady."

As he left, Mamma spoke once more to her visitors. "We've arranged a treat for you. Some Christmas music to get us all in the mood for the evening. Please go through to the hall and enjoy the carols."

Elizabeth set her glass on a table and prepared to follow, but Mamma caught her arm. "No, you're staying here. And so are your father, your brother, and Lord Fairchild."

Papa always made the most noise in the house, but when Mamma spoke in that tone, nobody dared to disobey. With varying degrees of reluctance, the guests trailed out of the drawing room. Scandal scented the air, along with all the fresh greenery, and nobody wanted to miss anything. A few Christmas carols as entertainment paled in comparison.

Mamma shut the door and turned to face her family and that duplicitous viper Stanton Morley-Bridges. She addressed herself to the duplicitous viper. "My lord, I must apologize. You must think you've come to a madhouse. None of this will make any sense to you."

Actually, there her mother was wrong. Elizabeth was sure that Tom knew exactly what was going on. She might have overestimated most of his qualities, but even now, she couldn't doubt his intelligence. In the hall outside, the singers broke into an energetic rendition of *God Rest Ye Merry, Gentlemen.*

"I regret to my soul that I seem to have offended Lady Elizabeth." Tom sent her another of those meaningful looks. Again, she refused to respond. He was trying to create a conspiracy of two, but she wasn't falling for his tricks again.

Her eyes narrowed on him, but she remained silent. Guy cast her a questioning glance, then spoke to Tom. "Sorry, old man. I'm to blame for this mess. When you said you were coming back to England and that you hoped to seek a wife, I couldn't help thinking of Elizabeth."

"Who is obviously at her last prayers when it comes to finding a husband," she snapped, heat flooding her cheeks. How much more mortification could she bear?

Her mother cast her a quelling glance. "Elizabeth, not helpful."

"And obviously not true," Tom said. Once the compliment might have charmed her, but she was no longer susceptible to his wiles. Or at least she didn't want to be.

"No, it's not true. You've broken hearts all over

London," Guy said.

Elizabeth's hands formed fists at her sides. She needed to stay angry. Otherwise, she'd cry her eyes out and that would be the last straw. Tom's double-dealing had cut her to the bone, but if she thought too much about how betrayed she felt, she'd collapse in a sobbing lump. "So I'm a witch, as well as past my prime?"

Guy ignored that. He went back to addressing Tom. "I thought the two of you would like each other. My mistake was telling Papa, who has clearly been up to his old tricks in trying to get his daughter wed. I'm sorry, Tom. If you and Elizabeth met without all the drama, you'd get on like a house on fire. I'd wager the crown jewels on it."

A house on fire was a disaster, which was how everything felt to Elizabeth right now.

Angry, stay angry.

"Her father decided to give Elizabeth an ultimatum before your visit," Mamma said with the fond exasperation that her husband's antics tended to arouse.

Tom's mouth turned down with a wry amusement that was so familiar, it set Elizabeth's heart cramping in regret. She'd been so happy in the park. She hated that he'd spoiled her treasured memories of their time together. "I'm guessing some dire punishment was on offer, should her ladyship decide against having me?"

Looking hunted, her father mumbled a reply. "I was going to send her up to Aunt Agatha in Caithness."

Guy looked appalled, as did her mother. "Not the incontinent pugs. Father, you wouldn't be so cruel."

"Henry, Aunt Agatha? I didn't know about that," her mother said in horror. "No wonder our girl's kicking up like a half-broken horse."

"I am here, you know," Elizabeth pointed out.

Her father rocked on his feet, as if preparing to slink away from the confrontation. "Well, she won't settle down. Four seasons. Acknowledged as a diamond of the first water. Proposals from a hundred good men. And no sign that she means to take a husband. It's...unnatural."

Tom surveyed them all with a thoughtful expression. Elizabeth might want to break a vase over his head, but she had to give him credit for his calmness in a storm. "I realize that I'm a stranger to all of you except Guy, but I'd dearly love the chance to speak to Lady Elizabeth alone and apologize for the trouble I've caused her. You have my word of honor I'll behave as a gentleman should."

"It's not your fault, Fairchild." Papa still sounded as cranky as a bear with a sore head. "It's the fault of featherbrained chits who don't know what's good for them."

"Henry," Mamma said in a warning tone.

Her father emitted a long-suffering sigh, as after a spatter of applause, the carolers moved on to *Deck the Halls,* including handbells. "Very well. It's a little unconventional, but perhaps you can talk some sense into her, Fairchild. My wife and I need to get back to our guests in any case. We don't want people talking."

Elizabeth could tell him that the family's behavior had already created a stir, but she remained silent. Having a few minutes alone to tell Tom what a nasty game he'd played with her suited her just fine. She couldn't do that with the family listening in.

Nonetheless, it would be nice to be consulted. "Do I get a choice? I don't know this man." Which was true in the most essential sense. The engaging gentleman who had flirted with her in Hyde Park would never set out to deceive her like this.

"There's no need to be afraid of me," Tom said at his most benevolent, although he must know that her turbulent mixture of emotions didn't include fear.

"I'd trust Tom with my life," Guy said stoutly.

"I'm not afraid," she bit out with a glare at both young men.

"Then what can be your objection?" her father asked. "Don't be difficult, Elizabeth."

Elizabeth meant to be very difficult indeed, as her mother seemed to guess. Mamma cast her another quelling glance.

"Guy can wait here while you two talk in the library. He'll be close enough to come to your rescue, should you need it, Elizabeth." Her tone indicated that there would be no such need and that her daughter was being unacceptably missish. Which was rich when they'd just met Tom and as far as they were aware, so had she. "The fire's lit in there, and nobody should barge in to interrupt you. Even if they do, Elizabeth isn't a debutante anymore. A few minutes alone with a man in the family home shouldn't cause a major scandal."

Even so, Elizabeth was surprised that her parents allowed her any privacy with her bugbear. It wasn't the done thing, and if Papa intended to marry her off, surely he wanted to preserve her pristine reputation. A suspicion crossed her mind that he might want her ruined, to force her into marrying Tom. Could her father be that Machiavellian?

"I'll treat Lady Elizabeth with the greatest respect," Tom said.

"I'm sure you will," Mamma said, as if it went without saying. Elizabeth couldn't help thinking back to his effect on Cyril and Bruno and her own foolish self before she woke up to what he was really like. It was just as powerful when it came to prospective in-laws.

"And I'll be within earshot," her brother said. "Not that you'll need me, sis. Tom is a good 'un. Anybody can see that."

Elizabeth begged to differ. But it was already clear that Tom's charm had worked its magic on her family. They all thought that he was marvelous. She shouldn't be surprised. She'd thought that he was marvelous, too, until she knew better.

When Elizabeth didn't protest again – what was the point? – Mamma turned to Guy. "Guy, go in and fetch them in ten minutes. Then you three can come out as if you've been together the whole time. That should counter any gossip."

"It's the least I can do," her brother said. "I feel like this is all my fault."

Mamma turned to a sulky-looking Lord Tierney. Papa didn't like it when his grand schemes went astray. He'd moped for a month when his American landscape designer eloped with a lady of the ton and left his extravagant new gardens in Cumbria unfinished. "Henry, shall we join our guests?"

"Yes, dear." Papa extended his arm to her and they left. Mamma prevailed. She always did.

Guy stood in the open door to check the corridor was empty. "I'll give you a quarter of an hour. Anything more and people will sniff out a scandal."

"Lady Elizabeth?" Tom asked, presenting his arm.

She didn't want to leave the room arm in arm with him, the way they'd walked together during those blissful hours in Hyde Park. She was having enough trouble clinging to her proud fury as it was. But an inquisitive glance from Guy made her curl reluctant fingers around Tom's forearm. That brought her close enough to catch the delicious scent that had stolen her wits when they met. How could he smell so good and do such horrible things?

Straightening her backbone, she indicated the room across the corridor. “That’s the library.” She glanced at Guy. “Thank you for doing this.”

He shrugged. “Sis, give Tom a hearing. He really is the best of fellows.”

Elizabeth disagreed, but she remained silent as Tom walked forward and shut them in the library.

CHAPTER SEVEN

To the sound of distant bell ringing, Tom released Elizabeth. She watched him close the door.

"You're angry with me," he said in the soothing tone that had allayed Cyril's terror when he'd been stranded up the oak tree.

It wasn't a tone that she appreciated hearing when he spoke to her. Elizabeth didn't like to be managed. Particularly by someone who had manipulated her feelings from the first. "You don't say."

She stood in the center of the room and glared at him, even as her trembling hands tangled in her skirts. Because despite everything that had happened, she hadn't mistaken how attractive he was. He'd looked appealing in winter outdoor clothes. In stark black-and-white evening dress, he was the most striking man she'd ever seen.

If she didn't know that he'd set out to make a fool of her.

He lingered near the closed door, as though he knew that if he came too near, he risked sending her running. His hands spread in an apologetic gesture. "I'm sorry."

"Are you?" The nervous movement of her hands in her filmy, rose-silk skirts betrayed that she wasn't in charge of her emotions. With an almighty effort, she brought her hands to her sides and kept them still.

"I'm sorry I've upset you. I'm not sorry I met you in the park. I'll never be sorry about that."

His gray eyes were sincere, and he sounded like he meant it. But he'd sounded sincere when they met, and look how that turned out. She sidled from one foot to another, until she remembered Papa doing that and how guilty it made him look. "You knew who I was."

He sighed and ran his hand through his hair, reminding her inevitably of the ruffled, laughing, magnetic man who had turned a bleak Christmas Day to gold. "Only at the end. For pity's sake, please believe me."

She folded her arms and resisted the heartfelt plea. "Why should I?"

His jaw firmed. "Because I'm not a liar. The minute you said you lived in Lorimer Square and your name was Elizabeth, I guessed you had to be the girl I was supposed to meet tonight. If I hadn't been quite so bowled over, I probably should have guessed earlier." He sent her a pleading look. "Guy described how pretty you are – and how spirited."

She narrowed her eyes on him. "Papa calls me wayward and headstrong."

Tom shrugged. "If you think that's going to deter me from courting you, you need your head fixed. I don't want a docile little cipher of a wife. I want someone who turns my life into an adventure."

She kept her defensive pose with her arms folded, although with every second, her outrage became harder to hold onto. "Wife, is it?"

He shrugged, as if he hadn't said anything of great significance. "Probably a discussion for a later occasion."

"There mightn't be a later occasion."

"Because you'll be in Scotland with Great-Aunt Agatha and the pugs? That sounds frightful. Is putting up with my company really a worse alternative?"

Elizabeth didn't answer that. Instead, she studied him with confusion in her heart. His gentle teasing chipped another layer off her resentment. "If you knew who I was, why didn't you say something? Why didn't you tell me who you are?"

He ran his hand through his hair again. It seemed to be a characteristic gesture. "You had to go."

"Yes, I did. I'd already taken enough chances. If I'd been capable of a moment's logical thought, I'd never have left the house at all."

"I assume you left home in high dudgeon because of your father's letter?"

She sighed, more of her tension draining away. "I'd been at a house party just outside London, but I came home early because my maid was sick. The letter was waiting for me when I arrived to an empty house. After I read it, I felt ready to explode. I was in such a fit, I decided to ignore good sense. A walk in the park seemed a preferable alternative to smashing every piece of the family china. Especially when Mamma was expecting guests."

"I wondered why you were on your own."

"I took a shocking risk," she said, bracing for him to berate her for breaking society's rules.

He didn't. "Perhaps, but it was lucky for me."

"Because you had a chance to see what I was like before you had to present yourself as a suitor?"

This time, he folded his arms and regarded her with an ironic eye. "I don't *have* to present myself as anything. Our time together in the park changed my mind about courting Guy's sister, however pretty she was. Instead, I wanted to court the lovely girl who kissed me behind a holly hedge."

She blushed. He made it impossible to remain in a snit. Her shoulders came down, and the tight clenching in her stomach eased. "So you didn't set out to trick me?"

"When I found out you were the Elizabeth Tierney I was meant to meet tonight, I decided fate worked in my favor. I hoped you might feel the same. I'm sorry if you think I was playing spiteful games. That's not my style at all, which I hope you'll discover as our acquaintance develops."

Her sigh would alert him that she surrendered. "I might give you the benefit of the doubt," she said begrudgingly.

Several rooms away, the carolers began *I Saw Three Ships*. More bells. Tom regarded her with unhidden relief. "Does the benefit of the doubt extend to a kiss?"

A thrill ran through her, although she hadn't altogether yielded to the Christmas romance in the air. "We'll see."

That charming smile appeared for the first time since they'd come into the library. "I should have borrowed some mistletoe from the drawing room. By George, I doubt there's a bunch of mistletoe or a sprig of holly left in Cumbria."

A faint smile lengthened her lips. "The family loves Christmas. You'll have to get used to that if you're marrying into the Tierneys."

His eyebrows rose, although a light in his gray eyes reminded her of how he'd looked after he kissed her in the park. "Am I marrying into the Tierneys?"

"I've known you for less than a day."

"And you've spent far too much of that time being angry with me." He stretched his hand toward her as he stepped closer. "Am I forgiven?"

After a hesitation to make the point that she hadn't fallen completely under his spell, Elizabeth curled her fingers around his. She liked how his hand felt in hers. It was pleasantly warm and firm and the calluses on his palm hinted at an active life. The Stanton Morley-Bridges she'd imagined had been weedy and soft and pale as a daisy. She was very glad that he wasn't the Stanton Morley-Bridges she'd imagined.

Unable to resist, she heaved a much more theatrical sigh. "I suppose so."

"Thank you." This time, his smile was one of the happy ones that set her foolish heart dancing. "May I kiss you now? Our quarter hour is nearly done and if I'm to play propriety from now on, I'm not sure how much kissing is ahead of us."

"If you must," she said, as a tide of expectation made her breath catch.

His smile broadened. "You're not going to make this easy for me, are you?"

She couldn't help smiling back at him. "I might have carried on like a hoyden today, but I don't want you thinking that you needn't make an effort. I do have choices other than marrying you, you know."

Tom was back to looking at her as if she was the brightest star in the sky. She rather liked it. "Great-Aunt Agatha?"

"Caithness is beautiful in its brisk way."

"Yes, gales and rain and heaving seas always make me feel the joys of spring."

"Me, too."

He edged closer. One hand slid around her waist. She was sure that he'd notice her shiver of pleasure. "Not to mention the hundred men who have already proposed."

Papa and his big mouth. "A slight exaggeration."

"Only a slight one, I'm sure," he murmured, bending his head but not kissing her yet.

He teased her, the devil. "If you're planning to kiss me, I'd do it now, or we'll have an audience."

Laughter turned those quirky, fascinating features brilliant. "You're so fierce."

"Do I frighten you?" she asked drily, sliding one hand over his shoulder.

"I'm absolutely bloomin' terrified," he whispered.

"Good," she said, knowing that he didn't mean it. She stretched up to close the distance between them just as he lowered his head the last fraction of an inch.

Their lips met with a sizzle that made her quiver with delight. Heat zapped through her, and her heart raced with excitement. She sighed and arched into his chest. Now that he wasn't dressed for outdoors, she could get close to his body. She ached to get closer still. To dispense with clothing altogether.

By the time he raised his head, she was giddy and dazzled and breathless and eager for more. Her anger was forgotten. As she struggled to keep her balance, she caught his arms. Her attention focused on his face. Tom looked as overcome as she did.

She licked her lips, tasting him there. He groaned and briefly closed his eyes. "Don't do that, or I won't be responsible for my actions."

Need extended between them, as tangible as a rope of gold. But then a burst of applause from the hall provided an unwelcome reminder that this was neither the time nor the place to succumb to their sensual impulses.

"I won't call you Stanton," she said.

The intensity faded from his expression. "That's fine."

"And I'm not making any commitments."

"I understand that. I'm not proposing."

That surprised her. "Ever?"

The teasing glint was back. "We'll see."

She couldn't help laughing as she stepped away. "You're a dreadful man."

"The worst." He caught her hand. "Now we ought to go and find Guy, who seems to have no concept of time at all."

"I do love my brother."

Tom laughed and reached out to tuck in a stray curl that the kiss must have dislodged. "The best of fellows indeed."

"And the perfect chaperone."

"Yes, we must employ his services again. I'd like to steal a few more kisses."

"Good thinking."

They drifted toward the door, then stopped at the sound of a discreet knock. "I've given you as long as I can, but I think the carols are nearly done," Guy muttered from the corridor. An excellent chaperone indeed.

"We're coming now," Tom said, although he paused to subject Elizabeth to a serious stare. "So we have an understanding, my lady?"

"That you're going to court me?"

"Yes, and that sometime very soon, I'm going to ask you to be my wife."

Excitement made her heart crash against her ribs, but she adopted an airy tone, as she released

Tom's hand and turned the doorknob. "Very well. But will I say yes?"

CHAPTER EIGHT

Elizabeth said yes.

She and Tom married on Valentine's Day, under the full gaze of society at St. George's in Hanover Square. The bride wore white velvet and walked up the aisle with five bridesmaids. The scent of massed hothouse flowers filled the cavernous interior of the church with the promise of spring not too far away. Never let it be said that when Elizabeth Tierney at last deigned to wed, she stinted in any way.

The extravagant gown was currently tossed with lamentable carelessness across the back of an upholstered chair in Richmond's best inn. The bride's undergarments were scattered across the carpet, along with the groom's elegant dark blue coat, gray silk waistcoat, neckcloth, and shirt.

She and Tom had been so desperate for each other, that the moment they came upstairs after dinner, they'd all but ripped most of their clothing away. Now only a flimsy shift covered her, and Tom was naked, except for the cream silk breeches that he'd worn for the wedding.

A silver tray of champagne and delicacies waited

on a sideboard near the closed door. Vases of more hothouse flowers adorned the chests and tables furnishing the room. In the huge four-poster oak bed in the corner, the sheets were turned down. A fire blazed in the hearth, and massed beeswax candles lent the opulent chamber a golden glow.

The bride released a blissful sigh, as her groom of nine hours raised his head from a passionate kiss. They were standing on a rich red and blue carpet in the middle of the room amidst the chaos of discarded linen.

"I've missed your kisses," Elizabeth murmured, rising on her toes and running her lips along that heroic jaw. She loved that Tom was so tall and strong. It made her feel lusciously feminine.

His laugh was low and as velvety as her wedding dress. "Fie, Lady Fairchild. Are you accusing me of neglect? I kissed you at the ceremony."

"A mere peck." She pouted and linked her hands behind his neck, as she glanced up at him through her lashes. When she arched her body, the beaded tips of her nipples grazed the bare skin of his chest. The sensation sent a frisson through her. "It hardly deserved to be called a kiss."

His lips twitched with the wry humor that she loved. "I kissed you yesterday. And I believe also the day before, if memory serves me correctly."

"You've forgotten." She adopted a shocked expression. "I'm devastated."

"You're a baggage, that's what you are." When he said it so fondly, she could hardly object.

After Christmas, their courtship had proceeded along conventional lines, with Tom asking Lord Tierney's permission to marry his daughter a month ago. The banns had been called. Elizabeth had met Tom's family and received a warm welcome that boded well for future relations. The union of sparkling Lady Elizabeth Tierney with distinguished diplomat and future Lord Blaydon, Stanton Morley-Bridges was the kind of aristocratic match that the ton applauded. Two fine young people from prominent families, neither tarred with scandal. A wooing conducted just as the sticklers decreed, with family approval bestowed upon the eventual engagement.

Less publicly, Elizabeth and Tom had found frequent opportunities to be alone. Their short courtship and engagement had featured plenty of kisses, even if hurried and always with an ear for interruption.

"I'm frustrated." She sounded like she was joking, but she was deadly serious. Since Christmas, their privacy had been measured in intervals of minutes.

With a groan as heartfelt as hers, Tom reached out to grasp her hips. Her stomach lurched with excitement, as the warmth of his touch seeped through the light shift to her skin beneath. The undergarments littering the floor included her drawers. Beneath her shift, she was completely naked.

"Tell me about it. Every time I got into my stride with kissing you, someone decided they had to talk to you about wedding fripperies."

It was true. Elizabeth had desired Tom from the first, but their snatched embraces had kindled that desire into a mighty inferno. Now she was mad with wanting him.

He caught her up for a kiss that had her bare toes curling against the carpet. Her heart took a dizzying swoop. Twining her arms about him, she pressed closer to that broad chest with its fascinating scatter of dark curls. She couldn't wait to discover all the mysteries of his body. She couldn't wait for him to discover all her mysteries, too. And of course, the greatest mystery of all awaited, when they joined together as husband and wife.

Tom drew away and leveled a searching stare at her. "Thank you so much for deciding that you'd rather marry me than move in with Great-Aunt Agatha."

"It was a close-run thing," she said, not meaning it. Great-Aunt Agatha hadn't traveled down from Scotland for the wedding, but she'd sent the newlyweds a Wedgwood vase of surpassing ugliness to mark the occasion.

Tom gave an exaggerated shudder. "Don't I know it? When your father looked so smug walking you down the aisle, I was terrified you'd take umbrage and pick up your skirts to scarper."

The memory of that moment made her smile. She was too happy to muster much resentment for Papa's machinations. She'd got what she wanted. If her father did as well, good for him. "He was rather pleased with himself, wasn't he?"

"I wanted to shout at him to stop looking so self-satisfied."

She gave a horrified giggle. "I'm glad you didn't. The vicar would have had conniptions. Anyway, Papa spends most of his life looking self-satisfied. You'll get used to it."

He angled her hips toward him. "So you're not going to run away?"

She shook her head and shifted from foot to foot, too jumpy to stand still. "I love you too much to want to leave you."

Oh, dear...

A bristling silence crashed down. Elizabeth regarded Tom in dismay. He looked shocked, then his brows drew together in what she couldn't help but read as displeasure.

She blinked against the sting of tears. She refused

to spend her first night as a bride bawling like a lost calf. That would be outside of enough. Sweet heaven, what a miserable henwit she was. Why didn't she keep her mouth shut? She'd guarded her secret throughout their engagement, not sure if declarations of love would place too much pressure on their brief acquaintance. Yet here she was, babbling out the fateful words and likely to spoil their wedding night.

"You've never told me that before," he said slowly. She couldn't interpret his tone. He didn't sound angry. Or was that just wishful thinking? "We've only known each other for a few weeks."

She bit her lip and tried to back out of his hold, but his grip tightened, keeping her where she was. "I know."

He still looked troubled. Which annoyed her. That was better than feeling like she wanted to disappear into the wallpaper or turn into a sniveling mess.

"Long enough to marry," she said with some vexation. If he told her that she was a silly girl who didn't know her own mind, she *would* run off to Great-Aunt Agatha.

At least he didn't say that. It wasn't much consolation. "Yes, but somehow love seems the ultimate commitment."

Shocked, she met his gaze. "More than vowing to spend our lives together?"

"I know it doesn't make sense. It doesn't have to."

She summoned all her pride, difficult when she felt so vulnerable. Elizabeth detested feeling vulnerable, which was why she'd hugged her burgeoning adoration for her fiancé so close to her chest. "I'm not asking anything of you. I promise I won't make emotional scenes."

To her surprise, he responded with sardonic

amusement. "Yes, you will."

Yes, she probably would. If he took a mistress, she'd pitch Great-Aunt Agatha's vase at his head and grill his heart on the drawing room fire.

"Can we forget I said anything?" she asked in a small voice. She'd imagined telling Tom of her feelings at some stage. Preferably after he'd already declared his eternal devotion to her.

His frown deepened. "Why would we do that, for heaven's sake?"

"Because you obviously don't love me back," she said in an even reedier tone. She didn't want to cry, but if this went on much longer, she wouldn't be able to stop herself.

"What nonsense is this?" Impatience edged his deep voice. "You know I've been head over heels with you from the moment you scowled at me in Hyde Park on that snowy Christmas morning."

It was her turn to frown in confusion, as her frantic mind winnowed all their interactions. "No, I don't."

He let her go and stepped back. It shouldn't feel like a distancing, but it did. "Well, you damn well should."

"You never said."

"Neither did you."

She swallowed, knowing that the next few seconds would set the tone for her entire marriage. "Tom, what are you saying? Please be plain. I don't want to get this wrong. Do you love me?"

He sighed again and ran his hand through hair already rumpled after their storm of kisses. Those lighthearted moments when they'd rushed up to the room felt like they'd occurred an eon ago. "Yes, I love you. I assumed you knew."

She shook her head as a new kind of happiness found a home in her heart. Tom had made her happy from the first. But this joy descending upon her now carried a weight and significance that would nourish the rest of her life. "I knew you liked me. Or else you'd never have asked me to marry you."

"I'd never have asked you to marry me if I didn't love you."

Of course he wouldn't. What on earth had she been thinking? Love had turned her brains to custard. An elated smile curved her lips, as she held her hands out toward him. "I'm a silly wigeon. I should have guessed."

"Yes, you should." He caught her hands and brought her closer. "I always knew how I felt. But I was never sure you loved me back."

More confusion as she peered into his face. "But I've kissed you every chance I got."

He shrugged. "That just means you love my kisses."

"I do. I also love *you.*"

His short laugh was rich with self-mockery. "Well, that's the best wedding present anyone could give me." His voice deepened into a sincerity that settled in her bones. "I love you, Elizabeth. I'll always love you."

Elizabeth stared at him and spoke with equal emphasis, so there was no chance of him misunderstanding her. "And I love you, Stanton Morley-Bridges. Forever."

For a charged minute, they stared into each other's eyes, as if they could hardly believe this gift they shared. Then they were kissing as though they'd die if they stopped. Somewhere in the hectic embrace, Tom released Elizabeth's hair so it tumbled about them in soft waves. Still kissing her, he combed his hands through the silky mass with a sensual delight that built her longing.

This close to him, she felt his rising excitement.

The heady mixture of anticipation and trepidation inside her made her feel like she whirled around in a giddy waltz. Soon, so soon, she'd become his wife in the fullest sense of the word. She couldn't wait, and yet she was utterly terrified.

He pulled away far enough to tug her shift over her head and cast it to the floor with the rest of her linen. She'd never stood naked before a man before. Shock blazed through her. Shock and surging awareness of what was about to happen.

His hands explored her bare skin with devastating effect, while he went back to kissing her. He shaped her arms and shoulders and back and lingered on her buttocks in a way that made her blood pound like thunder.

She crushed her breasts against him, relishing the soft friction of chest hair against the sensitive nipples. A fractured moan of desire escaped her. She thirsted to feel his hands on those tight peaks.

With a breathtaking show of masculine power, he lifted her in his arms and carried her across to the bed. She curled her arm around his neck, reveling in his strength and his uninhibited hunger for her.

"You're beautiful, my love," he murmured, setting her down on the sheets with a care that arrowed straight to her heart. She liked that he thought she was beautiful. She liked it even better that she was his love.

Elizabeth stared up at him from heavy-lidded eyes, as the empty ache between her legs intensified until it verged on unendurable. Shyness made her hands flutter to cover her bosom and her mound.

"You're superb from top to toe, my darling." He caught the hand doing an inadequate job of concealing the swell of her bosom and brought it to his lips for a kiss. "Won't you share that with me?"

She gave a raspy laugh, even as she was torn

between covering her pubic hair or reaching for the sheet. "I didn't think I'd be embarrassed. I've been so looking forward to our wedding. I've been picturing all the lovely things you'll do to me tonight ever since you kissed me at Christmas."

He sat on the edge of the bed and squeezed her hand. "You know what I'm going to do?"

"Mamma told me before my first season. She was sure that I'd find a husband straightaway. I've had a lot of time to imagine sharing a man's bed."

His adoring smile turned her insides to treacle. "I'm so glad you waited."

"So am I. Somehow I always knew there was someone special for me. There was nothing wrong with the men who proposed. But even if I liked them, I wasn't starry-eyed, the way my friends were starry-eyed about their choices. I hoped one day I'd feel like that, but I never did. Until I met a mysterious rogue in Hyde Park."

Tom leaned down and kissed her with more tenderness than passion, although passion hovered a mere breath away. By the time he lifted his head, her arms twined around him and she'd forgotten her self-consciousness.

He kissed her neck and shoulders until she wriggled with sheer delight. The heat in her secret places flared into irresistible demand. She wanted this man. How she wanted this man.

Tom lay on the bed next to her and kissed the upper slopes of her breasts. He cupped the lush flesh in his elegant hands. Elizabeth jerked with startled pleasure, then jerked again when Tom began to tease her yearning nipples. She arched up, seeking more. Rolling one pebbled crest between thumb and forefinger, he took the other between his lips and gently scraped his teeth across it.

"Tom," she cried in wonder, as lightning sizzled

through her. With a soft murmur of approval, she pressed a shaking hand into his hair. After a sultry interval, his lips moved to her other breast. Elizabeth was so caught up in the experience, she kept forgetting to breathe. Every inhalation turned into a shuddering gasp. The earthy scents of arousal weighted the air around them.

Still teasing her breast, he let one hand trail down her bare flank to her hip. She moaned and shivered under his exploration. He rolled to the side, balancing his weight on his crooked elbow, and watched the progress of his caresses with unabashed fascination.

Wherever Tom's fingers ventured, they set up explosions of heat. Along the curve of her hip. Across her stomach and the dip of her navel. Down to tangle in the damp, light brown curls that concealed her sex. When he slid his hand between her thighs, she sighed and spread her legs in instinctive encouragement.

"I'm...I'm wet there," she muttered, cheeks flushed with embarrassment.

"That's your body preparing for me. It means you want me." He bobbed down to kiss her briefly, as his fingers stroked her cleft. She gasped into his mouth when he found a place that was particularly sensitive. She'd never felt anything like this before. The sensation was extraordinary.

Elizabeth felt pressure and realized that he penetrated her with one finger. She squirmed again, even as her body adjusted to the invasion. Soon there would be another invasion. The idea made her tremble with expectation and a fresh flurry of nerves.

He stopped and withdrew his finger, which wasn't what she wanted at all. "Am I hurting you?"

"No," she said.

"You don't sound very sure."

She placed one hand on his chest, feeling the gallop of his heart under her palm. He gave the impression of control, but that frantic heartbeat told her how desperate he was. “I’ve just never…”

“I know.” He kissed her again. “It’s my privilege to introduce you to all the wondrous things your body can do.”

Her hands curled against his chest, feeling the pleasurable tickle of hair. “You’re still dressed.”

“It reminds me to take my time.” His lips turned down. “It’s your first encounter with a man, and I believe that can be uncomfortable.”

Tom was being considerate. This time, the warmth that filled her had nothing to do with passion. She’d noticed his essential kindness from the first. It was one of the reasons why she’d fallen in love with him. “Mamma said it might hurt.”

“I never want to hurt you, Elizabeth.”

She smiled at him with all the love in her heart and laid her hand on his cheek. “It will be all right.”

He smiled back. “I’m supposed to be reassuring you.”

With a soft laugh, she moved her hand in a caress. “Do you know what always reassures me?”

“Your cook’s ginger snaps?”

Her laugh this time held a note of surprise. “You noticed how much I like them.”

Tom rolled his eyes. “How could I not?”

“They’re very good.”

“They are. As I remarked on the single occasion when you let me have one.”

“I am rather greedy.”

“A man wants a wife with an appetite.”

“We’re not talking about biscuits anymore, are we?”

“No, but you’ll be pleased to know after much begging and flattery, I’ve managed to pry the recipe from Mrs. Dawkins's hands."

Her eyes rounded. "Goodness, it must have been a lot of flattery. That recipe is a family secret."

"I couldn't have you pining away in Dorset, longing for your days of maidenhood when you enjoyed endless plates of ginger snaps."

She curved up and kissed him with a deep gratitude that soon edged into desire. "I love you so much, Tom."

It was charming that her declaration took him aback. "Is that because of the biscuits? I can try and get her pigeon pie recipe, too, if you like."

"No, she's going to the grave with that one. I love you because you're the most wonderful man in the world."

More charming self-deprecation. "Perhaps not in the world."

"The world," she declared and reached down to pluck at the waistband of his breeches. "I think it's time you gave up your modesty, my lord."

Through the teasing conversation, she'd remained achingly aware of the hard masculine flesh straining against his breeches. She was curious and eager, and ready to take the next step on their journey into married life.

"In a minute. What reassures you? You didn't say."

Her smile reappeared. "Your kisses. Right from the first."

"Oh, my darling..."

Tom took the invitation – because invitation it was – and kissed her until her head reeled. She dug her fingers into his bare shoulders in a silent plea for him to keep going.

He groaned and rolled out of the bed. "I can't wait any longer."

His flavor lingered in her mouth. He might taste

even better than Mrs. Dawkins's biscuits. "Good."

He reacted with a grunt of amusement, as his shaking hands tore at the fastenings on his breeches. Tom was in general an even-tempered gentleman. Elizabeth approved of that, but she loved to see him reach such a pitch of craving now. With a sigh of anticipation, she stretched out against the sheets. She curled her toes and lifted her breasts in a blatant display. Her earlier shyness evaporated to nothing under his unfettered pleasure in her nakedness.

While Tom's attention focused on her rather than on his buttons, his attempts to rid himself of his breeches became more chaotic. "You're making life difficult," he complained, laughter warming his deep voice.

"You'll survive," she said, pleased to see him in such a dither.

Finally he tugged his breeches down and cast them aside without looking. Elizabeth didn't notice where they landed either. She was too busy staring at the impressive column of flesh rising against his flat stomach.

"Goodness me," she whispered. Would that fit inside her? No wonder Mamma said that the act would hurt. She pressed her thighs together as virginal nerves, temporarily absent, surged anew.

He laughed and kneeled over her. "Has my rampant manhood awed you into silence?"

"Yes," she said in a scratchy voice.

"I think you need reassurance," he said gently. He kissed her again, lingering. He went back to stroking her between the legs, until she forgot her trepidation. She was too busy trembling her way through reactions that she'd never experienced before tonight.

This time, when Tom eased his finger into her, her body gripped him in preparation for the ultimate union. Her hips bumped upward, as the blood rushed in her veins.

Rising on his arms, Tom shifted until he lay between her legs. Through the shuddering storm, she felt something blunt and hot press into the junction between her legs. She hooked her hands over his broad shoulders and stared up into his eyes. "It's happening?"

"Yes." His voice was strained. So were his features. His gaze burned down into hers, as if he could see right through to her soul. "Bend your knees."

She obeyed and tightened her grip on his shoulders. As he inched inside her, the pressure increased. He breathed erratically, and his gray eyes turned opaque. She ran her hands down his arms, feeling the way his muscles hardened. He was struggling for restraint.

"Are you all right?" he asked jerkily.

So far, the act was uncomfortable, but not painful. "Yes. Don't stop."

He bent to kiss her, then edged further forward. Her body stretched to accommodate his slow advance. Elizabeth bit her lip, as pain sliced through her. Despite her determination to endure, a muffled whimper escaped.

He stopped moving. "I'm sorry."

"Don't be sorry." Already the pain faded. She traced the line of his spine and caught his hips. With every second, his possession became easier to bear. "It hurt for a moment, that's all."

He kissed her with an open-mouthed appreciation that flooded her with pleasure. Her tension eased, and her body fitted itself more naturally to his hardness. She sucked in a deep breath of air redolent of their desire. Musky. A trace of sweat. Rich and animal and before tonight, unfamiliar.

Elizabeth slid lower in the bed and felt how that changed his angle. She made a faint murmur of curiosity as Tom shifted deeper. No pain this time.

Now that the initial shock passed, she was mostly conscious of the transcendent intimacy of what they did. The vicar had spoken of them becoming one flesh. She'd assumed the phrase was poetic, but that was how this felt. As though this act united the formerly separate Tom and Elizabeth into one being The insight was moving, and she blinked away tears as she stroked his lean flanks with more tenderness than passion.

"I should stop." He frowned down at her. "You're crying."

With a choked laugh, she lightly dug her nails into the skin covering his ribs. "Don't you dare."

"But..."

She gulped back a sob. She didn't want Tom going anywhere else right now and if she burst into tears, he might. He already looked ready to bolt. "I'm crying because I love you so much, and because this thing we do is so beautiful, and because I'm so glad I waited for you to come into my life."

She watched his face change, as he listened to the torrent of words. He bent and kissed her with a devotion that she couldn't mistake. "Oh, my beloved..."

He raised his head and pushed forward with purpose, going to the hilt. When their bodies first joined, her heart had clenched with overwhelming emotion. But this closeness carved a rift so deep inside her, it marked her forever. She was his. She would always be his. On a broken sigh of surrender, she arched until her breasts brushed his chest.

"That's...wonderful," she whispered. And it was. The momentary discomfort didn't count against the wonder of him filling her emptiness with his love.

When he shifted back, she couldn't muffle a disappointed whimper. She pressed up to prolong the contact. "Don't go."

His laugh was husky. "I'm not going anywhere. You'll like this."

She did. For a rapturous interval, his body rocked in and out of hers, launching her on a glorious flight to the stars. It was like when he'd touched her between the legs, but better. She panted, as she strove to attain some goal that lay just out of reach. Every time he slid fully inside, she verged closer to that peak.

Until on a blast of heat and light, she crossed the last barrier and soared free. The explosion of ecstasy outmatched anything that she'd ever imagined possible. She cried out his name, as she wallowed in transforming sensation and her body spasmed around him. He gave a grunt of approval and kept moving, until he shuddered in her arms and lost himself inside her still-quivering body.

Tom kissed her thoroughly, then rose on his elbows to stare down at her with eyes that shone with love. "I adore you."

Elizabeth touched his face, noting how his expression had changed since they'd mated. She could tell that he, like her, had touched paradise tonight. They'd experienced bliss together, just as together they'd advance into their new life. This was a love that would endure. "I love you, too."

He pulled free and rolled to his side, wrapping his arms around her and nestling her back against his chest. Tom's love surrounded her. It was the best feeling in the world.

Or perhaps the second best. She rested against him, her mind awash with memories of what had just happened. It seemed a gift beyond measure that they could do that again and again. She smiled into the candlelit room.

Behind her, Tom's rough breathing eased. The quiet interval had Elizabeth's eyelids drooping. Drowsing in her magnificent lover's arms was sheer delight. The night's discoveries came thick and fast.

She was almost asleep when Tom murmured into her rumpled hair. "You called me Stanton."

"Hmm?"

"When we made love, you said my name. Not Tom."

She shifted a little but kept her eyes shut. "I was carried away in the moment."

"I liked it."

"I liked what you did."

Male satisfaction tinged his grunt of amusement. "I'll do it again, once I've caught my breath."

On a shiver of anticipation, she curled her fingers over the hand that spread across her midriff. "Ooh, yes, please."

With a weary laugh, he pressed a kiss to her crown. "You've married a man who can't get enough of you."

She bumped her rump back against his stirring rod. "I approve."

His next laugh sounded like he was more awake. She was also losing interest in sleep. Who wanted to sleep, when a passionate man lay beside her, ready and willing? Not Elizabeth Morley-Bridges, Viscountess Fairchild, that was for sure.

"I'll be gentle. You might still be tender."

She laughed and turned around so she could see him. "I'm tender. And grateful and overwhelmed with what we just did. I'm starving for you. And I love you more than words can convey."

His eyes glowed with a joy that warmed her to the heart. "And I love you, Elizabeth. Let me show you how much."

And he did.

EPILOGUE

Hyde Park, London, Christmas Day, 1820

The park wasn't as snowy as last year, and so far they hadn't had to rescue any stray urchins from the top of an oak tree. But the scene was similar enough to last Christmas Day for Elizabeth to relive the magic of her meeting with Tom and the wonderful changes that had taken place since then.

"I was so angry and upset when you found me," she said, cuddling into his side the way that she'd shamelessly cuddled all those months ago. Her hand hooked around his elbow and their boots made a satisfying crunch on the new snow along the path.

It was their first visit to London since their wedding. They'd enjoyed a passionate honeymoon in France, before settling down to their new life on Tom's beautiful estate on the Dorset coast.

He glanced down and gave her a smile from under the brim of his stylish high-crowned hat. "Are you saying you're angry and upset now?"

Elizabeth giggled and nudged him with her elbow. "No, you teasing man. I'm revoltingly contented with how everything turned out. I can't hide it. My father will look like the cat that got the cream when we sit down to Christmas dinner."

They were outside earlier than last year. The sun wasn't long up on what promised to be a beautiful Christmas Day. In a couple of hours, both families would descend on the Morley-Bridges town house on Green Park and her chances to get her husband to herself would become very thin on the ground.

"You could make more of an effort to appear discontented with your lot. I don't think you're trying hard enough." He stopped and gave her a mock frown. "I mean, look at you now. You're staring at me with stars in your eyes. Anyone would think you're in love."

She laughed again. "But I am in love. It's your fault. If you weren't so wonderful, I could manage to summon up a pout or two."

He bent in and kissed her. That was another change from last year. No need for subterfuge. Lord and Lady Fairchild could wander Hyde Park alone together for as long as they wanted without raising comment. They could even kiss, within reason. Although that was the problem with Tom's kisses. They had a habit of sending her reason to the devil.

"I can't apologize for being so happy."

"Neither can I." She was warm in her thick merino pelisse with its sable trimming, but she was even warmer now that Tom had kissed her. "We'll just have to let Papa continue to take undeserved credit for our wedding."

"These things are sent to test us. Would you like to go home? We've got time for me to try to make up for your disappointment."

Anticipation ripped through her. He was asking if she wanted to go back to bed. They'd started the day with a vigorous encounter that left Elizabeth feeling like she'd breakfasted on starlight. No wonder she had stars in her eyes. The thought of spending Christmas morning in her husband's arms was tempting indeed.

But not yet.

She snuggled closer as they started walking again "In a moment, Tom. There's something I want to tell you."

"Oh?" He stopped again and turned to face her, taking her gloved hands in his.

For more than a month now, she'd been on the verge of confessing her secret, but every time she approached it, her nerve had failed her. But today, today she was resolved to share her news. After all, Christmas Day was their real anniversary. What more auspicious date to let Tom know that their life was soon to change forever?

"I'm...I'm going to have a baby," she said in a rush, then paused, surprised at how easily the words emerged.

Tom's quirky, beloved features melted into a smile of such joy that a lump of poignant emotion closed Elizabeth's throat. His hands tightened on hers. "Sweetheart, I'm so happy."

He leaned in and this time kissed her with a fervor that would have caused comment, if anyone had been around at this hour to observe them.

When he pulled away after a long, heavenly interval, she was breathless and her knees were rubbery. Being an old married woman of a year didn't seem to make her any less susceptible to her husband's appeal.

She stared into his face, while she waited for the world to stop spinning around her. His eyes blazed and he was clearly euphoric. And not half as surprised by her news as he should be.

"You wretch," she said, laughing. "You already

knew."

The wry smile that she'd fallen in love with curved his lips. "I...hoped."

"You guessed."

He shrugged. "We live in very close quarters, my love. The signs were there. Will you forgive me?"

"For paying attention to me? I think I can." She rose on her toes and kissed him again. "Are you truly pleased?"

"That the woman I love is going to give me a child in..."

"Late May, I think."

"A spring baby? How wonderful." He sucked in a breath, and his gaze told her that he thought she was the most miraculous being on earth. "Of course I'm pleased. I thought I was the happiest man alive when I met you. Until the day you said you'd marry me. But then we got married and you told me you loved me..."

"On that marvelous night." Oh, the extraordinary things he'd done to her on their wedding night. The wonder was that what they did in bed had only got better. She was so lucky, she could hardly believe it.

"Yes. But then every day since then, you've made me happier. The arrival of a son or daughter just places the crown on my entirely unmerited good fortune."

Elizabeth frowned. "It's not unmerited. You're the best man I know, Stanton Morley-Bridges. And I love you more than I can say."

Tom kissed her again with such tender emotion that her heart clenched with love. But when he raised his head, the familiar amusement turned his eyes to brilliant silver. "Happy Christmas, my lovely wife."

She smiled back as carnal interest stirred. She knew what that look portended. "Happy Christmas, my beloved husband."

"You know, good news and fresh air and seasonal spirit give a man an appetite."

She sent him a glance of mock disapproval. "You'll be eating like a king in a few hours."

With a laugh, he tucked her hand around his arm. He turned and began to head back toward home with a purposeful stride. "I'm not talking about food, my darling."

On a laugh of pure happiness, she fell into step beside him. "I can already tell this Christmas is going to be even better than last year."

"That sets me a challenge." He sent her a seductive glance from under his thick black lashes. "I'll do my best, my love."

"You always do." Tom's presence in her life was a blessing, on Christmas and every other day, and Elizabeth couldn't wait to see where they went from here. Wherever it was, love would light the way.

Miss Barton's Mysterious Husband

A Mayfair Christmas Romance

ANNA CAMPBELL

A heartwarming Christmas reunion story from bestselling historical romance author Anna Campbell

The Un-Festive Season…

Sir Roland Destry finds no joy in Christmas. Since his beautiful, spirited wife left him during their honeymoon, he finds no joy in anything. But an unexpected encounter on Christmas Eve may just change the gallant baronet's luck and show him that the age of miracles has not yet passed.

The fire still burns…

Since fleeing back to her family after an unwise marriage, Charmian Barton has reverted to her maiden name and kept her reckless elopement a secret. If only it was so easy to rise above heartache and regret. But when a rainy night brings her errant husband to her doorstep, as magnetic as ever, passion springs to blazing life and proves that this union is far from over.

A heartbreaking truth revealed.

Will shocking revelations of what really kept them apart divide them forever? Or can Charmian and Roland forgive the mistakes of the past for the sake of a love that never died?

CHAPTER ONE

Puddlebrook, Yorkshire, Christmas Eve, 1818

By heaven, he loathed Yorkshire.

Sir Roland Destry especially loathed it on a freezing, dark afternoon, when the precipitation couldn't decide whether it was snow or rain. Whatever it was, it knew that it wanted to blight his journey. As another rivulet of icy water trickled down the back of his neck, he shivered and cursed beneath his breath.

Not for the first time, he regretted agreeing to spend the Festive Season with his friend, Sir Hugo Brinsmead, and his family. But as he encouraged his exhausted horse to plod through whatever this godforsaken village was called, he regretted it with particular savagery.

There was the whole Yorkshire thing, for a start. The county had never been lucky for him. It wasn't as if Christmas was his favorite time of year either. These days, he preferred to hole up at his club for most of December and pretend the rest of the world wasn't elsewhere, cuddling up together in cozy jollification.

But Hugo's invitation had arrived when he was feeling lower than usual. He'd replied in the affirmative, before he had a chance to think through what he committed to. Not thinking through the consequences of a fleeting impulse had caused him more than enough trouble already, damn it all to hell.

Disaster was all but assured.

Having said yes to Hugo, he was duty bound to attend, but lack of enthusiasm meant he was late leaving London. Then the weather had turned on him – as it was wont to do at this time of year. Like Yorkshire and Christmas, winter was doing what it always did.

He probably should have brought his carriage. At least that would offer some shelter from the storm. But he'd looked forward to a good ride.

The journey had started out as a good ride. He'd taken his time, giving Titan plenty of rest along the way, and staying in luxurious hostelries, where he had private rooms and no obligation to wish anyone the compliments of the season.

But for the last twenty miles, travel had become sheer misery. He should have stopped at an inn somewhere. God knew why he kept plodding his way northward. He could only blame the stubborn stupidity that seemed to mark most of his actions.

So here he was, a good forty miles from Hugo's estate. He was cold, wet, and exhausted. And the horrors of a family Christmas still awaited. Some days, a man wished that he'd never got out of bed.

The road through the village crossed a bridge. Through his grumbling, he was aware of a roaring in his ears, but he didn't pay much attention.

Only when Titan balked at advancing did Roland emerge from what even he recognized as a colossal sulk to realize that while the road might once have led to a bridge, the bridge was no longer there. Instead, a raging torrent of brown water threatened to break the high riverbanks.

It seemed that he wasn't going to spend Christmas Eve with Hugo after all. He was in such a funk, the news came as a relief.

"Nowt will get through that, sir," a rough voice insisted from behind him.

Roland turned his head to see a portly fellow in a bedraggled sheepskin coat splashing toward him. A farmer, he guessed. He'd been riding through soggy fields all day.

Roland raised his voice over the thundering water. "I wanted to make Halifax tonight." Hugo lived about ten miles past the city.

As the man approached, he kept his sodden hat pulled low against the tumbling rain. "Reckon the only place thou will make tonight is Puddlebrook."

"Where's Puddlebrook?"

The man gave a grunt of derisive amusement. "Thou art standing in it. Though tonight, it's more Noah's flood than Puddlebrook. Bridge went two hours ago."

That was another thing that Roland remembered without fondness about Yorkshire. The denizens liked to make grim jokes.

"There was a crossroads about five miles back."

"Flooding at Muckly Marsh, if thou goes that way. Flit in spate. Muckly Marsh goes underwater."

Muckly Marsh didn't sound appealing. "Then what in Jericho am I to do?"

"Reckon thou'd best hop down to the Spotted Fox and see if they've got a bed. Mind, we've had a few strangers through today, so it might well be a bench in the taproom."

"The Spotted Fox?"

One leather-gloved hand waved toward the village behind them. "Aye, the inn thou passed on thy way. Did thou not mark it?"

Roland had been so sunk in a murk of misery and memories, he hadn't seen much. Now that he took the trouble to look, he noted that Puddlebrook was a substantial village, sure to have at least one hostelry.

He touched the dripping brim of his hat. "Thank you for your help. I'll take your advice."

What else could he do? Titan was close to done in. So was he.

"Aye, right canny. Big place on the left. Can't miss it. Merry Christmas."

"Merry Christmas," Roland muttered, the words sticking in his throat.

The man waded off as Roland turned Titan back the way that they'd come. He bent forward to pat his mount's neck. "You'll be glad to get into a nice warm stable, old boy. I'm sorry I dragged you through all this."

Titan must have sensed shelter and food were on offer, because he kicked into a trot rather than the discouraged plod that he'd progressed at for most of the day.

Once Roland reached the Spotted Fox, he wondered how he'd missed it. It was the most substantial building in the hamlet and it blazed with light as night closed in.

A groom rushed out to take Titan. As Roland dismounted, he tossed the lad a shilling. "He's done good service today. Treat him right, and there's another shilling in it for you."

"Aye, my lord."

Tired, wet, grumpy, he trudged into the inn's wood-paneled hall. The place was noisy and bustling with activity. Clearly, he wasn't the only stranded traveler.

A maid emerged to take his wet greatcoat and hat. "Do you have a room available for the night?" he asked, tugging off his leather gloves.

"Sir, we're that full, I'd have to check with the mistress. We might be able to find you a place in the taproom."

"More guests, Milly?"

The woman's voice from further down the corridor turned Roland as motionless as a block of stone. Three years, yet he recognized it from the first word he heard.

"Just a single gentleman, mistress."

The woman who had spoken came up the hallway and stopped beside Milly.

The last time that Roland saw her, she'd worn a fashionable muslin gown in autumn shades of gold and russet. It irked him that he even remembered the sodding color.

Today, she sported a modest gray frock under a cream linen apron. Her rich red hair was confined in a single plait. Plain clothing didn't play down her extraordinary beauty. If anything, she blazed brighter in her simple garments.

He couldn't even pretend that he'd forgotten that beauty. It had haunted him every moment since they'd parted.

When her gaze settled on him, she went as still as he did. Deep green eyes widened in undisguised horror. No question that she remembered him, too.

"Roland..." she said in a choked whisper, as her hands clasped together in front of her.

"Good afternoon, Charmian." An ironic smile twisted his lips, despite nothing about this situation striking him as funny. He mightn't be amused, but somewhere a malicious fate was laughing its head off. "How obliging of Father Christmas to arrange for me to spend the holy festival with my wife."

CHAPTER TWO

Charmian didn't even pretend to smile. Once, long ago, she'd enjoyed Roland's wry sense of humor. But once, long ago, she'd thought that they'd be happy together for the rest of their lives.

How did that work out, Charmian Barton?

The maid glanced open-mouthed between the two of them. Milly chattered like a parrot. The news of Miss Barton's mysterious husband's arrival would be all over the inn before they started serving dinner. "M-Miss Barton?"

He gave Charmian a sardonic smile that she hadn't seen before. *"Miss?"* You've been living under false pretenses, I see. Not to mention you've lost your wedding ring."

She hid a wince. The immediate numbing shock receded a little. The urge to run and hide faded, too. Stiffening her spine, she told herself that she could hold her own against Roland. She wasn't wide-eyed and innocent and nineteen anymore. If she was honest, most days she felt as old as the millennium.

Had he come looking for her? She hadn't had a word from him since they'd separated in York. But the marriage stood. They remained linked for life.

"It never meant much," she retorted, although she couldn't stop her fingers curling at her sides with a shame that she shouldn't feel.

"So I see," he responded, the line of his lips turning bitter. Bitterness had been alien to the man she thought she'd known. But then, she'd long ago understood that she hadn't known Roland Destry at all.

Seeing him stirred a storm of emotions. Shock. Confusion. Anger. Regret, her constant companion since they'd parted.

Anger emerged paramount.

A hundred furious words rushed to her lips, so it was perhaps lucky that her aunt appeared on the landing above. "Charmian, weren't you fetching hot water for the Whytes in room twelve?"

Charmian suddenly recollected that she was standing in the middle of a crowded inn during a natural disaster. She couldn't indulge in the luxury of a tantrum, much as she might want to. "Milly, please look after the Whytes."

Milly bobbed into a curtsy, although it was clear that she'd much rather stay and hear the gossip. "Aye, Miss.. Mrs..."

"Destry," Roland said in a low voice, without sparing the girl a glance.

He hadn't looked away from Charmian since he'd first seen her. She couldn't help wondering what he saw. Since their last meeting, she'd endured three hard years. These days, she approached the world warily, and she knew that showed on her face.

It was unforgivably vain to want him to think that she was still beautiful. If only for her pride's sake. She couldn't bear the idea of him feeling sorry for her.

With an incoherent murmur, Milly left as Aunt

Janet marched down the steps. "What is it, love?"

Janet mustn't have heard Roland say Destry. With so many guests, the inn was in uproar.

Charmian gestured toward Roland. "Aunt, this is Sir Roland Destry. Roland, this is Janet Barton, my father's sister."

Her aunt was capable and formidable, ready to withstand any challenge that life presented. A woman running a country inn needed to hold her own with patrons and staff. Charmian had seen her face down a pack of drunk bullyboys and triumph purely through force of personality.

Charmian also knew the kind heart beneath the forbidding exterior. That kind heart had provided unfailing support through the last years.

Now she expected to see dislike or disdain on her aunt's face. How puzzling that Janet's first reaction seemed to be fear. She wouldn't have said that Aunt Janet was afraid of anyone.

"Sir Roland," Aunt Janet bit out, although Charmian couldn't help thinking that she was apprehensive under the frosty welcome.

Perhaps Roland's exalted rank overawed her, although her aunt was used to dealing with the upper classes. The Spotted Fox was the only decent public house for miles, so it received patronage from the local gentry as well as travelers and farmers and agricultural workers.

Aunt Janet performed a curtsy so sketchy, it hardly justified the name. Roland's bow was more elegant, but then, he'd always had perfect manners. No wonder Charmian felt like a complete bumpkin in his company. "Miss Barton. I'm hoping you can offer me a bed tonight."

"I'm afraid we have no room. If you go back to Sorby, you may find a place." This was the voice that Aunt Janet used when she threw drunken yokels out at closing time.

Under that tone, yokels turned as quiet as lambs. Roland was made of stouter stuff.

He'd been a charming young man with a sweet nature. Or at least so Charmian had thought until that last catastrophic quarrel. His reply now conveyed nothing sweet. "Sorby is five miles in the wrong direction. My horse is exhausted. It's a deluge out there. And I'm frozen to the bone."

Janet folded her arms over her substantial bosom. "Nonetheless, you must go."

Charmian sent her aunt a questioning look. "I'm sure we could fit Roland in the taproom, even if on a chair."

"Don't forget I'm family." His dry tone indicated that he didn't feel like family at all.

Janet's eyes narrowed. "The taproom's full."

The conversation paused while the barman passed them, balancing a tray piled with empty tankards. He threw them a curious glance, but didn't stop. It was all hands on deck tonight. John should have finished at five and gone back to his family for Christmas Eve.

"I'll take a blanket and sleep in the stables if I have to," Roland said with a snap of his straight white teeth. "I'm not putting my horse out into that weather again."

He'd always been kind to animals and children. He'd been kind to her – at least at first. It seemed that hadn't changed. When it came to animals anyway.

"We can't help you, Sir Roland."

Janet's uncompromising attitude confused Charmian. There were good reasons for her aunt to dislike Roland, but people died in storms like this. Sending Roland away endangered his life. Charmian might have a few bones to pick with her husband, but she certainly didn't wish him dead.

She straightened, aware that she was about to make a mistake but unable to think of any alternative. "He can sleep in my room."

Her aunt paled, even as Roland tilted a doubtful eyebrow at Charmian.

"That's not suitable, Charmian." Now there was no mistaking the fear at the root of Aunt Janet's prickliness.

"It couldn't be more suitable." Charmian had had a long, tiring day. She'd had a long, tiring three years. She wasn't up to dealing with whatever was peeving her aunt. "We're married, after all."

"I thought you might have forgotten," Roland said with a snideness foreign to the lighthearted man she'd married in such haste.

"How could I forget? If I survived the plague, I'd remember the experience," she sniped back. When they'd wed, that nastiness wasn't in her vocabulary either. Clearly they'd both changed for the worse since their last meeting.

The door behind them opened, and a shivering family of four tumbled into the hallway. Two men emerged from the taproom on the right. "We're still waiting on our dinner," one of them said rudely.

Aunt Janet looked hunted, but she didn't respond to her customers. Sign enough that she was rattled. She prided herself on being an excellent landlady. "The taproom will be good enough for you," she told Roland in the voice that always summoned immediate obedience.

Roland's eyebrows rose in understandable annoyance. Not much obedience to be seen. "You said there was no room."

John emerged to deal with the new arrivals. He shot his employer another questioning glance, when he saw that she was still busy with Roland and

Charmian.

"I'll make room," Janet said grimly.

Charmian frowned. They couldn't stand here, airing their dirty linen in public. "No, I want him with me."

"I'm overcome, wife," Roland said. "You do care after all."

She bit back the urge to say, "I don't." It wouldn't help. Anyway, despite everything, it wasn't true. "We need to talk."

"It took three years to reach that conclusion?"

"I haven't noticed you beating down my door, begging for a reconciliation," she snapped back. He acted as if all their problems were her fault.

"That's all very well," the man outside the taproom said. "But where's our dinner?"

Aunt Janet sucked in an irritated breath and squared her shoulders. She set a smile on her face – not an entirely convincing effort – and faced the man. "I'll check with the kitchen, Mr. Smith. I'm sorry you've been kept waiting." She turned to Charmian. "Can you look after the new arrivals and get John to bring another beer barrel up from the cellar?"

"I'll show Roland to my room first," she said.

"I'd rather you looked after our guests."

Charmian frowned. It sounded like Janet tried to keep her away from Roland. Was she worried that he was a danger to her? Her aunt had always been protective of her only niece. "Roland won't hurt me."

"You haven't seen him for a long time."

Nobody was more aware of that than Charmian. She'd counted every minute of every hour of every day.

"This isn't getting my dinner," Mr. Smith barked.

A woman emerged from the parlor at the end of the hallway, clutching a screaming baby and Milly appeared from downstairs carrying two canisters of hot water. This corridor was busier than the Strand on a Monday morning. It wasn't the place for any sort of meaningful conversation.

"Come with me," Charmian said to Roland over the din. "I'll have to come down and help, but upstairs you'll have a bed and some privacy at least." She reached to pick up his valise.

"My wife doesn't need to play the servant," he growled. "I'm capable of carrying my own bag."

She flushed a painful red. Because for most of the time that they'd been apart, she'd helped her aunt in the inn. Playing the servant, as Roland put it. He must wonder what madness had led him to marry someone little better than a scullery maid. It was a question she'd asked herself in the depths of many a night during the long, lonely hours when the answers that she came up with were entirely depressing.

"Then please follow me," she said tight-lipped.

"Charmian, Sir Roland will be better off in the taproom," her aunt said with barely hidden desperation.

Aunt Janet definitely wanted to keep them apart. Did she fear that this reunion would distress her niece? Of course it did, but it was past time that she and Roland discussed their future. That was never going to be easy.

"No, Aunt. He's coming with me." She collected a lamp from a side table and mounted the steps, not needing to check if Roland fell in behind her. From the moment they'd met, she'd felt a preternatural awareness of his presence. That, it seemed, hadn't changed, despite their estrangement.

"She doesn't like me," Roland said.

"No, she doesn't. For good reason." Her aunt had been devastated when Charmian returned home, brokenhearted after her reckless marriage.

They continued up past two floors containing guest rooms to the attics. Only when Charmian pushed the door open did she wonder what Roland would make of her quarters. He was a rich man with a large manor house in Northamptonshire. Not that she'd ever seen Leeder Hall. They'd been on their honeymoon in York when they parted.

As he shut the door behind him, she set the lamp on a chest of drawers and folded her arms in a gesture that even she recognized as defensive. "It's not what you're used to."

His lips quirked with the self-mockery that once she'd found so attractive. She still did, plague take him. "No gilded halls and silk upholstery?"

Charmian didn't smile back. She was far too conscious of the fact that she and Roland hadn't shared a closed space in years and this was a minuscule room containing a bed. "No."

He set his bag on the floor and took off his coat, hanging it on a hook in the wall. He was a tall, lean man, and his head came near to brushing the low ceiling in the center of the room. He wouldn't be able to stand straight at the sides, where the ceiling followed the roofline.

This was her first chance to look at him properly. He'd been a handsome young man. Dark-haired. Dark-eyed. With a flashing smile that stole her silly heart from the first.

Three years of maturity had only built on his attractions. The harder lines of his face lent him character as well as charm.

"It's fine, Charmian. More than fine. I appreciate your generosity in sharing it. I'll do better here than I would in a taproom crammed with snoring brutes." He didn't sound as confrontational as he had downstairs. Instead, he sounded as tired as she did.

"Unless you snore these days?"

He was trying to put her at her ease. She should appreciate it. Meeting an estranged spouse was always going to be awkward.

"How would I know?" she asked sharply, before she kicked herself. Roland was quick enough to pick up on the implication that she'd slept alone since they'd separated, and she wasn't ready to feed his vanity by revealing that she'd stayed faithful to her vows. "Did you come looking for me?"

"No, our meeting is a pleasant surprise." She hid a wince at his sarcasm. "I had no idea you were in Yorkshire. I was on my way to visit a friend."

Of course he hadn't come looking for her. He never had. Although it perplexed her that he'd been so startled to see her. After all, he must know that she worked at the Spotted Fox. Unless he'd never even read her letters. Which was a very depressing thought indeed.

"I meant it when I said that we need to talk," she said in a rush. "But the inn's packed to the rafters and I have to help Aunt Janet."

"You need to go downstairs."

"Yes." She gestured around the small room with its sloping roof and plain deal furniture. "It's not fancy, but you should be warm and comfortable here. I'll send John up with hot water. He'll do the fire, too."

Roland was removing his gray waistcoat. Only his loose shirt and buff breeches remained. He crossed the room to dip his hand in the jug of water standing by the unlit hearth. "He's already got plenty to do. He doesn't need to be hauling buckets of water up three flights of stairs for me. This will do for a quick wash, then I'll come down and lend a hand."

"That's—"

"Beneath my dignity?"

The astringent edge to his humor was new. The young man she'd married had taken a sunny view of life. Too sunny, as it turned out, at least where his marriage was concerned.

She'd been about to say something along those lines, but another pair of helping hands would be useful, so she went for a less adversarial response. "That's very kind of you."

The look he sent her said that he doubted her sincerity.

"No, I mean it. We're run off our feet. Thank you." And she'd prefer to have him out of this room. Thinking of him waiting for her here, sleeping in her bed, handling her things, would torment her.

"It's the least I can do."

"You need to change into some dry clothes."

He arched an eyebrow at her. "That almost sounds wifely."

His sarcastic tone made her blush with chagrin. As if all the fault between them lay with her. Her voice hardened. "Then freeze, if you prefer. It's your business. Not mine."

His laugh was short and unamused. "Now you sound like you mean it." He began to untie his neckcloth.

Charmian took a shocked second to realize that he meant to undress fully in front of her. Her cheeks heated, and she jerked her attention toward the window. "I'll...I'll see you downstairs."

That evoked a derisive grunt. "Do you want me to save your maidenly blushes?"

"I'm not a maiden." She braced her shoulders and glared at him. "Thanks to you."

"I remember, but I wondered if you did, you've come over so coy. Don't you remember what a naked man looks like?"

He tugged off his damp shirt to reveal a chest that

had filled out from the slender man she recalled. Roland Destry had become a much more substantial presence since their last meeting. She suspected that these days he made an implacable enemy. The insight wasn't welcome.

"I've tried to forget," she said through stiff lips. Which was true, just as it was true that she'd failed miserably. Memories of Roland's naked body had pursued her since their parting. When his hands lowered to the fastenings on his breeches, she pushed past him and out of the room, even if that gave him victory in their little war. "I'll see you soon."

CHAPTER THREE

It was nearly two by the time Charmian trudged upstairs. All night, new arrivals had stumbled in out of the weather. There wasn't a spare inch in the taproom and while she'd saved Roland from sleeping in the stables, that fate had befallen several of the lone male travelers who showed up after midnight. Their guests would be with them for the festival. Goodness knew what her aunt would feed them all.

She was wrung-out and fed up and filthy. The fact that it had been Christmas for two hours already didn't chime with her sour mood at all.

She'd been in a sour mood for three years. No amount of Christmas cheer would change that.

Charmian pushed open the door to her room, fortifying herself for another thorny encounter with Roland. Given that her estranged husband was her Christmas gift this year, she couldn't help feeling that her lack of cheer was justified.

He'd come up about half an hour ago, after proving surprisingly helpful. Helpful, cooperative, and diligent. When he'd offered assistance, she'd expected him to retreat, once he discovered how much hard physical work was involved. But he'd hauled hot water and trays and coal and firewood without complaint. His lordly manner had even come in handy for solving disputes between the guests, inevitable in such crowded quarters.

She ought to be grateful, but it rankled to discover that her neglectful husband was as charming as ever.

Once everyone at last was settled, she'd stayed downstairs mopping the kitchen, until she'd realized that she was just being a coward and avoiding Roland.

Her stomach tied itself in nervous knots as she surveyed the small room, but she needn't have worried. The lamp was lit and the fire burned merrily in the grate, but no far-too-observant gentleman awaited her. Her troublesome spouse collapsed across her bed, lost in sleep.

Very carefully, Charmian edged inside the room. They had to reach some conclusion about where they took their unwise union. But it was a relief to put off the discussion until tomorrow. Or later today, given the time.

She couldn't help lingering to study Roland. He looked dead-tired. Hardly surprising. He'd been riding all day in worsening weather, then he'd been run off his feet this evening. But now that she had a chance to examine his features without fearing those perceptive dark eyes, she saw that the tiredness seemed more ingrained than the mere result of a difficult twenty-four hours.

Even in slumber, his lips settled into an unhappy expression and deep lines ran between mouth and nose. They hadn't been there when she'd met him. The man she'd married had been carefree, funny, one of life's victors. This man sleeping so soundly on top of her bed – he hadn't even turned down the covers – knew the acrid taste of disappointment and failure.

While she'd spent most of the last three years fuming at Roland, it was hard to maintain her ire when she looked down at him. She'd imagined that she alone had suffered with their separation. But seeing him now, she knew that wasn't true.

As she stepped back, he stirred. Through one burning moment, dazed dark eyes settled on her. For once, there was no trace of wariness. Instead, warmth flooded his expression and the smile that curved his lips swept her back to those weeks when she'd loved Roland Destry and he'd loved her in return. The happiest days of her life, when she'd been sure nothing could go wrong, now that she'd married this marvelous man.

Despite everything, she smiled back, even as her poor misused heart swelled against her ribs.

Then she remembered what had happened since. He must have, too. His smile faltered and disappeared, and his gaze turned watchful again.

Charmian wasn't quite so quick to return to the cold, unloved present. For a long moment, she gazed at the man she'd loved so passionately. Until she realized how revealing her expression must be and she looked away. "Go back to sleep. You've gone like the clappers all evening."

He didn't comply. Instead, he sat up and rubbed his eyes with unconcealed weariness. The fire warmed the small room to comfort, so he'd taken off his coat and boots. He was a long way from undressed, but having her husband sitting on her bed in shirtsleeves, breeches, and bare feet summoned unwelcome ghosts of former intimacy.

"Do you do that every day? If so, I take my hat off to you. I feel like I've fought Waterloo single-handed. And I only did it for a couple of hours."

Because he sounded genuinely admiring, she bit

back a gibe about being a skivvy who worked for her living. "Most of our custom is local. We get a few paying guests, but nothing like this."

"You must be exhausted."

She was. And like him, not just because of the current emergency. "I'll live."

One did, didn't one? Even when there didn't seem much point and every heartbeat just counted out loss.

"I'm glad to hear it." He gestured toward the washstand. "I brought you up some hot water."

"Thank you. That was thoughtful." He'd been thoughtful as a young man, too. Which was why his behavior since had caught her so off guard.

Because it hurt to look at Roland, she surveyed the room. He'd been tidy, too. That hadn't changed. His coat and boots were neatly stowed. "And you brought up firewood. Thank you."

He rose, towering against the ceiling, and moved to place another log on the fire and freshen it up with the poker. "A husband comes in useful."

Once they'd teased each other, but those happy days were long past. She didn't smile. "I wouldn't know about that."

His eyes narrowed on her, but he didn't give her an acerbic answer. He'd always been slow to anger, but as she'd discovered when he lost his temper, he held a grudge. "Do you want to do this now when we're both tired or shall we wait for the morning?"

She'd reached that point of tiredness where she felt too high-strung to sleep. Anyway, how could she sleep when she shared a room with her long-lost spouse for the first time in years? "It is morning."

"Yes, it's Christmas." She'd never heard him use that flat tone before. "Happy Christmas, Charmian."

Something about that joyless greeting made her want to cry. She'd lived with regret for so long. But it stabbed particularly deep tonight when Roland shared her room.

They'd missed out on so much. They'd never got to do any of the normal things that married couples did. Celebrate Christmas or birthdays. Set up a home together. Have children. In spite of everything, when she discovered that their fortnight of vigorous bed sport in York hadn't resulted in a pregnancy, she'd cried her eyes out.

At least a baby would have provided a focus for all the love that Roland didn't want.

It was too much. She either subsided into a sobbing mess – when she'd already cried more than enough over her disastrous marriage – or she fought. She'd only survived because she'd been angry. God save her, she was angry now.

She turned on the only man she'd ever loved and spoke with a voice as biting as acid. "Stop acting as if you're the one who's hard done by. Why didn't you answer any of my letters? You must have known we had to work out some way to go on. We were married, for pity's sake. You couldn't just sweep that fact under the carpet and go on your merry way, as if nothing had ever happened."

He whitened so fast that the shadows under his eyes stood out stark and purple. "Letters? What letters?"

She didn't have to try to keep up her anger now. Her hands clenched at her sides. "Don't pretend. I wrote you so many letters. It must have been hundreds. And not one word in reply. Not a single word."

His eyes were searching. "Is that true, Charmian?"

At this rate, she was going to clout him with the hot water canister. "I don't lie. Or have you forgotten that since we parted? I'm not surprised that you have. After all, you conveniently forgot you had a wife at all."

One emphatic gesture sliced the air. "I never forgot. Nor did I ever stop writing to you."

Roland had never been a liar either. Something told her that he wasn't lying now, mad as his claim might sound. "I don't understand." She'd stepped closer to Roland when someone knocked on the door.

CHAPTER FOUR

Roland bit back the urge to curse fit to raise the rafters. He and Charmian were finally about to sort out the trouble between them – and it was clear that there was some mystery to solve as well. After their years of no communication, he wasn't willing to lose this chance. She might go silent on him again. That had driven him to the brink of insanity. "Don't answer it."

Charmian didn't look any happier about the interruption. "There might be a problem."

"There is a problem. The fact that you left me three years ago and I haven't seen you since," he snapped.

She flinched as there was another knock. "I'm sorry. I have to..."

When she crossed to open the door, she revealed her aunt in the clothes she'd worn all evening. "Charmian, you're awake?"

Charmian didn't bother confirming what was visibly true. "Do you need me downstairs, Aunt Janet?"

Roland strained to hear some disturbance, but the inn was quiet, apart from the rumble of various snores and the distant roar of the river.

"No. No. Can I come in?"

Roland ground his teeth. He'd long ago realized that Charmian's family had interfered in his marriage. He only had to recall the stony reception that her mother had given him at Holden House when he'd turned up, determined to get his wife back.

Charmian cast him a nervous glance. "It's late. Can't it wait until the morning?"

Janet Barton bore a strong resemblance to her niece. The same red hair and fine features and green eyes. Those eyes were worried right now. "No. I need to talk to you."

"Should I send Roland downstairs?" Charmian stepped back to let the woman in.

"Yes. No."

Charmian looked bewildered. Roland couldn't blame her. He'd only met Janet tonight, but he'd seen enough to recognize a woman of strong character. Her current uncertainty didn't fit with that.

"Which is it, Aunt?"

"I think Sir Roland needs to hear what I have to say."

Roland stood. The room wasn't large. With three people inside, it was overcrowded. He noticed that the woman carried a leather satchel. His curiosity sparked. Janet looked as if she bore the weight of the world on her shoulders. She also looked unmistakably guilty. What the hell was going on?

Charmian now looked troubled rather than puzzled. "What's the matter?"

Janet looked guiltier than ever. "I..."

Instead of continuing, she slid the satchel from her shoulder and offered it to Charmian. Whatever it held, there was a lot of it. The worn leather bulged.

Charmian took the bag, but didn't immediately open it. "What is it, Aunt Janet?"

Her aunt looked strained and pale. She licked her lips and wrung her hands. "I just ask you to remember the state you were in when you came back to us. Your mother and I believed we were doing the best thing. I'm still not convinced we were wrong. But..."

With shaking hands, Charmian opened the satchel. Roland felt sick, even before Charmian checked the contents. He had an idea of what was inside.

She shot her aunt a killing look. "L-letters?" she stammered. "I don't understand."

Janet squared her shoulders in a way Roland had seen her niece do a hundred times. "You should sit down."

Charmian's shock receded and she flushed with anger, as she looked again at the satchel then at her aunt. "I don't want to sit down. I want to know what all my letters to Roland and..." With a shaking hand, she sifted through the satchel's contents. "...and his letters to me are doing in your possession."

Her voice was like a whiplash, and it was clear that Janet felt the bite of the strike. Her eyes were glassy with tears, as she regarded her niece. Tears and love, much as Roland didn't want to recognize it. "We, your mother and I, were so worried about you when you came home from York and your disastrous mistake."

"Our marriage, you mean," Roland grated out.

Janet leveled tragic eyes on him, and he realized that she'd concentrated so hard on Charmian that he'd hardly registered in her awareness. "It was a mistake. Haven't three years apart proven that?"

Charmian looked furious. Even worse, she looked devastated.

"Three years apart that you and my mother engineered." Her voice was flat. He could tell that she struggled to control her tumultuous reaction.

Janet adopted a persecuted air. "We feared for your sanity when you came back to us. Don't you remember? You couldn't eat, you couldn't sleep, you cried for a week, then you sank into a silence that was worse."

Charmian directed a glower at him. She was a proud creature. She wouldn't like him hearing this.

Roland didn't like hearing it either. He hated to think of her suffering. All this time, he'd imagined her angry and disdainful. Her distress didn't flatter his vanity. He'd always wanted the best for her. He still did.

"Perhaps because I missed the man I love," she said, as if the words didn't slice through him like a knife. Because he'd loved her, too, and losing her had come close to destroying him.

Roland didn't place too much faith in her declaration of past love. He didn't underestimate the changes that their separation had wrought.

Janet's jaw took on a stubborn line familiar from his acquaintance with Charmian. "There's no good to be had from mixing the classes. Someone always gets their heart broken, and it's nearly always the woman. I told your father he was wrong when he sent you to that ridiculous school in Bath. He was asking for trouble. I was right, wasn't I? The Bartons belong with the working people, however much money your father made. The gentry care for nobody but themselves."

"You've always said that, Aunt, and I've never known why."

Janet's face tightened, as if she smelled something fetid. "Because it happened to me, just as it happened to you, my darling girl."

Aghast, Charmian gaped at her aunt. "You married someone from the upper classes?"

Janet's grunt expressed contempt. "There was no marriage, but I fell for the squire's son's pretty lies, convinced myself I was in *love.*" The bitterness in the word made even Roland wince. "Then he went off and married a rich baronet's ugly daughter instead. I loathed that you went through the same thing."

Roland made a dismissive gesture. "But Charmian didn't go through the same thing. We married. We were set to be happy together."

Janet looked at him as if she despised him. "Then why did she come home with her heart broken?"

"My heart was broken because I never saw Roland again," Charmian said. "No wonder you and Mamma were in such a hurry to rush me off to Puddlebrook after that first week. Even if Roland came looking for me, he'd never find me here."

"I did come looking for you. Over and over." Memories of his grief and frustration threatened to choke him. "But your mother wouldn't tell me where you'd gone. She said you didn't want to see me again."

The satchel dropped to the ground with a thud, as Charmian stared at him in astonishment. "You came looking for me?"

"Of course I did. You were – you *are* – my wife. I wanted you back."

She looked unconvinced. "Even after that terrible fight?"

He shrugged, although he was as far from nonchalant about all this as it was possible to be. "We could have worked it out." He cast a fulminating glare at Janet, and his voice hardened. "Given the chance. At least I thought so, although you clearly bore a grudge. But, Charmian, you know where I live. Why didn't you come to Leeder Hall?"

Her hands twined at her waist in a gesture of distress that mirrored her aunt's. "I wasn't sure you wanted me to."

Roland frowned. He'd already told her that he wanted her back. He wasn't going to humble himself by admitting the devastation that she'd left behind after she abandoned him. Or not while her aunt remained to listen, anyway.

He was sure that his pride would be pulverized before they were done, whatever else happened. The question was whether he'd end up humiliated but still bereft, or whether this unplanned meeting offered a fresh beginning with his beautiful wife.

"Even so, we were married. That wasn't going to disappear for the wishing."

She flinched. "Did you want it to go away?"

"Did you?"

She made an apologetic gesture. "I thought of looking for you so often, but my mother and Aunt Janet said that if you loved me, you'd come for me. And you didn't."

"And you accepted what they said without question?"

Shame dulled her lovely green eyes. "I did for the first few months. Especially when you didn't answer my letters. After a couple of days of feeling very sorry for myself, I wrote again and again, and there was only silence."

Roland scowled at Janet. "And I wrote to you to receive the same silence in return."

Janet looked even guiltier. “There was no future for the two of you. I’m still not sure there is.”

“But that’s not for you to say, is it?” Roland snapped.

Charmian regarded her aunt with confusion as well as anger. “You must have had a plan. What did you imagine was going to happen as the years went on? Neither Roland nor I could marry again while the other was alive.”

Janet looked hunted. “I don’t know, Charmian. Your mother and I were so worried about you. We just wanted to make sure you didn’t do anything stupid. We thought we’d wait until you were strong enough to make your own decisions. That’s why we kept the letters. Your mother sent on anything she received in Somerset, so if ever you were capable of making a choice, you could read them.”

“But how could I make my own decisions when you hid Roland’s letters and stole mine, and nobody told me that he’d come looking for me?”

“We acted in your best interests.” Janet’s hands twisted so tightly that her knuckles shone white. “We couldn’t bear seeing you so distraught.”

“And you’d already had your heart broken by a careless rake,” she said.

Janet had never married, Roland realized. Clearly that early experience had scarred her for life. It was a pity, but it wasn’t an excuse. “It wasn’t fair to tar me with the same brush as your first love.”

Janet looked at him with genuine hatred. “Why not? It’s clear that you left my niece in pieces. You should never have met, let alone been foolish enough to marry. I told my brother that no matter how much money he made, he could never expect the gentry to treat him as anything except a trumped-up servant. The Bartons work for their living. You and your ilk sit around, drinking brandy and causing trouble. I wish to God her parents had never tried to raise Charmian as a lady. There's no disgrace in earning your daily bread. There is disgrace in leading innocent girls on, then forsaking them."

Roland was angry, an anger stemming from years of misery and loneliness and longing. It was difficult not to shout at the woman.

"You know nothing about me." His voice might remain soft, but his tone was acid. "And Charmian isn't you. What happened to you didn't happen to Charmian."

Janet looked stubborn. "I know what I saw."

"I was going to come to Leeder Hall," Charmain said, shooting a worried glance between her aunt and Roland. She must feel the rising temperature in the room.

"Why didn't you?"

"Celia Hibberd wrote to say that you were taking the Grand Tour."

He frowned. "Did she know we were married?"

"I didn't tell her. I didn't tell anyone except my family. It was just one of those gossipy letters between friends, you know. Did you tell her we eloped? If you did, she never mentioned it."

"No, I didn't tell anyone that I'd found a bride who left me within a fortnight," he bit out.

"Your pride again."

Charmian's disdain stung. Yes, he'd been proud at the start. Too proud. But it hadn't taken him long to realize that pride gave a man no comfort when his bed was empty and his heart ached for the woman he loved.

He wasn't about to admit that. It seemed that his pride retained its sway. "Pride was all you left me with."

She flinched at his answer. "If you were heading off on your travels, you weren't suffering too badly."

A protest died on his lips. After six months without a word from the bride he'd married with such joy, he'd been sick to the soul. England only held painful memories. He'd escaped to foreign climes, hoping that Italy or France might offer balm for his suffering. They didn't.

His only chance to restore his spirits was seeing his wife again. Three wretched years hadn't changed that. Even tonight when she was so prickly, she made him feel more alive than he had since she'd left.

"Once we heard that, we knew we'd made the right decision," Janet said. "When you're a rich aristocrat, it's so easy to run away from your sorrows."

He glowered at the woman. "Except I was only away a couple of months and I wrote over and over to Charmian the whole time. And I came to find her again, as soon as I returned to England."

By then, he'd realized that there was no future for him without Charmian. Or no future that he wanted.

Janet went back to looking guilty, while Charmian stared at him out of devastated eyes. "Roland, I'm so sorry you went through all that. I promise I didn't know."

When he met that troubled green gaze, he asked the question that had tormented him every moment of every day since that stupid quarrel in York. "Would it have made any difference if you had?"

He'd waited so long for the answer. It seemed he had to wait some more.

Charmian shot a glare at her aunt. "Aunt Janet, you should leave us now."

"But—"

"You've already interfered enough, wouldn't you agree?" The question's sweetness was poisonous.

Janet whitened and looked stricken, but her tone indicated that she left under protest. "As you wish."

Charmian waited until the door closed behind her aunt before she faced Roland. "Well, husband, what happens now?"

CHAPTER FIVE

Charmian's mind reeled after the revelations of the last half hour. The churning mix of emotions in her stomach made her feel sick. Anger was there. And sorrow. And astonishment and guilt. Definitely guilt. Guilt as gnawing and powerful as a disease. She'd promised to trust Roland when she married him, yet she never had. And she'd been wrong.

Roland stepped forward to take her arm. "Sit down before you fall down."

It was the first time that he'd touched her since she'd left him. The contact slammed through her like gunfire, cut through her roiling confusion. She caught her breath, and her eyes fixed on his face. "How could they do that? It was so cruel."

Roland's lips flattened. "I suspect they thought they were protecting you."

"That's...that's a very generous view of their actions."

"Oh, I'm not feeling generous. I'm not feeling generous at all."

Charmian believed that. She heard the controlled rage in his voice.

Her gaze searched his features. She wanted to know what he was feeling. About their situation. About her. Did his anger extend to his wife? It had, she had no doubt. Had what they learned tonight changed that?

She'd been angry with him, too. Furious and resentful and hurt. Hurt to the depths of her soul. But now, now only one question mattered. "What do you want to do?"

A grim smile lengthened his lips. "Apart from push your aunt into a snowdrift?"

She shouldn't laugh. Nothing about this debacle was funny. But a huff of bleak amusement escaped her nonetheless. "Can I help?"

His smile broadened, and for a charged moment, they stared at each other without animosity creating a wall between them. For a fleeting instant, she was the girl who had married him, who had adored the ground he walked on, who had been convinced that she'd found the other half of her soul.

Whether that was true or not, her soul had been in bleeding tatters since the day she'd left him.

The shutters fell back over his eyes. He couldn't have said "keep out" any more clearly. "Sit down, Charmian."

In a haze of misery, she let him settle her on the edge of the bed. His hand on her arm felt like the only warmth in the entire cosmos. As if to confirm that winter had conquered the world, a gust of wind rattled the windowpane.

When Roland released her, she wanted to howl like that icy wind. She'd been cold for three long years. She didn't want to be cold any longer.

Instead of sitting beside her – it was humiliating quite how much she wanted him to stay – he crossed the small room and sank into the

Windsor chair near the fire. Without speaking, he lowered his head and studied his linked hands. She stared at his untidy dark hair and wished with futile but piercing longing for a chance to do everything all over again and make different decisions this time.

Charmian prepared for him to rage at her, to blame her for the disaster that their marriage had become. Now that she knew the facts, she couldn't help but think she deserved it. Yes, her family had interfered. Unforgivably so. But she'd allowed it to happen. She'd gone along with her mother and her aunt's plans for her with no word of complaint. She just assumed that they were making the best decisions, when in fact their meddling had transformed a hiccup in a new marriage into three wretched years.

But when he spoke, his tone was gentle. He didn't look up at her which was something of a relief. Those dark eyes always saw too much.

"When I met you, I thought you were the most wonderful girl in the world."

She tried not to wince at his use of the word "were." What else did she expect? Whatever he'd done since they'd parted, and she couldn't imagine he'd slept alone every night like she had, it was clear that the estrangement with his wife had taken a toll on Roland, too. Contrary to her aunt's predictions.

"Everyone at Celia's house party admired you. All the girls wanted your attention. Heavens, even all the boys treated you like a hero. I couldn't believe you noticed me, let alone fell in love with me."

Slowly he raised his gaze, although she couldn't read his expression. Charmian supposed that he must be asking himself the same question. She was well aware that she looked a mess. She'd started work before dawn, and her dress was crumpled and stained. Not that it came anywhere near fashionable when it was clean. It certainly wasn't fit for a baronet's wife.

She looked, she was bitterly aware, like the peasant she was. And Roland would recognize that, which stung more than it should. After all, they had worse problems to sort out than her smarting vanity. But, oh, how she wished that he'd found her rosy-cheeked with health and wearing silks and satins and sipping tea in a salon. Instead of tired and worn and heartsick and wearing a frock marked by a day's physical labor.

Charmian struggled not to raise her hand to wipe her face or smooth her hair. She felt vulnerable enough already without revealing to Roland how her shabby appearance made her cringe.

So often, she'd fantasized about meeting him. The dreams that had hurt the most had him opening his arms and saying he'd always loved her and their separation was a tragic mistake. In other dreams, she was dressed to the nines and the toast of society, and he was crushed to realize what a glorious woman he'd lost.

None of her fantasies had involved her frazzled after a chaotic day and trying to make sense of a heinous betrayal from those closest to her.

His smile was reminiscent and surprisingly sweet. "How could I not fall in love with you? You were beautiful and vital and...real. All the other girls there were paper dolls in comparison."

The sadness in his answer undercut the compliments. The implication, Charmian was well aware, was that she was none of those things anymore. Too late to wish that she'd never left Roland at that inn in York. Too late to wish that she'd stayed and fought for her future. Too late – and pointless as well – to wish that she knew then what she knew now.

Charmian had met Sir Roland Destry at a house party at Lord Hibberd's Yorkshire estate. Her father had made a fortune as a brewer in Bristol and had ambitions to move up in the world. Ambitions that both his wife and his sister had derided, Charmian now recalled. After all, her aunt's favorite saying was "You can't make a silk purse out of a sow's ear."

Nonetheless Harry Barton had bought himself a pretty little manor near Wells and set up as a gentleman. He'd raised Charmian, his only child, to be a lady and sent her away to an expensive school near Bath, where the gentry educated their daughters. There she and Lady Celia Hibberd, whose father had hosted that fateful house party three years ago, had become friends.

The rambling old house in the Dales had been crammed to the rafters with eligible young people. Charmian mightn't be as blue-blooded as her friends, but she was her late father's heiress. When it came to marriage prospects, all that gold made up for any shady origins in trade.

But the moment that she met Sir Roland Destry, those other gentlemen might as well not have existed. He was four years older than her nineteen and had the polish of Cambridge and a couple of London seasons. More than that, he'd been sweet and funny and kind. And handsome enough to make any girl dream of winning his heart.

For Charmian, the dream had become reality because he'd fallen in love with her just as swiftly as she fell in love with him.

She hadn't thought back to those first golden weeks with Roland in years. The pain of comparing that euphoric idyll with the loneliness of life since was too excruciating. But seeing him again – still handsome – brought back a tidal wave of memories.

Within a week they'd decided to marry. Within another week, they'd hatched a plan to elope together in secret after the house party finished.

"Why did we run off together? We could have called the banns."

A bleak smile twisted his lips as he shifted in the wooden chair. "By heaven, you really have forgotten. I was mad for you, and we'd come very close to losing control a couple of times. Lord Hibberd wasn't much of a chaperone. You and I managed to spend a lot of time alone."

She hadn't blushed in ages. Roland's reappearance in her life seemed to have her blushing every five minutes. "The summerhouse."

"And the boatshed, and the woods near the lake."

"And that little room off the dining room."

"You were lucky you came to the wedding a virgin."

And, oh, that first night together after their dash to the Scottish border and their quick wedding, conducted by the village blacksmith at Gretna.

After all their naughty escapades on the Hibberd estate, Charmian hadn't been afraid, but she'd certainly been nervous. Roland had been careful and patient with her, and soon she'd been flying among the stars.

To her shame, when she left him, she hadn't just missed him, she'd missed having a man in her bed. Roland had awoken a volcanic passion inside her, shown her a dazzling new world of sensual pleasure. Then that glorious discovery was snatched away from her with agonizing abruptness.

Self-disgust flattened her lips. "I couldn't keep my hands off you."

"That's nothing to be ashamed of. I couldn't get enough of you either, if you recall."

She could most definitely recall. She'd recalled for three desolate, solitary years.

"We were in love," he said. More of that heartbreaking past tense.

She stood and sent him a direct look. "Then we had that terrible fight."

His expression was stark. "And you went away."

She made an apologetic gesture. "The things we said…"

"We could have come through."

"If I'd stayed and hadn't been such a coward," she said in a dull voice. "I ran for home faster than a rabbit runs for its burrow."

He didn't smile. "I should have followed straightaway. I was a fool, too bullheaded to know what I was losing."

"I thought you would come after me," she mumbled, looking down at her hands performing a distressed dance at her waist.

She couldn't endure looking at Roland. She'd spent all this time convinced that he hadn't suffered. Sometimes she'd been convinced that he didn't spare her a thought. How else to explain the long silence? In her imagination, he transformed into an unfeeling monster who had forgotten their marriage as easily as he'd forget a rainy day a year ago.

But much as she'd liked believing that she was in the right during their long separation, it was impossible when she looked into his face and read the marks of weariness and remorse and misery. The same things that she saw in her own eyes when she could bear to look in a mirror.

"I did," he said grimly.

Yes, he had, after her mother sent her away to work at the Spotted Fox. "I was in such a taking, my mother said I needed something to keep me busy.

She was sick of me staring out the window all day or curling up on my bed and crying."

"Charmian..."

Hearing about her grief upset him. He turned waxen, and those deep lines between his nose and mouth sharpened, making him look suddenly older.

She made a helpless gesture, wondering where her pride had gone, but not missing it. "I couldn't eat and I couldn't sleep. I was in tatters after we parted. My mother was genuinely afraid that I might do something desperate."

"I'm sorry." She couldn't doubt that he meant it.

"So am I. Especially when—"

"The cause of the argument was so petty."

She straightened and sent him a direct look. "No, it touched on something important, something we needed to sort out."

"You wanted to travel south to see your family before we settled at Leeder Hall. I could have agreed."

She shook her head, as her hands twined together. "Yes, you could. But the fight was really about how fully I was committed to you."

"It seemed to me—"

"That I put my loyalty to my family ahead of my loyalty to you."

He sighed and ran his hand through his hair. The familiar gesture made her heart squeeze in painful longing. "I should have been kinder. You were very young and an only child."

He was trying to ease the load of blame on her, when he really shouldn't. Both she and Roland had been wronged. She hadn't forgotten that. She never would. But she was sickly aware that the sin lay heaviest on her, not on her intrusive family. "We were both young, but that was no excuse. You told me I needed to grow up and decide I was a wife before I was a daughter."

He winced. "I told you a lot of things that I've had time to repent since."

"You were right. I'd pledged myself to you and our marriage. That should have come first. I wanted to be Lady Destry, but I also wanted to be pampered, spoiled Charmian Barton. Our separation is mostly my fault."

He looked devastated. "You're being too harsh with yourself. We could have sorted things out."

"If I hadn't run home to Mamma, like the stupid little girl I remained at heart. I can't blame you for hating me."

In a fit of temper, she'd hired a chaise from the inn at York and paid a maid to accompany her for the sake of appearances. She'd rushed back to Somerset and a useless attempt to retreat to her childhood. She'd cried the whole way.

"I don't hate you," he said in a dull voice.

"You should." She felt so weighted with guilt, she feared that she was likely to sink through the floor.

"No, I shouldn't. I should have put my pride aside and begged you to stay."

"But you did chase after me."

A bitter smile twisted his lips. "I was so desperate for a kind word from you. I was ready to crawl over broken glass for your forgiveness. But your mother treated me with such coldness."

"I should have realized that there was something in the wind. She was utterly appalled that I'd fallen into a seducer's clutches. I don't think I've ever seen her so angry. It took me forever to convince her that we really were married. Then she was sure that I'd fallen prey to a ruthless fortune hunter. She was so relieved when there was no baby."

Sorrow weighted his gaze. “I’d hoped there might be. I thought if you carried my child, you might come back to me.”

“You have no idea how I grieved when I discovered that I wasn’t pregnant. It was as if I’d lost all my links to you.”

His smile didn’t reach his eyes, but at least it was a smile. “Don’t be a goose, Charmian. Didn’t you listen to the words of the marriage ceremony? We’re united until death do us part. Even if I never saw you again, you’d be my wife.”

The warmth of his voice when he called her a goose swept her straight back to their first meetings. He’d been the kind of lover who teased the object of his affections with silly nicknames and absurdly extravagant compliments. Every time that he said something ridiculous, she’d melted. She still did. A shaft of agonizing regret sliced through her as she realized anew what she’d tossed away.

“You could have involved the law. You had a right to get me back. You had a right to claim my fortune.”

He shook his ruffled dark head and gripped the arms of the chair. “I couldn’t do that without the risk of alienating you forever. How would you have felt if I’d hauled your mother up in front of the magistrates? I might be a fool, but I’m not such a fool as that. I wanted the girl who loved me to come back. I wanted us to build on the joy that we’d already found.”

More past tense. How she detested it. “So you were content to let things drift?”

Her dismissive tone made anger flare in his eyes. “I kept writing.”

She gestured toward the stuffed satchel. “So did I. Little good it did me.”

"When I didn't receive a reply, I thought you wanted nothing to do with me."

"And I thought you felt the same." The enormity of her family's wrongs against her staggered her. She had an inkling that when she came to terms with what her mother and aunt had done, she'd be even more livid than she was now. "We should be grateful that chance brought us together to sort things out."

His hands opened and closed on his thighs. "I didn't expect to find my wife working as a skivvy in an obscure country inn."

"You must have been appalled," she said, starting to bristle. "I was never good enough for the noble Sir Roland Destry."

A decisive wave of his hand swept aside her remark. "Stop it, Charmian. You were perfect. Then and now. Seeing you so strong and capable makes me want to cheer – and weep like a lost child, because you always had that strength inside you, but it took unhappiness to bring it out. I'd give my right arm to have seen you come into your own."

She missed most of his explanation. Her longing heart had snagged on one word. Her hands drifted to her sides and she stared at him, as she struggled not to make too much of what he said.

Yet her voice cracked as she spoke. "Perfect, Roland?"

CHAPTER SIX

Roland stared at this beautiful, spirited woman he'd married in such haste and wondered how she could even ask the question.

"Yes, perfect," he said, standing.

He wondered if he set himself up as a target. Pride alone had kept him going since she'd left. Although pride, he'd discovered, couldn't compare as a companion to the woman he'd wed. If she shot him down, he'd crash so hard that he feared he'd never rise again. But if making himself vulnerable meant that Charmian came back, he'd take the risk any day.

"I've made you so miserable." She went back to wringing her hands. "You should hate me."

A wry smile twisted his lips. He felt like he'd smiled more in this last hour than he had in the previous three years. "I could never hate you."

She looked unconvinced. "You must have cursed me."

One hand cut through the air. "I did that, all right. You hurt me."

He waited for her to defend herself, but instead her lips turned down. "I did. And I'm so sorry. I'll sound like a witch, but I wanted you to suffer without me. Now I've seen you, I can't forgive myself for what I did."

He didn't even need to consider his reply. "I forgive you."

"That's very magnanimous."

"It's the only way forward. That is..." He swallowed to shift the great lump of trepidation that jammed his throat. "That is if you want to go forward with me."

She regarded him with an uncertainty that reminded him of the untried girl he'd married. Painful emotion cramped his heart. He'd missed that girl like the devil. He could already tell that the woman Charmian had become could do even more damage, if she decided she wanted nothing to do with him.

"I'm your wife." She spoke in a hesitant voice, as if unsure of the facts.

He smiled again. "Yes, you are, but we could arrange a formal separation if that's what you want."

She looked unimpressed. "As a follow-up to our informal separation?"

He shrugged, although he didn't feel casual about any of this. "If you like."

That troubled green gaze remained fixed on his face. "Is that what you want, Roland?"

He reached out to grab the plain mantelpiece and summoned all his courage to answer. If she turned him away now, she'd annihilate him. "I want you to be happy, Charmian."

It was true, as far as it went. But of course, he wanted so much more than that.

Her intense expression didn't ease. She didn't answer the question but continued with one of her own. "Do you want us to separate?"

"We've been separated for three bloody years," he said with a hint of bitterness.

"Yes. But do you want to make that official?"

"No."

"Then what do you want, Roland?"

He swallowed again. Speaking was so damned difficult. More difficult at this moment, when he had to lay his cards on the table and sacrifice all the protection of his pride.

"I want you back. I've always wanted you back. Never, not even one day during all these endless months and years, have I woken without wishing you were in my arms again." He waved toward the satchel. "If you doubt me, there's proof. I don't know what you wrote in those letters, but mine are nothing but a plea for you to see me, to speak to me, to live with me again."

She was so white that her rich red hair formed a shocking contrast to her translucent skin. "Some of mine are pleas. Some of mine are angry. I was hurt, too. You were always a better person than I was."

"If you thought I'd made no effort to get you back, you were entitled to hate me."

She bit her lip and sent him a questioning look. "I never hated you either. But I feared that you'd stopped loving me."

"Never," he vowed, before he could remind himself that it might be more tactical to play those cards a little closer to his chest.

A light sparked in her eyes, a light that he'd last seen the morning she left him. The morning before they had that horrible, destructive argument. Roland's aching heart surged, as he waited for Charmian to say that she loved him. Then dipped again when she subjected him to a lingering scrutiny. "There was a reason why I got so upset when I thought you didn't love me anymore."

"Because we were tied together for life?"

She shook her head and stepped closer. "No, because I never stopped loving you. The idea that you'd forgotten me broke my heart."

There had been too much misery for him to greet her declaration with unconditional happiness, but something black and sour and festering in the depths of his soul faded away. He felt lighter, as if someone had lifted a heavy stone that had been crushing him into oblivion.

Roland couldn't resist touching her, although he was aware that this reconciliation was too new to support the weight of desire. He felt like he coaxed a wild bird to accept food from his hand. One false move and she'd flutter away up to the sky and he'd never find her again.

He held his hands out, not surprised to notice that they shook. The second it took her to reach out for him seemed to last an eon. Then for the first time since she'd turned his life to endless frost, Charmian touched him of her own free will.

As her fingers curled around his, her breath caught. Her touch felt frantic, as if she, too, feared that this reconciliation might shatter if mishandled.

He stared into her eyes, seeking the truth of her avowal. She'd once regarded him like a hero who could do no wrong. He couldn't expect that again. He didn't even want that. If they'd been a little older and wiser when they'd married, they'd have known enough to recognize that they were meant for each other, whatever temporary friction might trouble their match.

Although he'd always known that she was the only woman for him, hadn't he? He just hadn't known enough to plead with her to stay before she left him.

"Roland," she said in a thick voice. "If you don't kiss me in the next minute, I might just explode."

His grip on her hands tightened, as he stared at her in shock. The heart that he'd feared dead expanded with a piercing emotion that could only be hope. When hope had been a stranger for so long. "Kiss you?"

Her smile was shaky, and her eyes shone with longing. "Don't you want to?"

"Hell, Charmian, I've waited to kiss you ever since you went away."

Tears choked her laugh. "Then I don't think you should wait another second."

"My darling..." He released her hands and caught her face, tilting her up toward him.

He read a similar fragile hope in her eyes. Her lips parted as she snatched a breath. He'd thought that if ever he had the chance to touch her again, he'd fall on her like a ravenous lion. But so much depended on this tremulous moment that he needed to be careful. He'd frightened her away once. He couldn't bear the thought of frightening her away again.

Because that was the problem with hope. It could lift a man up so high that if he fell, the drop was likely to prove fatal.

So he didn't grab her up against him in a fury of possession. His head started a slow descent toward hers. He paused a breath away from touching her lips with his.

She closed her eyes and strained upward. "Please," she whispered. "Don't make me wait. I've waited so long already."

He couldn't say who closed the final distance. When their lips met, Roland felt the contact like the blow of an ax. Heat shuddered through him, and a roaring cascade of sensory impressions. He thought that he'd remembered every detail of their time together. Reliving each second over and over had been both pleasure and torture. But this was like kissing his wife for the first time.

Her scent was rich in his nostrils. Her skin was warm and smooth beneath his palms. For a breathless moment, he sipped delight from her lips. She made an incoherent sound. Protest? Encouragement? Surrender? Perhaps all three at once.

She stretched up to deepen the contact and sucked his lower lip into her mouth. Desire shuddered through him as he opened his mouth over hers. She let him in and for the first time in years, he tasted the sweetness that he remembered. Except that Charmian seemed in many ways a stranger. A beguiling stranger. A gift from a capricious fate.

His hands firmed on her cheeks, as he pulled back to tease her with a rain of quick kisses. Tender kisses that verged on innocent. With a wordless complaint, she nipped at his lips in a silent plea for more.

He kissed her nose and her forehead and her closed eyes and the sweet space between her eyebrows. Another of those incendiary little murmurs brought him back to her lips. This time, he plundered their wonders. Using teeth and tongue, until her tongue ventured out to meet his. She shifted closer and threaded her arms around his waist. He angled her head and kissed her fully, glorying in the hot honey taste of her mouth.

When he'd first kissed her, she seemed uncertain, as if she hadn't kissed a man in a long time. She'd already admitted that she'd taken no other lover, but even if she hadn't told him, her kiss revealed that she'd waited for him.

The knowledge was glorious. He'd tormented himself so often, imagining other men touching her, kissing her, possessing that lissom body. But no longer. When they met, he'd trusted her immediately This was an honest woman. Now, when he didn't deserve such good fortune, he realized that she'd stayed true.

He already loved her so much, he was near sick with it. Discovering that she'd kept faith wiped away an ocean of rancid misery seething inside him.

That first hesitancy melted under the blazing kiss. She met him with rising passion, digging her fingers into his waist. He drowned in the joy of having her in his arms once again. For the first time since she left, Roland felt whole.

His hands slid back to tangle in her mass of russet hair. That vivid shade had haunted his dreams. It was unusual, but not unique, so every time he caught a glimpse of a woman with deep red hair, his heart leaped with the hope that it was Charmian.

But it never was, and he was left more disconsolate than ever. Worse because of the fleeting surge of hope. Since he'd lost her, he'd learned to despise hope and its lying promises. But it was impossible not to hope when the wife he loved was kissing him as if the world would end if she stopped.

He wanted to kiss her all night. Hell, he wanted to kiss her to the crack of doomsday. But sensual heat burgeoned between them and tenderness had long ago flared into desire.

While he wanted her like blazes, he didn't mean to rush her. So he pulled back and returned to little kisses. The way that he'd started what seemed like a century ago.

They were both panting when they finally drew apart. She stared up at him out of dark, yearning eyes. Her hands kneaded his waist. Her lips were red and swollen, and his hands had made a tangle of her severe hairstyle.

"That was..." she began, lifting a hand to those tempting lips.

"A beginning?" With the greatest difficulty, he made himself release her and he stepped back. The powerful urge gripped him to carry her across to that chaste single bed and bury himself inside her, to take the kiss to its ordained end. After losing her for so long, his natural impulse was to snatch and seize and capture. Make sure that she never went away again.

But all this time without her had taught him caution. He sought a lifetime with this woman, not just a quick tumble to satisfy years of frustration. Still, it nearly killed him to take another step away.

"It's late." His voice was gruff with reaction to that wild kiss and the effort it took to behave like a civilized man. "I'll go down to the kitchens and fetch you some more hot water. The water I brought up earlier will be cold now."

He shouldn't be pleased to see disappointment in her eyes. She'd gone up like a column of flame in his arms. The passion between them hadn't faded, he was grateful to note. Grateful and relieved.

But passion had never been their problem. From the moment that they met, they'd been voracious for each other. Throughout their hectic courtship, she'd brimmed with innocent ardor. His memories of their brief weeks together were tinged scarlet with the heat that they'd generated when they finally shared a bed.

"You don't have to. I can go. Or wash in cold water."

He smiled at her. “Let me look after you, Charmian. You’ll sleep better after a decent wash.”

Although she still looked puzzled, she nodded. “Then thank you.”

He went to the door and opened it, desperate to get out before he did something drastic to scare her away again. A Christmas miracle on a stormy night had brought them together. He couldn’t allow himself to shatter the frail bond of trust forming between them.

Losing Charmian once had nearly killed him. The prospect of losing her twice was too agonizing to contemplate.

CHAPTER SEVEN

Charmian lay in her narrow bed and stared into the darkness. The rain continued, slamming against the window and pounding against the tiled roof. But that wasn't what kept her awake.

Since the weather turned bad this morning, she'd been rushed off her feet. She should have fallen into bed and gone straight to sleep. But here she lay open-eyed, feeling like the storm outside raged inside her as well.

The reason for that wasn't hard to fathom. The reason lay on the floor in front of the fire wrapped in a blanket.

When her mother and aunt had cooked up the plan to get her away from home, they'd hoped to rescue her from the despair where she'd languished since leaving Roland. Or so they said. At the time, she should have guessed that some plot was afoot, but she'd been so heartsore that she hadn't thought to question their decision to send her to help Aunt Janet.

They'd schemed to keep her out of a ruthless seducer's clutches. Tonight the ruthless seducer lay silent on the far side of the room, with no designs on his wife's body, damn it.

She hadn't shared a room with a man since she'd run away from Roland. That was enough to make her restless. That, and those spectacular kisses that made her feel alive for the first time since they parted.

He'd kissed her as if he'd starved for her, then stepped away and acted like her brother. The passionate lover had given her grounds for optimism. The polite stranger made her feel like howling in denial.

Not to mention that those kisses had woken parts of her she'd done her best to ignore since coming to the Spotted Fox. There was a pulsing weight in the pit of her stomach and her blood raced with carnal desire.

Carnal desire that clearly she experienced alone.

Because instead of ripping her clothes off and uniting his body with hers, Roland had been kind and contained and considerate. He'd brought her hot water. He'd stepped outside while she washed and changed into her sensible white flannel nightdress. He'd hardly looked at her when he came back in to wish her good night and stretch out on the rag rug in front of the fire.

Charmian shifted again. She'd been doing a lot of that. She couldn't seem to find a comfortable spot. Mad to say that the bed seemed too big, when it was small even for one person. But that was how it felt.

Roland hadn't moved since lying down. He'd looked exhausted when he arrived at the inn. Then Janet had put him to work running up and down stairs and fetching and carrying. Charmian should be all wifely and be glad that he got some rest.

She *was* feeling wifely, but not about letting her husband sleep off his weariness. He'd said that he wanted her back. He'd said that he loved her. For pity's sake, he'd kissed her into next Wednesday.

How *dare* he leave her lonely, while he slumbered in front of the fire?

She shifted again and told herself that she had no right to be annoyed. Instead, she should be grateful and hopeful and happy. She and Roland had a chance to make up for the past's mistakes. She'd prayed for that to happen since she'd left him.

And it was Christmas Day. Surely that alone was cause for joy. A time for fresh starts and new plans.

As she lay yearning and stirred up and confused, Charmian didn't feel joyful. She felt frustrated.

Sexual frustration was a familiar companion. But it verged on unbearable when the object of her interest was mere feet away, rather than kicking up his heels in the fleshpots.

She sighed and turned onto her side to face the wall. Perhaps if she couldn't see him, she could pretend that her long-lost spouse wasn't within reach. She tucked one hand under her cheek and blinked away stinging moisture. For pity's sake, she'd already cried enough tears to fill an ocean. There shouldn't be a drop of saltwater left inside her.

"Are you all right, Charmian?"

"Did I wake you?" She didn't want to lie to him, but nor did she want to answer.

"I haven't been asleep."

He'd been so quiet, that surprised her. "I haven't either. You don't have to stay on the floor. There's the chair, or if we squeeze in, we could share the bed."

She thought that she heard a faint groan. Or perhaps a log shifted in the fireplace. "It's a very narrow bed."

She continued to stare at the wall. The view was misty. "Big enough for one."

"I'm better where I am," he said with a hint of

grimness that she didn't understand. "Are you crying?"

"No." The choked denial proved her falsehood.

"I thought I heard you."

"I just caught my breath."

He wasn't persuaded. She didn't blame him. "I apologise for upsetting you."

"It's been...an overwhelming day." *Now you don't want me, and I don't know why.*

"Yes, it has. I'm not sorry, though."

"That you made me cry?"

He exhaled audibly. "No, of course not. I'm not sorry that we met and we've had the chance to talk."

Talk. Yes, they'd done that. And needed to do more. But talk wasn't what she wanted. At this moment, she wanted his arms around her. She wanted his spicy masculine scent in her nostrils and his warmth to banish the chill inside her. She wanted the hard thrust of his body and that moment of perfect intimacy when he filled the aching emptiness at her core.

Then she wanted the inexorable climb to ecstasy, the blast of sensual lightning at the peak, and the gentle drift back to earth afterward.

She wanted him to treat her the way that a man treated a woman he wanted.

It had been three long years since Roland had used her body. But she'd forgotten nothing. She was in a fever for him. Why on earth was he so far away?

"Charmian?" he asked when she didn't reply. "Aren't you glad we've reconciled?"

"Yes, of course," she said. "We couldn't have gone on as we were. We had to make some decisions."

"Yes."

She wondered if she was wrong to hear a hint of disappointment in the single word.

"Some certainty about our future will be helpful."

She struggled to sound pragmatic.

"Yes."

A silence fell. She wondered if he'd gone to sleep, but some vibration in the air told her that he was as alert to her as she was to him. She swallowed another sob, although why she bothered, she couldn't say. Roland knew she was upset.

She heard him roll over. This small room offered a kind of intimacy, even if not the intimacy that she wanted. "If you're happy we're together again, why are you crying?"

What could she say to that? She summoned all her courage and decided to be honest. "I missed you."

"I missed you, too."

Wondering why he was so slow to understand, she licked dry lips. "I missed...what we did in bed."

She heard him move again. When she turned, she saw him sit up. Against the firelight, he was a black shape, but she caught the glitter of his eyes.

"Are you asking me to join you, Charmian?" His tone was neutral, but in the flickering glow, the line of his head and shoulders was stiff with tension.

She sucked in a shaky breath, and all her secret places softened at the prospect of Roland joining his body with hers. "You're my husband."

He sighed. "I am. But I don't want to take anything for granted. This is too important."

"Would you...would you like to sleep with me?"

During their few euphoric weeks together, she'd never had to ask. One come-hither look was all it took to lure him into bed sport. It seemed that she needed to work a little harder these days.

"I want what you want."

A hiss of frustration escaped her. "That's no answer."

"If I come to you now, I want you to be very sure

that you're coming back to me." His tone became resolute. "I couldn't bear losing you twice. Not after you take me to heaven again."

That dratted annoying lump in her throat was back. She swallowed to shift it, but her voice emerged as a croak. "Is that how it felt to you back then?"

"You know it did."

She swallowed once more. It didn't help. "I've had long enough to question whether I knew anything at all when we were together."

His hiss expressed contempt for that statement. "Come on, Charmian. Whatever else went wrong between us, we were always a perfect match in bed."

"Then why are you all the way over there?" Her voice was scratchy.

He didn't immediately respond. Her heart shriveled into a tiny, aching lump. He'd kissed her as if he wanted her, but she was out of practice with a husband. Perhaps she'd misunderstood.

Roland sounded on edge when he answered. "Because I don't want to frighten you away with how much I want you."

The tightness in her chest eased. She hadn't mistaken his desire. Something told her that they needed to come together as lovers before they could heal the breach between them. Anyway, she was desperate for him. Just the sight of him made her feel like she was a woman again, after three vile years of feeling like a ghost haunting her own life. His admission that he wanted her in return set the wanton blood rushing through her veins.

"I'm not frightened anymore." Which wasn't entirely true. Roland wasn't the only one who feared that this chance reconciliation mightn't last.

He made a convulsive movement in her direction before he pulled back to resume that constant watchfulness. She felt like he counted her every breath. "Convince me."

Charmian supposed that she owed him that. After all, she was the one who had left him in York. "I...I kissed you."

"Yes, you did."

"I've told you I love you."

"Yes." A single word, but it didn't sound quite so uncompromising.

"You say you still love me."

"You don't seem sure."

She wasn't. Not to the depths of her soul. "It's been a long time, Roland."

"It has."

She sat up and put her feet on the floor, wishing she hadn't extinguished the lamp. If he wanted her to strip her soul bare, it would be easier if she could gauge his expression.

Ever since she'd left him, she'd tormented herself. A vivid imagination could be a curse. She curled her fingers into the mattress underneath her and steeled herself to ask a question that she wasn't sure she had the right to pose.

Her voice shook with nerves. "Were there...were there a lot?"

Although she couldn't see his face, she knew his brows drew together in a frown. "A lot of what?"

Roland, don't lie to me. Not now. Not when it's so important. If we can't start out with honesty, what use is this new beginning?

"A lot of women."

"Charmian..."

One unsteady hand made a sweeping gesture. "You don't have to tell me about them. But it's driven me nearly mad, thinking of you with other lovers. I need to know."

"You're my wife."

She made a contemptuous sound. "Yes, I am, and you already know you're the only man who's shared my bed. I realize that it's different for men."

"Why is it different for men?"

The edge in his voice made her flinch. "Well, different for you. I've been stuck in the backwaters of Yorkshire. You've been out in the wider world. You can't tell me you had no chance to bed other women. For pity's sake, you traveled around Europe's pleasure spots. Anyway, I know you, Roland. I know how...insatiable you are. Celibacy would drive you out of your mind."

"So you've tortured yourself this whole time."

She'd gone past the point where she had any hope of preserving her pride. "Of course I have."

"I didn't think you'd care."

"Because I didn't answer your letters."

"Or come back to me."

"You were wrong."

"Yes, I was wrong. But I only discovered that tonight."

She raised her chin and told herself that she could endure this. If she'd lived through his absence, she could live through learning that he'd been unfaithful. "The uncertainty is the worst. Tell me. I'll forgive you, then we can move on."

"So what would be acceptable when it comes to adultery? One lover? Three? Twenty? A hundred?" His question held a sardonic tone that she didn't understand. Shouldn't he be grateful? Hadn't she said that she'd overlook his sins? And she'd almost meant it, by God.

"I wouldn't like it if it was one." Because that indicated a stronger connection than the urge to relieve a physical itch. No, she wouldn't like that at all.

"It wasn't one."

She sucked in a relieved breath. Although she shouldn't find too much comfort in the admission. She didn't want him making an emotional link with some faceless woman, but nor did she want him seducing any female who took his fancy.

Face it, Charmian, you want him to be all yours. Despite your long estrangement and his masculine needs. Despite you leaving him.

It wasn't a reasonable attitude, but then, love wasn't always reasonable.

"How many, then? More than ten?"

"No."

So somewhere between one and ten. How many could she survive hearing about? Two? Seven? "Stop tormenting me. How many, Roland?"

He shifted as if he'd like to avoid the question. She supposed that it couldn't be easy to own up to breaking his marriage vows. "You're so sure I did the wrong thing."

Her lips tightened. "Did you?"

Charmian heard him draw a breath, and she braced for the confession. She could bear it. She could. If she could bear living without him for so long, she could bear knowing that other women had enjoyed that lean, elegant body.

"No, I damn well didn't." As he rose to his feet, she felt his glare.

"But—"

"There wasn't one. There weren't five. There weren't a thousand. There was only one woman for me and I'd married her, whatever woe that might have brought me."

His temper slid off her like water slid off the pitched slate roof above them. Wide-eyed, Charmian stared at him, while the glorious news slowly made itself real. He hadn't betrayed her. There had been no other women. She knew immediately that he spoke the truth. His impatience was more convincing than any attempt to cajole her into believing him.

"But...but you must have wanted..."

He raked one hand through his already messy hair. "Wanted a woman. No, I didn't want *a* woman. I wanted *you*. I'd made promises to *you*."

"But I'd left you."

He gave a low growl. "Yes, you had, But I hadn't given up all hope of you coming back. I hadn't given up all hope of us making a life together one day. I never stopped loving you. Even though I felt like the world's greatest fool when I told myself that somewhere, somehow you'd remember that you loved me, too."

Charmian was ecstatic to know that so much of what she'd feared had lived only in her mind. So it made no sense that the tears that had come and gone all night now poured down her face. With clumsy hands, she dashed at her wet cheeks.

"I remembered," she said in a thick voice. "I hoped we'd have another chance, too."

He sounded more composed when he spoke, although deep emotion still roughened his musical baritone. "How could I come back to you and beg you to live with me again if I'd betrayed you with other women?"

"I'm glad you didn't," she said, knowing the words were inadequate.

He must have felt the same because his "good" was a little grumpy.

She gave a muffled giggle, even if one clogged with tears. "All right, I'm in alt. I'm elated. I couldn't be happier to know you were faithful to me." She stood. "It's just that you were so...energetic during our honeymoon."

"Meaning I'd run off like a wild beast and leap on

the first available woman? You do me an injustice, Charmian. By heaven you do."

"I know. And I'm sorry." She swallowed, but the tears didn't stop. "I'm sorry for everything. Please don't be angry."

"I'm not angry with you, now I know the truth about what kept us apart. I'm just heartsick at the thought of all we've missed, my darling."

The *my darling* was the clincher. "Then let's move on together now and not miss any more, Roland."

With shaking hands, she caught her loose nightdress and tugged it over her head. She heard the hitch in his breath, as she dropped the voluminous garment to the floor. Beneath her night rail, she was naked.

Roland made an unsteady movement in her direction then stopped. "Swear to me that you'll never go away again. I've barely survived your absence. You'll destroy me if you leave me now."

She managed another sketchy smile and stepped out of his shadow so that the firelight revealed her body. "I'll never leave you while I live, Roland. I give you my solemn oath."

That glittering black gaze remained fixed on her. He breathed in audible gusts. She couldn't doubt that her nakedness aroused him.

Charmian ought to feel shy, especially when unhappiness and hard work meant that she was no longer the voluptuous armful Roland had wed. But strange to say, she didn't feel at all self-conscious.

It was time to offer herself to her husband without subterfuge. He said that he loved her, and that he'd always loved her. She believed him. The man who had stayed true to her wouldn't care if there were a few more angles on the woman she'd become.

She was close enough now to read what lay in his eyes. Love. Familiar from so long ago, but never forgotten. A love that she now knew had never wavered. Desire. And a trace of uncertainty, as if he had difficulty believing that after all their trials, they might find mutual understanding at last.

He reached toward her breasts but didn't yet touch her. "What's that?" he asked hoarsely.

She glanced down to see him pointing at the chain that she wore around her neck. She'd forgotten it was there. It was always hidden under her clothes. "You know what that is."

"Your wedding ring? You wear it?"

"Every day." Presenting herself as Janet Barton's unmarried niece had seemed easier than trying to explain why she wore a wedding ring, yet had no husband.

"Charmian..."

When she met his gaze, her heart cramped at the fierce emotion that she saw there. "It kept me close to you."

She shivered as his fingers brushed her skin. She'd dreamed for so long of this moment when they came together again. He caught the chain and very gently lifted it over her head so it didn't tangle in her plait.

His trembling hands fiddled with the clasp. As if he handled something holy, he drew the ring off its chain and held it in his palm. "May I put this on your finger?"

"For pity's sake, will I ever stop crying?" she mumbled, extending her hand in his direction. It was as shaky as his.

"It's a significant moment." He shoved the chain into his pocket. "I'm feeling a little misty-eyed myself."

With that, she regained what she'd lost. Laughter

had marked their days as a married couple. Laughter had been yet another loss to her over the years. Yet now Roland returned it to her. Graciously. Generously. Without a hint of acrimony.

"I love you, Roland," she said, as he slid the elegant gold band onto her ring finger.

He lifted her hand to his lips and pressed a fervent kiss to her knuckles. She could see that this moment when he reclaimed her as his wife left him profoundly moved, too.

"And I love you." He ripped at the fastenings on his breeches and shucked them down his narrow hips. He was so desperate, his usual aristocratic grace was utterly absent. "Now I mean to show you how much."

She loved that overmastering desire made him clumsy. She loved *him*.

So when he was naked and sweeping her into his arms, she kissed him and held on tight in preparation for the splendors ahead.

CHAPTER EIGHT

Roland's arms enclosed his wife, and he kissed her back with all the aching hunger that had tormented him ever since she'd left.

More than hunger compelled him. Love was the driver. So much love.

So he didn't fall on her like the ravening beast that he'd likened himself to earlier. Instead, his touch turned tender. He kissed her face and her neck and her shoulders and her breasts. Little touches to confirm that she really was here and not a figment of his lonely imagination, as she'd been so often during their agonizing years apart.

She laced her hands around his neck, pulling him closer. Her breath caught with each contact of his lips and enchanting murmurs of pleasure escaped her. Dear Lord above, the memory of Charmian's fervent responses had haunted him.

Appetite strained like an unbroken horse against the rein. He'd hardened the moment she took off her nightgown, and he grew harder with every second. But he wanted this first mating after so long to express care and reverence and gratitude. They'd have time for the fierce tides of passion later.

Later...

A magic word to a man who had believed that he'd lost all chance of a future with his beautiful wife. Who stroked his neck and back and ran her hands through his hair. Who was warm and willing in his arms.

Who became impatient with teasing, he could tell. She clung nearer, and her hands curved around his buttocks in a shameless appeal for more than glancing kisses.

Despite having dreamed of her for so long, he was surprised at how familiar everything felt. The inn supplied lemon soap, so her scent held a citrus tinge, whereas the girl he'd wed had preferred a rose perfume. But beneath that, she smelled like Charmian. Smoky and musky and womanly. His nostrils flared to catch the earthy essence of her arousal. That hadn't changed.

When they'd met, she'd been plump and pretty and as luscious as a chocolate éclair. This woman was slender, and her body was lithe with muscle. Proof of how she'd worked since leaving him. But her skin was as smooth and creamy as he remembered, and her lips were just as soft and eager.

Lips he could no longer resist.

He kissed her with all the wild joy he felt. She gave a low hum of approval and used her tongue to whip him into a frenzy of desire. Her fingers dug into his buttocks. Need shuddered through him like an earthquake.

This was every fantasy come true. Charmian aroused and desperate in his arms. The promise of uniting their bodies in the most profound act he knew. Without his wife, his life had been intolerably impoverished.

One thing alone remained before the picture was

perfect. He withdrew from the kiss and studied her with his eyes and with his longing heart. “Take your hair down.”

She stood on tiptoe to land a couple of kisses on the corners of his mouth. “My hair?”

He found himself smiling at her. The sort of smile that came straight from the soul. The sort of smile absent since she’d abandoned him. “You have no idea how often red hair features in my dreams. I reached a point where I couldn’t abide seeing a red-haired woman, because the sight only made me ache for you.”

Her gaze softened. Already she stepped back and started to undo the thick auburn plait that snaked down across her bare breasts with their tight, rose-pink nipples. He bit back a groan and closed his eyes.

“Roland, are you all right?” she asked.

He opened his eyes and gave her a wry smile. “Your bosom might have featured in those dreams, too.”

Charmian released a huff of laughter and glanced down, even as her fingers worked on the plait. “You’re welcome to touch.”

“Oh, yes.” When he cupped her breasts, she gasped. He caressed the curves and brushed his thumbs across pert nipples.

“I’m...smaller than I was.”

The hint of apology made him lift his gaze from the delicious curves. “My love, you’re exquisite from head to toe.”

Her lips turned down. “I’m not the same as the girl you married.”

Roland kissed her with overflowing thankfulness. “No, you’ve grown up. I love the woman you’ve become. I love you, Charmian.”

The trouble faded from her lovely green eyes. “Have we learned to be wise, do you think?”

"I hope so. I'll never take love for granted again. We received a precious gift, yet we were careless enough to cast it aside."

"I pray that you're right. The world has been such a sharp, cold place since we parted."

"Nothing was right for me without you, my darling."

She touched his cheek with a loving caress that he felt all the way to the soles of his feet. "Then let's make it right tonight. It's Christmas. The time for second chances and new beginnings. I love you, too."

She ran her fingers through her hair, loosening it until it flowed over her shoulders. His heart slammed against his chest at the glorious sight. His wife was clothed in firelight and hair the color of flame.

Words had brought them this far. Actions would knit them together forever. Still gentle, he swung her around and brought her down onto the bed, cradling her in his arms as she sank into the thin mattress.

When he straddled her, she stretched out beneath him and circled his dick with eager fingers. Roland exhaled on a hiss, as a blast of heat threatened to incinerate him.

"Next time." He caught her hand. "I'm too close to the edge, and I want to do you justice tonight."

The hint of wickedness in her smile reminded him of the ardent girl he'd wed. "Do you remember our first night?"

He gave a short laugh. "How could I forget?"

The wicked smile deepened. "And it was even better the next day."

He stroked her thighs, trailing his hands toward the russet curls that hid her sex. "After that, I couldn't keep away from you."

One finger traced a line down his chest, stopping on the way to tease his nipple with a fingernail. A shudder of response made him gasp. He thought that he was already as het up as he could get, but it seemed there was more.

"I loved how much you wanted me. It made me feel like a queen."

He kissed the pale slope of her breast and slid his hand between her legs. She moved under his caresses and sucked in an audible breath. He smiled against her skin when he discovered that she was slick and hot already. "I still want you like the very devil."

"And I want you," she murmured. "We've wasted so much time."

He kissed the hint of sadness from her eyes, as he stroked her cleft. "Then let's not waste any more."

With a sigh of surrender, she bumped her hips higher. "Take me, Roland. I don't want to be lonely anymore."

Finding the site of her pleasure, he teased her until she writhed. He held back from taking her to her limit. That was a moment he meant to share with her.

He raised his head and shifted back. "Open your legs for me, my love."

The intensity between them reached such a pitch that it almost felt like a reprieve when everything turned to a disorderly scuffle. On such a narrow bed, trying to position their bodies almost knocked him to the floor. They were both breathless and laughing by the time she cradled his hips between her thighs.

She shifted up on the pillows. "Please don't break your neck, now I've got you back at last."

Kissing her again, he poised above her. The path to paradise lay open before him. After so long, he wasn't sure whether they would come together like strangers, but he slid into her as smooth as honey. She closed hard around him, claiming him in return.

Roland rose on his elbows to survey her. Her eyes were the color of wet moss and heavy with desire. Her lips were swollen and parted to give him a glimpse of small white teeth.

Her beauty sliced through him like a saber. It always had, but seeing her like this, lost in their connection, the feeling was overwhelming.

Roland was home after a long and arduous journey. The half of his soul that had been missing was finally returned to him. For the first time since Charmian left, he trusted in tomorrow.

He felt an invincible urge to lose himself in the passion flaring between them. But first, despite his fierce animal urges, he needed to bask in this closeness that had been stolen from him. A closeness that made his life worth living.

Charmian stroked the straining muscles of his arms before tracing the line of his back. As he stared into her eyes, he believed at last that their love was strong enough to recover from their separation. In so many ways that mattered, their marriage started tonight.

They'd both suffered. They'd both learned the value of what they shared. They were both strong enough to fight for their love.

She bowed up, brushing her breasts against his chest. The change of angle made his balls contract in needy craving.

"I wanted to have your baby. I wanted it so much," she whispered.

"Let me give you a baby now. I want us to be a family." Poignant emotion thundered through him. He pushed deeper in preparation for the sensual storm ahead. "I want this for the rest of our lives."

"Oh, yes, Roland, yes."

The stillness had been transcendent. Now he thirsted to give her everything he had. "Let me take you to the stars, my love."

For three hard years, Charmian had felt empty and lost. Having Roland back to fill all those longing parts of her felt like a miracle. Muscles that she hadn't used since she'd left him surged to throbbing life, as her body adjusted to a man again.

When he pulled back with a slow power that thrilled her, she sighed her pleasure and lifted her hips. How strange that she'd relived this act over and over since their parting, yet it turned out she hadn't remembered it at all. She'd forgotten how every part of her melted with desire. She'd forgotten the ferocious thunder of her blood. She'd forgotten the sheer animal pleasure of having Roland deep inside her.

She'd forgotten how love turned his physical possession to pure gold, so she felt as if they existed in a glowing bubble of light.

Charmian caught the glint of firelight on her wedding ring, worn for the first time since she'd run home to her mother in such a taking. Silly, thoughtless, careless little girl she'd been.

She was no longer that brainless ninny – although at least she'd been smart enough to fall in love with Roland. She'd grown into a woman who knew enough to cherish their love as the precious, unique treasure it was.

As he shifted forward, her frantic hands closed around his arms. She thought that he'd gone as deep as possible, but now he seemed to touch her womb.

"Oh, yes," she sighed, tightening around him.

"That's so good, beloved." Awe rasped in his voice. She wasn't alone in finding this an experience of the soul as well as the flesh.

But flesh had its own demands, demands that they'd both resisted for too long. That need could no longer be denied.

He rose on his elbows and began to move in hard, determined thrusts. The rise to climax was swift. All the pent-up desire rushed through her to charge her response to every touch. She welcomed him as he plunged inside her. Her fingers digging into his arms, she strove for that rapturous peak.

When he scraped his teeth over a sensitive nerve in her neck, Charmian shuddered into ecstasy. Rivers of fire. White light. Heat. Muscles clenching in helpless delight. She lashed her arms around him, clinging as she rode out the irresistible storm.

As she convulsed, she cried out. Through her fiery crisis, she heard him groan. He jerked in her arms, and the liquid heat of his seed flooded her.

Roland slumped against her and buried his face in her shoulder. She heard his hoarse breathing. He was heavy, but she didn't mind. The press of his body confirmed that he really was here. Ripples of ultimate pleasure ran through her, soothed the sharp edges of her long unhappiness.

After a few seconds, Roland shifted to the side, stretching out against the plaster wall. She stared at him, noting that he was no longer the troubled man who had arrived at the inn. He looked younger, easier, more like the carefree gentleman she'd married.

She shifted closer to kiss him with all the gratitude in her heart. "I'd forgotten how magnificent you could make me feel. Thank you."

His smile held no trace of his earlier bitterness. "I love you, Charmian."

"And I love you."

His expression expressed a wry fondness. "And

you're still crying."

As he brushed at the tears trickling down her cheeks, she gave a waterlogged giggle. "I'm just so happy. I thought this would never happen. I was terrified that I'd lost your love forever."

"Impossible." He kissed her with such tenderness that her tears spurted anew. "I'm so grateful we found our way back to each other. You're my reason for living."

She studied his face, as she struggled to control her wayward emotions. "I don't want to go to sleep. I'm afraid this might be a dream."

A laugh escaped him. "On my solemn oath, I'm here, and I'll be here when you wake up."

"That makes me happy, too. You make me happy, Roland. Don't go away again."

"Never." The word sounded like another vow. After so much heartache, they'd found each other. The magnitude of the gift was almost beyond understanding.

She cupped his jaw in her hand, feeling the faint prickle of whiskers. "I can't believe we've been so lucky."

Eyes alight with adoration studied her features. "You'll start taking it all for granted in twenty years or so."

She gave another watery huff of amusement. "What a lovely idea."

He kissed her with all the love that she read in his face. Love and weariness. They'd both had an arduous day, and they'd had to wend their way through a tangle of harrowing emotions before that perfect, passionate conclusion.

"Sleep now, Charmian. Sleep safe in my arms, as you'll sleep safe in my arms from this day forward."

"Roland..." Emotion welled up inside her, although she didn't want to cry anymore. She'd spent far too long crying. So she swallowed the lump in her throat and responded in a wry tone. "I hope the beds are bigger at Leeder Hall."

A brief laugh. "No risk of falling on the floor there."

"I'm pleased to hear it."

"Roll over on your side, and we'll manage very well."

It turned out that he was right. She shifted around to fit her back against his chest. Lying close like this, there was plenty of room.

He slipped his arms around her and curled one hand over her breast. The gesture was so laden with tenderness, those dratted tears rose again. Mistily, she stared into the firelit darkness and said a fervent prayer of gratitude for second chances and steadfast love.

Roland's familiar scent surrounded her and the warmth of his long, powerful body. Her heart settled into a steady beat, as she finally accepted that her long ordeal was over. She and Roland were together and would stay that way.

Roland's embrace tightened. He dropped a kiss on her naked shoulder. "Happy Christmas, my dearest wife," he murmured, his voice gruff with tiredness.

"Happy Christmas, my love," Charmain whispered, closing her eyes. For the first time since she'd left him, she felt at peace.

CHAPTER NINE

It was still dark when Charmian stirred. Roland's arms encircled her, and she was pressed close to his naked body. She was warm inside and out in a way that she hadn't been since that devastating quarrel in York.

She needed a moment to realize that the silence meant that at last the rain had stopped. Perhaps some of the inn's guests might manage to make it home for Christmas after all.

Very carefully, she shifted in Roland's arms. She had no idea what time they'd gone to sleep, but the weariness weighing down her body told her that it wasn't long ago. Strangely, given that she probably hadn't managed much more than an hour of sleep, she felt more rested than she had in years. Discovering that she hadn't loved in vain and that she and her husband were reunited had done wonders.

Her lips curved in a smile, as she gingerly perched on the edge of the narrow bed where she'd found such rapture. The chance to salve her sexual frustration contributed to her wellbeing. Although it would take more than a single tumble to satisfy her physical craving for the man she loved.

She glanced back at him. By heaven, he was handsome. The fire had died down a little, but it provided enough light for her to make out his chiseled features.

Her unruly heart did a little jig of joy. Even better, he was all hers, when she'd been so sure that he was lost to her forever.

The world couldn't have given her a better Christmas gift.

The urge rose to lie down again, to nestle back in his arms and let Puddlebrook go on its merry way without her. It was an effort to stand and collect her clothes ready to go downstairs. As she stood, muscles that she hadn't used in ages twinged, reminding her of that passionate swiving.

At least the water Roland had brought her last night was still lukewarm. Proof enough of how little time she'd slept. As quietly as she could, she sponged the traces of their lovemaking from her body. Pink marks on her skin where Roland's whiskers had chafed her provided another reminder of what they'd done.

"Good morning, my love," a sleepy voice said from the bed.

Charmian found Roland regarding her with such unconcealed appreciation that she shivered with desire. The traitorous urge to crawl back into bed strengthened. "I didn't want to wake you."

He shifted to sit on the edge of the bed and rub his eyes. With his rumpled dark hair and bare body, he was beguilingly disheveled. "What are you doing?"

"I'm going down to help my aunt. The inn is bulging at the seams. She'll need another pair of hands, especially when everyone starts demanding breakfast."

The lazy delight faded from his eyes. "After what she did, she deserves to rot."

Charmian sighed. "I know. But she's still family and anyway, it's not just her. It's John and Milly and everyone else here. I don't want to let them down. We have so much. We can afford to be generous."

His lips turned down in wry acceptance. "And it's Christmas."

To her relief, she saw that he wasn't angry. She slipped her shift over her head and reached for her stays. "And it's Christmas."

He yawned and scratched his chest. With another ripple of pleasure, she remembered that curling hair rubbing against her breasts last night when they'd joined together. "Can I help you to dress?"

"Thank you, but I can manage." Since coming to the Spotted Fox, she hadn't had a maid. Everything she owned these days fastened at the front.

"Stop it," she muttered, as she fumbled with the hooks.

Roland tried and failed to look innocent. "Stop what?"

"Watching me like a cat watches a mousehole."

He laughed. "You can't blame me for enjoying the show, when a beautiful woman gets dressed in front of me."

She blushed. "I'm so glad you think I'm beautiful."

"You'll be beautiful when you're eighty, my darling."

Her hands stilled, and she stared at him, lost in a fog of love. "You make it so difficult to go when you say things like that."

He gestured to the bed. “We could start the day in a much better way than you running off to wear your fingers to the bone.”

Charmian almost yielded to temptation. Then she remembered her responsibilities, and she went back to dressing. “Don’t tease me.”

His expression turned serious. “I’d like to take you away from here as soon as the roads are passable. You’re not saying you intend to stay on at Puddlebrook as your aunt’s dogsbody, are you?”

This was an uncomfortable reminder of their quarrel in York. She eyed him, but she saw no belligerence. He was asking her, not telling her. “I’m ready to go. The lure of a proper bed is too strong for me to stay here.”

His brief laugh was proof that this was a man who had learned cooperation and compromise during their separation. “I’m glad to hear it.”

She stood in front of the mirror and picked up her hairbrush. Her hair was a disaster this morning, but she did her best to confine it in its usual plait. She met Roland’s stare in the reflection. “Thank you.”

He lowered his head in ironic acknowledgment. “You’re welcome.”

She smiled and tied the end of her braid with a ribbon before she turned to him. “As soon as the crisis is over, we can leave. I’m dying to see Leeder Hall.”

“I’m dying to show it to you. Haven’t you forgotten something?”

She frowned, checking her plain frock, brown today. Despite the distraction of a splendid naked man observing her every movement, she seemed to be adequately clad. She wore stockings and shoes, and all her buttons were done up. “What is it?”

His lips curled in that seductive smile that had stolen her heart when she'd been a giddy girl of nineteen. "Doesn't your long-lost husband merit a kiss to start his day?" Unashamed of his nakedness, he stood and opened his arms. "Fie, Lady Destry, and it's Christmas, too."

She rushed across the room and threw herself at him. The kiss was intoxicating and threatened to continue far too long and lead to more than kissing.

Only with the greatest reluctance did she pull away. "Stay here and get some sleep. You have an insatiable spouse to take care of tonight."

He laughed and kissed her with the teasing fondness that always touched her heart. "Now that's what I call a Christmas present for a red-blooded Englishman."

Charmian rose on her toes to kiss him again. Briefly because if she lingered, she wouldn't go at all.

She drew away with painful reluctance. After so long without him, the impulse was to cling, never to let him out of her sight. She was clever enough to know that was no way to proceed. "I must go."

Roland watched her with a troubled light in his dark eyes. "Make sure you come back."

A rift opened in her heart as she realized that they'd both suffered too much to accept that everything from here would be smooth sailing. "I promise, my love. I promise on my soul."

This kiss was longer, but she did eventually manage to get out the door.

As she crept downstairs, the inn around her was quiet. It was too early for the guests to be about. Most days, the work of a country hostelry started well before dawn.

She realized with a shock that the pattern of her life was about to change forever. Lady Destry could lie in bed while the servants did the household work.

Lady Destry didn't need to bake and clean and launder and lug endless canisters of hot water. Her days of drudgery were done.

On such a chilly morning, she was grateful to reach the kitchens which were always warm. Her aunt stood at the oven with some loaves ready for baking.

"Good morning, Aunt Janet," Charmian said in a neutral voice. "Merry Christmas."

Janet swung around so fast that the tray tilted. She only just managed to save the bread from sliding to the flagstone floor. "Charmian!"

Her aunt continued to look sick with guilt. So she should. She might have meant well, but her actions had caused Charmian untold grief.

The deception angered Charmian, too. Her mother and her aunt had told her a lot of lies, if mainly lies of omission.

She and Janet had an enormous number of issues to negotiate. But first they needed to deal with an inn jam-packed with guests needing to eat and wash and decide where they went next. Not to mention that John and Milly would arrive soon, looking for orders from their employer.

Charmian focused on practicalities. As befitted a well-run inn like the Spotted Fox, they always put everything away the night before. But yesterday had been so chaotic that the usually pristine kitchen remained piled high with detritus. Gladys, the cook, had been preparing meals until past midnight. "Shall I wash up, or would you prefer for me to start putting breakfast together?"

Janet clumsily shoved the loaves into the oven and slammed the heavy iron door. "Perhaps bring in the breakfast things. Once everyone moves on, we'll have time to clean up properly."

Without shifting, Charmian sent her aunt a direct look. "Roland and I are leaving as soon as the roads are passable."

Her aunt twined her hands at her waist. It was a nervous gesture Charmian used, too. An unwelcome reminder that they were family, despite betrayals and wrongs. "You're going with him, then?"

She tilted her chin in defiance. "He's my husband. My place is with him."

Her aunt looked stricken. "You hate me for keeping you apart."

Charmian felt such a roiling mixture of emotions that she couldn't say exactly what she felt. She was angry. And hurt. But there was regret, too. And much as she didn't want to admit it, love. Aunt Janet had unarguably done the wrong thing. But she'd acted out of affection, however misguided.

Last night, when Charmian had learned the truth, she'd been livid and ready to banish her aunt from her life. Since then, she'd spent a blissful interval in her beloved husband's arms and she'd discovered that he still loved her. It was difficult to maintain quite that level of white-hot fury when waves of sexual satisfaction swirled through her.

"I don't hate you," she said, sure of that at least.

Her aunt didn't look reassured. "Perhaps you should. You love him."

"Yes, I always did."

"And he loves you. I...I didn't expect that."

"No, you thought I'd fallen victim to a fortune hunter."

"I realized last night what sins your mother and I committed against you. I can only say I'm sorry, Charmian. I know it's not enough, but it's all I've got to give you."

The apology shouldn't make any difference. After all, it couldn't compensate for the misery her aunt had caused. Not just for her, but for Roland, too. Neither of them had deserved to suffer through that purgatory.

Charmian sucked in a breath and surveyed the kitchen. It was a relief to avoid her aunt's despairing gaze. She could tell that Janet was eaten up with remorse and that she was frantic for forgiveness. She also saw that her aunt was realist enough to recognize that forgiveness wouldn't come easily, if at all. "You've been busy."

The long oak table groaned under trays ready for baking. Now she took the time to check, she could see that Janet had made a good start on tidying up after last night, too.

Her aunt looked like she wanted to push their awkward conversation further along the road of excuses and apologies, so it took her a few seconds to turn her attention to their surroundings. "I...I couldn't sleep."

Janet looked worn and older than her years. She'd also been crying.

Her aunt was the most indomitable woman she knew. Charmian had never seen her shed a tear. She shouldn't feel responsible for Janet's turmoil. After all, the woman ought to stew. But that would be easier to say if she didn't have a lifetime of kindnesses to recall, aside from that one huge, egregious act of treachery.

Janet pointed to a pot on top of the range. "There's coffee made if you'd like some."

The scent had teased Charmian since she'd arrived. For the last hours, her emotional troubles had occupied her attention. But standing here, she was aware that she'd had a huge day yesterday, followed by very little sleep. A hot cup of coffee would be welcome. "Thank you. Would you like some?"

"I'm awash with the stuff," Janet said.

"Yes, but would you like another cup?" Janet's never-ending fondness for coffee had become a family joke.

Janet's lips formed a shaky smile before they crumpled. Collapsing into a chair, she covered her face with trembling hands. She started to cry as if her heart was broken.

Stricken, Charmian stared at her aunt. She'd come in here feeling self-righteous and ill-used. It was more difficult to remain convinced of her moral superiority when her aunt sobbed in distress in front of her.

She and her aunt had always been close. Once her brother made his enormous fortune, Janet could have lived a life of luxury. Instead she'd chosen to maintain her independence as a country landlady. Hearing of her youthful romantic disappointment, Charmian couldn't help wondering if a mistrust of all males lay behind her aunt's stubborn dedication to going her own way.

"Aunt Janet..." She ventured closer, remembering that she was angry, but unable to bear her aunt's tears. "Please don't take on so."

Her aunt just kept crying, bundling up her loose apron and pressing it to her eyes as she swayed from side to side in an uncontrollable eruption of sorrow.

Charmian wanted to stand on her dignity, but it was impossible when faced with her usually unflappable aunt's grief. Without making a conscious decision, she found herself on her knees beside the chair with her arm curled around the older woman's heaving shoulders. "Aunt Janet, it's all right. It's all right. Please don't cry anymore. Please."

Janet hefted in a shuddering breath and cast Charmian a woebegone glance. "I can't bear that I've done you such harm. I can't bear that you never want to see me again."

"I didn't say that," Charmian protested, firming her embrace. "We can work everything out."

Her aunt didn't seem to hear her. Instead she laid her hand on Charmian's cheek. "You've always been the daughter I never had. It would break my heart if you never forgave me."

"She forgives you," Roland said behind her. "Of course she does."

"Roland..." Charmian turned her head to see him standing in the doorway, his face full of concern as he surveyed the scene before him. "Can you please pour my aunt a cup of coffee? The pot's on the stove. Just plain black."

While he prepared her aunt's drink, Charmian returned her attention to Janet who to her relief wasn't weeping anymore. She passed her a handkerchief. "Here."

Janet struggled free of Charmian's arms. "Oh, dear, I can't let John and Milly and Gladys see me like this," she said in a constricted voice. "What will they think?"

Roland carried the steaming cup over to her. "Here's your coffee, Miss Barton."

Her aunt wiped her face and blew her nose and stuffed the handkerchief into her pocket. When she took the coffee, her hand shook so badly that Roland had to reach out to help her.

His assistance upset her again, and she caught her breath on another sob. "You mustn't be kind. I don't deserve it."

He smiled at her, a gentle smile that surprised Charmian. She hadn't mistaken how outraged he'd been when he discovered that Janet had hidden his letters. "It's Christmas. It's a time for getting things we don't deserve."

"You..." Janet stared at him as if he'd sprouted wings.

"Aunt, why don't you go up to your room? John and Milly and I can manage. Especially as you did so much overnight." Janet would loathe the servants knowing she'd lost control of herself.

"And me. I came down to lend a hand." Roland set the brimming cup of coffee on the table and took Janet's elbow to help her up. Charmian waited for her to shake him off, but she accepted his aid.

Charmian met his eyes. "I'll take her upstairs. Can you stoke up the stove? We'll have to start breakfast soon. John should be here any moment. He'll tell you what else needs doing."

When Roland smiled at her, she read the steadfast love in his eyes. How had she lived without him all this time? One thing was certain. She'd never willingly do without him again. She swore that on everything she held dear.

"Perhaps...perhaps that's a good idea," Janet said, leaning heavily on Charmian and letting her niece lead her toward the stairs.

As they left, Charmian looked back to see her aristocratic husband pick up the coal scuttle and head outside to perform one of life's dirtier jobs.

CHAPTER TEN

Roland slumped into a padded armchair in the mercifully and recently emptied taproom. It was late afternoon, and he'd been on the run all day. He was filthy and exhausted, and his admiration for his wife had multiplied by a thousand.

Through eyes cloudy with weariness, he observed the room. To his surprise, he realized that it was decorated for the season with holly and mistletoe and other greenery. He'd been too busy and too distracted by the guests' demands to notice before.

A few guests remained, but the vast majority had moved on, eager to spend at least some of Christmas Day with their families. To everyone's relief, the weather had fined up. The sky even showed patches of blue before the early twilight. The bridge would remain out for weeks, even months, but most of the travelers had plans to take longer routes to avoid the flooding.

Janet had emerged before breakfast, showing few signs of her emotional collapse. She had, however, been notably less frosty with him, which left him with mixed feelings. She'd done an unspeakable wrong, keeping him from his wife. But he'd hated seeing her proud spirit humbled. Worse, he'd hated to witness Charmian's distress at her aunt's emotional disintegration.

"What a Christmas it's been," Charmian said from the doorway.

He looked up with a tired smile and held out his hand. "I got the only present I wanted."

The love in her eyes as she darted across the oak floor to curl up in his lap banished his exhaustion. His heart soared with happiness, as he enfolded her against him. A salty hint of female sweat tinged the clean lemon scent of her soap. Even after her exertions, she still smelled like paradise to him. He loved the earthy reality of having his wife in his arms after a long day.

When the chair creaked under their weight, Charmian gave a husky giggle. "I hope we don't end up on the floor."

"As long as I'm with you, I don't care where I am. Even flat on my arse."

"Ah, you sweet-tongued devil," she said with the affectionate mockery that he'd once believed he'd never hear again.

"Speaking of sweet tongues..."

The kiss was long and passionate and, yes, sweet. It spoke of love given and received. Love that had proven its strength. Love that would only deepen in the years to come.

He buried his face in the silky mass of her hair and said a silent prayer of gratitude that she was with him at last. At this rate, he might even stop hating Yorkshire.

"I do beg your pardon." Janet was turning away and shutting the door, when Charmian pulled away from Roland's kisses and called after her.

"No, Aunt. Wait."

Roland saw Janet's shoulders stiffen, but she was a brave woman, if one who had been tragically mistaken. She closed the door before she faced them. The rigidity of her stance hinted that she expected Charmian to berate her once again for keeping her from Roland.

Charmian scrambled off his knee, leaving him free to stand as politeness demanded. "Please, Miss Barton, sit down."

Janet Barton was an attractive woman who bore a marked resemblance to her lovely niece, especially when they were both blushing as they were now.

Janet linked her hands at her waist the way that Charmian did when she fretted. He found it harder and harder to maintain his anger. This woman had set out to do him ruinous harm, but she hadn't succeeded. He suspected that her conscience would provide adequate punishment without him reviling her. Nor could he forget her utter devastation this morning.

Janet remained standing. "I wanted to thank you both for helping today. I don't know how we'd have managed without you. Especially when..."

Charmian made a dismissive gesture. "I wasn't going to leave you flat. We're still family, whatever else has happened."

The generous response eased the tightness around Janet's eyes and mouth. "That's...that's more than I deserve." She directed a glance at Roland. "Sir Roland, I'm far too aware that I misjudged you. I apologise."

He bowed his head. "Thank you."

An awkward silence descended, before Janet crossed to sit on the settle near the inglenook. "You said this morning that you're going back to Northamptonshire as soon as you can. Are you moving on tonight?"

Charmian took Roland's hand. She didn't have to say anything. He already knew what she wanted.

"It's late and we're both tired," he said. "If you'll permit us to stay, I'd be very grateful."

Janet almost managed a smile. "I'd be delighted if you'd stay. I kept back a few choice morsels with the hope of having a small celebration of the season, now that the crisis is over. Milly can look after our remaining guests. John's gone home to his family. It would be just us. Or you can eat in a private parlor, if you'd prefer your own company."

Charmian's expression said that she found the answer in his face. He wanted to start as he meant to go on. That wasn't with setting up barriers between Charmian and her family.

She turned to Janet. "That sounds lovely, Aunt. It would be nice to do something to mark Christmas Day. We'd love to have dinner with you. Then we'll leave tomorrow morning bright and early."

The last of Janet's wary stiffness drained away. The gaze she leveled on them was misty. She stood and brushed down her dark blue skirts with trembling hands. "I'm so glad. Thank you. I'll go and get things sorted out in the kitchen."

"I'll help," Charmian said, but her aunt shook her head with something approaching fond indulgence.

"No, I can manage, and you've both been my drudges for long enough today. You deserve some time to yourselves."

They did. Roland was desperate to hold his wife close and bask in the fact that they were together again. "Thank you, Miss Barton."

"Please call me Aunt Janet. As Charmian said, we're family."

He wasn't completely convinced of his welcome, even now, but for the sake of future harmony, he said, "Aunt Janet."

And was rewarded with an approving smile from his wife.

"It's nearly five now," Janet said. "Shall we say eight for our dinner?"

"It's going to take me that long to wash the day's dirt away," Charmian said, which brought a smile to her aunt's face. An almost natural smile.

"I asked John to bring your things down to the front chamber on the first floor. Your bedroom in the attics isn't big enough for two."

Charmian's blush had ebbed as the discussion proceeded. Now it blossomed into pink again, which made Roland want to kiss her.

But then, he always wanted to kiss her.

"That's very thoughtful of you," he said.

"It's the least I can do. I'll see you both in the south parlor in a couple of hours."

As she left, Janet looked happier than she had when she arrived. Roland found his wife regarding him as if he'd set the stars alight in the night sky. "What?"

"I love you, Roland Destry."

He frowned in puzzlement. While he appreciated her feelings, she spoke the words with a particular emphasis that left him confused. "And I love you."

She smiled. "Even if I hadn't loved you before, I'd love you now."

"Because I was nice to your aunt?"

"Yes. When anyone even a fraction less generous would have ripped into her for what she'd done to us."

He sighed and ran his hand though his hair. "She feels bad enough already. Anyway, I don't want to cause a rift between you and your family, whatever they might have done. We have the children to think of after all."

Her eyebrows rose. "Children, is it?"

Roland caught her in his arms for a ravenous kiss. He felt like he hadn't kissed her for a month. After a faint huff of surprise, she joined in with commendable enthusiasm.

He raised his head and stared down at this woman he adored. "It's time we got to work on the next generation."

Her delicious gurgle of amusement reminded him of the peach of a girl he'd married. Although that girl, beguiling as she was, couldn't compare with the array of complex delights she presented now.

"Do you indeed? Oof!"

He'd swung her high into his arms and marched toward the door. For a few topsy-turvy seconds, he juggled her as he opened the door. "I do. Especially if the front chamber on the first floor has a full-size bed."

"It does." Charmian twined one hand around his neck.

He smiled down at her with all the happiness filling his heart. This was going to be the best Christmas ever. He couldn't help remembering his grim predictions for the day when he'd ridden into Puddlebrook. How wrong he'd been. "Then what are we waiting for?"

As he carried his wife across the empty foyer and up the wooden staircase, he could swear he heard angels singing alleluias. Or perhaps that was just what happened when a man was madly in love with the woman he'd married.

Love and joy had returned to Roland's life, along with the wife he worshipped. He was blessed indeed.

EPILOGUE

Leeder Hall, Northamptonshire, Christmas Night, 1823

Charmian, Lady Destry, gave a contented sigh as she entered the candlelit bedroom and moved toward her dressing table.

"Tired, my darling?" Roland asked from where he sprawled before the blazing fire in a brocade-upholstered armchair. He'd come upstairs before her and had already changed out of his formal wear into a royal blue dressing gown.

Outside it was snowing. Here, inside their beautiful bedchamber, all was comfort and warmth.

She gave him a radiant smile. "It's always a big job, hosting everyone for Christmas."

"Especially this year."

Her hand lowered to her midriff, over the place where a new baby grew. "Especially this year."

They hadn't yet told the family that they expected their second child in the summer. Their firstborn, a rumbunctious boy called Alfred, slept upstairs in the nursery under the loving care of Milly, who had taken up a place as nursemaid at Leeder Hall. He'd been born nine months to the day after their reunion, so Charmian and Roland had indeed made a baby during that ecstatic night of emotion and revelation.

On Boxing Day, they'd left the Spotted Fox in one of the inn's carriages for hire. Two days later, they'd reached Leeder Hall, but by mutual consent, they waited until New Year's Day to read their lost letters. It had been an occasion for tears and regrets and, most of all, a revelation that on both their sides, love had never faltered.

The five years since that rainy Christmas had seen the permanent healing of the wounds left from their separation. Charmian and Roland had established a life full of joy and purpose on their thriving estate, with yearly visits to London for the season to add a touch of excitement to their country routine.

Now Roland rose and prowled across to stand behind his wife. "We don't have to do a big Christmas every year."

She met his eyes in the mirror. It always struck her how right they looked together. He remained breathtakingly handsome, but these days, the first thing she noticed was that he looked like a man at peace with himself and his world. "I know we don't, but it's a nice way of getting the family together."

The annual winter house party mixed Charmian's aunt and mother with Roland's relatives. His sisters and their families, and his cousins and aunts and uncles.

"You enjoy it." He undid the clasp on her extravagant diamond necklace and laid it in a glittering pile on the dressing table.

It was a Christmas gift from her doting husband. He'd presented it to her during a private moment before dawn. She smiled now to remember the cool weight of diamonds on her bare skin and the passionate interlude that had ensued.

"I do. And I like that Mamma and Aunt Janet think you're the icing on the cake these days."

The first year, relations with the Bartons had been strained, largely because her mother and aunt were wallowing in a morass of guilt. But Roland's refusal to bear a grudge and Charmian's desire not to break off the connection had gradually eased the tension. Alfred's arrival that September had forged the final link in creating a loving family.

"I think you're the icing on the cake and the cherry on top as well," he said with a faint smile, as he started to unhook the back of her spectacular vermilion gown. It should clash horribly with her red hair, but the minute her London modiste had produced the patterned silk for her approval, Charmian had been avid to wear it.

"You're the icing on the cake and the cherry on top and the stars in the sky."

He gave a low laugh and placed a kiss on the pale shoulder bared under the sagging dress. "You win."

Sensual pleasure flooded her. She turned and laced her hands around his neck. "We've both won. I love you so much, Roland. Now kiss me."

He caught her hips in a firm grip as his lips explored hers. The sensual charge between them was as strong as ever. Charmian gave herself up to delight.

Delight that ended too abruptly when Roland pulled away to stare down at her with love glowing in his dark eyes.

She pouted with disappointment. "Why did you stop? I was enjoying that."

"You're tired."

She shaped her hand to his jaw and directed a meaningful glance at the large bed behind them. "Not that tired, my love."

He laughed with such elation, her heart melted all over again. He'd been right all those years ago in Puddlebrook when he said that their agonizing separation had taught them never to take love for granted. "You're going to give me a Christmas gift?"

It was her turn to laugh. "Another Christmas gift. Or have you forgotten what we did this morning?"

Roland kissed her on the lips, then whirled her away from the dressing table. A gentle push sent her tumbling back onto the bed in a froth of red silk. "Remind me, sweetheart."

Charmian caught his hand and tugged him down over her. "With the utmost pleasure, my superb and most beloved husband."

ABOUT THE AUTHOR

Australian Anna Campbell has written more than 50 historical romances. Her bestselling stories include 11 multi award-winning releases for Avon HarperCollins and Grand Central Publishing and over 40 independently published books. Anna has won numerous awards for her Regency-set stories, including *RT Book Reviews* Reviewers Choice, the Booksellers Best, the Golden Quill (three times), the Heart of Excellence (twice), the Write Touch, the Aspen Gold (twice), and the Australian Romance Readers' favorite historical romance (five times).

Anna loves to hear from her readers. You can find her at:

Website: www.annacampbell.com

facebook.com/AnnaCampbellFans

x.com/AnnaCampbellOz

bookbub.com/authors/anna-campbell

www.ingramcontent.com/pod-product-compliance
Lightning Source LLC
Chambersburg PA
CBHW030332030726
47499CB00003B/747

* 9 7 8 1 9 2 5 9 8 0 3 4 9 *